"Fans of *Downton Abbey* will devour this vivid tale of one nanny's unwavering love and sacrifices endured for the sake of the royal children in her care. Full of emotion and heart, Lala redefines the meaning of motherhood while Harper gives us a behind-the-scenes look into the lives of the royals."

—Renée Rosen, author of *White Collar Girl*

"This is a beautifully told novel of a woman who was surrounded by all the glitz and glamour of royalty but remained unaffected. . . . Readers will greatly admire the protagonist while learning about the quirks of the royal family and the events that shook the world in the early 20th century."

—Historical Novel Society

"There is nothing more fascinating than a behind-the-scenes glimpse into the lives of the rich and famous or, in this case, the royal, rich, and famous. Karen Harper does a masterful job of combining historical fact and fiction to create a rich and thoughtful view into the lives of Britain's King George V, Queen Mary, and their children."

—Melanie Stanley, *Ohioana Quarterly*

American Duchess

American Duchess

A Novel of Consuelo Vanderbilt

KAREN HARPER

WILLIAM MORROW
An Imprint of HarperCollins*Publishers*

P.S.™ is a trademark of HarperCollins Publishers LLC.

HarperCollins books may be purchased for educational, business, or sales promotional use. For information, please email the Special Markets Department at SPsales@harpercollins.com.

FIRST EDITION

Designed by Diahann Sturge
Frontispiece © Bettmann/Getty Images

Library of Congress Cataloging-in-Publication Data has been applied for.

ISBN 978-0-06-274833-1
ISBN 978-0-06-288429-9 (library edition)

19 20 21 22 23 LSC 10 9 8 7

American Duchess

Prologue

The Wedding of the Century, November 6, 1895
The Cage Door Closes

veryone was calling it the wedding of the century. I was calling it the worst day of my life.

Granted, I might have been watched like a hawk before—by a maternal hawk—but I had never felt my imprisonment in a gilded cage so strongly. Here I was on my wedding day, trapped in my bedroom with the door guarded by the biggest footman at the house so I would not flee.

"Miss Consuelo, can you please stop crying?" my maid Lucy asked as she sponged my red-rimmed eyes with cool water again. "I am afraid I will make drips on your dress."

My mother had purchased my wedding gown in Paris before my betrothed, Sunny—as I must now call him, short for Sunderland, one of his secondary titles before he became the 9th Duke of Marlborough—had even asked for my hand. He had become duke four years ago at age twenty. The sobriquet certainly did not come from his personality, because a less sunny person I'd never met. This marriage was all about dollars and no sense: Vanderbilt money for the Marlborough title, prestige, and power.

"I'm trying not to cry," I told Lucy with a hiccough. My voice was not my own. Mama had insisted on elocution lessons amid all the others, partly so I could speak loud and clear, but now I would sound so stuffed up declaring my vows in that huge church.

And where was my father? I needed him, and his presence has been scarce since Mother was divorcing him. But—ha!— she needed him today to give me away, needed his respectable presence as much as she needed the Vanderbilt fortune to cover all the outrageous wedding bills.

"Oh, thank heavens," I blurted out at the rap on the door. Swathed in silk and tulle, I managed to turn toward it as the footman hovering outside opened it for my father and he hurried in.

Ever handsome, always smiling—well, until the arguments had become so bitter and then the divorce loomed. Papa halted a few feet away, taking me in with his warm glance, and I burst into tears again, so glad to see him, so wishing he could spirit both of us away.

"My dearest, don't cry, not today," he said and carefully came closer, shuffling to avoid stepping on the long, pearl-encrusted satin train. "I know brides are nervous but—"

"You know it is more than that. Lucy, you may leave us now."

"But, Miss Consuelo, you cannot sponge your own tears. And I need to arrange the train and veil."

"Later. Soon. Please wait outside," I said and snatched the sponge from her.

Used to looking at my mother for confirmation, she glanced at my father, who nodded. She fled, probably much relieved.

"My dearest, beautiful girl," he comforted when the door closed. "Your mother has gone on ahead, so we have a few minutes to pull ourselves together."

"I need longer than that. A lifetime. You will visit at the palace, won't you? You are always welcome. The real vow I take today is to not change my beliefs to suit him, husband or not, duke or not! I do not care if the Prince of Wales himself comes to visit—and Sunny says he will."

Looking both worried and proud at that declaration, Papa came closer, reaching out his strong arms to carefully hug me around my shoulders.

"Of course I shall visit my dear girl, high and mighty duchess though she may be. And you and I shall write. After all, he has promised to love and cherish you, has he not?"

I shrugged. "But Papa, I tower over him by half a head. And there was the most cruel *Life* magazine cartoon by someone called Charles Dana Gibson of us kneeling at the altar where I tower over him and my hands are tied behind my back—and Mama is holding the rope to make me kneel!"

I sniffled as I stepped back and used the eye sponge to wipe once more under my eyes and then my nose. I cleared my throat and tried speaking louder. "But, yes, he said he would try to be a good husband."

"There, you see. You must learn to ignore the cruel press."

"It truly is not that which makes me feel oppressed. It is, well, lost opportunities."

"I know how much you loved someone else. Poor Winthrop too. I am sorry your mother had other plans."

I longed to scream at him that I had faced her alone on that, when I could have used his help—but then he would have lost anyway, as had I. We spoke a bit longer, lingering, perhaps pretending this was not real. He tried to buck me up, as my brothers would say.

Finally, I mentally squared my shoulders, which were already ever straight from years of wearing an iron brace to give me perfect posture. I tossed the sponge back into the bowl of water and lowered my knee-length veil over my face. Thank God for it, as I wanted to hide from all that awaited me. I could hear the crowd outside the house, and more would await us at and in the church. The numbers alone staggered me: twenty-five policemen outside the church to keep order, four thousand guests, a sixty-piece orchestra and fifty-voice choir, and a parade of churchmen to lead us through our vows.

Despite my lingerie, then four layers of satin, and the Brussels lace gown and veil, I felt quite naked and exposed. I wished I could hide forever. Someone—I feared I knew who—had released information to *Vogue* magazine, which had sketched and published each item of the enhancement undergarments I wore today. Suddenly my corset felt so tight I could hardly breathe.

"Ready, my dear?" Papa asked and held out his arm as if we were ready to tread the church aisle. Our cue would come just after the choir sang "O Perfect Love" before the "Wedding March" began. How romantic, everyone thought, but not I.

O perfect love, indeed. I had turned eighteen only eight months ago. I did not want to be the Duchess of Marlborough. I was an American through and through, however much Mama had taken me around the world, put me on display before French and British society, and bred me and sold me for this very event and the life to come.

Yet here I was, going to live on a huge estate still run by

feudal rules. At least my dear governess, who had been with me for years, had lifted my spirits by insisting that, once I was duchess, I could help others. Mama expected me to take over the British social world as she had the New York so-called four hundred. Then there was the need for what I had dubbed "an heir and a spare," when I knew next to naught about marriage bedroom protocol.

But I was a Vanderbilt and I would somehow—God willing—make the best of this damned gilded cage or die trying.

"Yes, Papa, I'm ready," I lied, but I kept thinking, *How did it ever, ever come to this?*

Part One

Debutante, 1893–1895

The Golden Cage

Chapter One

It was a blustery, gray November day. I could not believe how many New Yorkers had come to the pier to see my parents and their friends off. Of course the newspapermen were there shouting questions. But I suppose, since there were eighty-five people on board the Vanderbilt yacht *Valiant*, that some of the crowd could have been related to the crew of seventy-two and our French chef.

But the people on the pier were not what took my attention. Papa had invited his friend Winthrop Rutherfurd to come with us on our ocean voyage to India and France, and Win stood beside me at the rail.

To tell true, I adored him, however much older he was at age twenty-nine and I only sixteen. So handsome, even-tempered, properly protective and attentive. A trained lawyer but quite the sportsman. And how he looked at me, though his manners in public were impeccable.

On my other side from Win and Papa stood Mama and next to her from Newport, Oliver Belmont, a friend of both my parents. My youngest brother, Harold, nine years old, had come along, though my brother Willie, a year and a half younger than I, had stayed behind for his schooling. I would like to say I would miss him, but with Win along and his gloved hand so close to mine, well.

I jolted from my reverie when Mama spoke: "Consuelo, the next time you see New York, I will have brought you out in Europe. Your life will be different as a debutante—a Vanderbilt debutante."

Because I was tall for a woman, at nearly five feet and eight inches, I now looked down on her. After all she'd put me through—put me through my paces, she had called it, as if I were a filly to be trained. But there was no changing her—had I been twelve feet tall, she still would have steered me like this steam yacht, heading out into life's sea.

She immediately turned back to Mr. Belmont. I saw he dared to cover her gloved little finger with his on the teak rail. Though as was proper, flesh never touched flesh in polite society, it hit me hard that—could it be?—they were more than friends? But no. Mama never did anything to sully the Vanderbilt name. She only decorated it and flaunted it as she did our mansions on Long Island and in New York City and Newport, which she had built with her designing passion and Papa's money.

Win spoke, and I turned quickly to face him. Ah, he was nearly six-foot-three, though I did not need his height to endear him to me. Every kindly move, each smile and intense look in his eyes—

"Shall we stand at the other rail to see the Statue of Liberty go by—well, that is, we are going by," he said, gesturing with one arm and holding out the other for me to take. With a nod at my father, we walked together across the width of the ship to the port side. "Not only are you and I going by but we are going far, my dear Consuelo," Win added when we were out of everyone's earshot.

At that, I did not need this massive yacht at all. I could have flown.

I COULD HEAR my parents arguing through the wall between our cabins, however sturdy the mahogany barrier. Papa was shouting back at Mama? Never, never had I heard that. Usually, she ranted, and he walked out the door without fighting back, though now he was a captive audience on this vessel the rough seas were rocking.

"Alva, you cannot act that way with Belmont with the children and our guests about! His middle name isn't Hazard for nothing. He has been a friend to us both, but beware."

"Be grateful he is an honorable person, which is more than I can say for some of the paramours you have run to over the years!"

"Only when your social grubbing made our marriage a living hell, damn it!"

"And you have had a flaming affair with my friend Consuelo Montagu. Our daughter is named for her, for heaven's sake!"

I was astounded at that accusation. My godmother, the Duchess of Manchester, and my father? Surely not. Just before this voyage, Mama had ranted at me, *I do the thinking here. You do as I say!* But I would still side with Papa if I were ever asked for an opinion.

"You do not have time for me," he insisted, his voice a bit quieter now. "Only for spending money to buy our way into society, which we do not need—to climb the rungs of that ladder, not the money, I mean."

"We did need to take our rightful place among Mrs. Astor's so-called four hundred. We needed to show our true worth, and we have. And you need to show some appreciation for the houses I have designed and built, for they are works of art! Especially our Fifth Avenue mansion and Marble House. They make your favorite Idle Hour on rural Long Island seem tawdry."

"Just ask the children—especially Consuelo—which they prefer!"

I covered my ears with my hands and curled into a ball on my bed. I was starting to feel queasy from the rolling and tilting of the ship, and from what I was hearing. I could only hope that my governess, Miss Harper, who slept near the door, hadn't heard their fighting. But Miss Harper, who was bright and wise, no doubt knew more about my parents' rocky marriage than their own children did.

Except for me. When Mama and Papa were not speaking, I was the one who carried messages between them, both in the Fifth Avenue house and in vast Marble House, which everyone in Newport called a "cottage." I hated it when my parents did not speak to each other, but how I wished they were not speaking now.

"The wind is picking up," Miss Harper spoke from her bed across the cabin. So had they awakened her or was she trying to drown out their voices? "Getting a bit rough."

"I know. It scares me."

"This is the largest private yacht in America, maybe in the world. It does not roll as hard as their first yacht, the *Alva*."

"But the *Alva* sank."

Somehow, suddenly, that seemed the wrong thing to say. The big boat named *Alva* might have gone down, but not the real Alva. Like a storm, she, too, was a force of nature. Unstoppable, unsinkable.

AFTER SPENDING TWO days ashore in Cairo to get our land legs back while the *Valiant* passed through the locks of Suez, we reboarded the yacht to cross the Indian Ocean to Bombay. There the noise, swarms of insects, smells—the seething humanity of India—nearly overwhelmed me. My legs went weak and my stomach roiled, so I survived on toast and tea, despite some of the wonders we saw.

Win was ever attentive, and I began to love, not just like, him. We found we had a favorite Strauss opera in common, *Der Rosenkavalier*, so that became my private nickname for him. It translated to "the rose bearer," and he promised to have my arms full of roses when we arrived home. I told him my favorite was the American Beauty rose, and Amber, an amalgam of that name, was his secret, secret name for me, despite my dark hair and my dark eyes and olive skin. He teasingly said that my long, slender neck was the stem for my blooming beauty.

It was during the several days my parents spent away from us that I treasured most on the voyage, for, though Miss Harper or my maid Lucy always tagged along or sat nearby, I spent hours up on deck with Win.

"Your mother will have real visions of grandeur after staying with the British viceroy and the vicereine at Government House," Win told me. "It's not some plain outpost like it sounds. I hear they live like royalty as they oversee India for the queen."

"Then my mother will fit right in."

"Somehow we will win her to our side," he promised, keeping his voice low so Miss Harper, who was sitting on a deck chair holding a book, would not hear. "I come from acceptable 'stock,' and would not pursue you for your money—though I do not mean to say you are not worthy of great love without a dowry or settlement of any kind."

However sophisticated I was trying to be, I sighed. Staring at the passing life, as we anchored near the Bay of Bengal along the Hooghly River, it was so hard to picture a future with Win—to picture anywhere but here. I had glimpsed on the wharf below, amid food sellers and workers, that veiled and swathed women in the heat walked two steps behind their men, some bearing pots or pitchers upon their heads with one hand up for balance. So picturesque and exotic, but somehow strange and . . . and wrong. Wrong that the British rulers lived in luxury here when there was all this.

"You are trembling in this heat, sweetheart," Win said. "We had best go back inside. Miss Harper is coming over, as she must have noticed, too."

The three of us were barely seated in the stateroom when my parents came back from their two nights away. As faint as I had suddenly felt—though, who knew, perhaps the vapors were caused by Win's intensity as well as the sweltering scene below—I came to attention.

"They rule here as royalty!" Mama declared, pulling the pins from her hat and sailing it onto the spare settee. "Almost like a king and queen, or at least duke and duchess." Papa poured himself a tumbler of brandy from the sideboard and dismissed the footman with a wave of his hand.

"They are about to have a changing of the guard," Papa said, "but we were entertained in luxury. Lord and Lady Elgin will be replacing our hosts, the Lansdownes. Yet still there is a pall hanging over the place and—"

"Hardly a pall," Mama cut in, "and it is appalling you would say that. Consuelo," she said, turning toward me, "the wife of the viceroy, the vicereine, does much good here and has power of her own, quite independent of her husband. So, there is a British precedent for feminine power far beyond the duties or mere self-indulgence or luxury."

"I hope," I said, sitting up straighter, "she sees to the wretched masses I have observed, especially the women. And what is that you said about their practice of purdah, Win?"

Mama had seemed so engrossed in her opinions and observations that she turned to Win for the first time.

"It is the Hindu practice of secluding women," he said. "They wrap them in clothing head to foot or keep them behind high walls. It has just been outlawed here, but that does not mean the customs will change."

"Dreadful," Papa said.

Mama chimed in with "Despicable, primitive, and quite unfair!"

I bit my tongue to keep from blurting out something like "But isn't that how you have treated me?"

I shuddered at the thought and was grateful once again I was an American, though Mama and I had both agreed that women at home should be able to vote, else it was another, more civilized, kind of purdah, I supposed.

I saw that Mama studied and frowned at Win and me.

"Consuelo," she said, "let us leave the men to their brandy. Come with me. You looked peaked and need your rest before your first coming out event in Paris, and none too soon. You and I both need a change of scene."

Win made a move to help me rise, but she took my arm, pulled me up, and subtly elbowed him away.

Chapter Two

ama and I, our maids, Miss Harper, and our nearly one hundred pieces of luggage disembarked in Nice so we could then travel on to Paris. Papa journeyed on with the yacht, taking along Oliver Belmont and my dear Win, but we planned to travel through the countryside and would see them soon.

Yet barely were we off the *Valiant* that Mama took me aside and told me quickly and curtly that my parents' marriage was definitely over. She explained she would seek a divorce when we returned to America. She said Papa agreed that she would tell me, but I vow, it was so I would not throw a scene and cling to him. With the others, I tried to keep my chin up. I had seen it coming, but it still cut deep. I could only tell myself that perhaps Papa would be better off.

Though I was devastated, Mama forbid my moping about. We moved into a lovely hotel overlooking the Tuileries Gardens. At least the beautiful City of Light, as they called Paris, was balm to my soul. Mama and I walked and walked, talked and talked.

I blamed her and was angry at first, but she seemed to cater to me, taking me to museums and churches and lectures at the Sorbonne. We visited the Paris Opera and the Comédie-Française. I loved speaking French, and I loved the French people, so elegant and gay. The spring of 1894 helped to heal my heart and perhaps Mama's, too.

I was excited to have my portrait painted by the artist Carolus-Duran, whom Mama assured me was famous for his portraits of aristocratic women. So was I now, at age seventeen, an aristocratic woman? At least I trusted that the portrait would make me look that way.

"No, no, not red velvet behind her. Too heavy-looking!" Mama told the bearded artist in French when he tried to pose me before huge swags of tasseled draperies in his studio. "I want a classical look, a portrait to hang in Marble House, our Newport estate, for a while and then who knows, perhaps in an English palace."

My head snapped around. Whatever was she talking about?

"But the Prince of Wales in England, he is already married, madam, and his son the Duke of York last year, too," the artist protested with a roll of his eyes and a little smile that peeked through his mustache.

"Ah, but," she said, tugging me over to another backdrop, a realistic rendering of a classical landscape with an Ionic column, "don't you know there is one palace in Great Britain not owned by the royals? Its name is Blenheim Palace, and it belongs to the Duke of Marlborough. I have it on the best authority—Lady Lansdowne, an English aristocrat herself and the duke's aunt."

Why, I wondered, would Mama have been discussing that when she was spending time in a palace in India? I had briefly met Lady Lansdowne, too. How she had looked me over, a bit rudely, I thought, but that was almost all I recalled about her.

But I did love the painted backdrop Mama had chosen here and, later, the portrait itself. In it I stand as if I were indeed mistress of a grand house or palace, draped in white with the most calm, confident look on my face. One foot peeks from my gown, as if I were stepping forward into my future.

How I tried to emulate that feeling and look the night Mama brought me out into French society at the all-white ball for unmarried *jeune filles* at the palatial home of the Duc de Gramont. Yet however elegantly gowned in one of the many dresses Mama had bought for me from Monsieur Jean Worth's fabulous displays, I was frightened to death.

"MAMA, I LIKE this gown, but why should my hair be piled so high with curls?" I asked as my maid prepared me for the evening while Mama watched. "My hair isn't curly and it takes so long to get it that way. The height of the hair makes my neck look even longer. And everyone will have a necklace of some sort, so why only a simple white ribbon around my throat? You know my neck is too long, you have said so."

"Less is more with you tonight. We do not want people looking at your jewelry, but at you. My girl, your elegant, swanlike neck is part of your allure."

"Swanlike? Allure? But—"

"Consuelo, you have no taste!" she exploded, rising and pointing a finger nearly in my face. "I buy the gowns; you wear them. I decide the look; you display it. Believe me, I know what I am doing."

Still, that did not calm my nervous demeanor. The ballroom was vast. This was called a white ball because all the guests were unwed. It would have been deemed a pink or rose ball if married women were guests of honor. The men—and it looked to me as if there were an army of them—sat on one side of the room while we, with our chaperones, sat on the other quite on display. The men came across to ask for dances, and my card was soon filled, my evening a busy whirl. Yet wasn't this all a sham? I was certain Win would propose when I returned to New York, but I suppose I must go through this pantomime until both of us could present our plans. I tried to enjoy it despite my upset stomach and trembling hands.

Still, it was fun to whirl around the floor to a lilting waltz. I began to confuse names and, in some cases, the French titles of my dance partners. Mama was in her element, conversing with each would-be beau before and after dances or when one of them went to fetch us punch. I had strict orders not to go near the drink tables myself because, she said, that is where stains splashed on gloves and gowns.

And then, near the last dance, a handsome, dark-haired, blue-eyed man bowed before us to present himself. He had no title, and introduced himself as Jacques Balsan. Something about him, his assurance, his poise—his intent look—made me blurt out before Mama could give her yea or nay. "Yes, I would enjoy a dance," as if I had been a wallflower all night and was desperate. For the first time this evening I was happy not to be overdressed or glittering with jewels like many of the other maidens.

"Oh, yes, Balsan," Mama said after he made further introductions to both of us. "From the industrial family with the textile empire—the heir."

"I have traveled the world, Madam Vanderbilt, but, I admit, mostly to buy wool for our Balsan mills."

I thought Mama might not like such a plebian concern, but

she said, "Actually, my family dealt in cotton before our dreadful War Between the States. But as for the Balsans, of course, any family that is friends with the Gramonts is surely well respected."

He hastily signed my dance card, and we were off onto the floor. It was strange, but, as his gloved hand took mine, it was as if we really touched. He was not as tall as Win, just my height, so our eyes met and matched. He seemed to smile with his eyes as well as his mouth, which flaunted white, even teeth.

"Mama may be American and I too," I told him in French, "but she seems to know of your family."

"The Balsans' businesses are all earthbound, but I love to take to the skies. My passion—one of them," he added, smiling at me again. "My favorite pastime is ballooning aloft in the clouds."

"Oh, but is that not dangerous?"

"A bit, but worth it. To see the earth which mankind has tried to divide into fenced fields and roads and city blocks gives one a whole new vision for life. If our earthbound paths cross again, and I pray they shall, Mademoiselle Consuelo, I shall propose that I take you up into the heavens with me."

What an amazing conversation we had, when all evening I had heard little but comments on how beautiful I looked, questions as to whether I liked Paris and what were the Vanderbilt homes and businesses like, as if everyone did not already know railroads and more railroads had made my family's fortune. Of course, I should tell this Jacques Balsan that I could promise nothing in the future. That my mother would never let me go up in a balloon in a basket—oh, yes, I told him I had seen a newspaper drawing of such a daring deed.

I sighed and not from the exertion of the waltz. For the first time tonight, I did not wish that my dance partner was my dear Win.

"It sounds wonderful," I told him and felt quite let down to earth when he returned me to my mother with a smile and a quick squeeze of my hand before he bowed and left us.

"You will not believe this," Mama said.

"I know—oh, believe what?"

"You, my dear, have had five proposals of marriage this evening, brought directly to me, two of them in writing."

"Oh, no. I—from one dance?"

"From your beauty I—we—have showcased tonight, and your name, of course."

"Papa's money, you mean."

"The place I have made for us and you with it. But any French noble will not do, so do not fret."

I exhaled in relief, still a bit out of breath from dancing with Jacques. But there was something about the way she had worded that. Hopefully, she meant an American would be better for me, and I would convince her that Win, after all, from a respected and well-to-do family, would be quite perfect.

"Would you believe," she said as the evening ended, "that we have an invitation to meet His Serene Highness Prince Francis Joseph of Battenberg tomorrow? The great nephew of Tsar Alexander III, no less. He was not here tonight but an emissary of his family was."

My heart flip-flopped then sank. I could only hope there was no connection between Mama's European husband-hunting for me and that name and title. I didn't want a title and I didn't want to be linked with anyone serene and high. As much as I loved Europe, I wanted to marry in America to an American. And where was Battenberg anyway?

I searched the crowded room for another glimpse of Jacques but did not see him again. Not for many years.

MY DREAMY DAYS in France collapsed like a stuck balloon when I entered the evening salon of the grande dame Madame de Pourtalès to be presented to Francis Joseph of Battenberg. I had learned he was a German princeling, but I did not care a flip if he were a king or a saint. Mama had not exactly said so, but was she actually dangling me as a possible princess to an alien, distant, and no doubt backward Balkan state called Serbia?

The man I was to meet had a long, serious face and was attired in a military uniform heavy with medals and ribbons. He spoke French sharply and swiftly, and his quick smile did not reach his cold gaze as he assessed me. Was Mama mad? Even I was now onto the game of men who knew me not at all—and did not think that mattered—because they were mostly interested in being bankrolled by the Vanderbilt fortune.

It was a painful night as I sat next to him at dinner. Thank the Lord, Mama sat on his other side and kept him greatly occupied with her questions. I was so upset and so angry that I could barely eat the delicacies set before me. At least there was no dancing. Why, I would have taken any of my dance partners, especially that Jacques Balsan, and lived in a scow anchored on the Seine rather than live in any sort of palace with this man.

"Mama, I can only hope you did not intend him for me!" I insisted when we were back alone in our rooms at the hotel. "He is cold of heart and—"

"And not what I had in mind, though he is a prince, so do not fret and save your passion for England, where we are going next. I discerned tonight that the man is not really going to remain royal despite his title. His family has no palaces of their own, and his German arrogance toward women—oh, yes, I could tell—is despicable."

"Oh. Good. I thought—"

"I am sure the next titled man you meet will be of the true nobility—in character and heritage."

I was coming to grasp her game. She intended to marry me to nobility, even royalty. So Win and I must get Papa on our side, however much my parents were estranged now, then present our plans to her. That is, if Win would just propose when we get home, before some other catastrophe occurred.

BUT IT DID not take me long in London to feel I was on the marriage mart again. Instead of a conniving French grande dame this time, the liaison was Mama's distant acquaintance, the American Minnie Stevens, now Lady Paget, a friend of the Prince of Wales set, no less. Well, I told myself, I survived the maidens-for-sale ball and that dreadful German princeling, so I can survive here long enough to get home to Win. His letters, which were delivered to my maid so that Mama would not find them, were passionate and endearing. Mine were harder to sneak out, but with Miss Harper's willingness to look the other way, we managed to correspond.

But I was appalled anew when Mama and I had a meeting with Mrs. Paget. At least nothing was kept secret from me. Oh, no, they discussed my flaws openly, which they hoped to "work around" as if I had no ears or feelings.

"I know she brings a fortune trailing her skirts," Lady Paget told Mama, "but you will still have to dress her a bit more daringly. More bare flesh, lower necklines. The retroussé nose and long neck, not to mention her gangly height will be the drawbacks, not for the untitled, of course, but to win a coronet. She

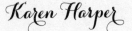

is not in the ugly duckling stage, but an awkward one, I am afraid."

I actually gasped at her blatant manner—or lack of manners—but Mama only nodded. "No more baby girl décolletage, I can see that," Mama agreed, "especially if you can arrange a meeting at that dinner party."

"He is young, only twenty-two, and somewhat attached to a person, but he loves his palace above all else, if you know what I mean. Unfortunately—or perhaps fortunately for you—the place absolutely drinks money, and the two previous dukes spent much of the family treasure to keep it going."

His palace? What duke? Indeed, I was being sold but, hopefully, not bought. I absolutely panicked. I was almost sick upon the Aubusson carpet in front of my small, gilded chair. My mother was mad to try to trade me for some sort of title. How desperately I wanted my father's help and to belong to my dear Win. I needed to go home! Of course, there were social classes and snobs there, but when I became my own woman, I could work around that, maybe change things. And had I just heard that this mystery man was also attached to someone he cared for, and that mattered not one whit?

"We will be ready and be there in fine fettle the moment you can arrange it," Mama told the woman and finally turned to look at me with a bright smile. I just stared back at her, quite distraught.

Papa had told me once that my mother, Alva, the former Miss Smith, had saved her impoverished southern family after the Civil War by stealing his heart and his hand. *Stealing?* I believed that now. But must she steal my wishes, my plans, my very life?

Chapter Three

felt like a lamb being led to the slaughter when Mama and I were invited to dine at Lady Paget's beautiful house on Belgrave Square in London shortly thereafter. I was to be seated on the right side of the Duke of Marlborough—the ninth duke. He bore the intimidating name of Charles Richard John Spencer-Churchill.

I was schooled repeatedly to the fact that he possessed the only palace in England that was not owned by royalty, and Mama—along with Miss Harper—lectured me thoroughly on the historical significance of Blenheim, a structure that held seven acres under its roof when completed. The palace was a gift from Queen Anne of England in 1704 to the first duke, a general, who had beaten the French and made them lose a great, famous battle.

Miss Harper read me a poem by Robert Southey that included the lines *Great praise the Duke of Marlbro' won* and *'Twas a famous victory.* I rather liked the poem if not the import of it for me. Actually, its deep message was against war, and I was all for that, at least. I knew much of America's so-called War Between the States, because Mother's southern family had lost much during those dark days.

Of course I would be kind to the duke, interested and polite and try not to blush at how much the bare flesh of my shoulders and the tops of my swelling breasts were on display. Then I would beg Mama to go home, though not tell her I wanted to see my father and ask his help to encourage Win, my beloved Rosenkavalier, to quickly tell my parents he wanted to marry me, ending all these on-the-market rehearsals and let's-bait-a-hook chicanery.

To my amazement, the duke indeed looked young—and, oh my, at least four inches shorter than I. I could tell that bothered Mama as she managed to get us seated quite quickly. He was slim with carefully combed brown hair and a wispy mustache. I found his face pleasant but nondescript, almost expressionless at times, as if he seemed to be somewhere else. He was fond of gesturing with his graceful hands. He did look me over carefully, mostly when he thought I was not watching him. In short—short was not a joke I told myself as I looked down on him—he was not a sighing maiden's dream of a fairy-tale prince—or duke.

"I understand your ancestral home is not only historical but beautiful," I observed after our introductions and what Mama called small talk.

His blue eyes lit at that. "Blenheim is a living entity, my heritage. It is my goal in life to see that she is taken care of, made more lovely yet," he told me, riveting his gaze to mine for the first time.

I could not help but think that Blenheim was his true love.

At least he had a purpose in life, something to protect and cherish. And he had referred to the estate as a "she."

He went on to describe the grand rooms of the vast building, the grounds and gardens, the estate workers and antique villages in which they lived. His voice became animated, and his hands drew pictures in the air. But then he because more serious again.

"I understand there are some family difficulties that will soon become full public knowledge," he told me between the third and fourth courses of dinner. "Mrs. Vanderbilt says you are going home straightaway, but that you will return for the next social season, so perhaps the two of you can tour Blenheim with me then."

Mama had not told me we were leaving soon, but I was glad for it. And perhaps, for someone like this man who cherished his home and honor, a looming Vanderbilt divorce would keep him away. Oh, if only!

"I am sure we would love to see the palace and estate," I told him, feeling much relieved that I—if not he too—might be promised to another before then. Mama may hope my absence would make this man's heart grow fonder—for my dowry at least—but I was praying that out of sight would mean out of mind.

Suddenly the food and wine tasted better. Our halting conversation seemed smoother. I might never see his beautiful Blenheim at all, because I was going home.

WE STEAMED BACK to the States in September of 1894 on the ship RMS *Lucania*, arriving in time to join the Newport social season. I was so relieved to be home and out of the clutches of titled Europeans and the women who acted as go-betweens for my mother. I was happy to be part of the demanding, breakneck Newport season. Mama was busy planning how to obtain her divorce and yet retain her place in society. Although I could tell she was keeping Win away from me, with Mama's attentions otherwise engaged, we could still correspond and we planned an autumn reunion in New York. I cherished each letter that came through my maid, addressed to "Dear Amber" and signed "Your true Rosenkavalier."

The daily routine for the young social set in season stretched nearly from dawn to the next daylight. Morning rides sidesaddle, then the first of many changes of attire to a day dress for a carriage ride. Before lunch, swimming at Bailey's Beach, though I detested the rocks and red algae there—and how long it took to change into my pantaloons, swimming dress, and huge hat. In truth, I thought a good deal of time was wasted in endless costume changes, usually from the skin out.

Next came noon luncheons in cottages or on yachts in the harbor or a picnic elsewhere with linen, china, and crystal laid out on tables or blankets on the grass. Tennis and gossip at the meeting place, called the Casino, and afternoon promenades. Tea later on the lawn and another change of clothes for dinner. Balls in the evening of various themes or decorated in a particular color. And then all over again the next day.

Papa spent his days on his yacht in the harbor or visiting his favorite place, Idle Hour on Long Island, to which I longed to escape. The few times I saw him, we quickly chatted somewhere outside since he was persona non grata with Mama, and I knew my friends might leak it to her, however loyal Miss Harper or my maid might be. Mama had sacked staff for far less before.

"Do not think she has given up plans for you with Marlborough," Papa warned me as we ducked inside one of the shops on Bellevue Avenue while Miss Harper pointedly looked around at the merchandise. "Talk about the Battle of Blenheim paying off for generations of those dukes," he went on, speaking fast and low. "Your mother's battle is big, too—first, complete the divorce and get control of you three children."

"No . . . that should be shared control at least," I dared. "What else is she demanding?"

"I have offered her all three homes in exchange for joint custody, but she is only taking Marble House—she's always hated the Vanderbilt home on Long Island. I thought she'd want 660 Fifth Avenue—well, she designed it, too."

"Designed and decorated it with your money."

"Do not talk like that. It takes two to make a marriage, and I am the one who asked for her hand, made the marriage decision, however much she steered me into it. But, what the deuce, I think she is going to emerge from this social disaster unscathed. She gave me a high-flying speech that she intended to pave the way for women being able to get a divorce without losing face—and then went on a rant about women getting the vote, no less. But, dear girl, how has all this been for you?"

"Everyone's talking, whispering behind my back about it. A few sniggers here and there. But, Papa, it is so outrageous if Mama thinks she can still marry me off well after this. I heard that at the mere hint of divorce or marital troubles and Queen Victoria tosses former friends to the wolves, and it is not so different around here."

"Well, Queen Victoria has not met Queen Alva. Your mama managed to best Lady Astor once, so I would put my betting money on her. But I am sorry, my dear, about the whispers, the scandal, which you are no part of."

"It must bother Win, too. Please tell him I will see him in New York soon. I hope his feelings for me will not change, if you know what I mean. He is from a respectable, well-to-do family so she cannot say he is only after my—our—money."

"No one who sees or knows you could be after only that, my dear. I had best push on now. I will tell Win you are looking exceptionally lovely. I would ask him down, but your mother is a powder keg right now, so take care of yourself and the lads."

He pecked a kiss on my cheek. How much I loved him!

Miss Harper knew to offer a handkerchief the moment she came back to me in the shop. "My mother will have my head if she hears I see him here and there," I whispered to her.

"My only assignment," she said, "was to watch out for Winthrop Rutherfurd lurking about. Let's go, or we will be late to the polo field to watch a few chukkers from the carriage. See and be seen, that is the best ploy to keep our chins up through all this."

I knew she meant the scandal of the Vanderbilt divorce. But the scandal that devastated me—that I must somehow escape—was the shock of being sold for a title to the highest bidder for my hand, and for the rest of me, too.

BUT EVEN WHEN we returned to New York that autumn, I did not see Win. Granted, I was ailing for a while, but his letters stopped coming, even after I wrote him, making me even more ill, especially when the Vanderbilt divorce was discussed and dissected daily in the newspapers. I did not miss the whispers of my friends, but could the "great divorce" have changed Win's mind about me?

Then, on a windy but sunny week in late winter, a few days before the divorce would become final, Mama announced that she and I were heading back to England on March 3, and that she was going to host a luncheon for my female friends on my eighteenth birthday the day before. She informed me that carriages would take me and my guests for a bicycle ride afterward, weather permitting.

Indeed, I thought, it would do me good to go out with a group of friends to get my stamina back and some color in my cheeks. In a way, but for having my brothers and Miss Harper around, I was in sore need of companionship.

I knew I looked pale, but painting was strictly for the demimonde, so I pinched my cheeks and enjoyed the luncheon—though Miss Harper informed me that several of those invited were "engaged elsewhere" when it used to be that no one missed any Vanderbilt event at the elegant 660 Fifth Avenue mansion. Then out we trooped to carriages that delivered us near to Riverside Drive, since the new bicycle rage kept horse-drawn vehicles away from that picturesque street now. And you might know that Mama actually rode along with us, including my brothers. And, suddenly, there was Win!

I never did learn how he managed to become part of our group! It hardly mattered. Here he was, at last, in the flesh, my handsome, clever Win. With the others around, Mama could hardly tell him to leave, and his presence made a public statement that the Rutherfurds, at least, still desired to mingle with the disgraced Mrs. Vanderbilt. He even doffed his hat to Mama as he coasted up beside me, and off we all went.

"Pedal fast so we can outstrip them, especially your mother," he said without turning his head my way. "Why haven't you written?"

"Only a million letters at least, and I have had none of yours."

"It is not *my* mother intercepting them."

"I am surprised I still have my maid and governess if she found out they used to pass them to me."

"But that would be tipping her hand. Consuelo, my beloved 'Amber,'" he added, using his secret pet name for me—probably secret no more, if Mama had intercepted our letters—"we will have to be strong through this. And I rejoice that you are of age today, as that may help."

"Or not," I said with a sigh.

We pedaled faster, ignoring the passing scene of the white-capped Hudson River, carriages, and other bicyclers. I was out of shape, out of breath—but out of patience, too. Indeed, I was of age! Must I be controlled by my mother yet?

"Then you still care for me?" I asked breathlessly as we increased our speed even more.

"I love you with all my heart. I play polo and think of you. I play golf and think of you. I have hidden here next to my heart a long-stemmed American Beauty rose to prove my continued constancy and pray that I am yet your Rosenkavalier. Would you consider a secret engagement until we can figure out how to best convince your mother?"

"What about your family—now with the divorce?"

"There is but one barrier as far as I can tell."

"Once she realizes how much we love each other, surely she will want to keep me here in society, not that of Europe. I have not heard one word about someone there I thought she fancied for me."

"Then, let's stop here and make our vow," he said, as we braked to a halt and glanced back at my laughing friends—and frowning Mama, all nearly caught up to us. He pulled a battered bright pink American Beauty rose from inside his buttoned jacket and seized my hand. The river wind ripped at us, loosening my hair and tugging at my hat. I clutched the flower to my breasts.

"Consuelo Vanderbilt, I love you with all my heart," Win said, in a rush. "I pledge you my undying love and admiration and wish to marry you—when—when we can manage it. Will you marry me?"

"I will. I will! To death us do part."

We dared not kiss but squeezed hands. I thrust the rose under my buttoned cloak as the other riders pedaled up to meet us. Somehow Mama managed to wedge the front wheel of her bicycle between ours.

"You are going much, much too fast," she scolded us. "Consuelo, you have been ailing and need to keep up your strength for our departure tomorrow. And Win, how lovely to see you again. But you, too, look a bit windblown and flustered. Are you quite well? Nice of you to ride along today to bid Consuelo good-bye."

"Hey, there, Win," someone shouted. "The wind is in my face but seems to be pushing you and Consuelo along!"

"Not a bit of it!" Win responded with a smile as we all remounted our bikes.

I sighed and shuddered with excitement as well as sadness that we were to be parted again so soon. But now I could imagine us riding a bicycle made for two through any gale or storm, way ahead of Mama's machinations, all the way through my now adult life.

Chapter Four

o my utter horror—but I could not let on until Win and I could get Papa on board and face Mama together—the Duke of Marlborough invited us to Blenheim on June 15 for what the British called a Saturday to Monday, their version of a weekend visit. I had danced with him twice at one of the lovely events of the season, the ball given by the Duke and Duchess of Sutherland, where I tried to converse politely and ignore that the top of his head came only up to my eyebrows.

Nor was I in the best of moods on that trip to Blenheim, for Lady Paget came along too, the woman who had so brutally assessed my weaknesses so that she and Mama could lay a trap for the duke—or was it to make a deal with him? So, for the trip to the Marlborough estate, I vowed to be polite again and not more. But that plan went awry when I first saw Blenheim. Though that had naught to do with Sunny, I plunged from curiosity to awe.

Oxfordshire was lovely in general that late spring day, but the estate was stunning—overwhelming. Sunny had said the park was almost three thousand acres and the palace had three hundred twenty rooms under seven acres of roof, but that had not prepared me for the absolute grandeur of the first sweeping view.

He had met us at the nearby railway station, and the carriage had taken us a short distance through mellow stone villages, past cottages surrounded by green fields to the weathered stone arch at the Woodstock entry to the estate.

"I hope you will see, Consuelo, why I love this place above all else," Sunny said, turning toward me. "And why preserving and improving it is the goal of my life."

"I understand completely," Mama told him when I but nodded. "My childhood home in Mobile, Alabama, was quite grand before the war ruined everything."

I prayed she would not launch into her stories of how many servants—slaves—her family once had, for that still bothered me deeply. But now, even as Mama fell silent, I could only bite back a gasp. Through and below the arch, guarded by a doorman in antique costume, lay an emerald man-made lake with a small island. The water reflected clouds in the vast sky, clusters of ancient oaks, and a honey-hued, massive arched stone bridge. At first I mistook the stretch of the palace itself for a palace *and* a village, but it was all one edifice. I did not love this man, but at first sight I did so love his Blenheim.

ONCE WE WERE inside the huge palace with its high ceilings and vast rooms, I thought it was all rather cold—a museum, not a home—a problem with which I was quite familiar but not on this grand a scale. Things were laid out so beautifully, so perfectly, here with balance and bravado. Why, the displays reminded me of my own bedrooms in New York and Newport in that nothing in the wardrobe or even on my dressing table were personal choices. Dusted and shined daily, all had been purchased and arranged by Mama, and in my younger days I had been afraid to touch them.

Sunny lived in this massive place alone but for his huge staff, yet we were introduced to the two unwed of his three sisters, who had come for the day. It was only then I learned, to my surprise, that his parents had been divorced and his father, the eighth duke, had remarried. Could that be something my mother had missed when she seemed to know everything else about Sunny? She looked at first surprised, then smug when she heard it, but not when she heard Sunny preferred his stepmother, Lady Lillian, the dowager duchess, to his mother, Albertha, now known as the Marchioness of Blandford. And oh dear, that stepmother was a rich American who had wed his father and brought in funds to repair and enhance Blenheim! Had that somehow set a precedent?

But would his parents' divorce—he admitted it had caused a scandal and royal ostracism for a time—mean that he would look more or less kindly on the daughter of divorced parents?

I also met his stepmother, Lady Lillian, that day. Meanwhile, his sisters, Lady Norah and Lady Lilian Spencer-Churchill also looked me over—not a good sign, I thought. Lady Norah didn't pay me much attention, but Lady Lilian, a pretty blond, who seemed sweet and kindhearted, reached out while the others only studied me.

"I know this place is rather much and can be a smashing bore—like dear Sunny," she whispered to me, "but give him a chance. By the way, of course the house is haunted," she added for my ears only. "The first duchess, Sarah, who oversaw the building of it just cannot let it go. Then there is the old male ghost that haunts the room where our cousin Winston was born, but he causes not a bit of trouble."

I learned that the Churchill name that the sisters sported was prominent in their family history and that Sunny's cousin Winston was a dear friend, and I must simply meet him sometime, his sisters said.

"Winston can talk about anything to anyone at any time," Lady Lilian told me on the sly. "I suppose Sunny did not tell you that Winston is his heir for all this, should Sunny not have a son. I hear you have two brothers, so I suppose, even in America, you know all about that."

She winked at me. I wanted to roll my eyes or shake my head, but she was so likable that I merely nodded.

"Besides," she chattered on, "however close Sunny and Winston are, it annoys my dear brother that Winston was born here at Blenheim and Sunny was born in India when our father was stationed there." She whispered the next words. "Secrets simply breed here, did ever since the first duchess walked these halls, you'll see."

That sent up red flags. Not that the place was haunted or that secrets hid here, but that she'd said, *You'll see.*

I could tell Mama wanted to know what young Lilian kept saying to me, but for once, she was keeping her hands off. Another danger sign was that she did not so much as turn her head—only her eyes—if Sunny steered me off into a corner or another room to show me some relic he fancied or was proud of, including the dusty battle banners of the first duke, Sir John Churchill.

Mama also happily sat off to the side with Lady Paget on Saturday evening when we dined in the massive state dining room, called the Saloon. The room seemed chilly even though logs blazed in both fireplaces. Fabulous frescoes with gods and goddesses gazed down at us from the ceiling and walls. Afterward, we moved into the Long Library—and long it was—to hear a concert by the duke's organ master on the tall pipe organ that seemed to soar to the ceiling.

I was impressed by the moving memorial inscribed on a carved and gilded scroll attached to the pipes. It seemed the magnificent instrument was paid for by Albertha's money. The inscription read: IN MEMORY OF HAPPY DAYS & AS A TRIBUTE TO THIS GLORIOUS HOME, WE LEAVE THY VOICE TO SPEAK WITHIN THESE WALLS IN YEARS TO COME WHEN OURS ARE STILL.

My nostrils flared at that, and I blinked back tears. So big Blenheim could be a home and not just a relic from the past. And a home to an American woman who married a duke and who managed to leave something beautiful behind.

But I quickly put all that out of my mind. I was getting silly and soft. Whatever writing was on the wall or on an organ, this place was not for me.

ON SUNDAY AFTER church, Sunny drove me around the grounds, just the two of us. He said he wanted me to see the people of the outlying villages of Woodstock and Bladon. The palace had been built, he told me, on land where once sat the Plantagenet kings' hunting lodge of Woodstock.

"I am glad you appreciate the past. History helps make the present," he told me as he adroitly handled the reins of our carriage pulled by two matched grays. Though I had much rather be on a bicycle with Win, I valued that compliment.

"It is living history here," I observed as we neared a field where folk strolled the street of the tiny village of Bladon. I then saw how true that was as, at the mere sight of us, men snatched off their Sunday caps and called out almost in unison with a little bow, "Good day, Your Grace." Women and little girls dropped a curtsy as we passed, and Sunny nodded their way. Some stood standing long after we had rolled by, gazing at us and pointing to others, as if they'd seen a saint pass.

"Living history indeed," I added. "It seems as if, well, somehow like feudal times."

"Not a bit of it," he said with a little smile, evidently at my naivety. "Tradition, indeed, but the present is built on the past. We provide for the working class and the poor, always have. Food is taken daily from the table at the palace to send to those in need, and, if they are ill and alone, they are cared for. They are rightly grateful to their lord."

"Lord with a small letter *l* you mean and not the Lord God. Things seem so . . . untouched here. In Americ—"

"This is not America, Consuelo. Things are as they should be. I show special concern, care, and charity for the estate workers as we Marlboroughs have since the first duke John."

"Maybe that's why some say the first duchess still walks the halls. Maybe she thinks the people's station could be better."

He did not frown but only shook his head as he snapped the reins to move the carriage even faster. "Such strange democratic ideas, my dear. You will see the old ways are best for all here."

I wished his tone had been angry instead of condescending, even amused. My friends and family had always said I had a good sense of humor, but I could not summon one smidgen of it, however silly some of this seemed. I bit my tongue. We were leaving for London soon and home thereafter. The beauty here was luring but deceptive. I felt suddenly so relieved to be departing that I blurted, "I do thank you for your time to show me the natural beauty of Blenheim."

He turned to look at me and leaned closer. For one moment I thought he might actually embrace or kiss me.

"Natural beauty is something that would suit you here," he whispered. He almost said something more, but hesitated. My stomach went into free fall. I sensed that he had almost proposed. "Best we head back since your mother has a headache," he added, sitting straight again.

No doubt she'd lied about that if he had asked her to come along. My mother never had a headache, never seemed to be ill. The fact she had maneuvered to get us alone together set off alarm bells in my own aching head again. She had not given up on pairing me with this feudal lord of all he surveyed. I vowed I would never be here again, certainly never live here, but I did have some vague ideas of what I would change if I had one bit of Marlborough power.

It was over wine and strawberries that night after dinner— just Sunny, Mama, and I, though a wigged footman hovered behind each of our chairs—that I had another glimpse that I might be doomed.

"Dear Sunny," Mama said to him, after a discussion on how he hoped to terrace the land above the ornamental lake and embellish some of the rooms of the palace, "how Consuelo and I would like to return your generous hospitality. I believe you said you were considering a tour of eastern America. We would love to entertain you at our home in Newport during the season in August and to invite you to a ball I am planning. You would be our honored guest, of course."

He put his crystal goblet down onto the damask tablecloth slowly, as if he were pondering that. "How lovely and tempting," he said, looking at me and then at her. "I could include it in my tour. I have never been to the States and feel I should understand its people better."

"Then we would be honored," she said and subtly elbowed me, a clear message to chime in, to say something.

Absolutely refusing to play her game, I said, "You will enjoy the sunny days cooled by the wind off the sea. I hope you like yachts. My father has a fine one."

Mama narrowed her eyes at that, but I told myself to keep calm. I planned to be publicly promised to Winthrop Rutherfurd by the time Sunny arrived. Perhaps then, the 9th Duke of Marlborough could find another heiress—a willing one—in America.

"Then I accept with pleasure," he announced, clinking his goblet to hers in a kind of toast—or to celebrate a business deal.

HIS AND MAMA'S plans were made. It was not until the next morning, when Sunny saw us off at the train, and it chugged away, that I dared to whisper, "Mama, if you are still thinking of matching me with him, it will not work. I am not suited to be his wife and live here."

She shrugged and did not answer, which frightened me more than if she had given me a chance to protest further or argue. The sway and jerk of the train seemed instantly to upset my stomach.

I turned away to look out the window at the blur of the passing scene. I did not need to set off one of Mama's fierce explosions with Minnie Paget just across the aisle. I would get Papa and Win's family on my side, then we would all plead our case to win her over. This was not feudal times, even though Sunny and his "serfs" acted that way. Mama could not force me to leave home and marry where I would be so alone and desperately unhappy.

Could she?

Chapter Five

y nightmare had only begun. Once we were home, I wondered if Mama had read my mind about Win. I became a virtual prisoner in Marble House, even in my room. She turned down invitations for me. Miss Harper said they were scarce anyway, because of the finalized divorce. Footmen were always at my door, if I chose to stay in my room, claiming I did not feel well—which was true. If I went for a brief walk outside, I had Mama, Miss Harper, sometimes my maid trailing behind.

In the house, everything swirled around the coming September ball with its special guest, the Duke of Marlborough. As bitter as I was, I saw that elegant, expensive affair was not only to get the duke here, hoping he would propose to me, but to ensure, even elevate Mama's social position here in Newport, and thus in New York, too. People who had shunned her over the divorce would never turn down the opportunity to meet British nobility. And if the Vanderbilt name was to be linked in wedlock to the Marlboroughs, that would be a famous victory, one to outdo the battle that had earned the dukes their beloved Blenheim.

"Brooks," I pled with my maid, "just get this letter into the post somehow." I extended a missive I had written to Win to tell him Mama was finally taking me to a ball on Saturday and could he be there? Her social invitations had suddenly gone sky high from people hoping to receive an invitation to the Marble House ball in return.

"Please, Miss Consuelo, not to ask me. She—you-know-who—asks me every day, me and Miss Harper, if we send a note for you, and we don't want to be dismissed. You would miss us too, yes?"

"Yes, I understand," I said and turned away to look out the window toward the sea. There had to be a way. I prayed that Win did not think I was snubbing him. Papa was at the Vanderbilt house on Long Island. Whatever happened, even if I did not have Papa and Win to help me, I vowed I was going to stand up to Mama one way or another. I was not going to wed the Duke of Marlborough and live in that massive museum in an estate run like one in the Middle Ages.

WITH THE DUKE'S visit barely a month away, I was deeply despondent. Each time I looked in a mirror, I thought no one, even someone off the streets, would want me with the shadows under my eyes and my moping about, listless, hardly speaking.

"Look, my dear Consuelo," Miss Harper said to me, "you must care for yourself better. You must cast off this gloom. You are going to a ball tonight at last, see your friends, enjoy yourself."

"I feel as if I'm on a leash with Mama holding the other end. I do not want to marry away from my home and family—except from my mother," I muttered. I was sitting in a tall chair, looking out a second-floor window, my favorite pastime, watching the sails of boats on the vast blue sea. They looked so free, turning, tacking, bending into the wind.

My dear, longtime governess pulled over an ottoman and sat by my chair. She took my cold hand in her warm ones.

"You must always look on the bright side," she said. "You are strong, Consuelo, with a charming personality and good sense of humor. You have always looked at the glass as half full, and I have admired that. Perhaps, as hard as this is, it is part of God's plan for you to become a duchess, the mistress of a great estate."

"Part of God's plan only if my mother is indeed God, and I am starting to wonder. Please do not take her side, or I will be completely bereft."

"Now you don't mean that! Whatever our position in life, we can make the best of it. I know the status of the Blenheim estate workers and commoners bothered you. Perhaps you could change things, carefully, slowly, do good. Bring some fresh American ideas to the duke's stuffy ways."

"Perhaps. But I cannot see that—cannot see myself—there, with him. I want someone else, my own life to live."

Miss Harper sat up straighter. I turned my head to look at her, really look at her. She always had her brown hair parted in the middle and pulled back into a stiff bun. The lines around her mouth had deepened, and her frown lines showed. Her lips thinned now to become almost white before she spoke again.

"Do you think this is the life I would have chosen for myself?" she demanded, her well-tempered voice more harsh than I had ever heard it. "Of course I have an excellent position and place, but do you never note or think I might prefer—

desperately desire—another situation in this one life I have to live? A home and family, a husband of my choosing? But here I am, governess, and I hope friend to a promising young woman who can do great things someday because, not only for her name and position in life, but because of her character and strength and good heart, which I have poured my life into these last ten years."

Tears burned my eyes to match the single one that tracked down her cheek. "You have been and are more to me than a governess," I told her, my voice breaking. "You have indeed been my dear friend. And, the Lord knows, I have needed that, needed you."

"Yes," she said as we now gripped both our hands together and leaned our shoulders close. "But there may come a time when you must go on, be strong without a friend until you can make new ones, stand on your own. My dear, I hear that your friend you are missing so deeply here in America will be at the ball your mother is taking you to tonight, but I warn you not to do something foolish. I repeat, be strong and stand on your own, but do nothing rash, only what is necessary."

Win would be there! So she still was on my side to tell me that! "What would I ever do without you? Thank you, dear friend," I cried, squeezing both her hands in mine as I started to stand.

"Consuelo," she said, snatching me back to sit again, "I mean you must bid him farewell and face your fate with the duke if it comes to that. Think of all the great things you can do, people you can sway, all—"

"Did my mother ask you to convince me of this?"

"No, I swear it. It is just I see that what she believes of your friend is true."

"What? What has she told you, tried to convince you to convince me? What is she saying against Win?"

"Think of this. I, too, have eyes and ears. I hear talk other than from your mother. Mr. Winthrop Rutherfurd is a trained lawyer who does not practice, and who would rather spend his time at polo, golf, horses instead of at work. Ask yourself, why has he not wed yet, when he is nearly thirty?"

"Because he is waiting for me, and don't you dare tell her that. I am sorry you are caught between us, and you must, of course, listen to her. But the fact you told me he is to be at the ball tonight means to me you are really on my side. Do not look at me that way," I scolded her for once as I finally dropped her hands and stood. "I will not run off with him—and how could I with my mother probably dancing with Win and me."

But even at that silly, dreadful picture, I felt better already. I could finally breathe. All I needed was a moment with Win to be certain he still felt as I do. And then I would stand up to Mama, end her plans for me with the duke, plan my own life. Yes. Yes, I would.

WIN AND I managed one short dance that night. "Yes, darling, yes, I still feel the same!" he told me. "We are engaged, betrothed, to be wed, whatever you may call it."

"Then I will tell her."

"But is it true about you and the duke?"

"She will try to force me, but I am done with that. He has not asked for me. You have, and I said yes. Papa thinks the world of you at least, so you must go to him soon and ask that he give us his blessing. One thing I have learned from Mama is to fight for what I want, and I want to be your wife."

"Oh, my dearest. I shall call upon you tomorrow, so she can-

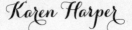

not stop our messages again, then see your father thereafter. Just after noon?"

"I will tell her tonight, settle things once and for all. She can still flaunt the duke as her guest. She can strengthen the position in society she fought so hard to build years ago, even this time without Papa."

"The music is ending, but our dance is only beginning . . ."

Over Win's shoulder, I saw Mama coming, like a steamship through a crowd of other vessels. Twice people tried to stop her to comment or chat, but she kept coming.

"Should we face her here?" Win asked.

"I will tell her alone tonight."

"I will always love and adore you, my Consuelo," he whispered as the next waltz began, and he beat a retreat into the crowd.

"Everything is settled then?" Mama asked.

"It is."

"Then let's head home. It is all for the best. You will see. Tomorrow is another day to talk and plan."

BUT I COULD not keep still. She seemed too calm to have understood what I meant by things being settled. A warning bell clanged in my head, but I could not go back to being kept in a cage only to be forced into another, foreign one, however gilded the walls and locked door.

"Mother, you reared me to be strong," I said back at Marble House the moment she told me to follow her to her room and we closed the door behind us. "So we need to be clear that I am not your prisoner or your slave. I know you had slaves to order about once years ago, but that was wrong and so is this."

She turned to face me, leaning back against her high bed,

for the four-poster sat on an elevated dais. And, overhead in glorious painted array, Athena, goddess of wisdom and victory, stared down at us.

"Ungrateful, foolish girl, however bright you are! I know what is best for you and your future! Your father and I are willing to pay the price for it and you must, too! Did not Miss Harper make herself clear to you?"

"That I should break off my betrothal to Win?"

"Betrothal! Utter rubbish!" her voice rose sharp and shrill. Her face reddened, and a tiny vein beat at the side of her forehead. "I told the duke you were free and clear to wed him and that—"

"You told him! Why did you not ask me? That is not true! You dragged me there and into all that. I am going to marry Winthrop Rutherfurd! I demand the right to choose a husband, the father of my children, the man of my heart like you did with father!"

"Oh, I chose, all right. But was he the man of my heart? No, he was the man my family needed then. My mother was dead, my father's cotton empire devastated. We were almost homeless, and there stood William Kissam Vanderbilt, handsome and easygoing, the son and grandson of King Midas, lord of all he surveyed!"

That outburst stunned me even more than the first. "I repeat," I said, trying to keep my voice and emotions controlled, "be that as it may, I mean to marry Win."

She seized my arm and pulled me toward the bed, nearly bouncing me off the side of the high mattress. Though I was taller, she tugged me down and put her livid face close to mine. "Consuelo, this is all for your good. Insanity runs in Winthrop's family. Why is he not married already, I ask you? I also have it on good authority that he cannot sire children. You are not going to marry into his family, and that is that. You are going to marry the Duke of Marlborough as soon as he proposes, and I am certain he understands that, so you had best, too."

"You are strong and have reared me to be strong, Mama. So I tell you true I will marry only Win."

"I shall make certain you do not leave this house until you leave it with the duke, one way or the other."

"I will not do what you say. I am eighteen. You cannot stop Win and me from marr—"

"You—oh—oh, I . . ." She gasped and lay back on the bed, one hand on her chest, the other clutching at the satin spread to keep herself from sliding onto the floor. I helped to steady her, lift her up to lay her on the bed, full skirts and all.

"What is it?" I demanded as she clutched her chest and gasped, screwing her face in agony.

"My heart. Oh, the pain. Listen to me, daughter. If you go to Win, I swear to you I shall shoot him. I will kill him so he will not ruin you and your life. I . . . ah . . . They will arrest me and hang me and my death—which may come right now—oh, my heart pain—will be on your head!"

I ran for her maid, and a footman went for the doctor. Surely, she did not mean any of that, I thought, all that hate and passion. And had she truly suffered a heart attack or had her own bile sickened her?

FINALLY, LATER, MISS Harper came to my room where I waited, pacing, still in my ball gown while the doctor was with Mama. "How is she?" I blurted. "She has always seemed so steady before, even if she lost her temper."

"I warrant she has never lost her daughter before. Her message for you is that she has had a heart attack and you are responsible. She meant, she says, what she vowed earlier. The doctor concurs with the medical diagnosis. He is giving her laudanum to rest, but she asked me for your response before she tries to sleep."

My legs gave way. My defiance fled. I sat right down on the floor amid the billowing poof of my skirts. My youth and my life were over. Could I even believe Mama's life was truly endangered—and that Win's could be? If I became Duchess of Marlborough, a stranger to myself, whatever would become of me?

"Tell her I understand," I told Miss Harper.

"Oh, and she says your father has agreed too, and will be proud to give you away to the duke, should His Grace ask for your hand."

"And the rest of me," I murmured with a sigh as I bowed my head and tears ran down my flushed face and spattered my satin skirt. "Please, tell her to keep calm and rest well. Tell her to get better soon, so we can plan for the duke's arrival."

She stepped closer and bent over to squeeze my shoulder. "I will tell her. And I will send Brooks in to help you undress so you, too, can get some rest. There is a lot of life coming, Consuelo, and I am sure it will be grand. It will be what you make of it."

I nodded and punched both fists into the pillow my skirts had made. At least, did not this all mean that I was soon going to see my father?

But I must write Win that I would not see him again. And I made another momentous decision that night. I would never call Alva Vanderbilt Mama again. That was a word of trust, love, and affection. From now on, to me, she would bear only the biological name of Mother.

Chapter Six

ou would think the duke's arrival in New York to-day is the second coming of the Lord, the way they are looking forward to it," Mother said to me over the breakfast table as she skimmed the day-old New York papers she had delivered to Newport. She didn't look upset at that but rather smug. "They even printed the time he is expected on the Cunard steamer *Campania*. My, but these journalists are stirring everyone up."

I twisted my linen napkin in my lap. "I hope the Newporters will be calm and quiet about it when he arrives later today."

"I would not bet on it," she said, trying to hide a little smile.

I had been aware that someone close to us was leaking news of Marlborough's coming visit to the States, and especially what galas awaited him here in Newport. Mother had remarked on it too, but had not seemed a bit put out with what I saw as an invasion of the duke's and our family's privacy. Granted, I should have been over that idea by now. Like the name Astor and the old Knickerbocker names like Roosevelt, the mere mention of Vanderbilt attracted publicity and rumors like flies.

Ah, but that little smile and the avid way Mother skimmed the papers . . . For the first time it crossed my mind that some of the details were known by such a few—not even me usually, so could it be . . .

That thought chilled me. I put my spoonful of coddled egg back in its cup. Suddenly, I was not hungry anymore. And here I had been making an effort to be at least polite, however distraught I still was over what I was coming to believe was Alva Vanderbilt's counterfeit heart attack. It seemed, as she snatched up another paper, this one local, that she was even proud of the wording, let alone the import of the articles laying out the duke's schedule. But I had not the strength to accuse her or argue again.

"It says here," she interrupted my thoughts, "that the duke is bringing his cousin with him and—"

"That Winston Churchill they all talk about?"

"No, my dear. Do not interrupt. Another Churchill, Ivor."

"Ivor," I whispered. "Winston and Ivor. Such unique names, and the duke's is merely a run-of-the-mill Charles."

She glared at me but went on, "When they disembark, the *Herald* says, they will be met by numerous members of the press, many of whom will follow the duke to Newport where he will be visiting at the Vanderbilt estate of Marble House."

"I am sorry if he has a raucous greeting. He already thinks most Americans carry on like crude cowboys or a band of whooping Indians. I do hope whoever is giving the New York press all this information will not live to regret it when it lowers the duke's esteem of America even more or, heaven forbid, frightens him away."

"Nonsense," she said, crumpling that newspaper and snatching up the last one. "It is reported that he and Ivor are supposed to go to the Waldorf to refresh themselves, then catch the five P.M. train—a parlor car has been reserved—for here. Well, enough of this, as we have our own planning to do. You are still looking peaked. You must eat, Consuelo."

"It seems I must do lots of things I do not wish to," I said, keeping my voice in check, though I still threw my napkin on the table.

"I will see to all the details here," she called after me as I murmured "excuse me, please," and headed for the door. "But you just be certain you are ready for his arrival. We will be his shelter here from the publicity and fervor."

I could not even bear to respond or look back at her as I walked past the breakfast buffet and out the door. How I wished I could just keep going.

UNFORTUNATELY FOR ME and for the duke—again, I was constantly reminded I was to call him Sunny—Newport, too, was soon in the throes of rapture over his visit. I swear, someone had been watching our house when he and Ivor arrived in their stiff summer white flannel suits and bowler hats late that Saturday, August 23, because a crowd had gathered outside the ornate iron gate.

I concentrated on introductions to Ivor. He was about the duke's age but with a much more open—and sunny—demeanor. My reunion with Sunny consisted of him holding my hands in his while he skimmed my face and person, then turned away to concentrate on talking to Mother. The five of us—her dear friend Oliver Belmont joined us—dined late that evening in our formal dining room that could almost have matched Blenheim in ornate grandeur, except Mother had been obsessed with copying French Versailles.

The next day, the social whirl began. After our family—my brothers included—attended Trinity Church, Mother held an afternoon open house for Newport society to meet the duke, and we were swarmed. "Have you met the duke?" I heard over and over in the crowd as people were presented to him across the room. Thank heavens, Mama—I mean Mother—did not make me stand at his side. I had heard her say to Mr. Belmont "not until the engagement could be announced." The whole thing made me feel not only dizzy but nauseous.

"Oh," a man whispered behind me, "is he the one over there who looks young—almost frail?"

"Yes, the pale, quiet one," a woman said. "Of course, in the eyes of most of our countrymen and women he is six feet tall and dashing as a fairy-tale prince."

I realized I knew that woman, Mother's new acquaintance Edith Wharton, who seemed to be on the fringe of her friends.

"Yes, there," Mrs. Wharton said, pointing. "The one who turns his head to look at all the pretty girls. But isn't he supposed to be promised to Consuelo, or at least the other way around? Oh, Consuelo, my dear," she said, beginning a blush as she recognized me. "We did not see you there. My, you look lovely this evening. And how tall you have grown. I mean I only see you in a carriage with your mother and the duke lately along Bellevue. I am sure you are so excited, absolutely on pins and needles."

I could hardly argue with her astute observations. And so the social swirl went on and on.

ON MONDAY, THE duke and Ivor played tennis at the Newport Casino courts, and a party was given for him at the so-called Gold Club where three hundred attended, but, thankfully, not me. On Tuesday nearly five thousand people crowded the Casino hoping to see him play, but he did not return until Wednesday, so he outfoxed them there.

He spent little time with me alone, though I had no doubt Mother would have permitted that, even promoted it. I was so grateful he was kept busy elsewhere on his so-called East Coast tour. Was he giving himself time to get used to the idea that everyone thought he was here to propose marriage to me? I could not imagine he was kind enough to give me time, or to find just the perfect romantic moment. He seemed not to have a romantic bone in his trim body, but I kept myself from gazing again at the American Beauty rose Win had given me, which I had pressed in my Bible. Or was the duke playing a cat-and-mouse game with Mama to up his bargaining power? If so, I wondered if he realized he was not the cat, but the mouse.

EVEN I, WHO was used to my mother's lofty level of entertaining, was awed by the fabulous decorations and display for the ball honoring the Duke of Marlborough at Marble House. She had so much to oversee that she let Papa help her in the preparations, though he had to promise to leave before the festivities began. Before he disappeared again, I had an opportunity to stroll the grounds with him.

"My dearest, how are you holding up? Sorry about Win, but think of all that lies ahead for you," he said in his usual effort to buck me up.

"What lies ahead is why you cannot console me."

"I daresay you think I should have stood up to your mother for you and Win, but the best-laid plans do not work out sometimes. I know you will do well as a duchess, my darling, use well that position and sphere of influence, so to speak."

"Some of his family studies me as if I am a brood mare."

"But I am sure you would like children. You would be an excellent mother."

"Since I have seen what not to do, you mean?"

Out on the back lawn where workmen were still stringing hundreds of lanterns, he took my shoulders to turn me to him. "Please, my girl, do not let this—or her—make you bitter. Look for the good as you always have. You have at least seen how to be strong from your mother," he added with a quick glance around. "Not a bit good for me to be here when everyone arrives, and you need to prepare. Consuelo, listen to me. Your Mama said you are wearing your grandmother Phoebe's gown tonight, one from a ball in Mobile before the war."

"Yes. I agreed. It means something to her."

"You know she lost her mother quite young and tried to bolster the family in their loss, tried to keep things together when their business collapsed and her father . . . well, fell apart. That is partly the reason she is the way she is, strong and determined."

"Good traits, I guess. In that regard I shall try to emulate her, but not with browbeating my children or selling one off for a title or—"

"Shhh. Here she comes. I had best be going. Did you hear the duke is coming to the yacht next week for luncheon with me? Just leaving, Alva," he said as Mama approached. "Things look as if . . . well, as if they have the special Vanderbilt touch," he added. He pecked a kiss on my cheek and hurried off.

THE HOUSE AND grounds did look amazing, as I stood there in my grandmother's gown of white satin and tulle with its full skirts. The papers had declared this fancy dress ball the highlight of the Newport season. Every single person who received an invitation had accepted. Crowds stood at the gate to see who arrived and had their invitations carefully checked. Once inside, guests were served by a vast parade of servants all dressed in the ornate style of the French king Louis XIV. Mother had also imported seven French chefs to add to the two who usually commanded the huge kitchen.

Three orchestras, two inside and one on the back lawn, played, not to mention the Hungarian band that picked up the dance tempo from time to time. Arrayed in white satin with a court-length train and dripping Vanderbilt diamonds, Mother greeted guests as they came in while the duke planted himself with Ivor where she had suggested—under my portrait painted in Paris now hanging in the Gold Ballroom. I supposed there was some symbolism there, but I was simply wishing Win would materialize among the crowd and whisk me away.

Fragrant flowers were everywhere, and water hyacinths filled hanging glass globes. The tables both indoors and out displayed artfully arranged orchids, ferns, and pink hollyhocks tied with pink ribbons. And a typical Alva amazing touch: scores of tiny, real hummingbirds buzzed among the flowers like iridescent jewels.

As was tradition with Newport balls, we began late because of the heat. Supper was served at midnight and breakfast was coming at three A.M. before people took their leave. And the coup de grâce of the night were the favors Mother had purchased in Paris and were meant to awe as well as please: tiny bagpipes that really worked, silk sashes, engraved lanterns, scrolled and scripted watch cases, fancy fans and fobs. I knew Mother had spent nearly five thousand dollars on those "trifling gifts" and was both amused and appalled to see how some guests traded for what they wanted and how some tried to make off with more than one hidden under a tailcoat or even a skirt.

As the festivities wound down, finally, the duke appeared at my side. "A grand evening. Interesting people-watching. Are you feeling quite well, Consuelo?"

"It has been a long evening."

"If you were a hostess in England, the outlay might not be so grand, but the planning, the balancing of people, the customs— all that—would be demanding, even daunting, I suppose."

"Different customs and people—a new country and life."

"Could you and would you do it?"

Was this his idea of a proposal? With people all about still and servants clearing the tables? The music had stopped. He had asked me to dance but once, and I had turned down other offers, which were few, since everyone probably thought I was permanently spoken for.

"As you can imagine, it would depend on who is asking. And from what country. I do favor France, but I am American, through and through."

His eyes widened at that careful rebuff. His nostrils flared, but he only studied me longer, closer. "Then we shall see," he said and lifted my gloved hand to bring it to his mustached mouth. He nodded as if in a half bow, turned on his heel, and left me.

Mother appeared as if from behind a potted palm. "Has he gone up for the night?" she asked me. "Whatever did he say?"

May the Lord forgive me, but on this night of nights for her, I was glad he had not said something romantic or promising or definite.

"He said naught of a proposal of marriage but he did say 'We shall see.' He and I are in agreement there, at least. We shall see."

Tonight, I thought, as I excused myself and walked into the house, I had managed a little victory, besting a Marlborough duke and a Vanderbilt general.

Chapter Seven

o proposal from the duke. Nothing. I felt as if a big clock were ticking in my head, louder, louder. I knew Mother was panicked. Could it be I would escape this fate?

The day was coming closer when he and Ivor would continue their East Coast tour. Other events came and went: Oliver Belmont's so-called Bachelor Ball, which simply meant he received guests alone, for he was long divorced from his wife. Since Mr. Belmont was mad for horse racing, the favors at this event honoring the duke were riding whips.

"I'd like to use one on the duke to make him cross the finish line," I overheard my mother tell Mr. Belmont.

All of Newport society decamped to New York City for the America's Cup yachting races. The duke spent some time with us there on the Astor yacht *Nourmahal*. We even sat alone on deck for a while. Nothing. Tick tock.

Back to Newport on Sunday, September 18. Daily drives

down Bellevue Avenue together or sometimes with Mother. Talk of Blenheim. No proposal, tick tock.

Conversation became awkward. I felt the duke was watching me like the proverbial hawk. For what? A declaration of love or loyalty from me? He did remark one day, "Your brothers are fine lads. Boy children seem to run in your family, an admirable trait."

Did I have no admirable traits? He was leaving on the morrow. Mother was distraught but hiding it. It was whispered everywhere, bandied about in the newspapers on two continents, that the duke was visiting Newport to propose marriage, to make Consuelo Vanderbilt the American duchess of Marlborough. If not, what joy for me. What shame for Mother.

"Mrs. Vanderbilt," he said after dinner the last night he would be staying with us, "would you mind if I took Consuelo off for a walk and a chat. Just to the Gothic Room, not far."

Mother managed a calm, almost sweet face. "Of course. Ivor and I will do just fine here. He has been telling me that another cousin of yours, Winston Churchill, is your heir unless you have heirs of your own. Consuelo and I should like to meet him. Is he married?"

"Looking," Sunny said. "Always looking at every opportunity is our Winston."

He gestured me toward the door and out we went. You might know, instead of outside on this starlit night, he'd picked the Gothic Room. That chamber had always frightened me with its medieval miniatures and collection of crucifixes. At least it did have a murmuring fountain, though that was decorated with the three stone masks of Greek tragedy. If I had not been so nervous—Was what he had to say farewell or forever?—I would have said the setting was perfect.

We sat on a needlepoint settee. He took my hand in his. His was cold but so was mine, and shaking.

"Consuelo, my dear, we are very different people from different realms, but I believe you will make a fine duchess for Blenheim and for me. You are beautiful and accomplished. I would like to do you the honor of asking you to be my wife. I will try to make you happy, and I am sure you will endeavor to do the same."

There it was. The clock in my head stopped ticking. Mother would be ecstatic. The newspapers would have copy for weeks. I would leave my family and home and be an American duchess.

"Yes. Yes, I would be honored" was all I could manage.

He lifted my hand and kissed the back of it. The deal was done.

BUT ACTUALLY THE deal was not done until the duke's lawyer came from England to negotiate with my father's lawyer about my marriage settlement. Now I really felt I was on the auction block. I had to wheedle information about the negotiations from Mr. Belmont because Mother would not discuss it.

The duke's settlement was $2.5 million in massive shares of stock in the railway company and annual payments of around one hundred thousand dollars. It was his for life, even if we did not stay married. Papa also settled a huge sum on me, independent of what went to the duke. All of it made me feel absolutely ill.

The duke and Ivor went off on their tour. I must say when hounded by the press, the duke said some very snooty things about America. He managed to even get arrested for "coasting" with his feet on his handlebars on a bicycle in Central Park. Oh, what fodder for the New York papers that was! Our wedding date was set for November 5 until Sunny protested that that was Guy Fawkes Day at home, the British celebration, I learned, of the exposure of a plot to blow up Parliament. I had a lot to learn about the British. And how I wished I could yet blow up my mother's plans. But too late. Much too late.

So the date of November 6 was decided on. Even I was put out—and Mother almost went berserk—when the duke skipped the wedding rehearsal because he thought it was just for me and my eight bridesmaids. So many differences between my America and where I was going.

Then came my wedding day.

I HAD ONCE seen Queen Victoria pass through the streets of London in a carriage with cheering, shouting crowds lining the way. She had been, of course, in her mourning black. I felt I should be now, though I was encased in white. And I kept telling myself that I was going to my wedding not my funeral.

With the help of the police, Papa and I made it inside old St. Thomas Church. We were twenty minutes late since I had needed repair from crying and clinging. The music of the orchestra and massive choir seemed to shake the stone foundations. My bridesmaids waited in the vestibule and fussed over my skirts and long train. I was handed a huge, heavy bouquet, since the orchids Sunny—yes, I had been told I must call him Sunny now—had had sent from Blenheim had not arrived in time. Tick tock, time to go. Time to become someone I was not and did not want to be.

"Your mother was so worried," Miss Harper said, appearing from where I did not know. "You are never late and she thought maybe you . . ."

"No," I said, then added the obvious. "I am here."

The hymn "O Perfect Love" swelled as my bridesmaids, one

by one, walked the long aisle ahead of us through massive bowers of blooms.

"Are you ready, Consuelo?" Papa asked and squeezed my arm tight to his ribs.

"I will make myself ready—for whatever befalls."

I was not sure he even heard those brave words for the orchestra suddenly swelled in the opening strains of the "Wedding March." Trumpets, no less. Again the walls seemed to shake. Oh, no, that was me.

Grateful again for the veil that hid my puffy eyes, I took one step and then another, tugging at Papa once to slow down. People were standing; faces flowed by. Up at the front, Mother was beaming. How I wish she had let me invite Papa's side of the family, estranged by the divorce she had demanded. I wished she had not made me return their wedding gifts unopened. Only my Vanderbilt grandmother was here. Sometimes I hated my mother.

At least she had not made me send back the pair of antique candlesticks from Win, but I would not have them shipped to Blenheim. I could not have borne using them, so they must stay unseen and their candles unlit. Strange how my mind darted away from all this: Papa had given me a diamond tiara "fit for a duchess," he said; my mother had presented me with a long strand of pearls that had once belonged to Queen Catherine the Great. Catherine, too, had been forced to change countries. And, how strange, but at the moment I recalled reading her biography—that she had not liked her future husband when she first met him.

I snapped back to now, to this—my wedding. With Ivor at his side, Sunny stood ready, looking small in the vastness, looking, well, stoic. He might be the Duke of Marlborough but he seemed nervous, too.

"Who gives this woman to be married to this man?" the words from the bishop rang out.

"Her mother and I," Papa said.

He stepped away to leave me there alone, now holding the hand of my future husband. Something rose up in me then, my Vanderbilt backbone. I can do this, I told myself. Somehow, I will survive and thrive.

AFTERWARD, THINGS WERE still a blur, both dream and nightmare. Despite the police cordon, the crowd outside the church surged at us. Two women tried to snatch my bouquet away. Some at least called "Good luck! May God bless you!" I felt I needed both, and yet a strange calm and acceptance had come over me. I was the Duchess of Marlborough. I had a new home, despite the fact we were taking a Mediterranean honeymoon first. And then there was the wedding night. After a reception for over a hundred guests at Mother's recently acquired home at Seventy-Second Street and Madison Avenue, Sunny and I were headed for a few days to Idle Hour, the Vanderbilt retreat on Long Island near Oakdale, before we left for Europe.

What I do recall when Sunny and I climbed into our carriage to leave was not the cheering crowds, nor even my teary goodbye to my brothers and Miss Harper. It was, as we pulled away, that I saw Mother in a first-floor window wiping tears from her face. Why was she not smiling? Laughing? Did I understand her at all?

SUNNY AND I took the ferry to Long Island City, then boarded a special train. We both sat, looking wilted, in our private parlor car heading for the first days of our honeymoon. Sunny perked up when he started reading congratulatory cables from England. He handed them to me after, telling me who was who. Some he was proud of, some he dismissed with a wave of his hand or tossed aside, a lesson for me of who mattered and who did not to my new husband.

"Ho!" he said and seemed to become much more animated over one. "One from the queen herself! I shall keep this. I have hopes you will be presented at court, even though Her Majesty's strength is waning these days."

"Mine is waning right now, too. But I feel I must be frank about something, clear the air a bit. We have been so busy—with others around."

He nodded, frowning, looking up at me at last.

I sat up straighter. I knew that expression, but I had to clear my conscience of this. I told him, "I am sure we shall both do our best to make the other happy, but I assume you know this marriage was my mother's idea, not mine. She insisted on it, even though there was another man who wanted me. She made me turn him away."

I expected he might mention that he, too, had given up someone he cared for. Would he be angry or wish to know more?

"Really?" he said with a small shrug as he looked down at the next cable in the pile. "I take it he was an American. I do not see much point in discussing it any further. As far as I am concerned, I never want to see your country again."

His lack of concern was like a blow to the belly, and his evident disdain for my dear country stung deep. How could I ever love or even respect this foreigner? How could I bear his children, though I swore to myself right then as I looked out the train window again as America rolled past, that I would teach my heirs—yes, mine—to love not only Great Britain but great and glorious America, too. I would indeed be an American duchess!

But however was I to get through my wedding night, my honeymoon, my new life?

AS I WAITED, exhausted and on edge, for Sunny to come to my bedroom at Idle Hour that night, I remembered something I had overheard Minnie Paget, of all people, tell someone once. It was a jest about a British bride on her wedding night not knowing what was expected of her. And, supposedly, her worldly maid had told her something like, "Just lie there and think of the British Empire."

I had been readied for bed not by Brooks, my longtime maid, who was not going with me, but by a new French maid, Jeanne, whom Mother had hired. Only Jeanne and Sunny's valet would be accompanying us on our wedding trip when we left here.

This grand, old Tudor house held such happy childhood memories. It was Papa's favorite place, though Mother had designed it. My brothers and I had sailed our small boat, gone crabbing and fishing in the Grand River, and hiked through the eight hundred acres of woods. My parents had the old bowling alley converted to a playhouse where I learned to cook and clean, and invited guests in for tea. I had kept a garden of flowers here and taken them in my pony cart to local convalescing children, one little crippled girl especially. Papa had said I had a good heart for children.

Sometimes here at Idle Hour House, Mama—Mother, I mean—had let me take off my iron corset. Strange, but waiting here now in what had been her bedroom while Sunny was next door in my old one made me feel I had put a sort of iron cage on again.

And it was here at Idle Hour that I had first met Win, when his parents were weekend guests. I thought he was so handsome, clever, and kind. If only he could be coming through that door right now . . .

Sunny knocked and came in wearing maroon silk pajamas and robe. "I like the sighing sound of the wind in the big trees here," he said, and I realized that was the most romantic, poetic thing he had ever said to me.

"You look, well . . . lovely," he went on. "So much beautiful hair when it is loosed." He came close, touched it, laced his fingers in it. I thought he would kiss me but he did not.

"Thank you," I said. My voice did not sound like my own. "I . . . I love the sound of the wind, too. Especially, I love to hear birds in the morning."

"You shall, at Blenheim. And if we visit the prince or queen someday, you will wake up to bagpipes."

"So much new to learn."

"Yes," he whispered, touching me at last, flesh to flesh, his hands skimming my arms under my loose-sleeved satin robe. "So much new to learn, and I shall try to teach you."

He drew me over to the bed and removed my robe. I shivered despite the fireplace across the room. It crackled. I decided then I would close my eyes and concentrate on sounds, remember the sounds if I did not like the . . . the feel of things.

Sunny's touch—his examination of my body when he laid down beside me and lifted my nightgown away—I concentrated on the sound of his increasingly heavy breathing. The house creaked, the fire crackled, the November wind no longer sighed but howled outside.

And something howled inside me at the thrust of pain and then our union. My heart beat hard, and I held my breath. The sounds of my new destiny, I thought, exhausted, floating . . . flesh moving against flesh.

After, when I turned over in the bed sometime later, he was gone.

Part Two

Duchess, 1895–1906

The Gilded Cage

Chapter Eight

ay the Lord God forgive me for thinking this, but our honeymoon seemed endless. A steamer to the Mediterranean, a rough Atlantic crossing with my husband suffering from mal de mer and I suffering from the reality of being married to him.

We disembarked at Gibraltar and visited chilly, late November Spain. Next, during Christmas in Rome, I was homesick and fell ill, becoming wan and weak. A doctor there actually told me I had six months to live, though he was so inept I did not believe him. I was appalled, however, to overhear that my husband had taken an insurance policy out on my life!

We skipped across the Mediterranean for a trip up the Nile. Then back to Italy. At Pompeii, where so many had died, I started to feel stronger. In January came the not unexpected news that Mother had married Oliver Belmont. By far, I was happier for her than I was for myself.

Even my beloved Paris did not really strengthen or soothe me, partly because of my own mistake.

"Time for the fashion houses here to dress my new duchess in grand style for going home and your first season in London," Sunny said during a carriage ride in the Bois de Boulogne. "I know some of your gowns are from Worth here in the city."

"That will be a new experience, for my mother always ordered my clothes. 'I chose them, you wear them,' she said more than once."

I thought he might be upset or think I was more of a ninny, but I knew he would believe me. To my surprise, he lit up and turned to me with a smile. "Then I shall help you. I have some styles, jewelry, too, in mind to show off my new wife!"

He proceeded to take over shopping for me, ordering things I would never wear by choice, overly elegant garments, not my taste at all. As with Mother, I did not see most of them before I went for fittings. His purchases included a nineteen-row pearl choker with diamond clasps that covered my entire neck. Truth be told, jewelry did not really appeal to me. But how appropriate a choker was, I thought, as we finally headed "home" to England with hundreds of new items in tow. Here I was a married woman, Duchess of Marlborough, and I had merely traded one manager for another.

My first days in London, before we even went to Blenheim, became a big blur. Most of the Marlborough relations met us as we arrived at Victoria Station. Cousin Winston Churchill was there, a carrot-topped redhead no less, round faced and instantly interesting and kind. Sunny had told me that Winston's father had died of syphilis only a year before. Missing Papa as I did, I felt great sympathy for Winston.

He was with his beautiful mother, Jennie Jerome Churchill, also an American, who had wed Randolph Churchill, Sunny's uncle. She had brought him a fortune in that bargain, too, another "Dollar Bride," as they were starting to call us imported American heiresses in the press.

Although Sunny had prepared me for the onslaught, I clung to the fact that we would see some of these family members singly in their London homes. There, I hoped, I could truly get to know them, not just be gawked at or talked about as if I could not hear. And then, while we stayed at Sunny's leased London townhouse, the visits began in the order of precedence in the Marlborough-Spencer-Churchill connections.

At the Grosvenor Square home of Sunny's grandmother, Sarah Wilson, a dowager Duchess of Marlborough, widow of the seventh duke, she said to me, "I do hope your country's war with South America wasn't too hard on your family, not to mention the threat of those red Indians."

I just stared at her a moment. No, she was not joking, as she sat papery-skinned and powdered in a chair in the corner of her drawing room.

"Your Grace, perhaps you mean the war between the northern and southern states," I said as she continually studied me with her lorgnette.

"I am referring to the war with South America in 1861, my dear."

Sunny shifted beside me, recrossing his legs. And then he dared to pop up to pace on the other side of the room to leave me to handle this myself. "Oh, yes, the North-South war," I said, rather than trying to correct her further. "Actually, it devastated my maternal grandfather's cotton import business, but good things came from that war, such as the freeing of slaves in our southern states, which went to war with our northern states."

"Slavery, a nasty business England handled much earlier than your country."

While what she said was true enough, it reminded me once more that the English upper class regarded even educated Americans as yahoos. I learned to fit in, however much everyone kept referring to my American heritage.

"My dear," the dowager duchess went on, her gray-eyed gaze piercing me again, "your first duty will be to bear a son, of course. Concentrate on that, not gadding about or entertaining more than you must. It would be intolerable to have that little upstart Winston who thinks he knows it all to become duke, however much Sunny likes him. Are you in a family way?"

"I . . . I am sure we will begin a family soon."

"I should hope so. And I must tell you about Goosey before Sunny comes back."

"Goosey?"

"The nickname for Sunny's mother—his real mother. Absolutely madcap, so keep an eye on her if he has her about again. Little jokes, inane ones. Something bloody dreadful, like an inkpot above the door or, like slivers of soap in the soup, you know what I mean, or, hopefully, not."

"A practical joker."

"Nothing practical about Goosey, silly as a goose. Albertha has bats in the belfry, as they say."

Oh my. So far I had discerned that Sunny's roué father browbeat him—or, perhaps actually beat him—and now I learn that his mother was too much of the wrong kind of fun. I thought again about my own parents, where the personalities were reversed, Papa great fun, even a rakehell at times, while my mother browbeat me—and literally used a rod.

Our next stop on the Marlborough spinning wheel was to

Sunny's uncle, the elderly Duke of Abercorn, at Hampden House in London. It was a charming place done by the fashionable interior designer Robert Adam, with grand and spacious rooms. The thin, nervous duke kept popping up to point out various family portraits and telling me I must know who was who despite the fact they were all dead. He wore a velvet smoking jacket and kept tugging the cuffs down.

He had fussed over removing my coat before Sunny could, then kept staring at the lining of it—Russian sables. "What a beautiful coat. Reminds me of one I own, but these may be better sables."

He rang for his butler who ordered his valet to bring his in. "Indeed, these are finer than mine, so I shall have to look for a new one. Sunny, you must tell me, my boy, exactly where you purchased this for Her Grace. You know," he said with a wink at me, "I can see that the future Churchills and tenth duke will be tall and handsome. Good news, eh, Sunny?"

Thirdly, though I was starting to wilt, we stopped at Lansdowne House in Berkley Square to visit the Marchioness of Lansdowne, an aunt whom I could tell Sunny preferred to his own mother. I breathed a sigh of relief for she was smiling, gay, and even gossipy. I had met her briefly in India, and my parents had stayed with her when she was vicereine, so we had a starting point, so to speak. It finally occurred to me where Mother got the inkling of pairing me with Sunny: His aunt must have mentioned that Sunny was available and Mother saw him ripe for the picking.

I was relieved not to have my corseted figure eyed again, as they were all hoping for an heir, but what I thought would finally be an easy visit turned into a "helpful talk."

"Now, Consuelo, since you do not know our ways, let me

give you some advice," Lady Lansdowne told me as Sunny nodded throughout. "A lady of your lofty status simply must not
walk alone in Piccadilly or on Bond Street, nor sit in Hyde Park
unless properly accompanied. You should not be seen in a han-
som cab, and it is far better to occupy a box rather than a stall
at the theater, and to even be seen near a music hall is out of
the question . . ."

On it went until my brain clicked off. Boring restrictions, I
thought. I was trapped in a gilded cage, and these new people
and new rules were the bars, at least the ones I could see so far.

AFTER NEARLY A week in London, it was on to Sunny's Blenheim—
my Blenheim now, too. That day was outright cold, so he insisted
I wear my sable coat. We went by regular train to Oxford where
a special train, with our parlor car decorated for a duke, took us
the rest of the way to Woodstock. Sunny had told me everything
would be both formal and festive to welcome their duke back
and their new duchess home. Yet I could not have been more
surprised by the turnout. It made the crowds on our wedding
day look meager.

"Good," Sunny said only as we disembarked to cheers and
huzzahs. "I would expect no less."

Women cried and waved, and men, some with little children on their shoulders, snatched off their hats or caps. The station flew bunting, British flags, and Marlborough coat-of-arms
banners. A red carpet had been laid on the platform. We were
welcomed by the mayor of Woodstock in crimson robes, who
greeted me with, "I must tell Your Grace that Woodstock had
a mayor before America was even discovered."

I was quite used to that attitude by now, but I was not prepared to control my emotions when the mayor's daughter pre-

sented me with a huge bouquet of pink roses. They were so lovely, so fragrant, not American Beauties, but it brought back to me Win's half-wilted rose that he had pulled from his coat the day he proposed on his bicycle and I accepted. I desperately blinked back tears and bit my lower lip—my upper lip not at all stiff but quivering. I had tried so hard to put the past behind me, but it kept lurking.

Speeches, welcomes, more cheers. To my amazement, our carriage up the road to Blenheim was drawn by estate workers rather than horses. That seemed off-putting, but the men looked proud, so I waved, smiling now much more than Sunny whose sharp nods indicated that all this was his due.

A triumphal arch had been erected. At the front door to the palace we were greeted by the chief steward, Mr. Angus, and the housekeeper, Mrs. Ryman, while a small band played "Home Sweet Home." I did love the schoolchildren's singing and promised myself I would visit their classroom soon. Tenant farmers, household servants, and other employees stood in separate groups, which bothered me, too, but apparently that was the way of it as we stood on the front steps of massive Blenheim.

Sunny, obviously their beloved duke, made a speech. "I did not plan to be so long away from you or that when I returned it would be the occasion of such good feeling and so kind a reception. Our new duchess has expressed to me numerous times that she hopes to become a friend to the people among whom she is going to dwell, and prays she might endear herself to your hearts."

And to yours, I thought. We had been intimate only in the bedroom, not in sentiment or emotion. I so missed that, longed for that. I still felt I did not know this man, let alone his people and all that would be expected of me. Suddenly, the roses and my coat seemed so heavy, even my hat and hair. I was swimming in exhaustion when I was about to face a luncheon for three hundred fifty people involved in these ceremonies in a chamber called the audit room.

I had never been so glad to see a hot bath. It had been prepared for me by my new English maid, Rosalie, for Sunny had not liked Jeanne and had sacked her. Sometimes I had the feeling he would give me the heave-ho, too, if I did not measure up. I had no time to soak in the bath, only to wash off the dust. Then it was time to be on display again.

As the pealing of church bells sounded near and far, Rosalie told me, "In your honor, Your Grace. Fireworks later too. And many trains coming tonight to take home people to their parishes, come to see their new duchess, they did. Mrs. Ryman says near thirteen hundred come in today."

Rosalie had laid out another outfit for me, perhaps one dictated by my husband, but I would change all that soon—as soon as I could. I actually liked that Rosalie was chatty, for I missed my American maid and Miss Harper terribly. For a moment, I almost missed my mother.

THAT NIGHT, SUNNY and I watched from a private tent in the park as fireworks filled the sky, great booming bouquets and whirligigs of colored lights. Strange, but I thought then of Jacques Balsan who had told me he loved to sail the heavens. He had promised me a ride in them someday, a someday now that would never come.

"Another ride through the streets, then home again," Sunny repeated over the noise. He took my elbow. "And what a night for our creating the next duke," he added, putting an arm around my waist.

I tried not to wilt. This was my husband and my new life. Of course I would love children. *Are you in a family way?* the words of the formidable dowager duchess sounded in my ear with the last of the booms that echoed through the trees followed by the gasps of Sunny's people, now my people.

"If you aren't tired," I said, trying to hint at my exhaustion.

"This place invigorates me and always will," he said, urging me toward our waiting landau.

And so I was now home in England, at Blenheim.

Chapter Nine

f I thought keeping Sunny's family straight was a challenge, I soon learned "commanding" the palace household staff of forty was more so. But my biggest surprise was that their rankings and domestic status seemed to be as important to them as were their places and privileges to the nobles of this land. Unfortunately, those above another, even belowstairs, seemed quite put out if the long-standing rules—which I was struggling to learn—were breeched by their underlings, or even by their new duchess.

For example, under the butler was the house steward, then groom of the chambers down to the numerous, lowly footmen. Yet Sunny's valet ranked high in his tails and striped trousers, too, and let everyone know it. Even when the housemaids had their meals downstairs, seating was strictly by rank of their duties and whom they specifically served, which gave my maid priority. And then there was another caste system in the kitchen from chef down to scullery maids.

I could have pulled my hair out with all the upsets and rows between our French chef and his staff of four over what went where on breakfast trays. I tried to settle the ruckus by telling them that, since the kitchen was a good distance from the bedrooms, keeping hot what should be hot should be their chief concern.

Of course we had had servants at home as I grew up, but I had never met with them, guided them, or corrected them. Sunny had said he would help, but he spent a good deal of time in London and, when home, immediately took to planning the water terracing of the grounds. So I relied on Mrs. Ryman, the housekeeper, as well as the butler and house steward and let them manage the other numerous workers. Sunny's tendency at all times was to criticize rather than help—both the servants and me.

Those first two months of Blenheim married life made me quite frazzled. I knew I must have control of things before we left for my first London social season in early May. At least, except for family, we did not entertain grandly those few first months.

My maid Rosalie was older than most in service and told me right up front that she would hate visiting away from Blenheim, because she would have to share a room with other ladies' maids. I should have stood up to "the duke," who had chosen her personally, and had her replaced right then, but I was already floundering in deep water.

I best summed up my struggles by relating it all to my mother in a letter, where I told the story of how I had asked the wrong servant to light a fire for me on a chilly afternoon. He dared to look down his nose and tell me, "The under steward has that task, Your Grace, and I shall speak to him for you, though his duties are not in this part of the palace at present."

"Never mind," I told him, rising from behind my desk—I had no secretary—"because I shall care for it myself. You see, we Americans do not mind sharing tasks and helping out in a pinch."

And what my mother wrote me back was most interesting. She didn't comment on my story. Instead, she went on and on about how her divorce—she was so happily married now—had set a bold precedent for an American woman to be able to escape the unhappy bondage of a bad marriage and yet retain her social status. I was such a frustrated bride that I decided to remember that scrap of information. She, too, applied pressure for me to bear an heir and said she would come to help out for the birth and christening of "the next duke."

What birth, what next duke, I thought, wadding up the letter. I could not even take care of myself, let alone a child—with a nurse and nanny hanging on and, no doubt, lording it over the downstairs servants.

The one person who greatly helped keep up my spirits was Sunny's sister Lilian, whom I had gravitated to when Mother and I had first visited Blenheim. She filled me in on not only gossip, but the history of the family and the palace itself.

"I swear, when I was young," she told me as we walked through the house on a rainy spring day when we could not venture out, "it frightened me that the first duchess, Sarah Jennings, haunted this place."

"Did you ever see her ghost? I know she is buried with the first duke in the chapel here."

"And under such a monument!"

"It does look so heavy and ornate, all that marble, so she would never creep out at night to scare little girls."

Lilian smiled. "When I was about seven, I did think I saw her in the bedroom that is now yours. I liked the painting of the golden cupids and the flowers there. And the fact it was not large like some of the vast, chilly chambers."

"Now you are trying to frighten me."

"I am not, dear Consuelo, I swear it. Well, you wanted to know all about her. They were a love match, you know, and she had to live here over twenty years after her dear husband died, and her goal was to finish Blenheim and make it grand in his memory."

"He is the one who should haunt these grounds."

She linked her arm through mine. "No," she said with a little smile again tilting up the corners of her mouth. "Sunny's planning never to leave, so he'll do that—if Sarah Churchill, First Duchess of Marlborough, lets him. I rather think she was the one to run the show in their marriage. Yet the first duke loved her madly," she said with a sigh.

I told her, "When I sit at chapel each morning at exactly nine-thirty, staring at the tomb as if it were an altar, it seems the first duke and duchess are to be worshipped. And maybe Sarah liked that dreadful saying on the marble mantelpiece in my room that reminds me of a tomb."

"Oh, I remember: *Dust Ashes Nothing*."

"Cheery to wake up to that," I told her with a little laugh, but I could not help but think that was an epitaph for Sunny's marital duty to get me with child. He tried, I cried, because I know I should feel happy, excited, something—and so far, nothing.

WE HAD THE entire family to a formal dinner on what I was remembering to call a Saturday to Monday, not a weekend. Everything went fine until my nemesis, the most senior dowager duchess, rose as if she were hostess to indicate it was time for the ladies to depart and the men to enjoy their brandy.

It was quite an affront to me and my place. Everyone looked up. Conversation ceased. Granted, when Sunny was unwed, as ranking duchess, she had that honor, but she was brazenly usurping it from me now

From across the table, Lilian mouthed, "Make her go alone—do not move!"

But I stood quickly and went to the door and met the dowager there. "Are you ill, Duchess Sarah?" I asked her and patted her shoulder.

She glared at me. "Ill? I am never ill, but strong and ready."

"Oh, I am glad to hear that," I told her in the best upper-class British accent I could manage at that point. "There surely was no other excuse for your hasty exit when I and the others are not yet ready to depart."

Her eyes widened. She colored and cleared her throat.

"Oh," she said. "I must learn to use my lorgnette at dinner. I must have thought you had given the sign."

Sunny's sisters and aunt hid smiles behind their hands. China, silverware, and crystal clinked again as the men turned back to their dessert. I made a show of helping her back to her chair. And that, I felt, was my first victory in the Battle of Blenheim.

However, I felt I lost most of the dinner table skirmishes when it was just Sunny and I who dined. At least I insisted our places be set, not at the far ends of the long table, but across from each other on the sides. Yet I felt at times that we might as well have been on distant planets. I tried hard to entice him to converse about his plans for landscaping the terraces, for fixing the roof, for information about the local tenants—anything! It simply was not his way to make conversation, and no one would have believed how little he talked, how little he even ate.

We were always both dressed to the nines, I in a satin and lace gown with Catherine the Great's heavy pearls or Marlborough diamonds about my neck. I hated to eat in the huge pearl choker Sunny favored, so had argued I was saving that for the coming season. He was always fully, formally attired as if we were eating with nobility—even the distant royals.

The servants served the first course, then retired to the hall so we could talk privately and intimately, which we seldom did, despite my attempts at conversation. "Sunny, I understand there is an elderly lady ill in the village. I should like to visit her. Rosalie says she is blind and loves to have someone read the Bible to her."

"Fine."

Although he had piled food on his plate, he often pushed the plate away along with his rows of silver utensils, even his drinking glasses. I felt rude eating, but I was not going to let his fastidious, fasting nature stop me after the first time or two. No wonder he was slight and slim.

"The food is delicious," I ventured.

"I am not that hungry."

Worse, he backed his chair away from the table, as if he wanted to get even farther from me. He crossed one leg over the other and proceeded to twist his ducal ring around his finger. After a period, where he was either brooding or sat deep in thought, he scooted close again and picked at his now cold food.

Between the long, drawn-out courses, I actually brought knitting, but he seemed neither to get my message nor care. I excused myself once and found the butler reading a detective novel in the hall.

He looked embarrassed and hid the book, but I told him, "I cannot blame you. I only hope the master of the house does not

die from starvation in that mystery novel. If so, I would like to borrow it."

I imagine that comment made the rounds downstairs, but I was at my wit's end.

I FELT MY personal, second Battle of Blenheim victory came the next day, and that was also over food at the table. We were dining with his sisters, Norah and Lilian. His mother, Albertha, alias Goosey, was there too, so we were all on edge. Sunny and his mother were like oil and water, though, I must say, I sympathized with Sunny this time around.

Having been warned about Goosey's antics, I had watched her closely to be certain there was no soap in the soup. But what I noticed—really noticed—for the first time was, when I lingered to be certain Albertha actually left the table after the meal with no hanky-panky, was the butler overseeing the dumping of leftover food into a tin pail. Although the meal had been delicious, the swirling mess it made mixed together almost turned my stomach.

"I thought that extra food went to poor people on the estate," I said.

"Oh, yes, Your Grace," the butler told me. "Straightaway."

"But the pudding with the bread, with the gravy, with the sweets, with . . . Why, it has turned to slop!"

Albertha said, "Always done that way. My dear, we cannot have an array of separate tins with everything wrapped up just so, you know."

The butler looked confused, caught between the two of us. He nodded, but I was not certain whom he was agreeing with.

"I'm going to the village on the morrow," I told him, "but I want breakfast and any other decent remains of the day to be packaged separately. I know you will take care of that, Mills."

"Oh, yes, Your Grace."

"Hmph," Alberta said. "You know, though, I did mix pudding with gravy once to teach Sunny he was not to stir things together on his plate."

I almost accused her of causing his wretched habit of staring at the food before he ventured to eat it, but I said only, "You know, Your Grace, my brother once put a frog in my bed, and I put it right back in his. I told him 'That's what happens to tricksters.'"

"Oh my," she said and dared a little smile. "I suppose some do take harmless jests the wrong way, but it sounds as if you were a brave girl."

But, I wondered, was I ready to be a brave duchess? I was going to the village on the morrow after church with some decent separated food and not slop fit for pigs. And if anyone else—including Sunny—protested about an American fouling up English tradition that was just too bloody bad.

THE NEXT SUNDAY, instead of being annoyed Sunny had stayed over in London on business, I decided to enjoy the day. He had spent much time looking for a place for us to live during the coming social season since Marlborough House, also built by the first duchess, was now the London home of the Prince of Wales and Princess Alexandra. They even had a close group of friends called the Marlborough House Set, which Sunny was not a part of because his father had been such a roué and had embarrassed the prince by naming him as a woman's lover in a public court.

So Sunny, now that he had a duchess, had let a place on

South Audley Street to "make do" for the season. However, when my father heard that, he promised us money to build our own London place, which would be grandly titled Sunderland House and would be ready for future seasons.

My, I thought, however were we to climb out of the prince's displeasure? And yet I was to be presented at court? And by the jokester Albertha? I would have to be certain my long court train wasn't booby-trapped somehow, for she had slipped some things past me at Blenheim, which sometimes, I swear, she wanted to turn into Bedlam.

So here I sat praying in the church service at nearby Woodstock not with Sunny, but with Lilian, for Norah was under the weather. I prayed for a child—a son—and for a much improved marriage and better relations with the Prince of Wales. I prayed for strength and some sign I was appreciated somewhere.

On our way out, while Lilian bustled ahead to speak to someone, the curate, standing off to the side, motioned to me. "I must tell you, Your Grace," he said when I joined him, "that the gifts and compliments you send regularly when the schoolchildren sing for the staff at the big house have been much appreciated. Even the flowers you sent their teachers at Bladon and here at Woodstock."

"I am pleased to hear that," I told him. "I learned long ago that children, too, love flowers. I had a garden at our house called Idle Hour and sent the flowers to nearby children when I was just a child."

"And now," he said with a smile and a slight nod, "your endeavors to meet and know people in the village are blossoming. The old ladies at the almshouse you visit are so appreciative of your time, especially Mrs. Prattley, the blind lady whom you read to."

"She loves the Book of John, especially the part where the Lord heals the blind man. I nearly have it memorized myself. She is such a gentle, patient soul and—I need to learn that."

"I have no doubt that 'Blessed are the meek' is difficult for a duchess. Well, the last thing I heard—and the old ladies all cheered—was that they now have food from the big house that they can tell what it is, not all swirled together like—mush."

"Good. Tradition needs to be changed sometimes."

"Well," he said, with the first frown I had seen from him today, "please do not quote me to the duke about that, for, of course, he always tells me that the aristocracy is the cornerstone of society—of civilization itself."

I did not blink an eye at that, Sunny's bedrock belief in a nutshell.

"I feel blessed by the village people and feel I derive more gifts from them than they do me," I told him as Lilian, already seated in our landau, looked around to see what I was doing.

"You know," he said, speaking even more quietly as others passed, "Mrs. Prattley calls you 'The Angel of Woodstock,' and I dared not argue with that."

I blinked back tears as I bid him good-bye and was helped into the landau by a footman. I felt calm for once, and cared for—really cared for her. For that blind, old lady and the others she lived with, the schoolchildren, the tenants in the streets and fields had given me a finer gift than any expensive costume or ornate piece of jewelry.

I felt I had done something good and worthwhile here, in the Lord's eyes, if not my lord's eyes. For the first time I glimpsed that I, as duchess, could make a difference.

Chapter Ten

ou indeed look like a Duchess of Marlborough!" my mother-in-law, Albertha, crowed, clasping her gloved hands together.

The two of us were waiting in the line of ladies to be presented to the Prince of Wales and his wife, Princess Alexandra, because the queen no longer undertook difficult duties. I was regretful I would not be able to meet Her Majesty, but Sunny had said he hoped for a more private audience with her soon. He was somewhere with the crowd inside, and the dowager duchess was my presenter. At least the two of us had worked well today so far.

It was the first time I had been in Buckingham Palace, which, I understood, the prince and his set had jauntily dubbed "Buck House." Today was the first time Sunny and I had ridden in the new crimson state coach he had purchased to be pulled by his favorite team of four matched grays. It was driven by a white-wigged coachman in a red coat with cape and guarded by two powdered footmen riding postilion in similar garb.

After being escorted through a series of small rooms called "the pens," I took my place in line outside the palace ballroom. I felt weighed down by my jewelry and garments and heavy court train, which was draped over my right arm. For once, I blessed my mother for making me wear that dreaded iron contraption years ago that made me stand so straight.

The neckline of my bridal gown had been cut lower to meet the proscribed style for presentation attire, since recent brides wore that gown by tradition. Short sleeves with over-the-elbow gloves were de rigueur. I wore a diamond belt, a recent gift from my husband, and the diamond tiara Papa had given me. Each lady to be presented wore three ostrich feathers upright in her coif. Sunny had said it was to honor the Prince of Wales's historic heraldic badge, but Albertha said it was so that, in the crowd, the prince could give his full attention to any pretty young woman approaching.

Oh my, I thought when the palace footmen swept open the double doors, at least the length and height of the ballroom was not so daunting, perhaps the size of Blenheim's long library. A band inside played military music, but we hardly marched in. Each of us in turn halted to give the card with her name to a lord-in-waiting, who then handed it to the Lord Chamberlain to be read aloud in his booming voice while the train was taken off my arm and arranged by Albertha and a page.

My name rang out, and I moved farther forward, leaving Albertha a few steps behind as planned. I sensed a stir in the attendants and the crowd, but I had known I would be a curiosity. I concentrated on gliding across the parquet floor and then onto the crimson carpet that led to the elevated dais where sat the prince and princess on thrones. Thank heavens I had practiced the court curtsy, for it was very deep with my head almost touching the floor, a real stretch for a woman of my height.

But I was well rehearsed. Probably fearful that his mother would come up with something silly, Sunny had insisted on watching while I curtsied repeatedly after walking the long library in this gown, dragging the train.

I managed both of my curtsies to the royals. Oh, the prince was quite heavy, indeed fat, and the princess so lovely. And how Bertie, as they called him, looked me over with an avid eye, more than most would dare. I found it a bit off-putting but for two things. I had heard he had a roving eye for any pretty woman, so it was not personal. And Sunny had said that if the prince approved of me, it would help the family climb back in his good graces.

And then, before I turned away, the most momentous thing: Princess Alexandra smiled at me, right at me! I was so grateful and liked her instantly. They said she was hard of hearing. I felt I not only saw but heard her sympathy, her good wishes for me loud and clear.

The worse part was yet to come, for one must not turn a back to the royals. So, after a page scooped up my train and placed it over my arm again, I retreated in reverse, gazing not to the right or left, inching away from the royal presence.

In the corridor outside, Sunny was beaming. "I have a beautiful, regal duchess!" he told the man next to him, though he did not tell me. That set me a bit on edge.

"Well done," Albertha said. "I must say, no one would take you for an American!"

I could not help myself in my retort to her, for I was full up with comments disparaging my people and my past. "I suppose you mean that as a compliment," I told her. "But what would you think if I said you were not at all like an Englishwoman?"

"Oh, but that is quite different," she protested, starting to blush.

"Different to you, but not to me. I am proud to be an American. I will ever be an American, even living here wed to the English, with English and American children, someday, I pray."

Sunny took my arm. I thought he might be angry, but he said, "Mother, Consuelo carried herself beautifully tonight, and as for children, we shall soon see."

As our coach swept us away from the palace gates that night to the music of the Household Calvary band, and as we rode down the Mall, I felt I had become in truth, duchess at last, if still an American one.

AMID THE SOCIAL swirl of polo matches, visits to Parliament to listen to and applaud speeches—sometimes Winston went along—theater visits, and numerous parties that first London season, came another important invitation. The Duke and Duchess of Marlborough were invited to be presented to the queen. The event was called a dine-and-sleep and was to be held with a small number of guests at Windsor Castle on very short notice. That, Sunny said, was because one never knew how strong Her Majesty would be from time to time.

We took the train, which the British called the railway. Again, I had been prepared for this by a family member, this time Sunny's great-aunt. I must speak only when spoken to by the queen and must keep my comments pertinent to Her Majesty's question. When presented, I would kiss the queen's hand, and because I was a peeress, she would give me a quick kiss on my brow as a blessing. Here we were, properly dressed in dark colors, but she was swathed all in widow's black. I know she still mourned her beloved Albert after all these years, but I vowed I would never go into eternal mourning, God forgive me, at least not for Sunny. However, mourning for losing my person and my past might suit me.

I was surprised that Queen Victoria was so tiny that I almost had to kneel to get low enough to receive the forehead kiss. I wore a diamond crescent in my hair that I feared might scratch her, but all went well. Her questions to me were about my country, and I caught the whiff of disdain there, too. Needless to say, I did not lecture her as I had my mother-in-law. Dinner was odd and a bit depressing with everyone but Her Majesty whispering. I found Windsor Castle somewhat gloomy and was amazed it made me long for—at least the gardens and rural spots—of Blenheim.

Funny, but in the midst of all this, I thought how very regal was dear, blind Mrs. Prattley in the almshouse with her black shawl pulled over her shoulders and her graceful, blue-veined hands folded in her lap while I read to her. She, too, had lost her husband years ago, and there was such an inherent, silent nobility about her. God forgive me, but I would have preferred to be spending time with her.

SUNNY WAS GIDDY with joy that autumn when we received an invitation from the Prince and Princess of Wales to visit their country estate of Sandringham in Norfolk for a Monday through Saturday—not even the shorter Saturday through Monday.

"He knows I am not like my father!" Sunny told me. "And I am sure he was taken with you too, Consuelo. He has a bit of a reputation with women, I must warn you again, though I am certain he would not pursue one who had not yet borne an heir."

"Nor would I 'take up with him,'" I retorted. "Not before or after an heir or ten of them. And since it is you he is favoring, you do not need me to earn the Marlborough way back!"

"Now, I did not mean that. Not a bit of it. You are a Marlborough-Spencer-Churchill now, too. You have been doing a fine job when we entertain here."

I just stared at what, I was certain, might be the first real compliment he had paid me, at least one he made directly, with no one else around.

"And you will be smashing there," he rushed on. "There will be a lot of shooting, of course, but you ladies will join us for lunch under a marquee outside, and you can become acquainted with the princess. Their heir, George, Duke of York, and his family live on the estate in a place called York House, quite small and provincial, but charming."

"Every house is small, compared to Blenheim. Do you think you could be happy in such a rural place? I have told you how much fun my brothers and I used to have at Papa's favorite house where we went after our wedding. My mother might have decorated it, but it seemed most like home."

"A place like that rather than Blenheim? Absolutely out of the question, so do not bring it up again. Blenheim is home! But one more thing. The heirs of George, Duke of York, Victoria's firstborn great-grandson and his younger brother, David and Bertie, their heir and the spare, as you like to say, live mostly at York House. Their mother is Mary of Teck. You must keep all this straight. And these two heirs were born a scant two years after their marriage and quite close together."

"I am sure hearing that, especially about their two little sons, will inspire others," I dared with a roll of my eyes. Then, to avoid a righteous tirade from Sunny and even a determined nightly visit to my bedchamber for my snide remark, I quickly darted in another verbal direction. "So how deaf is the princess and how is it best to speak to her?"

"I hear she somewhat reads lips, but be certain to speak directly to her. She will show you her collections of bric-a-brac, so she will do a lot of the talking, another way she tries to overcome, I suppose."

I wondered what she did to overcome and overlook her husband's infidelities, but bit my tongue on that. The kindly woman had smiled at me when I saw she did not necessarily do that to others in the presentation line. But how fortunate that she had borne children—sons—early in her marriage. And the message was always that I must do the same.

I MUST ADMIT I loved the country elegance of Sandringham. The "big house," as they called it there, seemed homey next to Blenheim, and York Cottage was a charming but cramped place to rear a family. We all ate ptarmigan pie and lobster salad at teatime, because that is what the prince favored. Dinner, blessedly, was not the usual four hours of a social meal, but one hour, because that was the way here. Despite the four major changes of attire each day, I enjoyed myself greatly because of the warmth and kindness of Princess Alexandra.

She was a beautiful brunette with a poodle-fringe of hair over her high forehead. She, too, owned a thick pearl choker, which she wore at dinner, so I was glad I had not brought mine along. I had seen that women imitated her limp with the so-called Alexandra glide, but I did not, for I found it faintly mocking.

"I must say, you have two beautiful grandsons at York House

I was honored to meet!" I told her as she showed me her large Fabergé egg collection. I tried especially hard to talk directly to her and raise my voice. She did not use an ear trumpet. Though she was some years older at age fifty-two and far above my rank, she seemed my age, my friend.

"My dear Consuelo, they are darling boys. We are on the lookout for granddaughters also."

"I was the firstborn, but two boys followed!"

"I am sure you miss your family. I miss mine in Denmark and visit when I can—or when they cannot come here. Now this egg opens up with a mere touch of this hidden pin, you see?" she said and opened the ornate, gilded and jeweled egg. To my surprise, within was a tiny, delicately decorated hot-air balloon with a gold woven basket and two gilded figures.

"Oh, it is lovely, Your Majesty! I know—I mean knew— someone who flew a balloon once."

"Someone is new, you say?" she asked frowning and tilting her head. I realized too late I had said that too quietly. Yet I felt I had blurted it out, so strong was my memory of my few moments with Jacques Balsan.

"He is a Frenchman! He flies in balloons!"

"I say, perhaps he will take us up someday," she added with a little laugh. "Oh, I see outside the window the men are returning. How many hundreds of partridge will they have dispatched today, do you think? Do come along now, and we will greet them before tea, then have time for a little lie down before dinner."

The prince was all eyes for me again, and Sunny was beaming in his proximity to the man. But I was well content to have only Alexandra take my arm.

BUT, ALAS, OUR newfound royal favoritism had its price—at least for me, though Sunny would never agree. During the yacht races at Cowes in August, he burst into my bedroom at our leased seaside home while Rosalie was lacing up my corset. I was surprised and Rosalie totally flustered.

"Wait outside," Sunny told her. "I need to convey something to the duchess straightaway!"

She fled, and I stood there, half-laced. I began, "Well, at least, I can tell by your smile no one has died, so—"

"The prince and princess will be making a visit to Blenheim! We are on the upward path, Consuelo! Do not look so dismayed, for this is a godsend for the Marlborough name and reputation, if not fortune, for it takes a lot of tin, as your American newspapers say, to host them. But this is an answer to prayer!" he insisted and came close to kiss me, something he almost never did.

"But when? Just the two of them?"

"Ah, November 23 for five days to be exact, but the two of them?" He laughed. "They are bringing some of their family, two of their daughters, no less, Maud and young Victoria. Then their staff, of course, two equerries with their valets, two loaders for shooting. Probably a total of twenty-four or -five, not including the servants."

He paused while I stared at him aghast. "Wherever will we put them—the royal party? We will have to move out of our first-floor rooms and house them there."

"Exactly. As well as redecorate some chambers. I do wish we had better plumbing, but they will have to make do. The benefits and beauty of Blenheim quite make up for that. So you need to plan breakfasts, luncheons, teas, dinners, and theatricals. The prince loves to be entertained. You will sit next to him at the table at dinner, of course, and you and the ladies will join us for luncheon in the fields the days we hunt—every day, I wager."

I still just stared. Granted, I had finally assumed control of the daily routines and our staff, but we had not been wed a year and now this? At first, the only thing I kept thinking was that my mother would be ecstatic and, as we crude Americans sometimes said, she would definitely "make hay" with this news.

Chapter Eleven

lthough Sunny oversaw the redecorating of the room the royals would use, but for Albertha's suggestions, I felt greatly on my own. I was even so desperate for advice that sometimes I wished my mother were here. But she was reveling in her new marriage and undertaking some political endeavors in her new zeal for reform. She cabled again, however, that she would come to oversee things when my first child was born, so that weighed on me, too.

"The royal reception is going to be an absolute repeat of our triumphant arrival as newlyweds here," Sunny said, with a clap of his hands. The Waleses would be arriving that afternoon, and we were heading out to the Great Court to take a carriage to meet our guests at the Woodstock railway station. "The same triumphal arch has been raised," he went on as if I hadn't planned and arranged all that weeks ago. "The same school-children prepared to sing for their arrival, and hundreds have turned out for a glimpse of their future king."

"I wish Winston was not off soldering in Italy," I told him.

"That is what one gets for attending the Royal Military College at Sandhurst. But he feels it is his best preparation for public service to the nation. He has always wanted to be a hero, and I can only hope he does not die for that cause. As different as the two of us are, well, we have been close. He has held me up through some difficult times, and I him."

"I was just thinking he would keep the prince entertained at dinner. You said he does not favor bluestockings, and here I have all this background of history and literature to discuss from my years of education."

Sunny laughed again, as he had at my frustrations and fears these last months of planning. "Granted," he told me, "the sort of bluestockings he would favor are those on a lady's legs."

He snickered like a horse as he helped me up into the carriage. This time, however, Sunny's favorite four matched grays would pull us back, not our estate workers. I carefully arranged my skirts so the rich brocade would not wrinkle, for I had needed to buy and be fitted for sixteen new ensembles, from tweeds to satins, for these few days.

"So tell me more about this Lord Arthur Balfour the prince has suddenly decided to bring along," I changed the subject as I settled my skirts. "The note said he would not join the guns but would bring his typewriter. He rather sounds like some sort of secretary."

"Not Lord Balfour. You must remember the word *secretary* here does not mean some lowly position. Balfour is about fifty, smooth of speech and manners, First Lord of the Treasury and Tory leader in the House of Commons."

"I do recall him from sitting in the strangers balcony in Parliament. A magnetic personality."

"But as for being sad that Winston's away, I say it is a blessing.

He would never let up on Balfour with his own dreams of grandeur. Winston is going to stand for office sooner or later, and I shall, too, locally here, of course, my ducal duty."

At the railway station, our greeting of the royal family and so many guests seemed to go on and on. I curtsied to the prince and princess, and she took my hands. "I cannot wait to see your collection of ornaments and bibelots," she whispered.

"Nothing like yours," I told her, "but Blenheim has some fine historical pieces—ah, crucifixes, battle flags, and such." I did not mention that Sunny's father and grandfather had sold off art and rare collections to pay Blenheim's debts.

I thought I had planned for every contingency of their stay with us, but I had not thought of that. And Sunny had warned that the princess had "an acquisitive nature" when it came to things she liked that others owned.

Oh dear, I thought, as the prince's laugh boomed out and we climbed into the carriage to be followed by others on the way back. I was already exhausted. However would I survive this "little" royal visit?

There was never a dull or even restful moment over the next few days. Hundreds of Blenheim birds were "bagged" each day, and the *crack, crack* of the hunters' guns permeated the air for hours. During the day, I entertained the ladies and Arthur Balfour and ended up admiring him immensely for his intellect and charm. He showed me how to use his typewriter, though I was slow since I had no time to learn the pattern of the alphabet laid out on it.

"One of the waves of the future, the keyboard to make print!" he told me. "Men will fly someday soon, too, mark my words."

"You mean in hot-air balloons?"

"Of course, but that is old hat. With wings, gliders like birds of the air. Hate to say this, but the Frenchies are far ahead of us with that."

I nodded, but had no time to ponder the "flying Frenchie" I had met once. Here came Princess Alexandra with the single lady-in-waiting she had brought and here came the guns back from another day of shooting.

"BLENHEIM IS A lovely place with a lovely mistress," Prince Edward told me at dinner the last evening they were with us.

"We are so honored you and the princess could visit."

"She is quite fond of you, does not take to many Americans or even some English, truth be told."

"She has been most kind to me," I said, starting to lift my champagne glass to my lips.

"And I hope I also," he said and clinked the lip of his goblet to mine.

"That goes without saying, sir. We have been glad to be able to return not only a bit of your hospitality to us but our gratitude for your past and future support of the Marlboroughs and the entire nation."

"Then to the queen," he said and his stentorian voice carried up and down the table.

Other conversation ceased, though I had noticed when he spoke to me, others tried to listen.

Alexandra, sitting to Sunny's right, smiled and nodded. Well, I thought, returning her smile, there was one who was not listening. She had told me she had such trouble with the buzz of voices in a crowd and missed things like the songs of birds and even human voices singing. And she had privately told me that to conceive a child, I should not ride horses or take hot baths—another person aware I must bear a son.

"To the Duke and Duchess of Marlborough!" the prince's voice rang out. "To their palace—the only one that is not Her Majesty's, of course—I lift a toast to their futures and contributions to the Empire."

Sunny rose, and the men all stood. I did not care if it was English precedence or not, I stood too, so the women got to their feet. It was a shining moment for both me and Sunny, who was beaming like the sun itself for once.

SUNNY KNOCKED ON my bedroom door after dinner one January evening since I had sent word down I did not feel well enough to eat. Truth was, I'd felt faintly nauseous all day.

"Shall we send for the doctor?" he asked, closing the door behind him. He seemed sincerely distressed.

"Not . . . not until later so he can agree with what I already know."

"Where does it hurt?"

I almost said, in my heart, but it was not hurt, though I had been a bit depressed of late. I actually felt contentment, mixed with a bit of anxiety. "I don't really hurt," I told him. "I think I am filled with joy—and relief."

His intense gaze dropped to my midriff, which I had covered with a warm woolen robe. The fire crackled in the grate behind the firedogs, but I felt warm all over. Triumphant. I smiled.

"Consuelo, if you think you are with child, tell me right out. If not, I will have the doctor here tomorr—"

"Yes. Yes! Though, of course, I am rather new at this, I believe I am with child."

He knelt before my chair and took my hands in his. "My dear wife!"

"Am I? And not just for this reason—and the other?"

"No . . . I . . . you have been a help to me in many ways. And now . . ."

"And now, other than improving Blenheim, you shall have another wish come true."

He lifted both my hands and kissed them solemnly. Tears gilded his eyes in the firelight and dropped onto my fingers. It was then, I swear, I saw a woman in a long, silk robe move in the darkness behind him and absolutely disappear through the door.

Goose bumps skimmed my arms. Had my maid come back in? Nonsense. Just exhaustion. A hallucination. Or just a surprise that Sunny, the 9th Duke of Marlborough, knelt at my feet as if he were at last being presented to me. Perhaps there was hope for us and for our future child.

I THOUGHT BEING pregnant would make me happy, but it only made me relieved. In truth, I felt lonely, however joyful I was supposed to be—especially when lacing tight was a complete farce and I needed to stay in more. I was so slender that I sometimes felt I had a, well, a child-sized hot-air balloon in my belly.

Sunny, after our triumph with the royals, spent much time away in London, but one day here I heard my doctor tell him in the hall, "She has narrow hips, Your Grace, and a first birth—with a big child. We shall pray no difficulties ensue. Though I can come here when her time is near, you might want to take her to London for the birth."

"Actually, I intend to. Since our own townhouse is not complete, I want the child to be born there in Spencer House, one tied to our family history. It will be good for her to attend a few events of the London season. The duchess's mother is coming from the States for the birth, and I shall endeavor to see she does not get in your way. Mrs. Vanderbilt—now Mrs. Belmont—has a tendency to take things over."

"So I gathered from what Her Grace said. I shall be back next week."

Meanwhile, I read German philosophers Mother had forbidden me, though I should have picked something cheerier. I spent a lot of time staring out my window at the pond where a butler, before I came, had drowned himself, or so Lilian, with her tendency to talk of ghosts, told me.

But I was immensely cheered when Winston came back from his military assignment in Italy and dropped in to see me before we removed to London. His energy and buoyant personality lifted me. He had been pumping me for any shred of conversation Lord Balfour had muttered when he was here for the royal visit.

"Let us walk to the monument and back," he suggested after lunch. "It is a lovely September day. We shall take it slow."

"You know ladies in the family way are not to exercise too much and I am big as . . . as a barn."

"Nonsense, you look beautiful as ever and can use the walk."

"Speaking of ladies, have you found a particular one you favor?" I asked him as I tied a scarf over my hat to face that windy day.

"Only one, but she is taken," he said with a grin and a wink at me. "But I am looking, looking. I must make my way, of course, first. It will not do to just be a war correspondent or soldier, even an officer. Consuelo, if I do stand for local office, will you attend my talks? Lend me your good graces?"

"Of course, and Sunny will, too. I envy your long friendship with him."

"Because we are so different. That is what people say. I am brash and hell-bent—excuse my language—and Sunny, circumspect and, well, inward."

"But blood is thicker than water. You are a formidable pair of cousins. Winston," I said and took his arm as we walked outside into the brisk breeze, "you do not seem to hold any resentment against this—our coming child, though if it is a son, it really sets you back from inheriting the dukedom if something should happen to Sunny."

"My dear, think of it this way. It would slow me down to have to tend to everything here if I were duke. Blenheim, an honor but a burden. It's like that tall pillar there, with the first duke atop it," he said, pointing dramatically at the monument in the distance. "How marvelous to be that lofty soul, but all alone, set in stone, way up there, instead of down here—with people who need help in war but in peace, too."

"Oh," I said, sounding quite inadequate after all that. I just stood there for a moment with the wind buffeting my skirts. The man did have a way with words. "I do see what you mean, though," I told him.

"I knew you would. If you bear Blenheim a son, that will be all for the best with me and for me, my friend Consuelo. And I hear your mother is coming soon."

"She is and batten down the hatches."

"I adored my mother," he said with a sigh. "Still do. But she was not around much. Quite the determined whirlwind, too. Truly, my dear nanny was my emotional mother, so be sure to get a good one for your brood."

"My brood?" I asked and stopped our walk across the grass. I had to laugh. "If I birth this one, that will be enough of a brood for now. And perhaps I shall have a daughter, as I was firstborn."

"But Sunny said your mother bore two boys after that."

"And I miss them both, my father too," I said with a sigh. I squinted upward at the rather too tall memorial with the first duke standing atop the Column of Victory in a Roman toga with his arm raised as if in blessing. I sighed, and the wind seemed to snatch my breath away. "I know I will not be able to do much in London, but it will keep me busier than here, make the time pass faster. Yet, I must admit, I am starting to think of beautiful Blenheim as home."

"Beautiful Blenheim for its beautiful duchess," he said quite solemnly. "Consuelo, I wish you well as you gift England with its next noble generation of us Spencer-Churchill-Marlboroughs. Now, here is one way I buck myself up in tough times," he said, lifting his right hand and spreading two fingers in a *V.* "It makes me look upward," he said with a glance up at the statue.

I lifted my right hand and made the same sign. We gently bumped our fingertips together. "Always onward and upward!" I told him, as we turned about into the wind to head back to the palace.

Chapter Twelve

unny seemed to care about me more during the days of my pregnancy, at least the times we were together. When he was planning the laying out of the water terraces he hoped to build, he would send for me to come out, be sure I had a chair, and explain his ideas. I agreed the sculpted, terraced beauty would soften and enhance the honey-hued building itself. More than once he promised that as soon as our child was born, I should invite my papa and some friends to see the setting for the future terraces my dowry would provide for the palace.

I spent some time overseeing the purchasing of a layette for our child, boy or girl. I spent so much time with the Bladon and Woodstock poor and elderly—and of course the schoolchildren—that Sunny insisted we head to London early. I will never forget my farewell to Mrs. Prattley as I held her delicate hands in mine. Her voice was like crinkly paper.

"I wish a blessing for yourself and the babe," she told me, lifting her sightless eyes toward my face as I sat beside her. "All will be well for Your Grace, our Angel of Woodstock."

"That means so much to me, my friend. It is like a mother's blessing."

"But she will be there, you say. Just remember that 'This too shall pass.' The difficult parts, the pain."

"I will bring the child, him or her, here to meet you someday."

"I do not know, Your Grace. Time weighs heavy on me."

And on me, I thought in the days after. This endless waiting. The avid expectations of my husband and his family. And my mother coming soon when I had not seen her for months after being under her thumb for so long. I was my own woman now, about to become a mother myself. Would she have changed? Dare she still try to dominate me, a married woman and a duchess?

The month before my actual lying in approached, Sunny leased Spencer House, a gray-stone, many-windowed home in St. James's, London. He took me on carriage rides and, at the doctor's request, escorted me on walks, mostly on the grounds or in nearby Green Park, which the three-storied house over-looked.

A week before Mother was to arrive, the most ornate, gilded, and crafted cradle I had ever seen arrived from her. It had been made in Italy, sculpted with twisted sea creatures on its base. A canopy of Belgian lace was draped over it. It belonged in some Baroque palazzio in Venice, but here it was in the room next to mine, close to our new nanny's bed, waiting, just waiting as were we all.

Since 1897 was the celebration year for Queen Victoria's Diamond Jubilee of sixty years on the throne, there were many London celebrations. Despite my girth, Sunny relented to let me attend the Devonshire House ball at the end of the season. I did not dance but sat with the dowagers off to the side and enjoyed the music and food. After dark, with a guard and two tall Marlborough footmen following us, we walked home through Green Park to lighted Spencer House nearby.

Our men held lanterns, the light of which snagged an occasional family group or old man as we passed. I gasped when I saw a young woman sitting right on the grass with her torn shawl wrapped partly around a baby who was wailing. It seemed as if these poor ragamuffins had emerged full blown from the grass.

"Perhaps I should have brought more men," Sunny muttered.

"Are they ill?" I asked him. "Not homeless, I hope. Even the poorest in Oxfordshire have a place to lay their heads. Can we give them coins?"

"I am pleased to hear you say that those near Blenheim are tended to. Sometimes," he said, pressing my arm closer to his ribs, "I worry that you think you must do more for our local poor when that is just the way of things—here too."

"I do want to do more. If we have to send cold, castoff food to them, if there are orphans or beaten or lonely women anywhere near the estate, if—"

"Consuelo, not now!"

"Why not now? Here we are in the heart of the city, the one you call the grandest on earth, head and heart of the British Empire, in this Jubilee year, and there are some of the queen's people—in mid-September when the wind will soon turn cold—who—"

"Sush! Do not turn back! See, you stumbled. Are you all right?"

"I just caught my toe. And we all stumble when you and I have just come from a feast and warm, lighted rooms and laughing people, and this is but a stone's throw away!" I swept my other hand in an arc to encompass the people huddled on the damp grass. How I wanted to go back to that woman with the baby.

He said naught else when I am sure he would have lectured me further had I not been heavy with child. It felt strange to have that power over him, to merely frown and have him inquire if I felt well, to hint I had not slept well and have him fuss.

Whether or not I soon bore an heir for the family and Blenheim or "just a girl," I vowed to love this child. And to someday, someway, speak out for the poor.

MY MOTHER HAD a knack for pretending nothing had ever gone amiss between us, but I guess I was glad for that.

"I am pleased you like the cradle," she said the day she arrived. I had told her twice that the gift was most kind and generous of her. "A little piece of Renaissance Italy," she added.

"A big piece of it, I would say. A work of art."

"I knew you would approve now that you are here with all this, including a doting husband and heir on the way."

"And if my firstborn is a girl—as with your own children?"

"Then you will marry her well someday—perhaps to royalty," she said with a little laugh. "And then try, try quickly again. I did. Never give up, Consuelo. Never stop striving."

It seemed to me her marriage to Oliver Belmont had mellowed her, though when I pointed out to her one night the ragged folks in the park, she ranted on about women's right to vote in America, though I did see a connection. Actually, I was amazed and pleased that she was in such fine fettle, and more pleasant than I recall, but then—so far—I was doing just as she, not to mention what Sunny, wanted. Indeed, I silently clung to

Mrs. Prattley's blessing as much as I did the spirited talks from my mother.

SUNNY AND MY mother colluded to keep the doctor around too much. From their being on edge, one would think they were having the baby. In a bad moment Mother had said to me, "You do not call me Mama anymore, Consuelo. Do duchesses feel no more devotion and appreciation than to desert their affection of the Mamas of their youth?"

Coward that I still was, I shrugged. "Mother does sound more formal, and using Mama is more girlish." I squared my shoulders as we sat across the breakfast table from each other. Sunny had gone to bid Winston good-bye at the railway station. Now was the time for this confrontation as well as for this baby to be born. I felt a thousand eyes were constantly on me.

Putting down my cup of hot chocolate, I told her, "I think of the term *Mama* as being one from a child, a dependent."

"Well, indeed you are not my dependent anymore."

"I mean in the way of trusting. You did so much for me— overly much—that I had not the slightest notion, for example, of how to buy my own clothes when I was on my honeymoon, let alone run a household. I am glad to hear you are concerned about and speaking up for women's rights at home, but did I not have rights—at least the right to choose my own husband and future?"

Her eyes widened. Her lower lip dropped. But that didn't mean she did not have a comeback. "I knew what was best, saw the opportunity for your glorious future," she insisted. "You were so young and—"

"Too young to know whom I loved, what I wanted, what country I would like to live in and rear my children in?"

I burst into tears when I was trying to be strong. My emotions were swelling, going to pop—and why wasn't this child ready to be born?

"Consider all you have to look forward to, my dear," she said, rising to come across the table to bend over me. I was amazed she was holding her temper for once. Her new marriage . . . my status, which pleased her . . . Had all that softened her heart? I could not fathom and would not accept that my dear Papa would not have been a good husband. But then, did people think the same of me and Sunny?

"Consuelo, I see you are still too young to understand. Perhaps when this child comes . . . someday later when you have a daughter to provide for and protect. I needed to save you from Win. Oh, yes, he swept you off your feet, but he and his family were not good enough, not for you, not for the Vanderbilts. Think of the status you have now, the things you can do for those beneath you, the very thing I dream of doing for America's women someday. The older and wiser you get, the more you will realize . . ." She plunged on, but I heard nothing else, wanted to say more, stand up to her even again, stand up to Sunny and just plain stand up, for a pain crunched through my middle and I doubled over to bump my head into my cup and saucer. The cocoa bled dark on the linen tablecloth, and I gripped the arms of the chair.

"Consuelo, did you swoon or are you in pain?"

I wanted to scream at her that I had been in pain for years. Since I could not have the man I had wanted. Since I had been in England. Since I was expected to bear a son.

"Yes," I managed as the power of that single vast pain still swept through me. "Yes, and I am sitting in . . . in the baby's water. Mother . . . it . . . . it must be time."

I WAS SWIMMING in the deep blue sea, rocked with waves of agony. I tried to push them away, but they kept rolling back over me, drowning me. My mother's voice . . . How had she done this three times? A man's voice, not Sunny's. Push? Push what?

"We can give her what Queen Victoria took for the births of her children," the doctor said. "Her Grace's hips are small. I will get the bottle of ether and the mask, but we shall not use them yet."

I pictured the queen, that tiny woman who had kissed me on the forehead. Mother had liked that story, but then she would. If she could have pushed me far enough—push, push—she would have turned me into the Queen of England instead of some duchess. Indeed, if that little woman could bear nine children with her narrow hips, I could too. Did being tall not count for something?

"Your Grace," the doctor's voice came again, "I'm going to give you something to help with the pain, but you must push hard first. We have the baby's head crowning but not the body."

We have the head. Have I lost my head, my mind, to be the Duchess of Marlborough?

Suddenly, I felt a screaming rip, as if a huge black curtain was torn in two. No, someone had screamed. It must be me.

Push, push. Push one's way into British society, let alone Sunny's family. Are you in a family way, my dear? I have to bear this child, make a family, make a life here when all I want to do is float up and away, up in a hot-air balloon, but it is so hot in here. I am soaking wet, swimming and here came yet another wave.

Someone was screaming again.

"All right, the baby has more than crowned. If we can just get one shoulder."

"Can you not give her the ether now, just a little?" a woman asked. That was Mother, but she should be telling him, ordering him. At least it meant she was on my side. For one shrieking moment, I almost called her Mama, almost begged her to stop the pain, stop telling me everything that I must do.

"I cannot do this, I cannot . . ." I cried. "I am going to die."

I felt a little wire mask pressed around my nose and mouth. Oh, it had a small cloth over it and smelled like the gilt paint Sunny insisted on using before the prince and princess came to visit. Were they here again? Must we give up our rooms and move upstairs at Blenheim?

Floating now, floating. Something left me, left my body. Was it my spirit? Was I really dying?

"Wait until the duke hears this!" a man said.

I just let myself sink farther under the huge waves. Under and far away.

Chapter Thirteen

ur son, John Albert Edward William Spencer-Churchill, Marquess of Blandford, was born September 18, 1897. I, however, was nearly unconscious and feverish for a week after, so I actually made my darling boy's acquaintance a bit later. The first day I finally felt strong enough, I insisted he not be put back in his cradle, nor simply shown to me by Nanny or my mother, but handed to me to hold for as long as I wanted.

"Oh, he is lovely," I said, looking into those pale blue eyes.

"Indeed he is," Sunny said, hovering by my bed. "Perfect."

We actually smiled at each other, really smiled from the heart. Whatever barriers lay between us, we had made this beautiful child. Bless Sunny, he gestured at Nanny to step outside, and my mother had the good sense to go, too. Actually, I liked Nanny, for she was also besotted with the baby, though she did not like the undernurse working with her.

"I want you to make a full recovery," Sunny told me, perching on the edge of the bed and patting my knee. "It was . . . well, a battle for you, but a victory, too."

"I shall wave that Blenheim battle flag over him when we get home."

"Do you mean that? Blenheim being home to you now? I thank God that Blandford, as we shall call him, has his mother and I my wife—my duchess back among the living."

I did not say so then, but I intended to call my son Bertie, for his second name Albert, to honor the Prince of Wales who had taken the Marlboroughs back in his good graces. Bertie's first name, John, was in remembrance of the first duke, but I did not care for the nickname Johnnie. And Blandford seemed so, well, so bland, but I would fight that battle another day. Granted, it was ducal tradition to call boys by their titles, but he was half American as far as I was concerned. He would not be treated with kid gloves but be allowed to be a boy. And he would learn to value all levels of people.

I could barely tear my gaze away from that little face. The shape of it was mine, I was certain. I ventured a quick glance up and saw my husband's eyes were shimmering with tears.

WHEN I WAS up and about again, we laid plans to return to Blenheim after the christening, which would take place in the Chapel Royal, St. James's Palace, with the Prince of Wales and the entire Marlborough clan—and, of course, my mother—in attendance. I was now the darling of Sunny's family for delivering what I overheard Albertha call "the future tenth duke."

I was ready to leave London soon, though, for I had long stretches of time with nothing to do. Mother was back and forth, visiting friends in London and Paris. More than once while she was away, without Sunny's knowledge, I sent coins anonymously out to the "park people" as I came to think of them, especially the woman with the baby.

But one day Sunny came home from a reception I did not attend because it would take so much standing. He came into the library where I was reading to announce, "I have brought you a special gift you will love! No, your mother is not back yet—ha! I have invited a new friend to visit, a young American lady, one even with ties to Newport!"

He was beaming and looked so proud of himself.

"Someone I know?" I asked, wracking my brain for who could be here visiting in the off season in London.

"Someone who knows of and admires you greatly—and would love to see Blenheim. I just met her today, and what a charming young woman, well-educated, well-traveled, even as you are."

"Do not keep me in suspense!" I demanded, standing. "You mean she is here now?"

In answer he went to the door he had closed behind himself and opened it. No footman in sight, just a lovely woman who came in, smiling and dipped me a slight curtsy. She had dove-gray eyes under perfectly arched brows, a rosy complexion, and Cupid's-bow lips. She wore expensive but not fussy garments. Her golden-brown hair and classic profile were so perfect that she reminded me of a painting by Botticelli, *The Birth of Venus*, I'd seen in Florence.

Yet despite the impact of her face and charm, I had no clue in the world who she was.

"Consuelo, I would like to present to you Miss Gladys Deacon, here on tour visiting, as you often were at her age."

At her age, I thought? But I am only twenty and a half, so how old is this lovely creature? Sixteen? Seventeen? Feeling as ancient as Queen Victoria, I extended my hand.

"I am so honored to meet you, Your Grace," Gladys—Sunny had pronounced it Glade-is—said. "Ever since I read about your beautiful wedding, I have wanted to meet you and the duke, and see your lovely palace someday."

"Someday soon," Sunny put in.

"I understand your mother is still in occasional residence with you," Gladys went on, with a sweet smile. "I envy you a loving mother, father too. I told His Grace," she added, with a glance at Sunny, "because everyone knows I have not been so blessed, and it has been hard to live that down."

It hit me then. This was the young woman whose father, a Boston millionaire, had shot one of her mother's lovers to death in a French hotel about five years ago. Since then the president of France had pardoned her father, and her mother had reared Gladys all over Europe. I would never have known about the scandal had I not overheard it during the Newport season.

And I thought my parents had created problems? How I felt for this girl, even thought I understood her. And Sunny evidently did, too, bringing home someone who must yet be the target of gossip—or had her charms won everyone over?

"Please sit down," I told her, "and I shall ring for some tea. How lovely to have a visit from another American, however continental your upbringing."

"Oh, I see you were reading in French," she observed, glancing down at my book on the table. "Such a romantic language, one of several I have fallen in love with and studied."

In the next two hours, I saw all that was true. For so young a woman, Gladys Deacon was very well read, spoke French smoothly and Italian far better than I. She was an excellent conversationalist and obviously awed to meet me. After a while, Sunny left us alone and went up to tell Nanny to bring Blandford down for a visit.

I found myself matchmaking in my head, but then, Gladys was too young for Winston—or was she? Men of all ages and circumstances would surely fall for this bright beauty. Poor Winston had managed to be turned down by two ladies already, one a young American actress named Ethel Barrymore and the other the lovely Muriel Wilson he had courted.

And so, I had a new baby and a new friend, a young one when so many around me seemed even older than my mother.

MOTHER CAME BACK to Blenheim to spend a few days with us. Although we got on well enough, she sided with Sunny on calling the baby Blandford and on my not visiting yet in the village—not until "you are yourself again, Consuelo." I was content enough to have her about but I must admit I felt smug when I came across the way to make her leave or keep her away if I wanted.

As we admired Bertie sleeping in his cradle in Nanny's room, the night before Mother was to leave, she whispered to me, "Whoever is that woman in the satin robe who bustles down the hall late at night? I try to talk to her, but she pays no heed, and she should be talked to. She acts haughty or else she's deaf."

Gooseflesh instantly skimmed my skin. I gestured mother out into the very hall she referred to and motioned Nanny to go back in. I knew full well that my mother was terrified of ghosts, some sort of encounter or superstition from her past having to do with losing her beloved childhood mansion during the War Between the States.

"I have seen her, too," I admitted. "Mother, do not panic now, but Lilian has seen her also and . . . and I saw her go through a door though it remained closed. We think it is an emanation of the first duchess, so perhaps it is an honor that she appeared to you, too."

She had gone stark white in the face. I put my hands out to steady her shoulders. "Of course, loving this house she built," I went on, "she means no harm, only seems to watch over it—and us." My voice was shaking now.

"What . . . what does the duke say?" she whispered, wide-eyed.

"He thinks it is a woman's silly whims. Perhaps she does not appear to men, dukes or not, because he thinks we are making it up."

"But the baby . . ."

"Will be fine. Bertie will be fine. She is protective of the house, of us all."

"Now, don't you fret your husband by defying him with that name Bertie!" she told me and shook a finger in my face as if I were ten again. Though she was obviously deeply shaken by what I had said, she not only seemed to accept it, but to want to just plunge ahead as if all were normal. She was obviously desperate to change the topic.

I both laughed and cried. "Mother, as if you never stood up to Papa or gave him a moment's unease."

"Do as I say, not as I . . . as I did."

"Divorce and remarriage? Perhaps I have thought of it," I blurted out, suddenly wanting to hurt and not assure her as I had about the ghost. Yes, I was my own woman now, finally. "But with little Bertie here, I will behave," I assured her. "Mostly."

I heard after she had departed that she had made her maid

sleep in a chair at the foot of her bed that last night. Despite Sunny's fussing, the day Mother left, I went to visit Mrs. Prattley and the ladies at the almshouse.

THE MONTHS AFTER Bertie, alias Blandford, was born were some of the happiest of our marriage. Sunny seemed more content. He went to London less often and brought Gladys back with him upon occasion, and she always cheered me up. My father, who was living in France, visited, some of the best days for me at Blenheim. The William in Bertie's string of names I had insisted on was to honor my father, William Kissam Vanderbilt.

Perhaps it was that I felt at home now, more relaxed, that I conceived a second child rather quickly, so that put Sunny and the Marlboroughs "over the moon," as the British liked to say. I was happy, too, though I prayed not to face such a difficult birth again. Well, I thought, this time round, I shall know much more about everything.

"My, aren't you a little brick!" Albertha crowed when she heard I was pregnant again. She promised no more tricks like the time a footman lifted the silver cover from a tureen of soup at our dinner table with family there and inside had been a doll in bathwater—with male genitalia painted on!

But maybe things had partly gone so smoothly because I *was* doing something behind Sunny's back rather than arguing with or riling him—that is, sending donations to a distant village. Sunny's estate agent had told us people were hungry from crop failures in the area beyond Woodstock. I had later told the agent to offer work to the men in the area to repair ruts in the roads with which I was achingly familiar. Only the agent knew I planned to pay the workers from my funds, and they weren't to know it was from me.

That was a huge mistake, however right I thought I was. The laborers sent Sunny a note of gratitude for something he had no idea about.

"You did this—through my agent—for my distant tenants—without a word to me?" Sunny shouted at me over our breakfast table when the note was brought in to him on a silver salver. Both the butler and the footman, on their way out anyway, scurried from the room and closed the door.

"You were busy and were doing nothing to alleviate their situation, as far as I could tell," I told him, calmly spreading strawberry jam on my toast. "How lovely that they wrote to you and that you will have the thanks for feeding their families until a better harvest."

"Consuelo, it just isn't done—going behind my back. What else is going on in that pretty little American head of yours?"

"Behind your back. Hm, let me see. I call our son Bertie rather than Blandford when I cuddle him. Of course, then, too, I have made peace with the Blenheim ghost, the first duchess, and—"

"Do not be flip with me. You and Gladys can giggle all you want, but this is serious!"

"Your Grace, Duke of Marlborough! You disapprove too much of charity, and can there be too much Christian charity? You have often told me these are your people. They were in need. I did not think you would object to their working to earn money rather than being on the dole or receiving funds through the church. It is payment for work to keep their spirits up and their bellies filled."

"You will not do such again!" he ordered, leaning toward me across the table. "This Angel of Woodstock thing has gone too far."

"But they obviously think their payment is coming from you, so I plan to take no credit. It increases the already good feelings toward the Marlboroughs, of which I and my son are now a part."

"But you are acting like a bloody socialist when I am going to stand for conservative office."

"I would certainly vote for you—for Winston too—if I could, but we women cannot, so we do what we can."

As calm as I sounded standing up to him, my stomach was tied in knots. He was actually quivering with frustration and rage. Poor Gladys had confided in me that her father used to beat her mother. If I were not with child again—if Sunny did not have that note of gratitude waded up in his hand—I wonder if he would have dared to strike me. I was sorry for one thing, though, that I had ruined our unspoken peace treaty.

And so continued the battles at Blenheim.

Chapter Fourteen

ur second son was born on October 14, 1898. This birth was easier for me. I teased Sunny that it was because "the spare" did not have to enter this world dragging quite so many names behind him. Ivor Charles Spencer-Churchill was small and pale at birth, but I was so happy all had gone well. Exhausted, I slept for nearly two days straight, but I was far from ill.

For this birth, we were at Hampden House, owned by the Duke of Abercorn—he of the sable-lined coat. He had kindly vacated for us and our entourage as, like last time, Sunny wanted his child to be born in a home tied to the Marlboroughs. Why that did not mean staying at Blenheim for the births, I never could completely grasp. At any rate, it made not only the Spencer relatives happy, but, of course, the Churchills too.

Ivor was named for Sunny's cousin who had been his best man at our wedding. I had considered asking that the baby be named Winston, whom I liked far better, but I did not want the nickname of Winnie. Sunny said Winston did not mind a bit and was pleased Ivor would continue the name Churchill.

"Winston," I told him when he dropped by on the third day after Ivor's birth, "I admire how you seem to take everything in stride. Here you are off again for who knows where as a war correspondent. I am in awe of your sense of adventure and self-confidence."

I was resting on a chaise in my sitting room while he perched on a chair nearby after having spent a good deal of his visit with Sunny.

"Compliments are always welcome," he told me with a smile. "Now, I brought you a present, Consuelo. You have told me how you love to hear the songbirds in the Blenheim park and that nothing but doves or pigeons hang about the eaves of the palace itself. So," he said, getting to his feet, "I have brought you a canary so you can always hear a tuneful bird."

He went out into the hall and brought in a covered cage and removed the cloth to reveal a beautiful golden bird with green hues on the tail. "A female, they say," he added.

"Well, it—she—is lovely. I shall call her Golden. Thank you for your kindness."

"She is keeping quiet for a while, I see, but she sounded lovely before. I say, have you heard that ballad about a bird in a gilded cage? Very popular for those who buy sheet music—written by Americans, too. It is some sort of tear-jerker about a girl who married for money but not for love."

"No, I have not, but I shall look for that. Perhaps I shall rewrite it to be about a duke who married for money and not for love."

Winston cleared his throat. "Well, I am sure little Blandford will like Golden, too, but best she stay in her cage with a new baby around. I am sure the doctor will get little Ivor over his breathing problem. Little lungs, as they say, will grow."

I stopped fussing with the bird. Breathing problem? Little lungs? I knew Ivor was especially small and pale, but . . . "Excuse me, Winston, and thank you for all that," I told him. I jumped up, kissed him on his cheek, and made straight for the door, just as the canary started to warble.

"Consuelo," he called after me, "I thought, of course, you knew."

I did not turn back and nearly twisted my ankle in my haste. One slipper came off my foot, so I kicked the other off and hurried barefoot down the carpeted corridor. I could feel the packing the doctor had put between my legs begin to loosen, but I did not care if I bled all over this house. I felt a bit dizzy and wobbly, but that hardly mattered.

They had told me the baby was sound asleep after that first day I held him. He had seemed fitful and fussy but breathing problems? Why had they not told me? Why had they said I should just rest even as the baby was each time I asked for him?

I did not knock on the door of the room we had made the nursery but simply swept it open. Nanny hovered over the cradle—not the baroque one. The doctor was leaning over it, too, and Sunny was pacing.

The door banged behind me. Everyone turned my way and gasped, so perhaps I looked like the avenging fury, just as I felt. But I forced myself not to shout at them as I strode in. "Why was I not told?"

"Now, Consuelo," Sunny said, making a grab for my arm, though I shook him off. "We did not want you to regress, to have a long recovery like last time."

"But little Ivor's recovery is of much more importance. Doctor, tell me flat out. How is he, and what can I do?"

"It's just a breathing complication, and you can see, Your Grace, he is holding his own."

"Now that I am not being misled and kept from him I can see that he is pale and fussy."

Ivor began to cough, more like a sporadic wheezing.

"I want to hold him," I said. "Perhaps that will ease if he sleeps upright against me."

I shouldered the doctor away and looked down at the little mite. Not robust like his older brother, and not the heir, but how I loved him. How my heart went out to him as I carefully gathered his small frame in my arms.

Nanny pushed a chair close for me. Sunny put his hands out to steady my shoulders as I sat barefoot and—I could feel I was bleeding again. Yet nothing mattered but holding and comforting this blessed little boy who needed his mother. I felt a fierce protective bond that—God forgive me—I had never felt before, not even with my firstborn.

Little Ivor suddenly seemed to breathe easier, and I did too.

TWELVE MONTHS PASSED, and when Blandford was two and Ivor just turned one, we received a message from Queen Victoria that she would be sending a large party including the visiting Kaiser of Germany, Wilhelm II, and his son, Crown Prince Wilhelm, to visit Blenheim. They'd be accompanied by the Prince of Wales, called Bertie, who was uncle to the Kaiser. But at the last minute, she decided to keep Princess Alexandra, whom I was eager to see again, and the Kaiser's wife, Empress Augusta, at home with her.

"I am sorry," I told the butler at nearly the last moment, "but the entire table setting will have to be redone. Still use the gold service, but I will give you the new seating chart as soon as I can."

It was even more difficult than the Prince of Wales's first visit, since Sunny fretted about how touchy the Kaiser was about being treated properly. "And," Sunny warned me as we set off in carriages to meet the party at the railway station, "be your charming best when the prince sees he will have to ride backwards in the carriage on our return ride. I, of course, will ride along beside."

"I shall ride backwards so the prince does not."

"No, as duchess and hostess, you must ride facing front with the Kaiser instead of with Bertie beside you. The two men detest each other—I thought it best not to tell you that, but I see I must—and Bertie absolutely will not ride beside his rude, pompous nephew unless he is cajoled or convinced. I have heard," he said, lowering his voice, evidently so our own staff did not hear, "the Kaiser refers to our Prince of Wales as 'that old peacock.'"

Sunny was right that the ride back was a nightmare. But we soldiered on, trying to please them both at dinner, even though the Kaiser—who had the largest handlebar mustache I had ever seen—dominated the conversation with self-aggrandizement and insisted on telling us all about the Battle of Blenheim, no less. He was only silent during the organ concert for which I had ordered German music.

But I did have to admire that he had managed to hide his withered left arm even when he ate. He had a special fork with a knife attached to his good hand so he didn't need his left hand. That deformity must have caused him much embarrassment and shame, though he was just the opposite of a quiet, shrinking personality.

"Consuelo," the prince whispered and pulled me aside after dessert and drinks, "I do not care if that pompous German is the queen's eldest grandchild or my nephew, he drives me to distraction. I will not ride in the inferior position again when we leave tomorrow."

"I have already told Sunny I will not go, but that means you must sit beside him, sir."

He puffed his big cigar, enveloping me with a cloud of sharp smoke, though I dare not cough or wave my hand to clear the air. "Good thinking, of course, but then you are a real benefit to the duke in so many ways. I shall not cause trouble for the lovely hostess you have been here under duress, though I have a good nerve to put tobacco in the Kaiser's breakfast tomorrow— just teasing, of course. Better it be something stronger than tobacco, but I shall behave."

He winked at me. I smiled. Ah, families not getting on, and Queen Victoria had one of the largest. At least, as Sunny had said, the prince had been convinced or cajoled to sit beside the Kaiser.

"You do Marlborough and Blenheim proud," he told me with that look of his that made me feel he was not only taking me all in, but undressing me with his eyes. "Two sons in the bargain, too."

A little bell went off in my head that Sunny had once said the prince would never approach a woman for a liaison until she had borne children.

I stepped back a bit and curtsied as if he had dismissed me. Holding his cigar behind his back, he reached down with his other hand to raise me. He kissed the back of my hand, then the palm. "Damn German royal relatives," he muttered. "I much prefer Americans. Good evening, then, dear duchess."

With that, he turned about and headed back into the smoke-hazed room where the men were gathered.

I WOULD NOT say Ivor flourished, but he grew. We watched him closely, especially since his older brother had such energy. I always kept an eye on my Ivor.

Things went on quite well with the children until one day when I scolded three-year-old Blandford—I had temporarily lost the battle to call him Bertie—for throwing stones at the footmen, who were taught to stand like statues, until needed. They were both strapping young men, six feet tall but, when Sunny did not react, and one of the stones hit too near Ivor, I said, "Blandford, stop that. You will hurt someone! Bad boy!"

Nanny was only tut-tutting as she was wont to do when Sunny was around, but I took Blandford's hand and tugged him off and away from the blanket. We had set up near the lake for a picnic while the footmen hauled out the food. I made Blandford drop the last stone and smacked his hand. And nearly went off my feet, when Sunny yanked me upright and away with him. He half-dragged, half-marched me to the far side of a big oak.

"He shall not be punished or told he is evil," he hissed at me.

"Evil? I just scolded him for being a bad boy for his own good, as well as that of others. We do not need him thinking he can stone our footmen, and what if he causes a wound or puts out Ivor's eye? Not be punished? Do you want to have the next duke be a heathen with no—"

He seized my wrist and pulled me farther away. "My father punished me cruelly! Berated me and hated me! Called me evil! I will not rear my son like that!"

He looked livid, wild-eyed and trembling. I was stunned. Of

course I had heard the whispers that Sunny's father was a roué, an immoral man, but had he actually brutalized his heir?

"We can discuss this later," I told him. "I had a very strict parent, too, you know."

"And you hated her for it! Spare the rod and spoil the child is a lie from the pit of hell."

"Perhaps, then, this Bible verse is better," I insisted, still keeping my voice down. "It's one my father told me, though I was a daughter and not a son. *For whom the Lord loves, He corrects, just as a father the son in whom he delights.* Sunny, we do not want to rear an heir who knows no boundaries."

He was still shaking. Despite the differences between us, I almost wanted to gather him in my arms and pat his back and tell him he was not evil and was dearly loved.

Almost.

THINGS BECAME EVEN more stilted between Sunny and me after that, perhaps because he had shown me the frightened child within the man and duke. More than once, I tried to have him tell me about his brutal father, but it was as if the outburst over Blandford had never happened. Now that I knew his secret, his insecurities, it seemed Sunny avoided me unless we had special engagements together. And that included one of my lesser favorites, the annual winter Quorn foxhunt meet in Leicestershire.

I loved to ride and had a mount I adored named Greyling—a great jumper—but I could not see pounding after yipping hounds to tear a fox apart. But after both boys were born, there was no excuse for me not to chase the Quorn hounds, one of the world's oldest fox hunting packs. And so, decked out in a fashionable dark blue, tailored jacket and long-skirted Busvine habit,

tall hat and veil, I settled sidesaddle onto my horse brought from Blenheim.

But I was still upset with Sunny for not scolding Blandford when he was naughty and nearly ignoring Ivor when he got his occasional coughing fits. So I vowed to myself, if I could not outride my husband, who prided himself on his horsemanship, I would at least match him.

Like all the men astride, Sunny did look elegant in white jodhpurs, red coat, and black hat. He looked smug, too, so sure of his riding prowess.

At the shrill sound of the horn and yipping of the hounds, we were off! The wind bit cold, and I could see my breath, but I gripped the reins with my leather gloves as Greyling smoothly vaulted the first railed fence in the crowd of other horses. I actually blessed my mother for my years of riding lessons. I had to duck low branches more than once. One ripped my hat back so it hung by my pins and veil, but I became one with the movement of the horse.

The nearly fifty hounds barked incessantly as we followed the blur of their brown and white bodies with the wagging tails. The fox was heading for the thicket, running into the wind, which made his scent easy to follow. More fences appeared, over which I nearly flew, trying to keep up with Sunny. I saw I had no hope of beating my husband, only staying with him, so that would have to do. He turned his head once, surprised to see me yet there before we both sailed over a hedgerow together.

I heard one of the women just behind us shout, "I am not going on. Oh, wherever is Louisa? Oh, no, unhorsed!"

I spotted the fox ahead, a red flash tearing through a dry grass field with the hounds closing in. It was then I lost my heart for this, the powerful people chasing an innocent, however much foxes preyed on other animals. I reined in and pulled Greyling off to the side and let the rest sweep by.

Our own groom dashed past, with a word of praise for my riding. I felt I had done well and hoped Sunny would say so. Later, after I stayed with the woman who had been unhorsed until a doctor came and finally went back to the barns, I heard Sunny say, "Mostly the ladies, the duchess, too, have acquitted themselves well."

He never told me such, but I was used to that. And used to the occasionally deep emotional valleys I found myself wandering in as if chased by hounds. But my spirits lifted when I received word that my father was coming soon for a visit.

I WAS SO happy for my father because he was happy. He still had a yacht but mostly lived in France and bred and raised racehorses there. He had a new circle of international friends—lady friends too. The few times I visited him, we went to the track to see his stable of horses race, and I could not wait to tell him how well I had ridden to the horn at the hunt. His mere presence cheered me.

I took the large carriage to meet him at the station, and a second one came behind because he was bringing four friends, all French so I would be able to practice that beautiful language with them, however much Papa and I spoke American English when alone. He had teased me the last time I saw him that I was starting to sound "terribly bloody British uppercrust."

I met him on the platform when he disembarked with the other gentlemen behind him. As we hugged, I fitted my chin perfectly on his shoulder.

"I have missed you terribly and am so happy to see you," I said.

And found myself looking into the handsome face of the man close behind as if I said that to him. Although I had not seen Papa's guest for years, I knew at once who he was, and my insides cartwheeled. It was the man who had promised me a ride in the sky while we whirled around the ballroom years ago, Jacques Balsan.

Chapter Fifteen

he first evening of my father and his friends' two-day visit spun by. Jacques and I chatted but in the presence of the others. We told everyone we had met briefly once, in Paris, long ago.

"Yet what a coincidence," I told Jacques after dinner their first evening at Blenheim when I had a moment to talk to him alone. We had not spoken in French so far, but I did now.

"Fate is kind for once, yes?" he whispered as we walked from the Saloon to assemble in the library. "And a blessing that we meet again and can now be friends."

"You have not married?"

"Not yet," he said with a shrug. "I found her once but lost her just as fast."

I nodded, feeling sad for him. I was not so conceited as to think he could mean me, not this charming, handsome French-man I had spent barely a quarter hour with years ago.

I had also told Sunny that I had danced with Jacques the night of my debut in Paris. I had received much the same bloodless reaction from him as when I had told him on our wedding day that I had loved another man. "What goes around comes around," he said this time.

"Well, just as with you and Gladys, it is possible to enjoy the company of another person," I had replied.

"Quite right. But you like Gladys, too. That Frenchman was not half as interested in our stables or even the estate when I gave your father's friends a tour. He is more interested in spouting off about how Blenheim would look from a hot-air balloon. Hot air—ha!"

It is true that Jacques was fascinated by not only that now—a passionate hobby, he said—but by the future of something he called flying machines. But I had found all of that quite daring and interesting.

At the first night's dinner, Jacques had proudly said, "Not only the Americans and Germans, but we French are at the forefront of this endeavor, have been ever since King Louis XVI watched a balloon ascent at Versailles years ago." The next day at breakfast, he had asked, "Can you imagine men flying over national boundaries, doing reconnaissance in war, let alone peacetime flights? We will need a lightweight engine for powered flight in the future, but I know a man, Léon Levavasseur, who is working on that."

My father looked interested. Sunny nodded. I was entranced, perhaps not so much by the idea of flight as with my own flights of fancy. Just as I had felt swept away in the brief dance I had shared with Jacques years ago, I sensed the same now. Perhaps Papa picked up on that for he asked me after breakfast, "Why don't you walk Jacques to the Grand Bridge, my dear? I and the others plan to go hunting with Sunny, but Jacques would rather not shoot birds in the sky, I take it—only fly with them."

I wondered if Papa—and perhaps Jacques—had set this up. Had Papa sensed some spark between this Frenchman and me? I know Papa thought my husband rather a cold fish, but surely he would not want to encourage me to stray. But with someone I had not seen in years and probably never would again?

"Yes, yes, a good idea," I told him.

"I CAN HEAR the banging of the guns already," I remarked to Jacques. "I prefer hearing birds sing to shooting them."

We walked together around the lake toward the massive bridge that the genius architect Sir John Vanbrugh had fashioned for the first Marlboroughs nearly two centuries ago. I had always loved the balanced beauty of it with its massive, honey-hued stone arches reflected in the lake the famous landscape architect Capability Brown had created from several streams.

"The banging of the guns?" he said. "I thought that was my heart—at the stunning view here."

He was a bit of a tease and a flirt but never seemed to over-step, perhaps because—even at my age and all I had been through—I was hungry to be courted. I loved speaking French with him. It seemed my senses woke up, the girl or woman in me sprang alive. Yet despite his words and the intense way he regarded me, he seemed so under control, so proper. But be-ware, I told myself, for he is a Frenchman. Allure and charisma are their stock-in-trade.

"But for London Bridge," I told him, "this may be the only bridge in England that was built to house people. Several of the chambers have fireplaces and chimneys, but I am not sure anyone has ever lived there. And there is one huge windowless room that had been plastered and fitted with an arch, as if for theatricals. The rooms are locked and off-limits now so that someone does not take up residence there or damage them—or themselves."

"A lovely place for a picnic or a great adventure. The lake, I believe, came later and put the lower part of the arches underwater. Still, so *magnifique*, yes? A work of beauty."

He took my arm and put it through his. His blue eyes seemed bluer with the sky above him. His mustache lifted slightly when he smiled, which was often. Our gazes locked and held. And then, something I had not expected. I had been quite tense but I suddenly relaxed. This man moved me deeply but made me feel safe, too, as well as respected and appreciated. Oh, what a heady mix that was.

We walked up onto the roadway over the highest arch of the bridge and looked down into the blue water of the lake. Despite the midmorning winter breeze, I felt warm, and it seemed as if this huge, solid structure under my feet was moving.

"Consuelo, your two sons are very handsome. The older one a handful, yes?"

"Indeed, he is. Do you recognize a bit of yourself in him?"

"I do. I was throwing toy soldiers off a bridge when I was young to see if they would sink or swim—the tin ones sank and the wooden ones floated, but none flew. As I said, it is beautiful here," he added. Leaning back, his elbow resting on the bridge, he looked up into the sun beyond my shaded face.

What did he really see? I wondered. An attractive woman, for I knew I had outgrown the gawkiness I once had. A married woman, a mother? A wealthy duchess? All that but still a lonely girl trying to find her place, trying to love and be loved?

"The offer to take you up in a balloon still stands," he told me as we walked slowly back toward the palace, taking the long way around the lake. "Perhaps when you visit your father next, yes? I shall take him, too, if he wishes, though he seems only interested in land or sea. And you, Consuelo?"

"If you think it is safe—because of my sons, I mean."

"I shall take care of you. But remember, some things worth having are not safe, at least at first. Ah, like flying machines, yes?" he added, turning to me again. He did not smile this time but seemed to study me. I think he wanted to remember me and this short time we had alone. I felt the same. And more. Even the Prince of Wales's stares and innuendos paled to nothing beside those of Monsieur Jacques Balsan.

SADLY, SOON, IN October 1899, England went to war, just when Sunny and I were trying to settle into a truce. The South African Boer War they called it because the Dutch Boer settlers in South Africa wanted Britain out of "their" territory. British forces overwhelmed the enemy at first, but the Boers fought back in what they called guerrilla style—unconventional and underhanded. Winston entered the action there as a war correspondent. He had been taken prisoner, made a bold escape, and was now considered a dashing hero here at home.

Sunny was slated to leave for the war soon, in early 1900, as part of the Imperial Yeomanry. I was appalled, not because he would go, but because a London paper intimated he was leaving not to do his duty but to escape marital problems. I thought we had been putting up a pretty good front and I never did learn who leaked the status of our non-marriage to the press.

"Now remember what I said about rearing our sons," Sunny said in the last few moments before he departed for who knew how long. We stood in the Great Hall at Blenheim, though we had said our good-byes with the children last night. "Boys will be boys, you know."

"I had two brothers, you may recall, and I do not think they were one whit damaged by learning there were some rules in life."

"Now do not argue. I am sure Gladys's staying for a few weeks will cheer you up."

"She does keep me up on things and is always kind, interested, and interesting."

"There, you see. Consuelo, my duchess, I know we had a devil of a time in the beginning," he told me, taking both my hands in his and standing closer than he had for quite a long time. The honorary medals on his scarlet dress uniform caught the slant of sun through the doorway glass and glinted. "And a rough patch here and there after. But you have gifted me with two fine sons and have been a grand hostess, helped me climb back into the good graces of the royals. I believe Queen Victoria is not long for this world, as they say, and then—Bertie as king and your friend Alexandra queen."

"That will mean a lot of changes, but England will weather them, war or not."

"Spoken like a true Englishwoman and not only an American."

"Only?" I said with the edge back in my voice that I reserved for when he lectured me, which was far too often. But I did not want to ruin this rare moment, for there had been so few like this. I realized, of course, that though he would probably be some general's secretary and not on the battlefield, he yet might not return.

We stared a moment into each other's eyes. The best I could think of to say was what he really wanted to hear. "I will take good care of our boys and of Blenheim."

"Dear Blenheim, my third son and heir," he said with a little shake of his head as he gazed away at the marble bust of the first duke over the Saloon door.

He held me close. His wool uniform smelled of the camphor it had been stored in, and I thought I would sneeze. Thank heavens, I did not, for he kissed me once hard on the lips. He did not want me to go to the station but to stand at the door of Blenheim where I would greet him with both boys when he came home.

"Be safe," I told him, "and take care of Winston, if you see him. He takes too many chances, but I know that you will be sensible."

He grabbed his helmet from the chair near the door. I followed him out and saw Gladys waiting by the carriage to say farewell. She said something and bobbed him that little curtsy she always managed as if she were one of his dependents hereabouts. He kissed her on the cheek and climbed into the carriage, which rolled immediately away while Gladys kept waving.

Chapter Sixteen

unny returned in July of that year. I greeted him on the front steps of the Great Court with Blandford standing beside me and Ivor in my arms. Sunny hugged the boys, quite equally, I thought, and ruffled Blandford's hair. He embraced me, too, and kissed my cheek.

"More later," he whispered, though I was not sure what that meant. More than a quick kiss? More time with our boys?

The months he had been away I had kept busy, yet I had pondered—even agonized—over what our marriage would be in the future. I had indeed missed him but not in an emotional or romantic way. I had missed his control of this big place, his concern, toward our sons at least. But as for the Duke of Marlborough and his duchess, even now that we were back together, unless it was with our sons, a stone wall loomed, one I did not know how to break through, one I did not know if I wanted him to climb. Even in the big ducal bed, when he claimed me again, I was getting used to a marriage that was as cold as vast Blenheim.

The Boer war was not over yet, but I was still glad to have him home. I had been right that he had not seen much action, whereas Winston had absolutely managed to be in the thick of it and was now planning to parlay all that into making a stand for Parliament.

"I had the tea table set up under the trees," I told him, gesturing toward the lake on that first day of his return. "Apricots and peaches, bowls of Devonshire cream and pitchers of iced coffee—things I am sure you have missed."

"Not as much as I have missed all of you. And scones for my boys, eh?" he added. "With fruit jams and cakes with sugar icing!"

Although Sunny had been gone barely six months, I had coached both boys about behaving and hugging their father. Besides, I was in a good mood. In the spring—ah, so far away—I was going to see Papa in Paris, attend the races at Longchamp, and accept the standing offer of my friend Jacques to take to the skies in a balloon.

IN JANUARY 1901, Queen Victoria died, and the nation and Empire were plunged into mourning. I even wore a traditional crepe mourning veil when I went out, as if I were a widow, especially, of course, when we went to London for the state funeral. Wearing black so depressed me that winter. I had the wildest urge to wear colors, not to dishonor Her Majesty's memory, but to cheer myself.

Sunny was pleased we had been asked to the services, which were in the smaller St. George's Chapel at Windsor, so only the elite and powerful were invited. Going to Windsor in our ducal train car, thinking I looked like gloom and grief itself, I was surprised when Sunny said, "My beautiful wife, if I die, I see you will not remain a widow for long."

I was sorely tempted to say something like, *And if I die, I believe the Duke of Marlborough will find a mate quickly, too.* I knew Gladys would take him in a moment, because, for some reason, he was her ideal of chivalry, her knight in shining armor. So often I saw her eyes follow him as she heaved a heartfelt sigh. I suppose I should have been jealous or worried, but I could not stir myself to that.

Besides, I understood fully. How foolish I was to be counting the days until I might see my favorite Frenchman again.

So, at least I had a compliment from my husband on my appearance. He seldom praised me for anything else, though I knew he approved of the way I cherished our boys. Sometimes I wondered if he were actually jealous of or resented my efforts to uplift the village folk, the way I got down from the carriage to greet or chat with them or—God forgive—from my little pony cart, which he thought not grand enough. At least he no longer chastised me for my democratic tendencies, perhaps when he saw the way the folk on the estate looked up to him for things I did.

The queen's funeral was solemn and striking, befitting a woman who had ruled England and the Empire for so long. But even as the Knights of the Garter, foreign rulers—including the Kaiser—colonial officers and ministers of state, and the lords and ladies of the realm like us rose as the royal cortège mounted the steps, I pondered her life when she was my age with a young family. But she had her beloved Albert then. She had wed the right man for her. And was not that just as important as being queen or even a duchess?

But after the pomp ended, after the funeral march faded and the clank of ceremonial swords in scabbards quieted, I found my spirits greatly lifted. Upstairs in the Waterloo Chamber, where a light meal had been laid out, I found myself sought for greetings and conversations—of course not by my husband—but by many of the powerful men of the realm including the charming Arthur Balfour and the influential George Curzon. I liked to think my conversations with them that day were a help for Sunny later being given the Garter and being named Under-Secretary for the Colonies in July 1903. As Sunny liked to say, "we" were really on our way.

And another great gift to me—although they were yet to have their coronation, Queen Alexandra asked me to be one of her canopy bearers for that ceremony. Also Sunny and I were in the very select party of companions asked to go to India for the Durbar next year, two weeks of festivities in Delhi to celebrate the succession of Edward VII and Alexandra—and Lord Curzon was to become viceroy there.

Oh, foolish and selfish though I sounded to myself, I hoped none of that interfered with my trip to see Papa and Jacques.

AT THE LAST minute on that trip to Paris, though Papa had said he would go up in the balloon with Jacques and me, one of his racing horses became ill and he begged off to go to his stables. The three of us had dined one night to make the plans, but at least I was still going. Jacques himself called for me at Papa's house, and we set off in a carriage for a field outside of Paris.

We talked about everything. There was never a dull moment. I told him about the electric car my mother had sent me and the boys from America. Despite Sunny's insistence I always be accompanied, that instead of my pony cart was my escape from problems and from him. I drove alone to visit charity cases and through the forests of Blenheim and Woodstock. I stopped on the bridge where Jacques and I had once stood. Sometimes I took Golden along in her gilded cage and just listened as her songs blended with that of other birds.

And sometimes I just watched the clouds and pretended I was flying. But now I was about to take to the skies.

"Let me hold your hand to steady you," Jacques said. He was speaking English to me right now, but French to the two men who would release the guy ropes yet keep their ends attached to a metal frame in the grass. Above us bobbing, waiting, was a beautiful blue and red balloon with big white stripes, the colors, I thought, of the American flag, the British Union Jack, and the French Tricolor.

Though I was trembling a bit at this ride and my nearness to Jacques, I climbed the wooden stairs next to the deep, narrow woven basket and, lifting my skirts a bit, climbed in. He came right behind me.

"We are going high but they will not cut us loose this time," he assured me. "Not for our first time, yes? No danger, for I do not want the Duke of Marlborough and the British crown after my head if we should just drift away forever." He laughed deep in his throat and reached up to adjust the burner over our heads.

"Now!" he called to his friends. *"Allons! Allons!* Let's go!"

And go we did. Upward, higher and higher, though still tethered to the ground.

I gasped at the magnificence of the vast view. This is what it was to fly. To my amazement, tears blurred my vision, and I blinked them back. He took my hand. His was warm and steady to my shaking touch. I leaned slightly against him as the breeze picked up. His arm encircled my waist.

"From the first moment I saw you," he said, his breath heating my cheek and ear, "I wanted to take you with me like this.

I . . . I wanted you. So, one kiss to celebrate our friendship, yes? This special moment we soar into the heavens, though I swear to you, Consuelo, we could even do better than this and on the ground."

"A kiss? Only a kiss," I told him, but my voice trembled and the breeze snatched my words away.

Our mouths met perfectly. He moved his lips, slanted sideways, seemed to drink me in. My knees leaned against him for support. He held me tight to him with one hand and steadied us with the other as the basket in which we stood swayed. Suddenly, I was not sure I had ever really been kissed before. I did not want this ride or his touch to ever end. When we parted, both breathing hard, still with our gazes locked, he looked ecstatic, yet tears gilded his eyes, too.

"Back to earth," he said and gave his men below the sign to pull them down. "But, whatever befalls, I shall always be your admirer and your friend. From afar, from across the Channel, from whenever you look up in the sky, know that I love you, Consuelo Vanderbilt Marlborough."

All I could manage was, "And I you . . . too."

God forgive me, I was madly in love with Jacques Balsan, but I would not be like so many others to have him once in a forbidden, secret while, yet never really have him for my own.

THE NEXT WINTER Sunny and I went to Russia with others in a delegation for court celebrations of the Orthodox New Year and to meet the czar. I do think Sunny just wanted an excuse to buy more outrageously grand costumes and jewels, to enjoy the pomp he so admired. He bought me a diamond and turquoise dog collar to go with a new blue satin gown. We took with us a retinue of valets, maids, even an armed detective to guard our jewelry. Yet I could not help but think that one single stone from our array could probably feed the Woodstock farmers or old ladies at the almshouse for years. Dear Mrs. Prattley had died soon after the queen, and I missed her terribly—Mrs. Prattley, I mean.

Despite the excitement and anticipation, I fell into a periodic depression while on our trip. The Russian landscape seemed stark and barren. In St. Petersburg, Russia's capital, we stayed at the Hotel de l'Europe. The décor and furnishings seemed stiff, strained, and stuffy. We went sightseeing and attended many an elaborate party, but I felt as frozen as the River Neva we so often drove by. Even sleigh rides and the lively dancing to Russian mazurka music did not lift my spirits during the long, dark nights—dark nights of the soul, I thought.

I missed my sons. I missed Blenheim. I missed Jacques, and could share that latter ache with no one.

We attended three stunning events at the czar's court. One was a ball at the Winter Palace that I shall never forget for its grandeur and glitter. Gold plate was fixed to some of the walls, and countless footmen stood about in scarlet livery. Sunny and I were surely attired for the grand occasion: I wore white satin with a draped skirt and a tulle train held to my waist by a belt of diamonds, a tiara in my hair and ropes of pearls dripping from my neck. Sunny looked magnificent in his Privy Councilor's uniform with a blue coat with gold lace, white breeches, and a plumed hat under his arm.

When the Imperial family entered to the music of the Russian anthem, we all stood amazed at the parade of Grand Duchesses and the Grand Duke, the heir to the throne since no sons had yet been born to the czar and czarina. Scuttlebutt about the czarina said that she was not only bewitching but bewitched by some of her advisors. It was said she ruled the czar, and that they were desperate for an heir despite the fact she had strange illnesses. I felt for her, for the pressure to bear a son.

At another, smaller event called the Bal des Palmiers, the Ball of Palms, since those trees had been brought in for decorations, I wore my blue satin gown and matching dog-collar necklace. I felt not as weighed down with that around my neck as I had by the stories and sights of some of the starved-looking Russians in the streets. Did not guilt hang heavy on this ruler for his people's grievances?

At the Bal des Palmiers, I was astounded to be seated next to the czar himself, perhaps by his request. He entered late, so I was rather taken by surprise. Seeing the thirty-two-year-old ruler of all the Russias at such intimate range, I noted how much he resembled his cousin, our new king's son and heir, George: same beard, pale blue eyes, and, shockingly, the kind smile and mild manners.

Small talk suited everyone during the meal, but I could not hold back on a question—a careful protest—burning in my mind. So others would not hear, I asked quietly, "Why is it Russia has no democratic government that works so well in England?"

The moment the question was out of my mouth, I feared his reaction, but he replied quietly and calmly, "I would like nothing better, but Russia is not ready for that. We are two hundred years behind Europe in the development of our national political institutions. Russia is more Asiatic than European and so must be governed by an autocracy for the people's good. Madame, I have inherited a government where my powers must be absolute. The great millions of Russia are ignorant, superstitious . . ." He cleared his throat and took a swallow of wine as if that ended the conversation.

I was relieved I had not brought up my dear, rambunctious, and rebellious America. Whatever would the poor, powerful man have said to that? Although I had hoped his answer might tear away the pall of doom I felt hanging over me here, after he said all that, it was worse, especially when he went on, "I tell you, Madame Duchess, this is how it is here in Mother Russia, what I inherited."

I saw people lean closer in the sudden hush of voices. It reminded me of how our guests at Blenheim had hung on every word Bertie, Prince of Wales, had spoken at our table.

But when the czar glanced and nodded at nearby guests, nervous conversation began again. "I must tell you something else, so you understand how things are here," he told me sotto voce. "I know everything you and the duke have done since you first came to Russia. My secret police send me dossiers on the movements of foreigners. We must keep control here, to know all, including the actions of the masses I have described to you."

That silenced me, though I wanted to make another remark about the poor people I had seen standing in the streets. All of that only worsened my view of "Mother Russia" as our hosts were wont to call it.

The weather worsened, too, and I fell ill with a cold and fever that crept into my throat and even my ears. I had to keep yawning or cracking my jaw to clear my hearing. We went on to Moscow, where I tried to stay warm but felt so cold inside. I attempted to bolster myself by thinking of the coming coronation in England, but we learned a sudden appendix attack on our king had delayed the first celebration date.

I came to hate Russia. I felt I was living in a barrel, with voices, music, church bells muted. I could not wait to go home and consult an English doctor.

But it was not until we returned home and my ear and throat problems hung on, after I saw a doctor, then a specialist—even after I saw Golden singing her heart out and could not hear one note of her tune—that I realized, to my horror, I was going deaf.

Chapter Seventeen

say, but they are cheering us so bloody wildly!" Sunny told Winston and me as the Marlborough ducal coach rolled toward Westminster Abbey for King Edward's coronation. "It is hardly for you, dear coz Winston, however proud we are of you for being a Member of Parliament for Oldham these days. The Marlboroughs are back in popularity indeed!"

"Such homage would be for Consuelo before you, Sunny," witty Winston teased him. "But I deduce the crowd madness is because the Marlborough coach colors come close to the royal ones. I wager those masses waiting in the heat too long think we are the king and queen. Consuelo is as beautiful as Alexandra and all decked out today, but neither of us have the girth or beard to be King Bertie."

Looking crestfallen and embarrassed, Sunny stopped waving. I had to bite back a smile, not only of amusement but as a silent thanks to Winston who understood my hearing problem and always spoke loudly and clearly around me. Queen Alexandra had included me in her lip reading lessons at the palace, though that did not help me much. Sounds seemed so muted, and it was such a challenge to stay in conversations. I only prayed that today, with all the vocal buzz and music, the pomp and tradition in the vast Abbey, I would be able to hear the service.

Winston had teased me earlier that I would be a fine ambassador to Russia, for Czar Nicholas had not only sent me a photograph of himself but had requested one in return as a memento of our conversation at dinner. "Not many," Winston had said, "could challenge his despotic rule and suggest British democracy and get away with it. He is smitten from afar, as are the rest of us, dear duchess."

Except for my husband, I almost said. Sunny and I sometimes avoided each other and did not speak. At other times, we bickered, even in public. I knew his family—except for his sisters and even Albertha, who were on my side—knew full well things were worse than ever between us, though we did try to be civil in front of the children. What we both especially detested were rumors and reports of our troubled marriage in both the British and American gossip papers.

Once we arrived at the Abbey, it took me a while to carefully emerge from the carriage, for I was dressed to the hilt to be one of the queen's canopy bearers today. At rehearsal, I had dared to suggest that four pageboys carry the poles of the ceremonial canopy when she walked, and that—to not trip over her trains or each other's—we then take the poles when she was seated. The other three duchesses so honored were those of Portland, Montrose, and Sutherland. I was the only American. I felt honored that my request to have help from the pages had been incorporated into the many hidebound ancient rules and regulations of this crowning ceremony.

But then things were in flux and a bit streamlined today, for the first coronation date had been set aside when His Majesty had suddenly been taken ill. His life was even despaired of, but it had turned out to be appendicitis, and a quick operation had saved his life. So here we were, not on the original date of June 26, but August 9.

It was warm, and I was swathed in a heavy, traditional Marlborough velvet robe trimmed with miniver over my heavy gown, my collar of pearls, and diamond belt. Sunny was robed, too, and would have the great honor of carrying the monarch's crown on a velvet pillow in the procession. The robes smelled faintly of the herbs and camphor they had been stored in, for they only came out for such rare, special occasions, and the last coronation—Queen Victoria's—had been so long ago.

When the new monarch's crown would be placed on his head, all the peers of the realm would also don their coronets. I had tried mine on and had it stuffed a bit to fit exactly over my coif and tiara, for it had been made for some earlier duchess with a larger head. I also had a chocolate bar hidden in a pocket that I had ordered put in my gown so that I would not feel faint from hunger or have my stomach rumble during the five-hour service where I would be mostly sitting on a hard wooden chair.

I did not mind one bit the blare of trumpets during the procession. Thank the Lord, I could hear them. And I could feel the vibrations of the great Abbey organ music through the floor. For at home, even my sons' high-pitched voices were difficult now unless they were facing me, and Golden's sweet songs impossible to enjoy. The sounds of my boys and the birds singing were what I missed the most, I thought as the Abbey's choir burst into a hymn that sounded so soft. But I would fight this. I had an appointment for treatment with a doctor in Vienna, and if that did not help enough, Mother knew of a surgeon at home who could operate.

I blinked back tears of dismay for my plight but also for the majesty and beauty of the service. For once, I almost felt more British than American, especially at the blessing and the crowning. But I had to stifle a laugh instead of tears when we peers of the realm lifted our coronets to our heads, for though mine settled in place as I had planned, I saw several men and women whose coronets had not been fitted, or evidently even tried on.

One too large ancestral coronet came down so low that it covered a man's entire head, and, when he had to hold it up, the ties to his heavy robe nearly choked him. I saw yet another coronet practically dangling from a man's ear. Just the raising of all the arms made several of the heavy, old ceremonial robes slide off and nearly topple their wearers. On top of all that, one countess I knew was evidently so famished and dizzy she could not even stand.

So thanks to a chocolate bar and planning and practice—good, old American ingenuity—despite the fact I could not hear half the service, I survived and even enjoyed the day and felt the most English since I had become Duchess of Marlborough.

THE NEXT IMPORTANT event we were part of came at the end of 1902 and into the new year. It was held in India and was called the Durbar, a magnificent ceremonial gathering of the Crown's Indian subjects so they might pay homage to the emperor, our king, now that the empress, Victoria, was dead. Sunny and I, along with other titled British subjects, had been doubly invited by the king—who would not attend—and by Lord George Curzon, Viceroy of India, who would oversee the days-long ceremony.

Blandford, age six, and my dear Ivor, age five, stayed home, and I missed them terribly the moment we embarked on the steamer *Arabia* for Bombay. We traveled with sixty-some guests, mostly friends of Lord Curzon and his American wife Mary Leitner. She was, as the American newspapers had rudely referred to some of us, another "Dollar Bride," a woman from a wealthy American family who had married a British title.

But I saw the Curzons were indeed a love match, and I envied them that. How far away did Paris seem now and that balloon adventure and kiss from Jacques, for I had not seen him for nearly two years, although he wrote letters full of his life and I dared to write back. Papa said he saw him seldom these days, but had not heard he was married or engaged.

If I needed to get my mind off missing my boys, my problems hearing, missing Jacques, and, actually, the sad and bad state of my marriage, at first India did that for me. We stayed with the Curzons in what could only be described as a fabulous palace, something out of *The Arabian Nights* tales. True, the representative of the new king and ruler of India must impress the people, but I, who had seen grandeur from my earliest days, was stunned at the extent of their posh, luxurious living quarters and servants.

Especially stunned because, once again, the gap between the ruler and the ruling class called maharajas was as wide as the ocean and the gap beyond that to the people of India a vast chasm.

"It took me a while to get used to the opulence and splendor, too," Lady Curzon told me as the two of us strolled the perfumed gardens of the palace amid mist-blowing fountains. The sun was warm within these walls, which stifled the breeze, so we both had parasols. I had told her of my hearing problem, and she was kind enough to speak loudly and directly at me. "Especially because of some of the sad things—many—to be seen, well, out there," she told me, gesturing at the inlaid mosaic wall.

"Yes, I saw the masses," I admitted. "You know, it is not so different from what I saw in Russia, even just outside the beautiful Winter Palace."

"We Americans have seen poverty, too," she said, almost defensively.

"Of course, both at home and in England," I agreed. "But to see the dead carried through the streets here in open litters to be burned . . . And the worst—I could not turn away from the sight of several corpses of dead infants floating in the Ganges. Mary, that was terrible enough, but there were cows as well as women and children bathing in that same water!"

"I have seen it. Time and British civilization brought here will surely help. In my position as vicereine, I will try to make a difference, and George, of course, is striving for that. At least the horrid tradition of suttee has been abolished, where the widow of a dead man threw herself on her husband's funeral pyre as if her life was over without him. And that poor water boy who walked in on you when you were bathing . . . I apologize again."

"He was horrified and terrified. I had to be certain he would not be beaten, you see, that is why I told you. I heard that used to be what happened if a male servant, even inadvertently, glimpsed in any stage of undress, an Indian woman of the higher classes."

"Castes, they call it. Yes, he would have been severely beaten or even killed, but not today. See," she said, reaching out to touch my arm as we stopped by a fragrant jasmine bush, twirling the handles of our parasols, "progress will be made, and I intend to help."

I thought again of the poor folk in the villages near Blenheim, of dear Mrs. Prattley in the alms house, even of the ill child I had taken gifts to when I was young and stayed at Idle Hour on Long Island. But I could put no mental distance between myself and the faces I saw packed together in the streets of Delhi, the lepers, naked children, the masses of beggars.

And so later, as I watched the parades of elephants with silken-clad riders vowing obeisance to the viceroy and the king, as I toured the beautiful Taj Mahal or watched fireworks gild the skies, or went on a falcon hunt, mounted on a beautiful horse, I still saw the poor in my mind and heart.

It was not fair. It was not right. It was not moral. I decided then, however much Sunny might protest, once I was home, that I would try, at least in my own small realm, to do more to help those in dire need.

ALTHOUGH MY HEARING was not improved by the painful drainage and scraping treatments I underwent in Vienna, and Sunny kept me overly busy being duchess, two events occurred that warmed my heart. My father planned to remarry very privately in London to keep the Vanderbilt-hungry press away, and Sunny and I were to be among the few guests. And the London house Papa had paid to have built for us was finally finished.

But there was a sad event, too, which was a warning to me, I thought, not to try anything too dangerous to amend my hearing. Poor, beautiful Gladys Deacon, our mutual friend, had a beauty treatment go all wrong.

She wore a veil and did not remove her hat when she came to explain to us at Blenheim after our return from India. "I have something shocking to share," she told us. "Please sit down. I must have the light through the window exactly right to explain this."

Whatever was she talking about, I wondered. I expected a scar she could somehow cover up. She sounded and seemed all right to me. Sunny, however, looked ready to leap off the settee beside me to comfort her.

"I always wanted to have a classic Greek nose," she told us, gripping her hands together as she stood before us. "I have often been told of my—my cameo beauty, and I suppose, in a way that went to my head, and I do not mean that as a pun."

Sunny cleared his throat and sat farther forward. I sensed a certain tension between them. Did she have me here for some sort of admission because I was her friend, too, or because she needed support if Sunny erupted as he often did at me?

"So I heard of this special doctor in Paris while I was there with my mother this winter and you two were off on your exotic India adventure. A doctor who works absolute miracles of facial perfection, so they said."

"And you did what?" Sunny prompted. "He did what? You are a beautiful woman."

"Was," she said and began to tremble and cry.

I recalled the time I went to Gladys's guest room to walk her to dinner here and found her just contemplating herself in the mirror so long she had evidently lost track of time.

"You see—here, I must let you both see—I had a paraffin wax injection in the bridge of my nose to form a straight classic line from my forehead down to the tip. At first it seemed perfect, but then, it slipped—the wax—inside my face," she said and finally removed her hat and veil.

Her nose was swollen, but, that aside, there was an obvious

puffy place where the wax had settled low between her nose and cheek to unbalance her features. And from other things Gladys had said off and on during the time we had known her, I wondered if she was sometimes unbalanced in other ways, too.

Sunny stood and examined her face closely with his hands on her shoulders. "It will pass," he told her, then whispered something else to her I could not hear since he was turned away.

"You must not obsess over it, dear friend," I put in, rising and stepping between her and Sunny to give her a hug. "His Grace is right that you are still beautiful. And it is the way people act, what they do that makes them beautiful, isn't that right, Sunny?" I added.

We had been arguing lately more than ever. We had spent time apart. I could not help myself now because I sensed, truly for the first time, there was more between these two than I had ever seen. Oh, yes, I knew she had adored me because I was the duke's wife, but had there been more—that I was close to the man she adored . . . and wanted?

We both comforted her, but as I lay in bed that night, I rehearsed in my head all that I knew about an English separation in a marriage and even—yes, I said it to myself for the first time—divorce. And not because of what feelings and acts might lie between my husband and Gladys.

I had heard that an Englishman could obtain a divorce by proving his wife had committed adultery. So much of that went on among the upper classes so that was de rigueur, except it then ruined one socially, the woman at least if it had become public knowledge. But for the wife to obtain a divorce meant proving desertion or bodily harm in addition to bedrock proof the husband had been unfaithful. I had no doubt Papa would help me obtain a good lawyer, but what would that mean for my helping to rear our sons? I could not bear life separated from them, even though they would be away at school in the future and lead their own lives.

But, I thought, I must try a separate life at least. Now that the London house was completed, I would furnish it, find excuses to stay there more, have the boys visit, especially Ivor, who needed me so. My mother could hardly scold me after her divorce and remarriage, and Papa had finally found his way to a new love.

Divorce? I could not think nor plan that far. Remarriage? A distant fairy tale. Yet living separate from Sunny—whom I now vowed I would more formally and properly call Marlborough—I would be able to travel to Paris more to see Papa. I would visit America, which my husband still vowed never to see again. I needed that ear operation. I could spend more time with charity causes without being forbidden or criticized. Somehow, now at age twenty-eight, I would begin to forge a life of my own.

Part Three

Champion, 1906–1919

The Open Door

Chapter Eighteen

I wanted to have privacy when I told Marlborough my plans to leave Blenheim and obtain a separation, so I went outside to talk to him. For once I had seen out the window that we would be alone—no hovering servants, not even his gardeners for once, who were working a ways off. It felt like such a long walk out to him, through endless cavernous rooms, down grand stone staircases, away from the massive bulk of the building, which hovered like a great, great creature over us all.

He stood in the area where the new water terraces had been staked out in intricate patterns with a reflecting pool already being dug in the middle. All of this as well as many improvements inside the palace had come from my marriage settlement. He did not see me until my shadow crossed his feet.

"My plans and hopes for this are ready to become reality," he said with an all-encompassing sweep of his arm.

"I can understand how good that feels. I need to talk to you about something else, something very serious."

"If you want to ask about furnishing our new London house, go ahead, but make it grand."

"But livable. I intend to live at Sunderland House full time, you see."

He looked up at me, squinting into the setting sun. "You cannot be serious. You cannot mean to endanger all this," he added with another sweep of his hand, but his voice was deadly calm. "Us. Our heirs. Our solid place with royalty. Now, if you intend to live there frequently to lend our name to some London charities, I can see that. But I take it you dare to mean that will be your home while I am here. Consuelo, I know that house is in your name, but your father promised it to both of us. And what about our sons and what everyone will say? Are you quite mad?"

I fought to steady myself, to keep calm. "I shall have them visit me, as you, of course, may do also. Learning about London will be an important part of their lives, and of course I shall visit them when they are here or at school."

"Bloody hell! You have had this scheme for how long? What are you really saying?"

"What you already know. Let us just say what you declared a moment ago. Your hopes and plans are ready to become reality. I now claim the same for my life. You know we are husband and wife in name only, and it is so obvious that our friends, and even our families, have realized that for years. Our beginning was difficult, and our marriage, despite two fine sons, is even more so."

"Is there someone else? George Curzon is taken. Surely not Winston, however much he adores you, for he is finally mooning over someone else, that Clementine what's-her-name."

"Clementine Hozier. Clemmie is wildly popular and pretty, so who knows if it will work out?"

"But you—wildly popular and pretty—have your rabid admirers by the scores! That French balloon man, your father's friend you danced with once back in the dark ages, perhaps, who just happened to turn up here once."

"There is no one I am keen on being with right now except myself and my boys. I did not choose this marriage, but you did, knowing I didn't love you. Now that I am my own person, I have decided that—"

"You are not your own person!" he shouted so loudly I would never have known I was going deaf. "You are Duchess of Marlborough, wife of the ninth duke, mother of the tenth! You are hostess of Blenheim, part of the British aristocracy! You are favored by Queen Alexandra, even by King Edward! What the deuce, Consuelo! You bloody well know that such a move on your part will sully the Marlborough name, after I've worked so hard to make sure it has fully been restored."

He was red in the face under his hat. I had expected something like this, an explosion, so I was prepared, or thought I was. I did love Blenheim and my sons. Yet I could do no other than this.

"You are not contemplating asking for a divorce?" he demanded, lowering his voice.

"Not at this time."

"Thank God for that. And, without my permission—my cooperation—you would never obtain one, no matter how much Vanderbilt money you could get from your doting papa."

"Do not dare to disparage the hand that feeds you and your real passion, Your Grace," I said with a sweep of my arm at his precious water gardens and all of Blenheim.

His hands were balled into fists as if he would strike me. I recalled how his father had abused him, how Gladys had told me her father beat her mother.

Sunny took a step closer, but I held my ground, kept my chin up, and my eyes riveted on his.

"Call it a trial arrangement if you need to tell others and save face," I suggested, keeping as calm as I could. "It's not unusual for married couples to live apart, and as I said, you are welcome to visit me at Sunderland House, and perhaps we can entertain togeth—"

"Hardly. In our circles here, Mrs. American Consuelo Vanderbilt, most—and there are many—who do not get on in a marriage manage to 'live apart' as you say, but they do it in the same great house. This will besmirch the Marlborough name all over again. We will be barred from proper society, though some will no doubt stick by us—by you. You can say good-bye to your friendship with Queen Alexandra."

"Sad, isn't it, that His Majesty continually breaks his marriage vows to his faithful wife with Mrs. Keppel and others, then comes down so hard on anyone who breaks those same rules or wants to legally leave a marriage. His motto seems to be to couple with whomever one wants at country weekends and the like, but do it secretly. Still, if you mean our separation will be a trial for you, that you would miss me in any personal, heartfelt way, Your Grace, then that is perhaps one of the few, best compliments you have ever given me."

"You will disappoint your family, especially your mother."

"Who took control of her life to divorce her husband and marry for love."

"My sisters, my mother, and Winston who championed you from the very first will be horrified."

"I am grateful to them, for you never really championed me, not in my difficult beginning here nor in these last thorny years. If I had had your real support and affection in the beginning . . . Well, enough said. I will only tell the boys for now that I am leaving to furnish the new London home and will include things they will like since they will visit frequently. When you are in London you must come see them. I do not want them upset. After all, you have several other places you can stay in London. Perhaps even with Gladys."

I turned and started away, but he was so quiet after that jab that I looked back. He stood, watching me, his mouth open, stunned. He called after me, "I had hoped you would not let me down." I was surprised that I read his lips at this distance, or did I just know what he would say?

"And I had foolishly hoped the same of you, from the very first day you proposed marriage to me in the country you hate and I still love. I will tell you my plans for departing soon, but I say good-bye now."

I turned away again and headed back for the palace. Poor Cinderella had gone to the ball and not found her prince, but I would go on. I had to find myself, be myself. I knew that this was so right that I did not waver or cry.

ALTHOUGH I KNEW it would take me several years to really finish and furnish huge Sunderland House in the Mayfair area of London, I set to it with a will. I did regret that years ago, when Papa offered to have it built for us, we had decided on the name of one of the duke's early titles, the one that had given him his very misleading nickname of Sunny.

The house was grand, of gray stone on Curzon Street, and had a fine stable out back. Four stories, many spaces to fill, and—I admit, like my mother—I had decided to give the décor a Louis XVI French flavor. How I longed those first few months living in London, not as much for Blenheim as I did for America and France. But I would visit each soon, very soon, I promised myself.

Sunny would not share the massive painting of the four of us, which the famous painter John Singer Sergeant had completed at Blenheim last year, but I did take the painting of Ivor and me by Giovanni Boldini and hung it in the dining room. In it, my younger son leans against me as if for comfort and support, and that was truly the way things were between us. He was never fully hale and hearty, but he was not weak or ill anymore.

As for the grand family portrait by Sergeant, the American artist who had made his name and fortune painting the aristocracy of England, I always thought he had read us perfectly. Because I was taller than the duke, he had us stand apart, with Blandford between us and our sons close by me with their two puppies. So Marlborough stood a step down cloaked in his black garter robes, his hand propped on an unsheathed sword. Above us, looming ever over all the Marlboroughs, was a bust of the first duke surrounded by battle flags.

That ever-present bust of the first duke gave me an idea for decorating the long gallery of Sunderland House. I commissioned bas reliefs of the founders of our two families, the first duke at one end—to be expected, I am sure, of those I entertained there. But at the other end, in an equal position, Cornelius Vanderbilt, "the Commodore," my great-grandfather, who had founded my family and its fortune in his railroad business. He had led an early hardscrabble life and was quite a character—typically a work-one's-way-up person, which had always embarrassed Marlborough and caused no end of shocked looks by my guests that he was honored equally to the grand English duke.

When my husband saw that and got the message, shall we say, he was not amused. Of course Papa loved it and Mother understood. Both of them supported and visited me whenever they could, and I had received an amazing number of kind letters from friends. I was amazed and honored how people rallied round me. Had my husband been disliked, or had I done something right?

Once things were reasonably presentable at the house, and when the boys were visiting for the first time, I asked their father to stay for dinner, for I had invited his family members who had stuck by me through this difficult time. That included—I was so grateful—my mother-in-law, Albertha, and his sisters. Winston was here, for he had politically managed to stand by both the duke and me, and he had brought the woman he was hoping, he told me, to propose to soon, Clementine. Since I had tossed proper protocol out the window in separating from my husband, I threw caution to the winds even further and would have both boys at the dinner table, too. Thank heavens their father had declined my invitation, for he would never have allowed that.

As we went into dinner, I saw that Albertha, I never could call her Goosey, had added small American and British flags to the new bas reliefs, so it rather looked as if both founders of our dynasty were waving the small flagpoles with their mouths.

"Mother, really!" Lilian said without so much as a blink. "Sorry, Consuelo," my sister-in-law told me as I led both boys in by their hands.

"Quite all right," I assured her. "Rather spiffy too."

I had found I had better hearing with fewer people about,

especially if they were close or I could look into their faces as they spoke. The truth was, it had not grieved me one whit as it had Marlborough that the king had indeed cut us from his favorites, and I cherished the kind letter the queen had sent me, giving me her secret support. I wondered if she wished she could leave the king, but she was duty bound so much more than I.

"Mama, can I have both those flags?" Blandford asked, obviously annoyed because he thought he was too big to be holding hands with his mother. "And tell Nanny you said so, too."

"You may have the British one and Ivor the American one. After dinner. Remember now all I told you about proper manners and being polite to your elders."

"So Ivor has to be polite to me," Blandford insisted.

I merely sighed as our footman—I used but one here rather than an entire army of them—helped me lift the boys onto the cushions on their chairs. They settled down well as the others took their seats, Winston hustling in last as he was always busy at something or other. He seated his Clemmie. I had thought about asking him to give a blessing for this new house, but I had asked him to pray at table once before at Blenheim and he had gone on so long asking for guidance for some contrary back benchers in Parliament that the first course had grown cold even under its lids.

So I had decided to do that duty myself. I might as well. I was head of the new household here. Everything else in my life was different, topsy-turvy as my own nanny had once said about my dollhouse when she had scolded me. But this mansion with real people was not a dollhouse, nor was this an evening for scolding or regrets. It was my declaration of independence, and I meant to find my way with worthwhile endeavors beyond my children. Several opportunities were waiting in the wings where I would help those less fortunate—and there were so many needy people.

I raised my voice and began, "Dear Lord God, please bless this new home and the dear people assembled here and those who are not but who also need your love and care . . ."

As I went on, Ivor reached over and put his little hand on mine, which were clasped in my lap. And that made everything just fine.

Chapter Nineteen

s I adjusted to my new life—the first time I had ever felt, more or less, in control—I lived in several worlds. I was a mother first, seeing my boys in London, or even at Blenheim, whenever I could. Their nanny and a governess had given way to valets and tutors, but at least their father did not try to keep them from me. After the groundswell of support I had received and the fact I was still invited to some social events, though not those where the royals were present, perhaps he felt I still held some sway.

Over the years, I had called him Sunny to his face or to his family members, he of the long frowns, sighs, and disapproving, narrow-eyed glances. But I now referred to him more formally as "the duke" or "Your Grace," but most usually Marlborough, his formal title.

I finally really felt a part of my own family again. Even Mother and I mostly got on, though I felt we were on tenterhooks together, perhaps because I now understood a lioness not only defending her cubs but wanting to choose what was best for them. And what could my mother say, after she had left her husband and children? Papa was ever helpful, my rock for advice. He and his new wife, Anne, visited me, so I had not been to France yet. As Papa and I sat over an early breakfast at Sunderland House one morning, he suddenly surprised me with a topic I had decided not to broach.

"Was it a shock to you," he asked, "that my new wife was the widow of your long-lost first love's brother? It never came up at our wedding or our earlier visits, and I just wondered. You and I have always been close—honest with each other. Now that you are heading toward freedom and Win is out there . . ."

"Anne's in-law relation to Win was not exactly a shock. The moment I heard she had been married to a Rutherfurd, I knew it must be some relation, and I quickly figured it out. Actually, I had never really known Win's brother Lewis, so I simply called it a coincidence and that was that. Papa, I have moved on far beyond that."

"And I know your mother would not dare to bring it up."

"Mother aside, I like Anne very much, and I am so happy for both of you."

"A second thing I want to mention is that my friend Jacques Balsan is here and there in Europe, testing and working on his precious flying machines, so I have not seen him for a while. But I mean to keep in touch with him and think you might, too."

I was so excited to merely hear Jacques's name that I told Papa, "His work sounds exciting but dangerous. He said in a letter that he holds 'Balloon Pilot Certificate Number 90' and has set the record for altitude by going up to a height of five miles once and another time went a record distance of eight hundred fifty miles from near Paris clear to Russia! But another letter said that he had moved on from balloons to buy his own heavier-than-air machine, for which he holds 'Pilot Number 18' license in France."

"I say, my dear," Papa said, smiling and leaning back in his chair to study me, "but you have all of those statistics down by memory, and that is not usually your bailiwick. I thought he might be keeping in touch, as they say. So was there something sweet in those letters?" he asked, putting another lump of sugar in his coffee with such perfect timing that I had to laugh.

"Now, do not assume. He just knew I was interested since he took me up in that balloon."

"Right," he said with a wink. "Wait until I tell Anne. She partly snagged me into a marriage proposal by memorizing the blood lines of sires, dams, foals, and racing schedules."

"Oh, she did not!" I protested, but I felt myself blush. He had caught me there. I had read Jacques's letters over and over until they were ragged. "But he is busy there and I here," I added lamely.

"Not too busy to write multiple letters to someone he has only seen a few times, and, as far as I know, he is wed only to his aeroplane. Of course you too, despite this new life of independence, are still wed, and not to an inanimate object. I know it will take time, but you must admit there is a precedent in our family for moving on from a bad, well, a marriage that does not work out, even ones that have produced beautiful, talented children."

I reached across the corner of the table to touch his arm. "For the foreseeable future, that is the way it is yet, Papa. Separation, not divorce."

"Yet. Time will tell. Maybe Sunny—Marlborough as you call

him now—will really want to move on, too. I hear he was at the theater with that Deacon woman, and that is quite public. So, have you seen her since you left Blenheim?"

"Interesting that she has not called or even written. Perhaps I was naïve to think she was a close friend—my close friend at least."

"Ah, never did the course of love or false friendships run true—or something like that. Your mother and I are both better off, though I hear Oliver has been ill now and then."

"I know. As if she needs something else to fret about when she would like to have all the women of the world—perhaps the universe—vote in the next American presidential election, or else rise in full revolt. Still that is all opinion and no action from her."

He smiled and shook his head. "You have her gumption and her backbone, my dearest girl, but rather a softer, sweeter side, too."

I SOON BECAME part of the international steamer set, back and forth to the homeland I had missed so much. I had an operation on both ears in the States, which did not help as much as I had hoped. So I wore a hearing device tucked up under my hat, paid even closer attention to people when they spoke, and went about my business.

My business—philanthropy and charity, but not simply dispensing funds from afar. As I had done at the almshouse near Blenheim, I jumped in with both feet. I used my position—and my genuine concern—to help out. Widows of the London tramway men were one group I visited and supported. How moved I was to be received by rows of capped and uniformed men—their guard of honor, they called it—at the opening of a hall for the Tramway Brotherhood in Kensington.

They doffed their hats to me, then put them back on for a photograph. "Your Grace, we are beholden to you for all you done for us," the spokesman's voice rang out.

If that was not enough to give the duke apoplexy about the "strange sorts" I was mingling with, next I took up the cause of prisoners of the crown, male prisoners. I was working with a churchman—well, that was acceptable—named Prebendary Wilson Carlisle, head of the Church Army, who was attempting to help first-time offenders so that, once released, they would go straight and not re-offend, which would be the final ruination of their already poverty-stricken families.

"Those men just released from prison have good intentions," the prebendary told me. "But too many cannot find gainful employment and so take the easy way out and go back to crime. The Lord would want us to help them and their families. Of course I could just ask you for a donation to hire someone— someone impressive, who could get us good press coverage and more donations, to interview and counsel them, but, well, it is overwhelming."

"I have thought myself overwhelmed more than once in life," I told him. I could not help but think of my canary Golden in its gilded cage, singing her heart out, when I could no longer hear her songs. I had given the bird to Ivor and made him promise to take care of her. Oh, yes, I understood some of what it was like to be in a cage.

"How can I help?" I asked. "I mean, besides leasing those two adjoining houses in Endsleigh Street you have your eye on. What a good idea to have laundries and sewing rooms there where their wives can earn a living to support themselves and their families while the husbands are in prison. I shall donate funds so we can also have a nursery with baby-tenders to free up those mothers to work there until their men come back."

"Then only by the grace of God can I ask you this, too, Your Grace. The men themselves, when released, you see . . ." he said, almost stuttering as if beset by a sudden rash of nerves. "It would be such a blessing if you could somehow get others on board, find places where these men could be gainfully employed."

"Since I would be spending time at the center for the women where I could encourage them, read to them, I could interview the newly released men to assess their talents and then have volunteers with jobs waiting."

"Oh, I did not mean yourself, to sit down with them, I mean."

"I do think that would be the best. So shall we get busy on all that?"

I ALSO TRIED to help with the many tragedies I saw as I visited the slums in Southwark on a regular basis. But observing the grief of others was not limited to my work with the overwhelming problems of the British poor. My stepfather, Oliver Belmont, took seriously ill in 1908, and his life was despaired of. In June when I heard that, I took an immediate steamer to New York. I found my mother, who had truly loved him, as tough—yes, that was the word—as tough as she was, truly inconsolable, for he had died the day before I arrived.

"He and my father—the only men I ever truly loved," she said the moment I arrived and she burst into tears. It felt so strange to hold her in my arms while she sobbed on my shoulder. Though we had tolerated each other in the years since my forced wedding, we had not yet truly had a heart-to-heart to clear the air, though the morning I had gone into labor for my oldest son, we had come close. The funeral was tomorrow, so I had barely made it in time for that. I knew Mother was also on edge because my brother Willie's marriage was, as they say, on the rocks. Was there some dreadful curse on us Vanderbilts?

"I MISS HIM dreadfully and always will," Mother told me the week after the funeral when we had gone to Marble House in Newport for peace and privacy. More than once she had said she must lie down for a while, but she kept coming back into my sitting room. Her hair, now with silver threads, streamed loose to her shoulders. She wore a robe of black bombazine; the circles under her eyes were like dark half moons. Outside, the summer social season went merrily on, but we stayed inside, she mourning her loss, I mourning my dead marriage and missing my sons.

"So, can you convince the duke to really release you?" Mother asked, sitting down on the chaise next to where I had been writing at the desk in a guest room, for I had not wanted to sleep in my girlhood one.

"It is both complicated and embarrassing for him," I told her, looking up from an article called "The Position of Women" I was writing for the *New York Times*. Although I felt that paper was not the scandalmonger other papers had been, I had come to detest most social sections. Still, I could not pass up a plea in my homeland for the betterment of women whether that meant getting the vote or not. The editor had told me that my name and position could do much good for the downtrodden. As that was exactly my battle cry in England, I had consented.

"Believe me, I know the worst of a divorce," she told me, dabbing a damp handkerchief under her bloodshot eyes. "I take it an Englishman must be seen with another woman in a compromising position and then not deny that charge."

"You have been reading up on it. Yes. And although I believe the duke has another woman, he would certainly not bring her name into it."

"I shall just die. I shall just die of boredom. Widowhood, worse than being a divorced woman. But I soldier on for my causes. And, bless you, Consuelo, you do too. I . . . I do have regrets about the way things were, perhaps yet are, between us, but I wanted so much for you. I prayed your husband would not tread you down, and I see that, however powerful, he has not."

"Mother, I fight for downtrodden women because I got some of that fight from you. Papa says I inherited your backbone."

"Did he? Well, that is something then," she said and blew her nose.

"Listen," I said, suddenly feeling as if I were the senior person here. I swiveled in my chair, leaned forward, and held her hand. "We have had some terrible times between us—your dreams, your ambitions running things at any cost—even any cost to me. But I admire that you have never been one to give up, even against difficult odds. You have said you believe this country would be a better place if women could speak out more strongly. Perhaps I learned that from you."

She nodded fiercely, tears in her eyes again. "Here, that must mean they should be given the vote. Suffrage, as they dare to call it when women are suffering now—even you and I— sometimes together."

"Yes, together. Would that not be something grand? I believe that in England women can still speak out and do great, important things without the vote, but—"

"As I said, not here. It must be the vote. Oh, that would be a war for me, if I got tooth and nail into it," she said, almost wistfully. "We women must have the vote!"

"I am sure you can work for it carefully, not with stunts or violence as some of the British women are threatening in order to make their case. Speaking out, writing an article—like this one," I added, "though I am not demanding the vote here or abroad."

"I did not rear you wrong, did I?" she asked, leaning forward and squeezing my hands.

"Well, you were a bit harsh at times."

"But look at you now! I am proud of your strength of character, not just your beauty. Did you detest me terribly? I wanted to help you, save you, make you strong."

"You know, I shall never forget that time my pony bolted and dragged the little cart with me in it toward the water. While others merely screamed, you picked up your skirt and chased that horse, stood nearly in front of the panicked beast and grabbed it by the reins and maybe saved my life. Even in our worst moments—especially at the end when I was so distraught—I knew deep down you loved me and thought you were doing the best you could."

She tugged me to sit beside her, and we held tight, both sobbing like babies. "My beautiful girl! My beautiful, strong girl," she said, stroking my hair as if I were but five instead of thirty-one. "You have a position not only here to be asked to write for the *Times*, but influence yet in England, so you can stand up for what is right. And—" she said with a huge sigh, as she sat back away from me, "separated or not, divorced or not, widowed or not, we go on!"

"We do! Together, if we can."

"Spoken like an English duchess—and an American one, too!"

Chapter Twenty

It made my spirits soar to know I was not socially ostracized in the States because of my marriage separation, and that even among some of my London friends, few seemed perturbed. Of course, I knew that going through with a divorce might be a different situation altogether.

In London, my godmother Consuelo, Duchess of Manchester, had invited me to one of her popular literary circle soirees. Oh, how I loved this sort of gathering, where, rather than social tittle-tattle, ideas and books and plays were spoken of and argued and often by the very men who had written them.

I was especially excited that I was sought out by many of the guests. Grinning, but shaking a finger at me, H. G. Wells said, "One more good deed from you among the so-called underclasses, my dear Mrs. Marlborough, and your former friends will have to brand you a socialist, and welcome to that club!"

He took a good gulp of wine, then raised his goblet as if he were toasting me, for he was a bit radical with all his criticism of the government—in fiction, at least. I had read his books

The Time Machine and *War of the Worlds* and thought him terribly clever, however much I read a threat of doomsday beneath his stories.

"Do not threaten this lovely lady," John Galsworthy, standing on my other side, insisted.

I thought Mr. Galsworthy rather a nervous sort. He spoke quietly, unlike the others who raised their voices over the buzz in the room, so I had to strain to hear him. I had thought at first he had gravitated to my side to pump me for inside information about the aristocracy, since he had begun a series of novels about a fictional Forsythe family, but he usually said hardly a word. He was, I thought, an observer, not a talker. He had, however, asked me if I had ever thought of authoring something like *The Marlborough Saga*, to which I answered, "I dare not, for truth is stranger than fiction."

The most interesting man today—not counting Winston who was here for once and had been kind enough to bring Clemmie to accompany me—was the very handsome, dark-haired and mustached Bernard Shaw, not to be called George, I had heard. His Irish accent was charming, though the tenor of his thoughts was not. It seemed he liked to criticize everything English, but then, I suppose, that was natural for a theater and music critic.

"The duchess is not a socialist, Wells," Bernard told his fellow writer, "but a fine example of my independent-thinking 'New Woman.' I will have to write a play called *The Duchess of Destruction*, for I believe she is out to declare war on slum landlords and even champion 'women of the night,' to get them out of that profession."

I was taken aback by that comment but not insulted. His drama *Mrs. Warren's Profession* was about a prostitute, and the author Henry James, who was not here this time, championed independent career women in what he considered an unfair male-dominated society. I took this banter seriously, for Henry James had told me once at such a gathering as this that I was the bravest of the new women. He had said that I had "plucked myself from the sinking mud of the aristocracy then jumped in with both feet to pull disadvantaged women up after me."

"So, Consuelo," Winston said, appearing suddenly as if to rescue me, "I imagine the heroine of the next British plays and novels will be a rebel from the upper crust, standing up for everyone's rights—and authored by this creative British brain trust."

Bernard laughed, Mr. Wells smiled, and Galsworthy beat a quick retreat, evidently when he saw the outspoken guest Nancy Astor stroll over to our growing group. She, too, was an American, one who had made an important marriage to Waldorf Astor, the American-born millionaire, now a British citizen. She was, as people put it, "frightfully outspoken" with a sharp wit. Winston usually liked that in a person, but the two of them got on like oil and water—or more like fire and turpentine.

It was a brave or careless hostess who invited Winston and Nancy Astor to the same event. I could see they were in the midst of some sort of contretemps even now. Nancy, trying to catch up with him, who must have snubbed her, was saying—and I could hear her from here over the background chatter—"I tell you, Winston Churchill, I do not know how that sweet lady Clementine puts up with you. If I were your wife, I would put poison in your coffee!"

"And if I were your husband," Winston shot back, "I would drink it!"

The chatter of our little circle stopped. My godmother must

have sensed disaster and came rushing over. Bernard smiled, but Mr. Wells bellowed a guffaw.

I admit I grew wide-eyed at that rejoinder but I had to laugh with the men. My godmother fanned her face. Nancy Astor, evidently unable to top that, harrumphed and hurried off.

"I swear, Winston," Wells said, "you may be wishy-washy between Conservative and Labour, but I like your style! And I like your American duchess, so better get her out of here before that Astor harpy tries to take it out on her."

"She dare not!" my dear godmother insisted, still fanning her face. "This younger duchess Consuelo stands up for herself, even as this older duchess Consuelo has learned to do!"

I hugged her while our little circle, especially Winston, applauded.

At that moment I decided, wherever I lived, I would be bold to mix such dynamic, fascinating personalities—however outspoken—at my gatherings, too.

LIVING APART FROM the duke but keeping tabs on my growing boys, with all my other interests, kept me busy. I must admit that I was often exhausted, but that helped me to sleep. I was able to obtain one of the first Akouphone carbon transmitters, an electric one, to help with my hearing. When I visited Papa and Anne at their home in Poissy about twenty miles from Paris and went to the races with them, I could more clearly hear Papa's recital of the order of the horses, despite the cheers all about us. I suppose it was pure nonsense, but I came to believe I could hear better in France.

But while there at their château, more than once I dreamed I was flying, looking down at the ground passing under me. I soared with the birds, hearing the lovesick songs of a canary named Golden who perched on the rim of the woven basket of the balloon. Below me I saw children on the playgrounds I had promoted in the slums of cities and saw Grace waving good-bye to me. I was looking for a country house, a place away from London, a retreat, but where was it in the fields and forests below? And I was trying to plan the Sunderland House Conference to help protect the poor working women, where they bent over dim tables making lace or matchboxes or chains all day with so little pay.

Chains . . . were my balloon and basket still chained to the ground, or was I lost? My fantasy turned to nightmare for I was all alone, and the balloon was drifting I do not know where, and Jacques was not there to save me.

I sat up in bed, sweating, my heart pounding. "Oh, a dream, good and bad!" I said in the silent guest room. It was already daylight. I remembered that Jacques had telephoned my father to say he would try to visit me here before I went back to England tomorrow. He and other pilots were preparing for war if worse came to worst with the terrible Kaiser and the Huns, but I was certain that could not be.

If Jacques did not come today, I would be gone. I had to leave, for I had scheduled the conference organized by two trade union charities, both headed by women, this time to convince people to protect women in the sweated trades. I was going to be daring in my methods. If the attenders accepted my invitations either to just see the inside of my London home or to hear some pretty speech from me while my helpers passed a basket for donations, they were in for a surprise.

"Surprise, madame!" a housemaid called out after she knocked on my door and opened it, carrying a breakfast tray. "Your papa, he says you have a visitor downstairs, Monsieur

Jacques, the airman, yes, did land his aeroplane in a field near here, only can stay a little while."

I threw the covers off and scooted out of bed. "Leave the tray, please, and call my maid at once," I told her in French. "Time, you know, flies too!"

"I AM SO proud of you!" Jacques told me the moment we were alone after spending a few minutes downstairs with Papa and Anne. He had already praised me for how well I was doing with my new hearing aid. "You are making a life for yourself, stepping away from a man who did not deserve you!"

He had borrowed Papa's motorcar to take me to the nearby field to see his aeroplane. The rural road was bumpy, and I bounced against him. "Much smoother in the air," he told me as my hip seemed to stick to his, "but this has its advantages! And there she is, my other passion."

Did he mean other than me? I dare not ask as he stopped the motorcar, and we got out in the rutted entry to the field. "At least the people who gathered have gone away for now," he told me, taking my hand and pulling me after him into the grassy meadow with bobbing daisies, though there was a mown path he must have landed on that stopped at the very edge of the uncut area.

"But is . . . is it dangerous for you?" I asked as we approached the silver aeroplane, glinting in the midmorning sun.

It had double wings, two front wheels and one small back one and a large rotor kind of thing on its nose. The pilot had no covered place to sit, so I could see his head must be out in the air behind a short windscreen. Still holding my hand, Jacques turned and looked at me, his gaze so intense.

"Everything worth having—and possibly losing—makes flying and other things in life precious. Consuelo, I did not trust this thought to writing in my letters in case you were, well, being watched, but I am hoping you are considering the final step to end your unhappy marriage. Granted, my strict Catholic family would never want me to wed a divorced woman and a Protestant, but I would risk all that if, well, if I could court you, see you. If you would allow me to come to England—or wherever—I do not care, to see you."

"But I thought you are married to . . . I mean . . . to this metal lady here," I said, with a gesture at the silver creature sitting so solemnly alone in this French field.

"So," he said, lifting my hand and kissing the back of my fingers, "you will never have to be jealous of her. My dear, that first night we met and danced so briefly, long ago, I went home and told my mother I had met the girl I would like to marry. Yes, I swear I did!"

He put an arm around my waist, kept my hand in his and tried to turn us as if on a dance floor. But a few steps away from the aeroplane, the grass snagged our feet and a clump of daisies nearly toppled us. Laughing, he took me closer to the aeroplane, and we leaned against its metal skin in the shade of one wing. He held me to him. How famished I had been for the intense attention of a man, all those years of marriage when I was duchess indeed but the duke was so cold. And since then, too, as busy as I had kept myself. But this man, when he looked at me, listened to me, spoke to me—I swear time stood still and I felt all that clear down to the pit of my belly. If Jacques had proposed it, I would have lain down with him in the meadow and loved him forever.

"So," he said, "the bold crusader who speaks out for downtrodden people's rights I have heard about and read about has nothing to say for now?"

"I am cherishing each moment. I do not want this—us—to end."

"Then I believe that is a yes that when I can I shall visit you, court you. I swear I shall win you!"

I almost told him he already had, but this was too quick, too brief, as had been all of our encounters. Was this even real? For I had dreamed of him, wanted something like this. And if war with Germany became a reality, that would mean Jacques would be gone to fight to protect France, or that I could even lose him before he was really mine.

We kissed and caressed until some farmer's boys shouted that the "pilot man" was back and everyone should come see.

"I must take you back before I go," he told me, frowning at the growing crowd we had not noticed along the fence of the field.

"I can drive back. I know how. I want to see you fly your other lady."

Despite the cheers and a few hoots from the farm boys, Jacques kissed me hard again and climbed up into the well that must hold his seat and the controls.

"Oh!" he said down at me. "I forgot the key to the motorcar!" He tossed it down to me. "Consider it the key to my heart!"

He put on a leather cap, goggles, and a scarf. The rotor on the nose started to turn, and the engine hummed. I moved away and stood in the staring crowd of rural French folk as the aeroplane rolled away onto the cut strip and rolled faster, faster, then took to the blue sky, sailing over an orchard.

"Long live love, yes?" one of the farm women said in French with a wink at me.

I just nodded and kept shading my eyes to look up toward the sun. Jacques made one pass above, a circle with a dip of both wings, then disappeared into the heavens. The little crowd cheered. I did too, but when would I see him again? And if war came to this lovely, peaceful land, would I ever?

Chapter Twenty-One

I did not know what was coming next in the European political situation, but then neither did the nearly five hundred guests know what was coming the next morning at my Sunderland House Conference. I imagine the engraved invitations and the tea and strawberry delights had made them think this would be a lovely, proper social occasion.

With Winston's help, I had invited important people who were kind but complacent. My friend was quite the liberal then in his political beliefs, but I noted even those of the conservative bent were here. As the program began, I could see my true purpose was dawning on the brightest of the churchmen, parliamentarians, business owners, and newspapermen and even some of the aristocracy who were here today: I had something not only entirely serious but shocking in mind.

I took the stage at the podium, but from behind the curtain out came six elderly working-class women from each side, a total of twelve, to sit in chairs. They were women I had chosen because they had labored long in the sweated trades, been paid little and treated nearly as slave-laborers here in the heart of England and throughout the Empire. I introduced each by name, but they boldly did all the speaking.

"Gents and ladies," the first silver-haired, frail-looking speaker said, "I been twenty years hard working in a factory what makes confections for sweet tooths, if you know what I mean. Eight shillings a week I made and from that provided for schooling and food of my child, since my husband been sent to prison. All those years I never eaten a dinner costing more than a penny."

An eighty-four-year-old, bent-over woman with a Cockney accent talked of being fifty years as a shirt maker in a factory and at home. "This here is a shirt I made and right proud of it, too," she told them, holding up the item. Her arms shook, but her voice did not. "Mrs. Marlborough says just tell true, so here's the end of it. Last week me and my husband worked from five-thirty morn till eleven at night at home after a day's work in the factory and made fourteen dozen of these, earned us ten extra shillings, but got to pay ten pence for cotton."

So on it went. Some of the crowd kept silent, some murmured or fidgeted. A few women wept, and some men blew their noses. I imagine some were offended that I had dared to bring in the old ladies to tell their own tales, but my dear friend Mrs. Prattley had done that so well. A few of my guests looked askance at me thereafter, a few thanked me. But the donations for the charity for Silver Haired Women of the Trades went as sky high as, well, as Jacques could soar in his silver aeroplane.

THEN, ON JUNE 28, 1914, a Serb named Gavrilo Princip shot to death Archduke Franz Ferdinand of Austria and his wife, the

Archduchess Sophie, in Sarajevo. This destabilized the delicate balance of that city, that country, and Germany, just lying in wait for a trigger to attack, took advantage. From those few bullets of an assassination came what was soon called The Great War or The War to End All Wars as fighting and destruction spread like wildfire through Europe. I was soon doing war charity work and fighting another battle, since, for the first time in our separation, the duke and I became engulfed in a face-to-face dispute.

"Bloody hell, Consuelo!" he shouted the moment he entered the library at Sunderland House, a place he so seldom visited. He stalked to the window and stood there frowning out as if he could not bear to look at me. "How dare you tamper with—even advise—Blandford on which regiment he should become attached to in this damned war! I fear England will too soon jump in with both feet and then it will not just be sharp uniforms, patriotic posters, and parades!"

I sat on the settee not far from him. "He is my son, too. And I am only looking out for his best interests. You are the one who approved of his leaving Eton for a course in officer training at Sandhurst, so he had that idea of joining the guards in his own head already."

"Don't try to shift this off on me as you have everything else. You've swayed most of my friends, even convinced Winston, to believe that the failure of our marriage was *my* fault."

"I have never said such a thing about you, except to myself!"

I almost feared he would strike me, but he only pierced me with a frown and stood his ground.

"Besides," he went on, finally turning to look fully at me, "did we not have an agreement that I oversee the upbringing of the next duke and you supervise Ivor?"

"Hardly! The only agreement I had with you about Blandford is that I can finally call him Bert, and only then because the boy insisted he prefers that he not be called Blandford."

"Never mind all that. What's important is that after I had arranged everything for him to serve in the War Office, where he would be safe, that he suddenly prefers the First Life Guards where he could well go into battle. He was perfectly content with my arrangements a week ago, and then you and some high-ranking friend talked him into changing to a second-rate regiment!"

"Marlborough," I countered, "if you would just listen to Winston, he believes there will be a conscription if things get bad when we get in this war, so why should Bert be cowed into serving in some office here, which he does not want?"

"I swear, I will have Winston's head, too, if he has advised you on this! He'd best stick to his royal navy work as First Lord of the Admiralty—a political position in a London office!"

"He has not advised me, at least not on this. But I have learned that the Kaiser is building aircraft called Zeppelins that could drop bombs on England—and so, no doubt, they could target the War Office where Bert would not be safe. None of us will be safe."

"Nonsense. Come clear over the channel, drop bombs, and make it back to German bases? But do not try to get me off the topic of Blandford."

"All right then, look at it this way. The Life Guards appointment is what he desperately wants. To serve with honor, to be with his friends. Do I want him in harm's way—never. But if you believe an appointment to the Life Guards is second rate now, surely *your* son and heir will soon make it first rate!"

"If you were any sort of mother, you would beg me to lock

him up during this bloody war mess. I believe we will go to war against those greedy Huns and the damned Kaiser. I am going now to try to undo the mischief of your meddling!" He stormed out just as the tea I had ordered came in on a rolling cart.

I imagined the duke was even more livid the next day, for I soon heard that Bert had already signed with the 1st Life Guards as a second lieutenant. And, Albertha said, that Bert had told his distraught father that he was old enough to make his own decisions as a loyal British citizen and next Duke of Marlborough.

To make the memory of that visit worse, I shortly thereafter received the first communiqué from Gladys in years, in which she dared to inform me that, *Sunny is so distressed over this, and it will be on your head if anything happens to his heir in this dreadful war that is surely to get worse if England jumps in with both feet and that is surely coming.*

SADLY, GLADYS WAS right about us getting into the fight as King George, the deceased King Edward's son, four years now on the throne, declared war on August 4, 1914. Winston had already ordered a test mobilization of the Royal Navy Home Fleet.

France especially came under German attack, which added Jacques to the long list of those I endlessly worried about. My dear Frenchman's letters had stopped, making me wonder if he was somehow fighting in that aeroplane of his.

When Papa and Anne came to stay with me in London, able to travel across the Atlantic since the United States was still neutral, Papa said he had word that Jacques was doing "reconnaissance."

"What does that mean?" I demanded. "Tell me right out. I want to know."

He glanced at Anne, who nodded, so she must already know. My insides twisted even tighter. Surely they had not come to tell me Jacques had been . . . been lost.

"He has volunteered for duty to fly over enemy forces and report their positions and strength," Papa told me, putting a firm hand on my shoulder. "And he is going to serve in Morocco to take part in early tests of aerial bombardment. He has become a captain in the new French air force, and he asked that I give you this," he added, taking a folded envelope out of his suit-coat pocket. "He was not sure how well the mail would get through from France to England right now and so sent this to me—sealed."

I held the letter in my hand. Though warm from Papa's coat, I imagined it was because Jacques had held it, maybe kissed it.

"Thank you, Papa, for telling me the truth and for bringing this. I shall continue to worry for Bert and Jacques and that Ivor does not get conscripted. I will be back in a moment, if you do not mind."

Anne—no wonder Papa had fallen in love with her—put her arm around my waist and whispered, "Take all the time you want, dearest Consuelo. We understand. As we grow older," she said with a glance at Papa, "the head and heart work together to know what and who one really wants."

I kissed her on the cheek and fled to my bedroom. I had known from the first, even in my youth, that I did not love the duke, and, strangely, known from my first time with Jacques, that dance, that he was special. I broke the seal on the envelope and pulled out the one-sided, one-page letter. Was it my imagination he had hastily written this? That he longed for me, but his mind was elsewhere, for he was already in love with his dear France?

I sat on the divan at the foot of my canopied bed and read:

My dearest Consuelo, I am writing this in haste, but, sadly, I fear our entire relationship so far has been in haste. I long for this war to be over and fear it has barely begun. I long to be with you, to formally court you, to win you. Granted, there are many obstacles to that, but we can win. We can win this dreadful war and we can win the right to be forever together.

Be very careful, even in London, for the Huns have their own deadly big balloons called Zeppelins that can drop incendiary bombs, and they will send aeroplanes in the near future. Perhaps find a small place of your own in the nearby countryside for a refuge, but I hope you will not return to Blenheim.

Lest I do not return from my part in this tragedy, know that I have admired and loved and wanted you from the first and that will never change, no matter what happens. I pray we will have our chance to be together, if you are willing, for I am more than ready.

I must tell you one thing. Eleven years ago I was married briefly, in a civil ceremony because the bride was going to bear my child. I never loved her, a fling with sad consequences, for the child died and there was nothing but that to keep us together. The marriage was never truly sanctioned and is long over. But I long for a true, a real one we both choose for the right reasons, if I can earn your care and trust.

Forever your Jacques, whether or not you wish it to be so.

A captain in the new French air force, but you are captain of my heart

The lines of the letter blurred as I blinked back tears. I read it again. It was so emotional, so open. That was one thing about this man. He shared his intense feelings, always had. It was a heady thing for a woman who had longed for love all those years I had lived with the duke. I clasped the letter to my breasts. He was right that we had far to go to really be together. I prayed so hard then and thereafter that we would have our chance.

I KEPT VERY busy to cope with fear and looming destruction. I quickly became involved with the Women's Emergency Corps, which promoted women taking over the work of enlisted men. I feared conscription, for that would involve dear Ivor, too, and he was never really strong. In school at Eton, he failed his medical tests for the army. On occasion, Winston used him for office work, for which I was so grateful. When Ivor could, he spent much time with me.

I also became chairman of the American Women's War Relief Fund, which supported a military hospital in Devon. When I had time, I scoured areas outside London for a pied-à-terre like Jacques had mentioned, not only for my safety lest London were hit by Zeppelin or aeroplane bombs but for my own sanity—an escape for the soul. But nothing right had turned up yet.

Meanwhile, I volunteered Sunderland House as a shelter should there be a Hun aerial attack on London. I had thought it could become a nursing home for wounded soldiers, but it proved unsuitable for that. I learned it was considered unpatriotic for one person, or even a few, to live alone in so huge a house when the nation was at war.

However, it was known in the neighborhood that the sturdy building with its extensive cellars would accept on immediate notice people off the streets who needed a safe haven during an attack. I prepared the cellars, which mostly stored food and wine, with lanterns and seats of various kinds. My women servants were mostly working in munition factories now, so, as exhausted as I was, I did much of the preparations myself, but nothing happened, except some Zepp attacks out by the docks.

And then it did. Not the huge floating, gas-filled airships, but on May 31, 1915, horrible, buzzing aeroplanes.

IN LATE AFTERNOON, the neighborhood sirens screamed, screamed, screamed as people ran to my front door. As my last maid and I welcomed them in, I glanced up to see three of the evil metal birds overhead, then I felt the vibrations and the muted *boom*, *boom* of bombs somewhere nearby. Why bomb such a residential neighborhood? Perhaps the Huns thought important people were here—and so they were. Yet people of all classes and ages streamed in, and I guided them quickly down to the cellars. The *crump*, *crump* of bombs was more muted here, and I prayed they would not come closer.

Huddled in the dim light of lanterns, no one said much at first, though several children and one baby cried. I took a little boy, perhaps two years old, onto my lap and bounced him a bit.

"We are so grateful," a man next to me said. I strained to hear him. "Hope a hit here will not harm all this wine."

I suddenly felt guilty. Sunderland House, like Blenheim, was so elegant, so massive and well stocked, but at least it had been used for important causes, helping, saving—I hoped—people.

"As soon as the noise stops," I declared, "we shall open some bottles and toast our fighting forces."

"And hope the Yanks get in the war."

"Yes!" I said. "I am sure they—we—will."

We sat there on edge for a good hour to be sure the attack was over. Rather than breaking out the wine here, I gave each family or lone adult a bottle as he or she left. Several of the woman curtsied to me as if I were Queen Mary. Many thanked me heartily. I hated to hand the little boy back to his mother.

Outside, as I stood in the door to the street, I felt so lonely. How I wanted to find a rural retreat, someplace small, someplace Bert and Jacques, too, could love when—if—they came back from the horror and madness of this war.

I turned to go back inside the mansion. It suddenly seemed a ghost house to me now, haunted by what might have been.

Chapter Twenty-Two

oon after, I found the country home of my dreams. A friend told me of a Tudor-era farmhouse for sale in the gentle hills of Surrey, a two-hour motorcar ride from London. I contacted the family who owned the house but hardly used it. And so, on a sweet summer day, I met with the Reverend Mr. Gainsforth to look at the property that had been in his family for four hundred years, quite outdoing the lease the Marlborough dukes held on Blenheim.

"We truly do not want to sell, Your Grace, but when I heard it was you, well."

"Because you think I will pay a pretty penny for it?" I asked him with a little laugh.

"Why, no," the portly man said, as he drove me in a carriage toward the property. "I mean . . . the duchess connection. You did not know that the first duchess, Sarah, briefly owned Crowhurst? Well, that is, she leased it to house some veterans of the first duke's campaigns."

"No, I did not. How wonderful," I said, craning to look down the lane for the first glimpse of the house and barn, but I was remembering what surely was Sarah's ghost at Blenheim, and I had wondered if she missed me there. I had a feeling she had not wanted me to leave.

The night I was overseeing the packing of my things in my bedroom, items had kept falling on the floor, and my maid had not known why. Twice the door to the hall had opened of its own accord to bring in a chill draft, and someone had turned down the covers on the bed when the maid was downstairs and I was undressing in the next room.

"Duchess?" Mr. Gainsforth broke into my reverie. "Are you quite all right? Crowhurst is its original name and bad luck to change it, family lore says. You can see the tall yews up ahead," he said pointing. "The lane just beyond that."

"Oh, it is just lovely!" I cried as we turned down a curving lane. I realized that was no way to get a reasonable price for a place, but I did not care. Charming, secluded—everything I had wanted, and, no doubt, Jacques had wanted for me.

The old barn was ready to fall down, but the ancient, half-timbered manor house looked sturdy and welcoming. It had a steep, slanted roof with stone chimneys. Thick windowpanes sealed with lead glinted in the sun. And the frame for the house was terraces of flowers in wild bloom, honeysuckle and roses, phlox, lavender Canterbury bells and purple iris. Around the back, lay a sunken herb garden, and beyond, a pond with four swans swimming!

The housemaid who lived in a room at the back, Hatherly, came out to greet us, a charming young, blond woman with rosy cheeks and none of that worried, gaunt look so many London girls wore now.

"Just cutting flowers for the table, Your—your Duchess!" she said and bobbed a curtsy after we briefly chatted. She went about her business in the herb garden as Mr. Gainsforth took me inside.

Clean flagstone floors and creamy white, unadorned plastered walls greeted me. The great hall reached upward to the raftered roof, and an oak staircase led to a great chamber upstairs with smaller bedrooms, too. A large oriel window threw light inside. I could instantly picture where an oriental rug would go, my French paintings, velvet draperies, and my chintz-covered easy chairs.

I knew I must have this place. I not only pictured escaping here on weekends and longer visits, but also inviting my London friends and my sons, but especially Jacques when this wretched war was over. I did not even fret that Duchess Sarah might haunt Crowhurst, the first property, at age thirty-eight, I could really call my own, here in my new home.

CROWHURST BECAME MY salvation. I loved being there, entertaining or just alone. Hatherly stayed on, and I needed only two local gardeners beyond that, even when I entertained, for things seemed so much simpler and safer here. I paid some local men to tear down the rickety barn and extended the stone patio. I spent much time in London at my war work, but fled to Surrey whenever I could manage.

Besides my literary and family friends, two of my favorite weekend or Sunday guests, not counting Winston and Clemmie, were Prime Minister H. H. Asquith and David Lloyd George, Chancellor of the Exchequer. The duke was now in the House of Lords, an aristocrat to his toe tips, the very group that Asquith was attacking to lessen their power. I suppose the duke knew Asquith was a friend of mine since I now leaned closer to the Liberal left. Getting along with the duke no longer mattered to me except for our not upsetting our sons.

I only hoped that when this dreadful war ended everyone would be so relieved that, if I asked for a divorce, the duke, who seemed ever swayed by his longtime lover Gladys, would be happy to oblige. I had realized far too late that her goal from the first was to be Duchess of Marlborough, and she was quite welcome to the duke and the title, though that would mean going through the grueling steps for a divorce.

I regretted that this September Sunday, H. H. Asquith had brought his wife Margot with him, not because I had designs on him, but because that woman completely annoyed me. She had nasty opinions of everyone, so I wondered what she said of me behind my back. She was the most skilled woman I had ever known at subtle or blatant digs.

"Those wretched little owls are back up there in the very tiptop of your ceiling," she told me, covering her wineglass with her hand as if their droppings would plop into her martini when they stayed way over in their little niche. "Really, Consuelo, how can you live out here like this? You had best have those creatures caught and tell that country girl of yours to bring in a man and a ladder to toss them out."

"I do get an urge to toss people out sometimes," I told her, straight-faced. "But the owls are wise little things and only observe and do not give a hoot."

"Oh, well, that reminds me of a comedy routine I saw the other day in London at a theater, the same one your eldest attended with that sort of chorus girl. My, your Blandford does have a good eye for beauty, skin deep at least, and he looked so fine in his uniform. I heard Sunny said simply—about Blandford chasing chorus girls—'It's his common American blood.'"

I chose to ignore that jab, for it was her bread and butter, though I would have much liked to have forced it down her throat.

"Bert is home for a brief leave," I told her, keeping calm, "and you are right about his appreciation of beauty. His good taste is why he likes Crowhurst so much—owls and all. He suggested I change the name to Owlhurst, but Ivor enjoys it here, too, just the way it is. I do think there is something so clean and pure here, unsullied by critics or all sorts, at least until recently."

The moment that was out of my mouth I regretted it, but the woman irked me to no end. Oh dear, now I might lose H.H., too, and he was such a brilliant conversationalist, especially with brandy in his hand and a week of fighting the House of Lords behind him. I imagined he rather liked being with people he did not have to argue with—except for Margot, that is.

"Well!" she huffed. "Do let me know if you ever take another suggestion from me, let it be that you rid yourself of Sunny. You do not even feign to be married anymore, and he has that other American on the string. I would give the heave-ho to H.H., lord of all wartime parliaments of the world, if he did that."

"I thank you so much again for your advice," I told her, my voice dripping honey. At least I kept from splashing my glass of wine in her face. "I shall remember that next time the owls call out *Who, who*, and I shall tell them, Margot Asquith, that is who needs your wise words."

"Really!"

"Time to head back, Margot," H.H. said, coming up and putting his arm around my shoulder instead of hers, but he still had brandy in his right hand.

"Margot does not like my pet owls, or a few others either."

"Ah. News to me," he said rolling his eyes. "I thank you, Consuelo, for this respite from the war. I fear we are going to have rationing soon, probably of sugar, even bread, maybe after that meat, but your food and drink has been excellent today. The conversation, too, most of it," he added with a quick glance at Margot behind her back. I nearly burst out laughing but bit my tongue.

"I just bet your government never rations brandy," Margot said.

He ignored that, but I had to laugh at last. I accompanied him to the door, and Margot followed, scooping up her purse and another drink.

What would I do without my friends during these war years, these years of separation from the duke and from Jacques, waiting for the right time to say I wanted a divorce, despite all the shenanigans we must go through with the damned newspapers on two continents all looking our way. But like a wise owl at the ripe old age of nearly forty, as soon as this dreadful war ended, I was ready.

IT HELPED SO much when my American countrymen finally entered the war in April of 1917. Mother had been predicting they would, but then, she had also predicted American women would get the vote. She was the perfect rabble-rouser for that, marching, giving speeches, and making a general ruckus in the American press, something she had been skilled at for years.

I spent some of my beautiful days at Crowhurst fretting for the safety of my loved ones: Bert, who was now in France; Ivor's health; and certainly for Jacques. Despite not being fit for service, Ivor had been taken onto the staff of the Quartermaster-General at his headquarters at the War Office—so the duke finally got his wish that a son of his served there safely. Also, Winston was kind to take Ivor with him on one of his tours to inspect the front in France, and he wrote to me—perhaps to the duke also—how well Ivor had acquitted himself in the war zone.

I seldom attended social functions now and had closed and vacated vast Sunderland House, taking a small place near Regent's Park where Ivor lived with me. I was so busy with war work that it was a rare delight to snag more than one or two days at Crowhurst.

King George declared the royal family would no longer be designated by its string of German names but henceforth be known as the House of Windsor. I imagined old Queen Victoria was rolling in her tomb at that, but it was best to cut all ties with the demented Kaiser.

The dreadful Spanish flu that was sweeping the civilized world hit both America and England hard, and, once again, Crowhurst was my refuge. With the "Yanks'" help, armistice was declared and the Treaty of Versailles was signed June 28, 1919. And later that year, when autumn turned the deciduous trees around Crowhurst glorious colors, Jacques was sent on a mission to England, and Papa telephoned to say my long-lost love would call on me at Crowhurst.

I did not know the exact time he would appear. Waiting, pacing, I looked out my windows toward my swans huddled together in the chill wind at the edge of the pond. With my pair of owls cuddled in the ceiling boards far overhead, I made two decisions: I wanted Jacques in my life forever; and despite the legal hoops we both must jump through, after nearly fifteen years of separation, I would ask the Duke of Marlborough for a divorce.

Part Four

Wife and Benefactor, 1919–1938

Chapter Twenty-Three

acques had telephoned to say he would drive to Crowhurst to see me. I wanted to tell him so much, to see him here, on English soil. I was nearly hysterical with joy and went on and on at first as to how grateful I was he was safe, was here . . .

"Dearest," he interrupted me. "We have been apart too long for too many damned reasons. Just give me the directions for when I get close, and I will be there as soon as I can."

I explained the twists and turns of the lane, then made him promise to drive carefully. He laughed. "If I told you the places I have been and things I have done these last few years, you would not worry for a motorcar drive to peaceful Surrey. Your father gave me the directions out of London—twice—but I needed to know which lane to turn in, that is all. If I could, I would fly and drop myself right in by parachute, but I hear there are no good farmer's mown fields nearby. I will see you soon, hold you soon, my too-long long-distance love."

And he was gone—but coming soon. I paced a rut in the flagstone floors waiting, waiting after all this time. I walked outside in the brisk autumn afternoon air, then back inside, out again. I had forgotten to so much as get a warm wrap, so went back in and up to my bedroom and stared at myself in the mirror, still hearing his words, his lovely voice in any language, for we had spoken in English just now.

Give me the directions . . . when I get close, he had said. What direction would our lives take? I had felt he was close to me for years, for so many difficult years, and now it was almost real.

Here I was forty years old, and he forty-nine. I had several silver strands in my dark hair and worry lines at the edges of my eyes. How would he look after the horror of the war? We both had long lives behind us but what was ahead?

I went back downstairs to rearrange the bowls of asters and dahlias yet again. "Mrs. Marlborough?" Hatherly called, coming in from the kitchen, wiping her hands on her apron. She knew to get right in front of me when we talked. "You be sure you want me to go, and you do the serving and all for your guest? You can just leave the dishes."

"Perhaps I shall. Yes, I will be fine and thank you for preparing that lovely shepherd's pie, salad, and trifle."

"All right then. Be here tomorrow afternoon."

"I do not know what I would do without you," I said, and gave her a quick hug.

Beaming, she went out the back door. I saw her go by the window, as she rode a bicycle and had only two farmhouses to go to her big family, though she lived here. But she was grateful for the time away because her father was ill.

I don't know what I would do without you, my own words rang in my ears. How had I done without a man to love all these years since, well, since I lost Win? And that was girlhood infatuation. Papa had mentioned that Win had been married for years. But there were big barriers to Jacques and I really being together, at least as man and wife. I was sure he wanted that and I did, too.

It was perhaps the one hundredth time I glanced out toward the lane when I saw a small, black roadster pull in. Yes. Yes!

I ran outside, trembling, fighting tears. Jacques leaped out so fast he did not close the motorcar door. We came together hard, and he picked me off my feet and spun me.

"Thank God, thank God you are safe and here!" I cried.

"My love. I want this dance for the rest of our lives." He put me down and kissed me so hard I could not breathe. I clung to him, kissing him back. I was dizzy with joy, dizzy with love as we finally stepped apart and studied each other.

He looked thinner, and his hairline had receded a bit. Crow's-feet perched in the corners of his eyes, and little shadows etched them deeper. He had a single slash of a white scar on his fore-head that had not been there before. But nothing mattered ex-cept that we were together.

He picked me up again, slammed the motorcar door with his foot and carried me over the threshold as if we were newly-weds. This was real. This was real!

In a golden splash of sun through the big oriel window, we talked for hours, holding hands, kissing, perhaps unbelieving we were really together and no one had to rush away.

"Yes, my love, I admit I was in great danger more than once," he answered my repeated question he had shrugged off at first. "I flew over German troop movements when night was falling on the evening before the Battle of the Marne. I was able to give

French and British troops information about German general Alexander von Kluck's advance, and that helped us give the Huns a devastating defeat."

We clinked our wine goblets to that.

"I was promoted to colonel after that and oversaw a group of scout aeroplanes," he went on, his eyes so intense that I thought he must be seeing scenes in his mind. "It was when I received that command that I sent you the short letter, about my past, my marriage. I wanted you to know everything, to understand—even if I did not come back."

"And my father said you did more than all that. He told me he had wanted the Americans to get into the war even when the president and Congress were dragging their feet. He said when some American aviators wanted to help out and were rebuffed at first by France, you said they should be able to contribute."

"True," he said, putting his goblet down and tightening his grip on my hand. "But he perhaps left out two things. One, I only convinced my superiors to let the American pilots in when we French lost so many men and aeroplanes. And second, your father donated $20,000 to the support of what we called your Yank flyers, the Lafayette Escadrille. I honor your father as someone who may have inherited his fortune, but who uses it for the good of mankind—as well as for the good of his sons and his beautiful daughter. And the fact you are an heiress has nothing to do with my devotion to and passion for you. I must soon become the chairman of the Balsan family business and will need to serve as director of other companies."

"I never thought you were after Vanderbilt money, unlike a certain duke I could name. I know your family is wealthy, too. I vow, I never even considered that."

"I like that—*I vow*. Let's work on that, now that I have lived through that damned war and you a difficult marriage and lonely, long separation. And you understand about my earlier marriage and dissolution, then?"

"I am hardly one to criticize anyone for a forced marriage."

"Yes, that, but yours was not your fault, so your father tells me. But now we must decide how to proceed about us, if you are willing."

"More than willing!"

"I will remember those words, too! I am hungry for our time together, for you."

"Oh, the food!" I cried, shifting forward on the sofa to jump up. "What if it is all burned or dried? I must rewarm things and feed you, for you have lost a bit of weight!"

"Rewarming things—everything you say, my sweetheart—has me thinking of other things," he teased and patted my bum as I rose to go to the kitchen. I wanted to feed him well, but I could hardly wait until the meal was over.

AFTER OUR SIMPLE, yet somehow sumptuous meal—how wonderfully normal to share food together—Jacques built a fire, and we sat on the sofa, looking at the leaping flames and each other.

"I should bring in my satchel from the motorcar," he said. "I even brought you a gift I almost forgot about."

"Hm, something wool from your family's textile business for this chilly weather?"

"You will not be cold, I promise. No, a piece of jewelry I should have brought in with me, an antique piece that was my paternal grandmother's. An overture to an engagement ring, someday, yes?"

"Yes!"

"Then just one moment," he added and popped up to go out into the darkness and back in with a battered-looking satchel he dug inside of.

To my amazement, he went down on one knee. "How could I forget I meant to give you this? *Sacre bleu*, it is your fault for being the ultimate distraction."

I knew Frenchmen were skilled at lovely words and at love, but I was so certain this man meant everything from his heart. The pin was stunning, oval-shaped, all graceful golden filigree scrollwork with two emeralds in the center. And then I saw the scrollwork was of two clasped hands. Tears blinded me before I blinked.

"It is just beautiful!"

"Perfect then. We will face a common future, get the path cleared so that we may be together for whatever days the good Lord gives us for the rest of our lives."

I nodded wildly as he pressed the pin into my hands and pulled me to my feet. His arms went around me. I embraced him and held hard. He lifted and carried me up the stairs to my room and slowly, sweetly undressed me as if we had world enough and time, as if we were starting all over again, young and in love, dancing, spinning around . . .

As he made delicate yet deliberate love to me, I realized I had never been really physically loved before. Taken but not loved and adored. Slow, sweet but with leashed passion. So intimate that it seemed to me we became one in more than two bodies uniting. Time stopped, though I wanted to remember and cherish each moment.

After, exhausted, we slept naked together under the covers, huddled close on our sides, as if I sat in his lap. I felt so safe, so alive. And so loved. It was what my wedding night and marriage had never been, a mutual giving of pleasure and trust.

But when I turned to him to tell him so, he kissed me again and ravished my senses.

WE COULD NOT bear to part, so I left my motorcar at Crowhurst, and we drove back into London together, laying plans.

"I know who I will try to get for a divorce attorney," I told him. "Sir Edward Carson was H. H. Asquith's attorney general and knows Winston, too, as they have both served in admiralty offices. I have met him at several parties, and he is most impressive."

"But is Winston to be trusted since he is the duke's cousin?"

"Absolutely. He has stuck with me and will be your friend, too. After my father and you, I would trust Winston Churchill anytime, anyplace. Sir Edward has a fine reputation and, I hear, is sharp-witted and sharp-tongued. A terror in the courtroom, Winston told me once."

"Which will make the duke back off?"

"Encourage him to cooperate at least. I think he would have given me the heave-ho, as we Americans say, long ago but for Vanderbilt money. He has carried on an affair with a woman who had been a friend to me for nearly ten years. Since her goal in life is to be the Duchess of Marlborough, and she holds some sway over him, she will be on my side."

"But can he afford to lose Vanderbilt money for that huge place?"

"Our financial marriage agreement states that he will still receive some funds. But everyone says property and death taxes are going up and up, and the duke is land poor, but I shall leave that up to Sir Edward and my father. Perhaps Blenheim should have paying guests to see its grandeur—ha."

"Now that is who I would trust with anything—your father."

I turned to him on the slick leather seat. A bit of rain was starting to spatter on the windscreen. "And I am betting, my dear Jacques, that Papa would trust you with anything, too—including me. He is greatly to be thanked for keeping us in touch through hard times, isn't he?"

He nodded but kept his eyes on the wet pavement. "And I suppose, since you say you are getting on better with your mother lately, we shall thank her, too, for bringing you to that debutante ball years ago, or I never would have seen you, we never would have danced—and declared we must fight to be together. Consuelo, my love, that fight is not over, for I still do not trust the duke, and I hear a woman seeking a divorce can be shunned and banned."

"Yes, but times for women here are changing. Besides, I did not closely observe my clever steamroller of a mother for nothing all these years," I assured him. "Sunny wants my permission for our heir Bert, dear Blandford, to wed a girl not yet twenty and needs my permission for that and for us to present a united front when we attend the wedding. Also, I have kept up a correspondence with the dowager queen Alexandra, and I am sure I can talk her into attending their wedding, hopefully to bring King George and Queen Mary with her, and that would mean the world to the duke. Oh, he owes me in so many ways."

"Ah, I am dealing with a Machiavelli!"

"Best remember that, my man. I hope to get what I want against stiff odds, and get you, too."

"I surrender."

I started to laugh but screamed, too, when a bolt of lightning and a huge crack of thunder came close as if in fierce punctuation. Jacques stomped on the brake pedal as a tree crashed down before us on the road and we swerved sideways.

"Are you all right, sweetheart?" he asked, after bringing the roadster to a skidding stop. "We shall get around that obstacle, too. And the fact it missed us—that is a sign we are on the right road, yes?"

We were both shaking, but I managed, "Together, yes!"

Chapter Twenty-Four

uge postwar events swirled around us. The Treaty of Versailles formally ending the war was signed in June of 1919, five years to the day after Duke Ferdinand and his duchess were shot to death. During the war, British women who were landowners and over thirty years of age had been given the vote, which still left out most English-women, so that struggle went on with protest marches, hunger strikes, forced feedings, imprisonment, and worse.

Jacques came and went to Crowhurst, though he was knee deep in family and business matters in France. Amid all this came my momentous attempt to attain a divorce from the Duke of Marlborough after a ten-year marriage and thirteen-year separation.

I'd spent time with my lawyer Sir Edward, planning how best to deal with the duke, and now the divorce drama had begun. It was to be played out in carefully orchestrated acts. There were nine steps for obtaining a divorce in England, and each must be documented, observed, or recorded. The duke and I had both agreed to play our parts, and I could only hope the British and American press would not broadcast every one of them in detail.

First, as if we were reading a hidebound script, the duke had written me a note requesting to see me to discuss an issue. *Dear Consuelo*, it began and ended, *Yours ever, Sunny*, per Sir Edward's specific directions. I had then replied to him in writing, citing a specific date and time and signed it *Faithfully, Consuelo*. What a farce these laws were but as the Charles Dickens character Mr. Bumble said in *Oliver Twist*, "The law is an ass."

Second, we must cohabit for a time. The duke, pretending to try for a reconciliation, had come to "live" at Crowhurst, bringing his sister Lilian, who I was still friendly with, so that it seemed we were living together, for I refused to go back to Blenheim for this part of the sham. Gladys had quite taken the place over and the duke had ordered her face—I heard from Lilian that Gladys's paraffin wax had shifted even lower to her chin—to be carved on some sort of statue there to assure her she was still beautiful.

For the third step, pretending to have tried to save our marriage, the duke had departed Crowhurst—he had never been there before and, I vowed, would not darken my lovely haven again. The note he had left me, again dictated by Sir Edward, read in part, *We have grown too far apart to live happily together again.*

Continuing the scripted drama, I had written a note to the effect that it was sad that he believed our marriage was over. I told him I was bereft and going away to rest for a while, to see my mother. Indeed, that was not skirting the truth, for I was exhausted through all this. I saw a doctor who recommended a rest away from England, and I went to my mother who had recently bought a villa in the hills above the village of Eze on the French Riviera. But I intended to be back in London soon, to carry on the fight and for our son Bert's wedding, in the middle of this grueling charade.

"MY DEAREST GIRL," Mother murmured as she embraced me in the sunny doorway of her charming new pied-à-terre called the Villa Isola, which she was decorating to the hilt. So exhausted from events and from my travel here, I held hard to her. This time it was her turn to comfort me, and she did. Papa had always been so good at that, but I saw now Alva Smith Vanderbilt Belmont had that in her, too.

"Come in and rest, here on the patio with the view of the sea," she insisted, pulling me by the hand as if I were four again. "It is restless in the winter, but always so beautiful."

She rang for tea and little cakes, and we sat out of the wind but in the sun.

"Has it been terrible?" she asked, scooting her chair closer and wrapping her hand firmly around my wrist. "At least you do not have the entire Vanderbilt clan against you as I did."

"No, the duke's mother and sisters and the Churchills have been supporting us both. Well, they have all seen our train wreck coming from way back."

"And the boys?"

"They see it as inevitable, I think. Ivor certainly understands. And since Bert is really in love for the first time—well, I never quite know about him. Sometimes he is Bert and sometimes he is Blandford, the next duke, so he, like his father, is caught between the devil and the deep blue sea of drowning debts at Blenheim and the heavy weight of heritage."

"So now to happier news. Your Frenchman has tracked me down and written. He would like to meet me and see you."

"Oh, when? Here?"

"He thinks not here at the villa, in case the duke's lawyers—or even yours—would not like that. And when have we ever been able to hide from the snooping press, who seem to hide up in trees? So I told him you and I would be taking a picnic along the shore tomorrow, and should he wish to join us exactly where. After all, my dearest, you no doubt need a good watchdog chaperone since he is obviously such a charming and determined Frenchman."

She laughed. Though I was ready to cry from exhaustion and emotion, I laughed too. My mother with a sense of humor. My mother on my side. My mother protecting my interests and wanting to meet the man I adored when she had caused my sad, bad marriage in the first place. But she was taking steps to make up for that now.

I hugged her so hard that I spilled my tea.

FEBRUARY 17, 1920, I was back in England for a Marlborough family affair: Bert's wedding to the lovely Mary Cadogan, daughter of Henry Cadogan, Viscount Chelsea. King George and Queen Mary were in attendance. Neither Gladys nor, of course, Jacques were there, but what a coup that the royals were.

That meant that the Duke of Marlborough was beaming. It was a feather in my cap, too, for it was through the Queen Mother Alexandra's friendship to me that she had convinced the king and queen to attend. I felt, since the duke was cooperating so far with the difficult steps of divorce, it was my final gift to him.

My mother had not come to the wedding because she heard Papa and his wife would be here. Yet what a blessing on this day that both my parents were on my side in the divorce.

My thoughts skipped back to the windy picnic she, Jacques, and I had shared on the deserted beach, getting behind some rocks to break the wind and to hide from possible prying eyes. They both had to shout over the wind so I could hear. I should have known she would ask him about his intentions, but she also encouraged us and urged us to move nearby when we were able to marry.

And, I daresay, Monsieur Jacques Balsan charmed her to the extent she left us alone for an hour to plan while she sat like a guardian on a rock a bit away from us, watching, she said, for some prying newspaperman or the duke's lawyers. I believed she was doing penance for making me marry someone I hardly knew and did not love.

Each time Jacques kissed me, his lips tasted of wind-blown salt water, and it was the most delicious delight. We both tried hard not to laugh at my mother since she looked like Lot's wife turned to a pillar of salt after her vigil.

"Who gives this woman to be wedded with this man?" The bishop's words brought me back to the present scene.

"The viscount and I."

Bert and Mary said their vows in this traditional venue for aristocratic weddings, St. Margaret's Church in Westminster. I glared at the back of the duke's head as he sat in the row before me. In contrast to this mutually agreed upon marriage, ours had been so wrought with tension and tears. At least, I thought, he dare not change his mind about the divorce, though a rather embarrassing step was yet in his control.

I shifted on the hard pew next to Winston, with Clemmie on his other side. Drat, there was one thing that still worried me. I knew the duke was angry over the information someone had given him that Papa had recently settled fifteen million dollars on me and a million on each of my brothers. Surely the duke would not insist we stay married to try to get his hands on that, though Gladys might have stayed with him at Blenheim anyway.

In the reception line after the ceremony, Queen Alexandra came up to me and took my gloved hand in hers. "My dear friend," she said, "I so hope that you are happy, at least as happy as I was with my own Bertie."

She was stone deaf and nearly shouting, but I knew she was too set in her ways to use the hearing devices I kept updating and hidden in my hair and hat. Had no one told her I was seeking a divorce? Or was she assuming I loved someone else? And how happy had she been with her roué Bertie, really?

"I am working on it, Your Majesty," I said loudly.

"Working on what?" the duke said, coming up to us after again speaking with the king and queen. I was so grateful they had come and that they had even mentioned that Queen Alexandra had reminded them of this event more than once. At least King George was not such a stickler for propriety as his father had been, for rumors were rampant that the duke and I would permanently part. But could I trust this man to finally let me go?

"I want Consuelo to be happy," Queen Alexandra told him, tapping his arm with her gloved finger. "I expect to see her again and know that she is content, so, sadly, you must do your duty, Sunny."

"Oh, ah, yes," he stammered, and the tips of his ears actually turned pink. So she did know of my attempt to turn our separation into a divorce, and she must be referring to that, bless her? Could she even know about Jacques?

After the royals had departed, the two newly united families went to Sunderland House for a reception. I could tell Ivor, the best man, was tiring, but I was too, light-headed and nearly swaying on my feet.

After everyone cheered the smiling, departing young couple—and I said a silent prayer that Bert's fascination with showgirls was over—and Mary's family had departed also, the duke came up to me and took my elbow to steer me aside from his family.

"I am writing a scathing letter to the *Times*," he told me.

"Not about our situation?"

"Hardly. About the wretched mess our liberal P.M. Lloyd George is making of things. Taxing the aristocracy to death. My key line in the letter is *Are historical homes to become merely museums and dead relics?*"

"I see. Of course, you are worried about Blenheim with all the new taxes."

"Go ahead and say it," he whispered. "And without much Vanderbilt money, despite the so-called allowance I receive when you decamp. And then to be made to jump through hoops to obtain a divorce—which I should have had years ago!"

"Really? How I wished we had discussed that years ago. And perhaps you had best keep your voice down here."

"I want you to hear this loud and clear. I still say you may have it—our damned divorce. I will do the rest that is required of me. I have someone who truly cares for me, and I have no doubt you do, too."

"Then thank you for carrying out the last important step. I am grateful, for I will no longer be told what I must do with my life."

"You have not listened to me for years on that! And that is

what is wrong with America, always was and still is, rabid, out-of-control independence mania, my American duchess!"

I surprised him by seizing and shaking his hand. "Nothing like a good American independence day," I told him. "Thank you again for your part in that. And on a happy marriage day, we discuss for the last time ending our sad one. It is for the best for both of us—Sunny."

Still clasping my hand in return, he nodded, but his frown seemed etched on his brow. "Consuelo," he said only and turned away.

Good-bye for good, I thought. And that made me feel good.

THOUGH I WAS terrified that the duke would yet balk at having to be seen cohabiting with another woman—though it would certainly not be Gladys, though he was actually living with her—he went through with it. Before Bert's wedding, the duke had sent me a letter declaring we could no longer cohabit together happily. As ordered, I now took that to London to my lawyer to petition a judge to restore my conjugal rights.

Again, I thought, what a sham, but the duke stuck to the rest of the plan. Followed by a detective hired by Sir Edward, whom the duke knew was two steps behind him, he took a lady hired for the occasion to the Hotel Claridge in Paris. They stayed in the same room the night of February 28, 1920, and were seen leaving the next morning. I can only imagine that the woman earned her money that night, not for any sort of coupling, but for having to stay in the room with a very upset, angry man.

Finally, the nightmare of pretense was over. The duke took a train to Nice to escape the press, and I hied myself to Sir

Edward's to ask for a court order that my conjugal rights be restored. The newspapers got the news of our pending divorce on March 23 and went crazy with it on two continents.

Finally, freedom was within reach! I would soon get my divorce decree. Then, six months later—if Jacques proposed again as he had almost already—I could legally wed him. I knew his very Catholic family would be upset he was marrying a divorced woman, but nothing mattered except our being together.

Only, I had no idea a tragedy, careening around another of life's sharp corners, would ruin my joy and tilt my world.

Chapter Twenty-Five

he telegram from my stepmother read: YOUR FATHER WAS OUT WATCHING HIS HORSE RUN AT AUTEUIL. TERRIBLE HEART ATTACK. I HAVE NOTIFIED YOUR BROTHERS. CAN YOU COME? ANNE.

I rushed to Poissy, arriving before my brothers, who were coming from the States. Papa looked so pale and thin—so still, though he was fully awake and talking. The prognosis was not good, and I grieved even the possibility of losing him.

"You have always been on my side," I told him the second day, sitting by the bed and holding his hand while Anne went to take a nap.

"I should have stood up for you when you married the duke."

"Water under—and over—the dam. I believe I will soon have my divorce decree and be able to marry Jacques."

"Ah," he said, slowly moving his hand to his chest outside the coverlet, "I would like to be there for that."

"You will be. You must be. It will be small, of course, private like your and Anne's wedding. We shall hide out from the world.

But, Papa, I must thank you for keeping an eye on him for me those years we were apart. You saved him for me, didn't you?"

"I cannot convince the man to like horses more than his blasted aeroplanes, but when he told me of your first, brief meeting . . . when I saw how he treasured it still and remembered . . . Ah, so much to remember."

"Rest now. I will sit here until Anne comes back and the boys—well, they are hardly boys now—will be here tomorrow."

"But just in case—in case they take so much time—you know—I must tell you how proud I am of you. Always was. But what you did as duchess, what you will do . . . your charities. *To whom much is given, much is expected.* That has been my motto, horses aside, to give to other less . . . less blessed, so—"

He fell asleep in the middle of that thought, but what fine thoughts and words to cherish.

THE NEXT DAY, it was a sad reunion with my brothers. When Papa improved a bit, they went home and I back to London to finish my divorce business. How I hated and feared to leave him.

However, on the day evidence would be given in open court for our divorce trial, Sir Edward advised me to be "indisposed" rather than face the newspapermen. In November our case was heard in London. The duke must attend, and his lawyer would deny accusations, Sir Edward had told me. But when the duke offered no evidence in his defense and was accused of a night in Paris with an anonymous femme fatale, the judge granted me a *decree nisi.* Unless, Sir Edward explained to me, the judgment would be contested within the next six months, I was divorced and free. I was not sure whether to laugh or cry that I was ordered to pay paltry court costs, when I had already paid with years of my life.

Although I yearned to celebrate with Jacques, we had to make do with a relieved phone call because word came that my father was dying. I was with him when he passed away, calmly, bravely, my champion over the years of my life. Exhausted and grieving, I had the terrible thought that the Lord had exchanged Papa's life for my new life, but that was foolishness, and I was done with all that.

Jacques came to Poissy to comfort me, to hold me. "He was a good man," he told me. "He did great things for me, kept me in line to wait for you. He was a special friend."

PAPA WAS BURIED in the huge Vanderbilt family mausoleum on Staten Island, there to sleep forever with his ancestors. The place was heavy stone, heavy on my heart. I cried as his polished coffin was slid deep into one of many vaults.

I vowed silently I would never be buried here. I had lost my beloved father, but I would always keep him in my head and heart, for he was, as Jacques had said, a special friend to me, too.

As we all turned to leave, I felt the weight of this mausoleum, the weight of the Vanderbilt name, which so many desired and envied. Yes, I was proud of the heritage, but it was a burden, too, like dear Blenheim was to the Marlboroughs. I could not wait to become just Consuelo Balsan.

Mother, of course, did not attend, though I knew she was grieving, if not Papa's loss, then for some sad things that had passed between them and how generous he had always been. In his will, my brothers and I had received even more of an inheritance, which I vowed would go greatly to good causes.

I stayed with Mother on Long Island where she had built yet another place. This one resembled a medieval castle, frowning down on Long Island Sound. She lightened my heartache some because she was celebrating the Nineteenth Amendment to the U.S. Constitution, which gave the vote to American women, a long struggle, a great victory, in which she had had an active and vociferous part.

"It is not so bad living alone, when one has one's causes," Mother said, trying to buck me up, though the design and décor of this place depressed me as much as had the mausoleum. I longed for sunlight, for a small, charming place like Crowhurst, but anyplace with Jacques would do.

"I cannot believe I have lived away from my marriage from my twenty-ninth year to my forty-fourth," I told her with a sigh. "I cannot say 'time flies,' but I bet it will—at least once this waiting period is over."

"You must bring your Jacques to visit me everywhere, and not just on the Riviera."

"Mother, he is running his family business, and I intend to take a good deal of his time—but we will certainly visit you. I thought the two of you got on quite well."

She moved from her favorite chair to the settee where I sat, and put her arm around me. "I thank God," she told me, leaning close, "that you and I get on well now. Consuelo, I am mourning that I made you marry the duke, but you did great things for his people, have become a strong, loving woman and have your sons, still have Ivor, at least."

"I pray he finds someone to love the way Bert has. The way I have, at last!"

WHEN WORD WENT round that I would be leaving England to live mostly in France—though I had not yet announced why—I came to realize I would be missed in England. George Curzon asked if I regretted leaving. I told him, "Only in leaving behind good friends like you and the people I have been able to help. I shall always miss Crowhurst but must let someone else find a lovely refuge there now, for I will find a country place in France as well as a home in Paris.

"And I admit," I went on with a sigh, "it will be an adjustment to step back into private life. I shall miss my friends and charities, but I shall find something worthwhile to do."

I did so regret leaving my causes, especially because Papa had said I had done well with them. "To whom much is given, much is expected," he had said, and I took that as my credo. I found it was from words the Lord had spoken in the Bible, in the book of Luke: *For unto whomsoever much is given, of him shall be much required.* Indeed, I vowed to myself that I would find good causes in France once I lived there as Madame Jacques Balsan.

But to my surprise, perhaps to flaunt the fact he was glad to be out of our marriage, too, the duke rather quickly wed Gladys in Paris with a civil ceremony at the British consulate on a Saturday, and then the next day in a religious ceremony. Bert, his bride Mary, and poor Ivor attended.

Ivor, age twenty-three, home from Oxford on holiday, told me, "I overheard Father was angry with her though. Gladys got what they call soft feet at the end."

"Cold feet?"

"That's it. I heard him yell at her—heard it right through the door—'Haven't you had time enough to make up your mind? You set your trap for me from the first, though it took me a while to catch on, and Consuelo, too! So do you want to be duchess or not?'

"I mean, I know they argue," Ivor went on as if imparting some state secret, "but they should not fight about something big like that. You and Jacques don't argue, do you?"

"Not yet, my dear, but you never know. Married people, even if they are in love, have to disagree sometimes."

"I am just glad I do not have to worry about being duke and all that. An honor, but not one earned, and a lot of trouble. It has made Father testy at times."

"Indeed it has."

"Besides that, I will choose a wife very carefully. Then we will not have to muddle through that divorce business."

I sighed. He was so innocent yet and always seemed to be younger than he was. Still delicate-looking with a blond tress always falling in his eyes, he resembled the duke whereas Bert looked more like me.

"I am very sorry you had to worry about all that, Ivor. I will miss you when I move to France, but promise me you will come and visit, and I will be back to visit you."

"I cannot wait until we can explore all the art museums in Paris. Art is my real interest, not most of the things I must study at Oxford. And one more thing, Mama. As much as I like Monsieur Balsan, I do not want to go up in his aeroplane. I do not think I could," he said, his face so serious. "Feet firmly on the ground, that's me."

"I will tell him, and he will understand. And maybe someday you will change your mind."

"Not on that. Would you change your mind to fly back to Father, even if he had not made it final with Gladys? And I will never call her Mother!"

I bit back a smile. "I shall miss the beauty of the land around Blenheim, but, no, I will never go back to being Duchess of Marlborough, and she is welcome to all of that now."

"Righto. I will never be duke and never go up in an aeroplane, and that suits me just fine," he said, folding his arms over his chest.

I hugged him and rested my chin on his shoulder, treasuring the moment. My dear boy had lived and flourished despite his weak constitution that had set him back in life at times. He and Bert and the dear charity friends I was leaving behind were my true heritage as the once Duchess of Marlborough.

JACQUES HAD PROPOSED to me numerous times, but not lately. Instead the mad aviator took me flying. He had borrowed a plane with two seats, and I was behind him. He kept yelling back to me, but I could catch only part of what he said, with the wind in my ears and the close-fitted leather cap that buckled under my chin. But even through my glass goggles, it was glorious to see the English countryside slip beneath us, farms and fields and forests.

Despite how happy we were to be together, I hoped he would make our private betrothal public soon. The landing was a little bumpy but it was on a grass strip. He slowed our speed and turned the machine around, but then, right in the middle of the meadow, hopped out and helped me down. I took off my cap, and the bounty of my hair spilled loose. Under that tight cap, I had not worn my hearing aid.

"I feel I am still flying!" I told him. I blushed, for I realized that was how I felt when he made love to me—stomach flutters, insides spinning, soaring high.

He dug for something from the inside of his leather jacket and hauled it out. In a satin pouch he opened lay a ring with one big, square-cut diamond and two smaller ones on either side.

"Oh, Jacques!" I cried. "A family heirloom, like the pin!"

"No—I could not—did not get a family ring," he admitted, raising his voice so I could hear, but suddenly stumbling over his words and frowning. "I bought it—wanted it to be only yours."

"It is so beautiful."

"As it must be for you. Here, give me your hand. Will you marry me, my beloved, Consuelo Vanderbilt?"

"Yes. A thousand times, yes!"

He slipped the ring on, and it was perfect. The sun caught the gold around the stones and gleamed.

"The glitter and the gold," I whispered as tears crowded my eyes. "I have seen the glitter but you are the gold."

He knelt, gripping my hand so hard it almost hurt. "I ask again and give you my pledge of constant love. Consuelo, will you be my wife? It does not matter one whit that we are getting a late start and had to go through hell to get this far. Onward and upward together forever, yes?"

"Yes!" I cried again and really cried now. I tugged him to his feet and threw my arms around him. "Finally, forever!"

FOR OUR WEDDING, I chose July 4, 1921, for it was truly my own American independence day. We wed in a private, quiet London ceremony that morning in a marriage registry office in Covent Garden, and then, the same day, in an Episcopal service at the Chapel Royal, Savoy, near the Strand.

Bert, who signed the guest list as the Lord Marquess of Blandford, and Ivor, Lord Spencer-Churchill, escorted me up the short aisle. I saw nothing else during the ceremony but the love in Jacques's eyes.

For the ceremony and reception—no expensive, elaborate changes of costume this time—I wore a sea-green satin dress and pinned primroses to my black satin hat that hid my hearing aid. The one thing I missed from my first, forced wedding was not having Papa here.

After the service, we went to a reception at Bert's London home in Portman Square. My mother had wanted so to come but knew her arrival would signal that it was time for the newspapers to pounce. Winston and Clemmie had sent a gift, but regretfully stayed away. We knew Winston, now Secretary of State for the Colonies, would be watched by the press.

Yet all that aside, I was a blushing bride, if not with innocence and youth, with joy. I did not think I had ever been happier. I did not think I had ever been so blessed.

That very day, we left England for France by aeroplane. My duchess days were really, finally over.

Chapter Twenty-Six

acques was worth the wait, the pain, the loneliness, and the longing. As we began our honeymoon, everything to me seemed like a fairy tale, a dream.

We moved into the house in Paris that Papa had given me when things went so wrong with the duke, but it seemed a different place now. Yes, it was the same earthly address: 2 rue de General Champs de Mars. The lawns reached down to the Seine where its waters rustled against the stone embankments as if it were a moat protecting our castle.

Our gardens were surely like the Garden of Eden, fragrant and colorful with lilacs and golden acacias on the terraces and—something that reminded me of Crowhurst, which I had sold—swans in our pond. One of them trumpeted to wake us up at times, but we only laughed and snuggled close and went back to sleep.

Out our windows, beyond our gardens, we could see people reading newspapers under the trees and galloping cavalry officers along the bridal path coming or going from the nearby

École de Guerre. Best of all, during the day, children were at play along the river. In the evenings, we often strolled its banks to talk to and play with them. Of course we would never have children of our own, but I was touched to see how good Jacques was with them, and they made me long to help children again.

It was so normal, so peaceful, a world away from prying newspapers, gossip, and watchful eyes. If people knew who either of us were, they did not let on. It was always just a friendly, "*Bonsoir, madame, monsieur.*" Being just another Parisian, not a Vanderbilt, not the notorious Duchess of Marlborough, was a blessing.

At night, lamplights silhouetted the Seine, and the twinkling lights of the nearby Eiffel Tower danced above our roof. Sometimes we stayed in, but often we went to the opera or accepted invitations to parties at the British embassy or mingled with the French diplomatic corp. I was thrilled to learn Jacques was regarded as a French war hero, one who had been awarded the Legion of Honour.

During those first weeks as a couple, we had such fun scouring little antiques shops to finish furnishing the high-ceilinged, elegant rooms. I had the furniture from Crowhurst shipped over. We used some of that, two easy chairs, even the bed, for it was where we had first made love.

We walked the quays and rues hand in hand like young lovers. At night, we shared the same hunger for each other, but not in haste, savoring each caress and kiss. Again, I felt I was new at this—the motions, the teases, the wild heights of physical passion. Jacques Balsan did not need his aeroplane to make me fly.

"So, SHALL WE begin to entertain?" he asked me one spring morning as we sat sipping coffee in our bedroom with the

French doors flung wide open to a view of treetops and sky. "And I need to get back to the family business."

"Could I go with you someday to meet a few of your cousins at your office? I know they are against your marriage to a divorced woman, but could we not work to win them over?"

He frowned and did not reply at first. He shook his head almost imperceptibly. "They are Catholic to the core, my love. I believe time will not matter, and pushing it could make things worse."

I reached for his hand across the little table. "I am sorry, my dearest."

He breathed out hard. "I knew it could be this way, but you are worth the cost. Perhaps, someday, we will find a way."

"Would it help if I could get my first marriage annulled?"

His head snapped around. He almost scowled, his eyes piercing me. "And make your sons illegitimate? And it would be for you like jumping through hoops of fire—perhaps in a public circus arena. And what would you say, that you were forced to wed the duke?"

"In a way, I was."

"And your mother would admit that, testify and say 'mea culpa'? I think not, for she values her public reputation as a worker for the good of women. Let us not mention that again. But shall we ask people in then, I said—begin to entertain here?"

I felt depressed for the first time in days, sad for him, for he had a big, boisterous family I knew he loved. And they must be so proud of him. What a burden to try to make up for all that. "Of course we will entertain," I told him. "We must pay back everyone's kindness and acceptance of me here."

Everyone, I thought, but those who should be family to me

now, the Balsans who had shunned their beloved son, and it was my fault.

WE BEGAN TO entertain with a will, the more the merrier, but almost always without family. Ivor stayed with us on holidays, occasionally we were visited by my brother Will, his wife Rose, and, of course, by my mother. Dinners, gatherings after the theater, even afternoon soirees when Jacques could get away from business early. For weeks, we did not speak again of his family shunning us because of me, though it was the only cloud on our horizon.

We were happy, very. We did not always stay in Paris but went to Monte Carlo for the tennis championships, to Nice for horse races, and visited on the yachts of friends in Monaco's harbor. When we were home, we went over our guest lists together, especially when Mother visited so that we did not have her grandstanding about a cause with someone. I made certain that the authoress Edith Wharton wasn't invited when Mother was around, because the two didn't get along at all. Mother was always critiquing Edith's books, insisting that so-and-so character was someone she knew and the details were not quite right.

But it is fiction, not facts! Edith had actually shouted at her once.

But based on facts, just hidden ones! Mother had insisted.

I cannot say I was simpatico with Edith either, but it was not over her stories, for I rather liked *The House of Mirth*. However, I found her personality overly forbidding and even cold—that is, unless we were discussing our mutual passion for flower gardens. I always felt that she was studying me as if I were a butterfly pinned to a board.

"How lovely you have been accepted by the rather snooty

French," she told me as she sipped a martini before dinner. "I mean after the Marlborough situation and your obvious ties yet to all that through your sons."

"I find the French friendly and charming," I said, forcing myself to keep from adding, *but they only respond to those of like kind*. Yes, she was fishing for inside information from me again. Why didn't Jacques or someone else walk up to us?

"Well, you must admit you have had quite a life on three continents. And to have won the hearts of not only the French but your charming Frenchman, leaving so much behind in both America and Great Britain. I am thinking of a new project about the bold American mothers and heiress daughters who conquered English aristocracy, you know."

"No, I did not know, but I am certain I will enjoy your inside information when I read that."

"Well, it is down the pike a bit, if you know what I mean. What do you think of the title *The Buccaneers*—like the pirates of old who sailed into rich ports and took ships and captains by storm?"

"Better a title, I believe, than something like *The Money Mammas* or *The Dollar Princess Dealers*."

She almost choked on a swallow of her gin. "Well," she added, "I would expect you to be clever at titles."

I was asking myself why I included this woman on the invitation list, when Jacques came up as if to rescue me. And more than once in my life, rescue me he had.

I MUST ADMIT my mother had always been what I had heard my son Bert once say—and had scolded him for it—"hell on wheels." As she aged, she became even more so, not merely becoming involved with causes but attacking them.

"Mother," I began tentatively as we sat together overlooking the Seine one late-summer day when she was staying a fortnight with us, "must you take on the Catholic church at home?"

"At home? Well, I am interested to hear you speak of America that way after years in England and now your happiness here. I suppose you do not mean my still working for women's rights, but refer to my new battle, which is still women's rights, Consuelo, really it is."

Though we were in the shade, a ray of sun sneaked through to make her hair gleam. She had died it brick red with henna. Redheads had a reputation for tempers, and I especially felt I was skating on thin ice with her lately, just as when I was a girl, but I was stronger now. I wondered if the high blood pressure with which she had been diagnosed was actually making her more active and irascible when it should have been a sign she should slow down.

I plunged on: "I was talking about your taking on the Catholic and Episcopal clergy in New York for the church's treatment of women."

She turned to me in her wicker chair, reached over, and tapped twice on my arm. "Just because you are wed to a Catholic now, my girl, do not let that color things. Granted, you have not tackled women's rights head on as I have, but, yes, I have publicly taken on even the Episcopal bishop of New York, William Manning, let alone the Catholics. Of course, as usual, the newspapers have picked up on it all like a dog with a bone."

"Which has always been one of your tactics, to turn publicity your way."

"The papers are still rabble-rousers, always have been! Women must be permitted to become priests! I wearied long ago of sermons about the downfall in the Garden of Eden being

Eve's fault. I mean, where was Adam, if he was supposed to be in charge? He should have been with her, not off somewhere when that serpent showed up for a long, seductive chat! And women being the weaker vessel . . . really! I believe you and I both have shown that is not the case, and how many women have you seen, in the charity work you have told me about, where the wife and mother kept the family together when the husband disappeared or even went to prison!"

As well as I knew my mother, I felt as if I had been ambushed. Jacques was no doubt right. The idea of her giving a statement to a tribunal of Catholic bishops that she had sinned and repented from forcing me to wed would be either impossible or a disaster. I had dared to bring it up twice more with him, but had received a definite no, so I was biding my time. The grandest gift I could give him, I was sure, in addition to a loving, loyal wife, was to reunite him with his beloved family, however Catholic to the core.

My other worry was that nothing seemed to stop Alva Smith Vanderbilt Belmont, even though she was in her upper sixties and had health problems, as well as the fact her phobias were worsening with age. She had become increasingly claustrophobic and superstitious, and how well I recalled how panicked she had been at the mere mention of a ghost at Blenheim.

So I decided to calm her down and change the subject before she caught on to my fishing expedition to see if she might ever consider helping me obtain an annulment, however much Jacques still tried to nix that idea. Once a tribunal met her, I was certain they would believe she had forced me to wed against my will.

I decided to try a diversion. "Wait until you see your new great-grandchild, Bert and Mary's sweet girl," I told her. "We had a wonderful trip to meet her. However much of an infant she still is, I plan to use her entire name when I am with her, so she will always know where she got it. It meant a great deal to me to know I had been named after my godmother Consuelo."

"Ah, yes," she said, sitting back with a sigh. "Sarah Consuelo, the little darling. But you realize," she went on, turning to me again and shaking her finger at me, "that if Bert and Mary do not produce a son, the dukedom should go to her, the firstborn, female or not. Why, the peerage rules in Britain are as unfair to women as those of the Catholic and Episcopal churches!"

"And that is the way things have been and are, though the first duke and duchess lost their sons and the title went through a duchess just that once by royal decree," I could not help but argue.

"Hmph! So there, they would not have a leg to stand on if the next head of the Marlborough family was Duchess Sarah Consuelo. I will tell Bert about that, Sunny too, if I ever run into him again, which I hope I will not. No backbone! Too traditional. And so—"

On she went, like a force of nature. I did agree with her on many of her crusades, but I still did think that sugar was better than vinegar to win grand causes, especially if, as often happened, the enemy were men.

Chapter Twenty-Seven

 s much as we loved Paris and its people, one of the special joys early in our marriage was finding our country house, Lou Sueil. We both loved the beauty and the climate there, for it was perched along the Riviera coast where people grew vegetables for market, and their fields were colorful and productive. The entire area just felt healthful and rather private.

We purchased one hundred fifty acres from the growers. I was proud and amazed at how Jacques bartered with and cajoled them to sell their extra fields, which we patched together for our flower gardens, the lawn, and a house. Lou Sueil meant "the hearth," and that meant heart and home to us when we took time away from Paris. We hoped the prying newspapers would never find us there.

We planted glorious gardens of flowers to complement the already exquisite cypress, mimosa, and eucalyptus trees. The latter were tall, slender evergreens that seemed to guard our privacy like sentinels. I loved the pink, feathery flowers of the mimosa and how the tiny leaves closed like hands if they were touched, even by raindrops. It was as if to say to outsiders who might wish us ill or want to spy on us, "Stay away or we will close right up!"

We built the house of stone to blend with the area. Eze, where Mother had a villa, was just across a ravine from us—a blessing but a bit of a curse, too, when she was with us. She seemed possessed by fears at times, other times by anger at the injustices to people here and at home. Always a builder and decorator of her own places, she at least approved of my furniture choices—the pieces that had been in storage from my dear refuge of Crowhurst and not used in Paris. We had a mix of deep sofas, easy chairs, and writing desks in the paneled rooms and white wicker furniture with cushions on the long porch.

"You enjoy writing, Consuelo," Mother told me one day. "Perhaps you should write a book about your charity work in England. Of course you could mention how you helped me with women's rights when you visited me at home, too. I intend to write my life story. But don't you want to do more than lend your name to projects now that you are no longer duchess? I have certainly proved no title is necessary, only hard work, gumption, and funds."

I turned on the wicker sofa to face her instead of enjoying the sprawl of fields and sea below. I had seen Jacques walking up the lane, swinging his arms. He had so much energy and was very popular here, even though few around knew of his war hero status.

"I am concentrating on my marriage for now," I told her. "I was not able or allowed to do that before. It will be my foundation for helping others again, children's causes, for, unlike the duke, Jacques will support my efforts."

"Your love and care for Ivor is at the root of your special concern for children, is it not? That he was sick and weak for years."

"That and, perhaps, that little girl I helped when I was so young and we spent time at Idle Hour. I took things to her—she was ill—in my pony cart."

"I remember. I suppose you think of all those outings with your father there."

"Yes, but I recall the playhouse you made for us, too. I led a gilded life and did not know it for the longest time. I would like to find a way to shed a bit of that on children who are ill or not so fortunate as I."

"Fortunate. Because of the Vanderbilt fortune, you mean."

"Mostly, but I will be honest with you. Despite the problems between the two of us when I was growing up, I was fortunate with my heritage. I always loved my easygoing Papa. You were strict and domineering, but you meant it for my good, and I see that now."

To my surprise, she began to cry in big, sucking sobs just as Jacques came in to join us. I motioned for him to stay back. He nodded and went into the house.

"I am sorry," I said. "I did not mean—"

"It's all right. I was too harsh, too much the general. But you still want me here, care for me—thank God for that."

"I will always love and admire you for the many good things you have done, for me and for others."

She nodded, kept nodding, with her hands gripped around the handkerchief she had used to blot her eyes.

"Consuelo, I've been thinking. No matter what happens to me, if you want to convince Jacques to let you pursue an annulment, I will testify. I will tell them I forced you to wed, for I have learned that can be grounds—a reason for that."

I leaned forward and gripped her hands. "They say it would all be private, kept within the Rota of three priests who hear the case. I was thinking Miss Harper could testify, too."

"Good. Yes. She knew how I arranged everything, even leaked things to the newspapers, as much as I hated their continual prying when I could not control it."

"You did? I wondered who, but I should have known!"

"Confession time all around then. But we must keep this attempt for an annulment secret, both before, during, and after, if they let us petition and testify. I can help you convince Jacques if you want."

"I will let you know, but I think he will be grateful. It grieves me to see how he longs to be back in the good graces of his family, and how I would like to know them, too."

"All right then, mum's the word," she said, blotting under her eyes again and giving me a tight smile. "The two of us together can do this for your dear Jacques."

THOUGH JACQUES, MOTHER, and I agreed to pursue an annulment and keep it quiet, the peaceful area of Lou Sueil was soon under attack by the press, and not for our endeavor. Newspapermen seemed to be behind each tree, on the beach, the lane, in town. We built a better fence and installed gates. Our news had not leaked, but the Duke of Marlborough had made a big splash with a publicized visit to the pope and then a well-heralded request that his marriage to me be annulled.

"He beat us to it," Jacques said. "I cannot believe that man is still plaguing us." He glowered off into the distance, down our lane at two men still hanging out by the gate. "Those are the two American reporters again, I think, not the British ones that dogged me yesterday."

"I had planned to buy fresh vegetables and other goods for our gathering tomorrow, but those reporters will cling to me and alienate our neighbors and friends. Mother just tells them off or starts explaining one of her new projects. Me they see as fair game for a statement beyond my standard one: 'That's the duke's business—no comment.' I cannot believe he has become a Catholic and, suddenly found religion, as they say. Sorry. I did not mean anything against the Catholics. I would remarry you in a Catholic or any sort of ceremony anytime."

I sighed and felt deflated as I sank on the sofa overlooking the view. Jacques sat beside me. "I just wish, if he gets his annulment, it would apply to you also, but it will not," he said. "You—and your mother—would still have to testify, and now that the duke has blown the lid off privacy—well," he said with that charming Gallic shrug.

"I detest how dirty the publicity is getting. My brother Will says one New York paper suggested that since the duke insists there was no marriage, he might want to consider returning his American millions. And the Episcopal Church is attacking the duke for suggesting that a Protestant marriage is less valid than that of a Catholic mass. Such vitriol but at least it has not touched us—yet."

I turned to embrace him but he was quicker than I, and he had me sprawled across his lap with both arms tight around me.

"I suppose we could do something outrageous in the middle of the day," he said, his voice that raspy tone I could hear without my ear aid. I had thought at first that the air was different in France for a hard-of-hearing person, but it was just my bond to my Jacques. I swear, I could almost feel his voice like a caress.

"Such as?" I said and felt myself blush under his intense perusal.

"How about something that would shock them all and maybe not get you an annulment, but get me, strayed Catholic though I am, a delightful afternoon?" he added with an exaggerated waggle of his eyebrows that he had copied from one of our British friends who had visited here last week, Charlie Chaplin.

"In the middle of the day—in broad daylight?" I asked and giggled. How quickly and smoothly this man could make everything awful go away.

"They may all go to perdition!" he said and set me aside only to bend down and scoop me up in his arms. "Because we have staff here today and are already a scandal, we shall continue this discussion in the privacy of our bed."

He bounced me once to tighten his grip and headed for our bedroom. Again, as ever with him, the outside world, even people stalking us, faded to nothing. We were newlyweds again, young, expectant, and happy. I was so desperately in love—but one thing did remain: However much the Duke of Marlborough still played havoc with my life, I was going to follow his lead to annul my marriage, whatever it took.

AT LAST, SIX years after my divorce and five years after my marriage to Jacques, I obtained an English lawyer and prepared to testify before the Catholic Rota with Mother and Miss Harper as key witnesses. With my mother's permission, two of her sisters also gave corroborating and quite damning statements about her treatment of me.

Our British lawyer, Sir Charles Russell, warned me, "Unfortunately, I believe the entire Catholic Church must know that your mother has publicly taken on a New York Episcopal bishop over the taboo issue of women in the priesthood, and that could prejudice even the Catholic Rota against her. So you will have to be very convincing, Mrs. Balsan."

My fear that my sons would be made illegitimate was not a problem, for this was indeed an ecclesiastical trial. The duke would never have threatened Bert's future inheritance or title with his own legal annulment.

Just as in the complicated steps to get my divorce, these proceedings seemed so antique and unfair to me. I had learned that the Holy Rota which would hear my case had not changed since it came to power in 1326, and that it was the same governing church body that had refused to annul the marriage of King Henry VIII and Catherine of Aragon. Well, I could see some similarities between that king and the Duke of Marlborough!

I testified first. I had been coached for the terrible—and true—things I must say. "My mother tore me from the arms of a man I loved and took me abroad," I told them, my voice steady. "She even swore she would shoot that man and willingly go to prison if I did not give him up and marry the man she had chosen for me, the ninth Duke of Marlborough."

The three priests nodded, frowning. I could hear and feel my heart beating. When they did not ask a question, I went on, "She had chosen the duke for me and brought him to America, though I had met him before in Europe. She said I would be the death of her if I did not agree to be affianced to him. He proposed and I, under great duress, accepted."

My dear, now elderly governess, Miss Harper, testified next to corroborate what I had said. Then—I held my breath—my mother.

"Yes, I forced my daughter to marry the Duke of Marlborough," she admitted under initial questioning. "It was, as you may know, an Episcopal ceremony, not a Catholic one. She disliked him for his arrogance—which, I must say, is understandable but has never abated. He is still very overbearing."

Oh dear, I thought. She is already off the script she was advised to use and had practiced. And she might as well be describing herself. What would these priests think of a modern-day Joan of Arc? Word was in even the European papers that Mother had attacked the Episcopal and Catholic churches at home over male priests.

She went on, "Consuelo was quite upset, but I did not soften my decision. I admit I coerced her, even put a guard at her door so she did not escape before her wedding, but the young man she had been infatuated with was mostly interested in athletics, and as for charitable causes, was a bit of a layabout. Although good things came of the union of my daughter with the duke—mostly through Consuelo's strength of will and care of the poor, and two fine, upstanding sons—their marriage and the resulting contract for Vanderbilt money was my fault.

"Surely," she went on, gesturing now, her voice rising, "their unhappy marriage, the lengthy, resulting separation and divorce all speak to their union being wrong and unsanctioned by heaven from the start. Again, I say, I take the blame."

She had said it. I fought to keep from rolling my eyes at that "unsanctioned by heaven" embellishment. I was amazed and grateful, but regretful to put her through this, however much she had ruined things years ago. But, I must admit, if I had not wed the duke, even if I had wed Win Rutherfurd, would I have lived a worthwhile life? More importantly, I never would have borne my dear Ivor and Bert—and, no doubt, never would have wed my Jacques.

FORTUNATELY, THE ROTA'S decision was to grant me an annulment since I had felt "deferential fear" of my mother and what she would do. Unfortunately, it all became front-page news on two continents. I partly blamed the duke for that, blazing the way as he had with his own public annulment.

Again, we were stalked by newspapermen both in Paris and at lovely Lou Sueil. Neighbors were harassed for their comments. Back in America, my mother was followed, and Miss Harper and my aunts were sought out and badgered, though my aunts—and, surprisingly, even my mother—said simply, "No comment."

Mother, who had strived so long to be recognized as what was now being called a "feminist," and who had fought to become a public figure of import, became depressed and almost solitary in reaction to her ruined reputation. To my grief and amazement, she said she wanted to be left alone. My brothers told me she hardly went out and merely wandered from house to house where she kept skeleton staffs and the curtains closed.

So great guilt crashed in on me even as we were privately— through much subterfuge and changing of vehicles—remarried in a Catholic ceremony in France. But I was ecstatic about one thing on the horizon. The press had not managed to sniff out Jacques's family, and he had been in touch with them. We were going to motor a roundabout way to meet them, which frightened me at least as much as facing the Rota had.

Chapter Twenty-Eight

I must admit I was terribly nervous as we motored up the curved lane to the Balsan château at Châteauroux in the heart of France. The family lived in a sort of compound with houses on grounds that looked like a well-tended park. Jacques had pointed out to me their cloth factories as we passed them, huge structures that had founded the family fortune back in the days of Napoleon when the Balsans had first clothed the French army in a blue cloth with the name of "the blue horizon."

"That is what is facing us, my darling," he had said to me as we motored through the grounds, closer to the imposing main building. "From now on, only blue sky on our horizon."

Someone must have been watching, for the moment we pulled up, several young adults on the porch became a crowd of waving, chatting people of several generations. I saw Jacques blink back tears of joy, which made everything worth it: my years of loneliness, missing my sons, even Mother's now ruined reputation for the way she had treated me years ago—

everything. Family first, I had once heard Jacques say, and loss of that had been a tragedy.

I was hugged, kissed on both cheeks, my back patted as people, young ones mostly at the entry, embraced me even as they did Jacques. His brother Étienne was easy to pick out, for, as Jacques had said, they looked much alike. I heard the voices of little children floating down the grand staircase, but they had evidently been banished upstairs for now.

But then came squeals and cheers and cries, some so loud I could easily hear them from behind me. French words from at least twenty throats came at me like a chorus, dancing on the buzz of some whispered conversations. What if I could not hear them when they spoke to me or asked a question? More than once I thought I heard, *"Belle, belle! Elle est belle!"* She is beautiful.

In the press of people, we were greeted by his parents. Jacques also resembled his father, so I knew them instantly, but especially from a photo of them Jacques kept in his study. His mother was crying; I was too. No kisses on the cheek here, for she simply hugged me hard. Then more kisses on both cheeks from his papa. They looked me over, smiling and crying while Jacques beamed.

With a strong hand, he led me the rest of the way inside, into a large, lovely room with tall windows. Like a queen, a frail, silver-haired woman was seated across the way under a tapestry.

"Even if you have met them, you must be formally introduced to my brothers, sisters, and cousins," Jacques told me, though he had explained that earlier. "You must meet our grande dame, for the formal introductions are hers."

We had rehearsed names and connections in the motorcar, so I was somewhat prepared. He had told me I would be formally welcomed by the doyenne of the Balsans, Madame Charles Balsan, Jacques's aunt, and the traditional head of the family. But I wondered if it would not only be a welcome but an approval. Strange, but the memory of the time I met Queen Victoria and she kissed my forehead flashed through my mind. How my mother would approve of a matriarch heading this family.

Everyone seemed to understand the importance of this moment, for the chatter muted, and it was as if the sea of people parted. Even Jacques's smiling father and teary mother stepped back to clear our path.

I sucked in a sharp breath when I saw madame. It was as if I were looking not into the face of Queen Victoria but into that of dear, long-departed Mrs. Prattley from the almshouse at Blenheim, though this woman was obviously not blind. Her gaze went quickly, thoroughly over me, then she smiled at Jacques and then at me. She even spoke loudly for an old lady, so perhaps she had been told about my deafness—or she was hard of hearing herself. No matter: I felt instantly at home with her.

"Welcome to our family, and I shall present to you each one," she declared in French.

"I am so happy to be here and to be the wife of Jacques Balsan," I said and somehow kept myself from dropping her a curtsy.

"And part of us now," she said. She seated me next to her in a chair and Jacques on the other side and began to recite names as people stepped forward in turn as if this had all been rehearsed. When the introductions were through, she presented me with a family heirloom, a small golden box. I knew instantly it was where I would store the antique pin Jacques had once given me and perhaps my engagement and wedding rings, too, if I took them off to bathe or sleep.

We went into a dining room lined with family portraits for a lovely dinner. I was seated between this kindly mater familias and Jacques at the head of the table, with his aunt just across the corner near his mother and Jacques catercorner from his father. My years of social training served me well, for I kept myself from sobbing with joy to see my husband so proud and happy. Surely nothing could ever go wrong again.

I DID WHAT I could to raise money for children's charities but also reveled in my own grandchildren. When Jacques was especially busy with the Balsan woolen factory empire or even training other pilots, I spent a bit more time with my sons in London. Bert and Mary now had three beautiful children, and they let me spoil them with my gifts and attention.

Sarah Consuelo turned ten during this visit in 1931; Caroline was eight; and the heir, and future duke, was five. Their mother, Mary, much relieved after John George Vanderbilt Henry was born, told me the third time was a charm, for she had felt the pressure to produce a boy, too. No heir and a spare, she told me, but this would have to do. Despite the fact I was no longer a Marlborough, she and I shared a certain understanding, and I valued her greatly.

Bert, all six and a half feet of him, was always very sure of himself, unlike Ivor, but then he had been showered with love from his father, more than had Ivor. I was happy to see that Bert did not seem to overly favor his son and very grateful that the Vanderbilt name was part of the boy's heritage, too. I did think that Bert was especially happy when I was visiting and Ivor was not there to distract me, as I had overheard him say to Mary once when they were first married.

"I say, Mother," Bert called to me—he always spoke very loudly, bless him—"but you are good hands on with the children."

"That is one of the most lovely compliments you have ever given me. They have wonderful parents and a good nanny, but sometimes it takes a grandmother's special fairy godmother touch."

"Grandmother Alva would have just smacked me," he said with a little laugh. "Still might next time I see her."

"So you do not mind if I go up to see the children tucked in?"

"Sarah C would like that so she doesn't see the ghost. But, truly, she only mentions it when we're at Blenheim, not here in the city."

I jerked alert and pulled the child toward me to hug her. "Did you think you saw a ghost there?" I asked with a smile, but goose-flesh peppered my arms. It had to be of the first duchess Sarah. And that long dead woman had a namesake with the child's name and mine. I did not really believe in ghosts, but I believed in the first duchess Sarah.

"It's bloody fine," little Sarah told me.

"Do not say 'bloody,'" her mother corrected.

"Well, she is a nice ghost," the child insisted.

My gaze met Mary's. "Have you seen her, my dear?" I asked.

"Oh, she is only in Sarah's dreams when we stay at Blenheim," Mary tried to assure me with a roll of her eyes, which was evidently meant to merely humor Sarah. "She is just pretend, right, my girl?" her mother prodded. "Just in your dreams?"

"She is oodles nicer than Duchess Gladys," Sarah insisted. "Duchess Gladys yelled at Grandpapa to get those children out of here, and that means us."

My gaze snagged with Mary's startled look, but neither of us said anything. For now, at least, I kept quiet on that. Later, I went upstairs, holding Sarah's hand while the younger ones went up with the nanny. The staircase was lighted, and I was relieved for Sarah about that. How often I had been frightened in the New York or Newport houses by darkness on the vast staircases. We sat on Sarah's bed as the city night sounds quieted outside and we waited for Nanny to tuck Caroline and little John in.

"If you do think there's a ghost at Blenheim, do not be afraid," I told her.

"She is not a dream. She goes up and down in the hall," she said, her eyes wide, "and she is not Duchess Gladys. You used to live there with Grandpapa, right?"

"Yes, a long time ago before his Gladys."

"Well, Gladys—I am supposed to call her Grandmama but I don't. She screams and throws things, but the ghost only comes in and covers me up and then Nanny says why ever did I open that bedroom door to let in the chill air, but I didn't."

The mention of the ghost had given me pause, but this news of Gladys was worse. Surely, this child hadn't dreamed any of that or made it up. And why was Bert letting the children stay there if Gladys was screaming—at whom I wondered?—and throwing things? I would have to find out, but I wasn't going to ask little Sarah.

"Do you know who you are named for?" I asked her after Nanny came in to change her to a nightgown and I tucked her in.

"You, of course!"

"But the name Sarah. What about that?"

"The first duchess long ago like in a fairy tale. She built Blenheim because the queen liked her and liked the duke and he was a good soldier, but he didn't fly planes in a war like Grandpapa Jacques did."

I had to smile at that. Jacques loved these little ones as if they were his own, and, in a way, they were.

"I want to tell you something I think you are old enough to understand, my dear," I told her.

"But Caroline and especially Sunny are not. I won't be duke, but I am firstborn."

There it was again: The name Sunny for the heir apparent to the dukedom, this time Sarah's little brother. The specter of my former husband seemed to haunt me, as the ghost of Sarah Churchill never had.

"All right, here is what I mean," I said, scooting forward to the edge of her bed and taking both her hands in mine. "I have seen that ghost, and she is kind and friendly, not bad or a bit scary."

"I believe you, Grandmama. Mother says the same, but she thinks I made her up, but I didn't—did I?"

"No, and she is our secret. I am so proud and happy you have part of my name and I believe ghost Sarah is, too." I leaned down to kiss her soft cheek. I had to talk to Bert about Gladys.

I went downstairs and found him at his desk with a whiskey, reading a letter. I knocked on the open door.

"Mother," he said, popping up. "I thought you'd be turning in since you are off to see Ivor again tomorrow."

"I do want to tell you how much this visit has meant to me—to see the children and Mary, but especially you, too."

He bit his lower lip, either in emotion or to keep from a rejoinder, but he took my elbow and ushered me in to sit in one of the leather club chairs that were pulled up before his big desk.

"Bert, I am proud of you, and it has nothing to do with the fact you will be the next duke."

"I know," he said with a shrug as he twisted toward me in his chair. "An accident of birth, an honor and yet a burden. Look at Father. Listen, I try not to so much as mention him around you, but—"

He stopped mid-thought and turned away, staring at the large photograph of Blenheim on the wall behind his desk.

"But what?" I prompted. "Bert, Sarah says that Duchess Gladys screams and throws things, and—"

"It is more than that," he interrupted. "That is more or less what I was going to say. They both shout at each other, bicker before guests even. I've had a real row with Father over the children not spending time at Blenheim right now. I know he can be moody, but she is, well, I had no intention of telling you this, but she is—unstable. Frankly, she's officially moved out of Blenheim, though she keeps going back, but now she's gone to live in London for a while, I take it. I think he is bloody well relieved that she's gone for now, because she made it a living hell there."

"I am sorry to hear, after all the grief and publicity he has been through, that he is unhappy—really."

"Mother," he went on pivoting toward me, "she breeds dogs she calls Blenheim spaniels, which wouldn't be so awful but she keeps them right in the Great Hall! She had the space divided into dog pens, and the smell was horrible! Her trust fund, I hear, was ruined in the crash in twenty-nine, and they're still fighting over the money. Worse, she kept a revolver in her bedroom and told Father she would shoot him if he ever came to her bedroom door again. Damn, I'm sorry, for I did not mean to tell you all that, and we're terrified the papers might find out, even if she's in London lately, because she comes back— for the dogs."

"But then she is doubly dangerous!"

"Father doesn't even stay there when he goes home now from London, but puts up at the hotel in Woodstock. I think . . . I am pretty sure he is going to find some way to permanently evict her. Sorry to dump all of this on you, but Mary and I . . . we trust you. I used to hope they would calm down and get back together, but it was and is a battlefield there—perfect for Blenheim, right?"

"I see you are worried for your father, but above all you must think of your children first, that they steer clear of all that. Bring them to us in France next holiday instead of Blenheim, even if Gladys has been sent away."

"I would like to, but Father would, well, you know."

"Yes, he would protest or sulk or worse, but he will have to see this is best for the children. You know, I used to believe Gladys was my friend, but she turned on me, had plans all along to take my place, and I was too naïve to know that at first. If I had not left of my own accord, who knows what she might have done. This knowledge of her screaming and a revolver in hand, well, above all, protect your children."

He sniffed hard and pressed his lips together in a straight line. "I will not tell Father we had this talk, but I will tell Mary. I do see why you left him." He said this in such a rush I had to almost read his lips. "Children sense things, the truth, early, even if they are told something else. I know that, I remember that."

"Dear Bert," I told him as we both rose, "you are tall in stature and tall in my heart. Remember that, whatever happens."

He nodded, sniffed again, and stooped to hug me hard.

Chapter Twenty-Nine

adly, we were still at times stalked and spied upon by European and even American journalists. It somewhat tarnished our love for Lou Sueil and made us wary in Paris. We began to think we should find an even more secluded place for a summer escape, close to Paris, not one on the busy Riviera.

Jacques and I clung close to our friends who enjoyed visiting us in Paris or especially at Lou Sueil in the winter months. We loved hosting people from all walks of life, including having open houses for our neighbors. At either of our homes, we mixed pilots, French dignitaries and generals, and British friends with artists or even entertainers like Charlie Chaplin. We often had Winston and Clemmie, for they had remained loyal friends, though they still saw much of the duke.

This Saturday through Monday we had them with us, Ivor was visiting, and our longtime friend George Curzon was here, and I was tending to them all. Ivor always needed encouragement in his endeavors, and poor George was ailing but so appreciated the winter sun. A government servant and longtime Member of Parliament, he had been devastated when he was overlooked for prime minister, but he had physical problems, too.

I walked down to the first terrace near the mimosa trees where he was drinking tea at a small table. I sat on the other side of it, and he looked over to smile at me.

"I did not know if you were taking a nap," I told him.

"Just enjoying the view and the warmth. And watching Winston argue with your husband."

"So I see," I said, glancing over the boxwood hedge at the terrace just below us. Ivor was with them, too. He had always loved being with Winston. Ivor sat back a ways, but I saw wild gestures from Jacques and gyrations of both the cigar and the paintbrush from Winston. "I do hope they are getting on."

"Winston is peeved over Herr Hitler in Germany, the new chancellor. He says that *heir*, as in inherits the power in the country, is just a few steps from becoming dictator and causing trouble with his rampant nationalism."

"Surely not after Germany was so shamed and devastated in the Great War."

He shrugged, and I saw him flinch in pain. He had a childhood spine injury that had kept him from athletics all his life, so perhaps that is why he excelled in intellectual ways. He was a charming though driven man and lately a mere shadow of himself, which was why I was so glad he was here resting. He had been quite melancholy, and that was rubbing off on me. Now with Winston on this anti-German rant, it did not make for the most restful of weekends.

"Consuelo," George said, "though I will, of course, thank you when I leave, I want you to know how much your friendship has meant to me. Your entertaining, your kindness—even though you turned me down for more than that when you and Sunny were first having trouble."

"You both insulted and honored me by that proposal. It worked out that we could just be friends."

He sighed so hard his body heaved. I fancied he might collapse but for that iron brace he wore. I sympathized greatly. My thoughts flew to my mother. She had suffered a slight stroke, and though she had mostly come back from it, finally—finally—something had slowed Alva Vanderbilt Belmont down.

"I had best walk down and calm them," I told George and patted his shoulder as I rose. It seemed bony. So much of the old days was passing away, the Victorian and Edwardian eras as they are called now, looking back. And what era was this? Surely not one between two German wars.

I walked down the flagstone steps. "That will be a lovely painting of the sea," I said to interrupt what appeared to be a Winstonian tirade, one I hoped was not aimed at Jacques. Ivor stood to give me his seat, but I put my hand on his shoulder and remained standing.

"Wonderful light here," Winston said, obviously changing the topic from whatever he had been saying.

Jacques stepped close and put his arm around my waist, so I stood between my dearest of men. If anyone here was upset at the other, it did not show, for Jacques, despite a flamboyant personality at times, could calm himself in an instant.

"I thought, perhaps," I told them, "you two were disagreeing about the view—or something."

"Winston is predicting another war, a German one again," Ivor said.

"Surely not!" I repeated the protest I had made to George. "They were beaten down by the loss and the treaty they signed."

"And," Winston said, blowing out a smoke ring the breeze ripped away, "that's part of the problem. They are bloody bitter and coming back hard under that Hitler fellow. Trouble on the horizon, though, thank God, not this one," he added and went back to painting on his canvas where the sea met the sky.

"I like the way Winston blends his colors," Ivor said, stepping closer to watch the man I considered his mentor. "His style has a touch of French impressionism but with a sheen of reality."

"You have always had a good eye for art," I told my son.

Jacques put in, "Ivor is thinking of investing in some paintings and promoting fledgling artists."

"That sounds like an excellent way to use your interest and talents," I said.

"Ha!" Winston put in with a guffaw. "Here is how I would like to use my interests and talents. I must get stubborn Parliament to name me P.M. soon! If not, I shall just resign and peddle my paintings."

"And 'ha' to that fairy tale!" I responded. "Ivor," I said, pulling away from Jacques just enough to peck a kiss on my son's cheek, "I do think that dealing in art is a marvelous idea and plays to your strengths."

"Wish I had a few more of those," Ivor whispered so wistfully that my heart went out to him again. He was still pale and a bit frail with headaches and a constant cough, but the doctors only diagnosed it as "weak constitution" and could find no real malady.

"I had best go find Clemmie," I told them, quickly blinking back tears that threatened despite the beauty of this place. For with all this talk of Germany again, I felt a cloud cover this sunny day. It was a strange foreboding, the most oppressive feeling I had felt since I had spoken with Czar Nicholas, and look what had happened to him.

WE FINALLY FOUND the place for the summer escape from Paris we had longed for, especially since we were still easy game for international journalists and wanted a getaway to hide out in privacy. On one of our weekend drives, we came upon the little town of Saint-Georges-Motel near the border of Normandy at the edge of the forest of Dreux. The town was small, with a population just over three hundred fifty we soon learned. We also learned a walled and gated château with a good piece of land was for sale by an owner who had thirteen children. The family had quite outgrown the main house, let alone the small cottages also on the property. The meadows of the estate bordered on the River Avre, which fed the water in our moat, then flowed into the larger River Eure.

We loved the area, the town, and the estate, which we promised to purchase that very day.

I was thrilled to see many children playing in the village street, the Cour d'Honneur, and the fields just outside our walls. Very few of the youngsters looked well-to-do. Ponies for a few but hoops and tops and balls tossed in the air for most. Ah, I could see it now, a yearly fete for the village children. All would be welcome, but especially those ill or less blessed, which I must admit—as happy as I was—would be almost everyone.

"WE BOUGHT THIS the way I fell in love with you—at first sight," Jacques told me the day we took possession of the property. He reached over to squeeze my knee before he drove us through the gates the groundskeeper opened for us with a nod and a grin. Massive linden and chestnut trees seemed to guard the entry gate, which fronted the village itself. We had discovered the name of Louis XIII stamped in the iron gate.

"We will love the summers here and so will our guests—the invited ones, not those crashing in for a sensational news story," he assured me.

"Seclusion and safety," I said with a sigh. "We shall make some changes inside and out of this old château, but I love the pink brick and bluish slate roof. And to have a moated home with two towers, so romantic and another barrier against intrusions."

I gazed round with a sigh, thinking of our solitary walks here, planning to invite all the people we loved.

"A penny for your thoughts," Jacques broke into my silence.

"What I want to do here for our new home and the people will cost a bit more than a penny."

"Do send me an invitation," he said with a little laugh as he pulled our motorcar to a halt before the front door. "Look," he said, pointing, as he came round to open the car door for me, for his charming manners and tender care for me had never ceased.

I turned to look where he pointed. A stag drank from the water of the moat, then lifted his big head crowned by the proud rack of antlers. He gave us a condescending stare as if to say, *This place is really mine, you know*, then trotted off toward the thick trees beyond.

"Magical—and so quiet here," I said as Jacques produced the key with a flourish as we walked toward the front door.

We went through the rooms to the back where I had planned so many pleasures and posies. I would plant hydrangea, iris, and lupine within trimmed bushes of fresh-smelling boxwood. Jacques had agreed we would add fountains and terrace the gardens. Strangely then, I thought of the duke, forever working on the terraced gardens at Blenheim. How was he faring now since Gladys's trust fund had been pinched by the American stock market crash? Had he evicted her from Blenheim as Bert had predicted?

"This place has been rather neglected," Jacques's voice cut into my agonizing. "Especially the little cottages but this château, too, which we will soon put to rights."

"Besides envisioning games and food tables out here to welcome our friends and local guests—the children, especially—I am thinking we could sponsor writers and artists, when the scattered cottages become livable again, for them to have a sort of summer sabbatical here."

"I am sure our favorite amateur artist, Winston, will set up shop here with Ivor advising him—if, that is, Winston has time to stop haranguing England about the threat of the new Germany."

"I regret that his colleagues and the newspapers think he is a bit of a crackpot. No one wants to hear war is coming after what Europe has been through. I hate to say it, but the best way to have him elected P.M. is to have some of his dire warnings come true, which I dread. Jacques, if there is a war, you would not go back into service would you, I mean at your age?"

"Ah," he said, turning me to face him, "am I ready to start walking with a cane now and lose my teeth?" He squeezed me hard and patted my bum.

"Hardly. But I— You have started flying more again, not just teaching others."

"Just to keep up with the innovations of the aeroplanes. If there is another war, it will be bombs away."

"Do not joke about that!"

"I am not, my love. Just being realistic as, I fear, is Winston. Hopefully the British and French, too—even your American countrymen—will get their heads out of the 'peace in our time' sand. Meanwhile, we shall love this new place and each other, yes?"

I turned to smile into his eyes. "Yes!"

THE BRISK, CHILLY autumn in Paris that year seemed to creep into our home and my bones. Fallen leaves skittered across the street as I gazed out my sitting room window, missing both Saint-Georges-Motel and Lou Sueil. And missing Jacques, who was working late at his family's business today.

Though we had closed up our greatly renovated new château for the winter, I was still mentally there, for I had been making notes and sketching the layout for the first fete I hoped to offer the local folk next September before we closed up the château again. It would take a lot of planning, but I reveled in that.

I sighed and drank some of my tea, but it had gone lukewarm. I had not been in the kitchen for a while to talk to Cook, so I thought I would not ring for it but walk down for a chat. But when the telephone jingled, I picked up the wood and ivory voice receiver.

"Bonjour," I said. "Consuelo Balsan here."

"Consuelo, I have found a lovely little cottage just on the other side of your new village, so we will be neighbors again!"

My mother. How like her to just announce, and not ask! Once she saw how lovely the area around our new château was, she had hired an agent to look for a nearby place for her. She was not walking well after her stroke and had actually found a wheeled beach chair that she had been assured had once been Queen Victoria's. Considering it was my mother, I believed that.

"That's wonderful!" I told her, though with her age and health, I rather wished she would stop buying property.

"Of course it needs redoing, much as your house did. If you two want to take an autumn jaunt some weekend, I will go along and give you a tour. My dearest, I do not know what I would do if I did not have a house to decorate. Sarah, first duchess, of Marlborough, has nothing on me for building, building. I must run now—well, you know what I mean. I must walk or be wheeled and quite carefully at that. Give my love to Jacques."

"Yes, of course. You can help me with the fete I am planning for the villagers when I see you next."

"And we can have a special event or two for women only, wake up those rural Frenchies to their femmes' rights!" she said, and the line went dead.

I did not know whether to laugh or cry. Perhaps I should suggest to Winston that he simply send Alva Smith Vanderbilt Belmont to deal with Hitler and get everything over with right away.

I stood and went out into the downstairs hall to head for the kitchen to talk to Cook. But there, stepping out from underneath the staircase, ripping off her veiled hat and holding a revolver pointed directly at me in a shaking hand was Gladys, Duchess of Marlborough.

Chapter Thirty

y heart began to pound. Gladys, after all these years. With a gun!

I thought she was in England, but now she stood right in front of me.

She came closer, still holding the revolver pointed directly at my chest. Surely she would not shoot me, I reminded myself, but then again my own son had called her unstable. Despite my instant feeling of drowning despair and panic, I decided I had to remain calm. I must humor her but seize hold of this situation. I found my voice before she spoke.

"Gladys, I did not know you were in Paris. You should have rung at the front door, and I would have invited you inside. Won't you please come and sit down? However did you get inside?"

"Through the back—the man putting things out in your dustbin—I waited until he turned away and just walked in."

"Anyway, welcome. Come, sit down and rest."

As she came closer, I could see with horror that her attempt to perfect her beauty with the wax injection was worse than ever before. The implant had slipped down beneath her skin, making her now look as if she had a huge lump on her chin. It unbalanced her once classic, stunning appearance—unbalanced her indeed, so why had she come here? I had to humor her, call for help, but how?

"Come in and sit down, won't you?" I repeated with a nod toward the open door I had just come through. I was afraid to make a quick, strong move, even to gesture. Was that loaded and would she shoot me? And why? That is what I must learn to really disarm her. What would happen if my maid came in? Jacques would not be home for several hours.

She gestured with the gun that I should go in. I thought about slamming the door in her face, but the pull of a trigger could be faster than that. I must not startle her. I went in sideways, afraid to turn my back to her.

"Sit down, please," I said yet again, risking a slight gesture, but all the time I kept thinking about what I could use to knock the gun away and run for help.

I sat in the chair I had been in. To my dismay, when I had hoped to put the table between us, she pulled the other chair closer, facing me, the gun now propped on her knee, still pointing at me. The black pinpoint of the barrel seemed as big as a rain barrel.

"Sunny hired detectives to evict me from Blenheim, the bastard," she said. "He fired my staff. He tried to turn out my dogs. Then he cut off the gas and electricity as if I were some intruder, but I fixed him, cooking by candlelight and smuggling food in."

Poor Blenheim, I thought. The glory of the palace reduced to unlit and stinking dog kennels.

"He threw me out, but not you," she went on. "You left of your own accord. Tell me, did he ever hit you? He blacked my eye once right before a party, so I showed everyone what he did. More than once, I shouted at him in front of guests."

"Well, I guess that served him right." I tried to keep my voice steady. "No, he did not strike me, but there were times I could tell he wanted to. But Gladys, he married you. He wanted you."

"I think a child between us would have kept him calm, but I couldn't. God knows, I—we—tried, really for years. But you had two sons, bang, bang, just like that."

I nearly dry-heaved at her saying *bang, bang—just like that*. I recalled in that moment her father had shot her mother's lover dead. That horrible heritage must still haunt her. Was she this upset at me because she had no children, or was it because the duke threw her out while I managed to leave on my own?

The telephone rang, so shrill. Again. Again. I dared not answer it, though perhaps the staff had for it stopped.

She glanced at it then went on, "If that is a reporter after you like they dog me, do what I did. I dumped a bucket of water on one and screamed at him to go away."

Ordinarily, I would have laughed at that, cheered that, but I just nodded, staring at her, trying to get control of this deadly danger.

"I hear you raised dogs," I said lamely as my frenzied mind darted about for something calming or distracting to say.

"Which he hated—hated, that is, once there were quite a few of them. I think he wanted me for my beauty and body—but then neither of those suited him. Or my trust fund, which was ravaged by the stock market mess at home. Or he wanted me to get back at you because you did not want him at all. And I had wanted him for years. I knew I was destined to be the Duchess of Marlborough."

Her hand holding the revolver shook. How many bullets would that hold?

"Gladys, listen to me," I dared, sounding a bit stronger. "We have both been the Duchess of Marlb—"

"I still am, of course."

"Yes, and—"

"My goal in life was to be something you threw away, but I am glad you did."

"There, you see. A gift to you, for we have so much in common."

"No, you still are rich, and I am not. He has cut me out of his will, so I am glad he is ill—sick of me too, so that is rich!" She began to laugh in little, jerking breaths, and then stopped cold. "But he still wants you, and he does not want me!"

"The duke—Sunny—does not want me. He hates me, so—"

"No, he called me by your name when he was making love to me! Well, not love really. Pinned down, riding me like a horse, he called me Consuelo. I am sick to death of it all and just want it to end. My father beat my mother," she gasped out, sobbing now. "Everyone knew I had such scandal in my past, and I am a scandal now, just like you, but he still wanted you when I—"

The door to the room opened. We both jerked our heads in that direction. Rosemary, my maid stood there. She could not see the gun.

"Oh, madame, I did not know of your guest," she said and started to back away. "The master, he called and said he would telephone you soon and could not wait to see you and—"

I stood. Gladys did too, raising the gun. "Does he call here?"

she screamed at me. "Is that why I was beaten and hated and sent away? Is Sunny still seeing you and comes here after he cast me out?"

"No, that was my husband on the tele—" I got out before she straightened the arm that held the gun.

Ducking low, I threw myself at her, my shoulder butting into her knees. The gun went off, but I felt no pain. I knocked the gun from her hand, and it slid away. We both went down in a crash of china from the small side table. Rosemary screamed, or was that me?

"Get help!" I cried. "The butler, not the gendarmes!"

Gladys only struggled for a moment, then went limp, wracked with sobs. "I want to shoot him!" she gasped out. "He's ill, in pain, but I want to shoot him anyway! It was your fault, too, that he said your name after years, after all I did and wanted and . . ."

Her words became garbled, gasping sobs. I held her arms down at her sides, so she would not attack me further, but I found her clinging to me, hysterical, so I hugged her back, silently cursing the father of my children. I had often wanted to comfort and help poor, desperate women, but I wanted this woman to be helped by someone else—now.

JACQUES HELD ME very close when he came rushing in while the butler and his valet guarded Gladys, who kept sobbing on the floor. I had carefully put the revolver in a drawer. Jacques set me back in his arms, mussed from my struggle with her and ashen-faced from grief. Ironically, I sported a black eye like the one she claimed the duke had given her. Jacques hugged me hard, then tended to the demented woman, who finally lay silent. We did not make a formal report with the police, for her sake and ours, too. We were sick to death of newspaper notoriety.

My maid and the butler sat with Gladys until Jacques phoned a doctor he knew at a *maison de sante*, a facility for the mentally ill. The doctor came and took Gladys away. Jacques asked him to phone the duke to inform him of what happened. Then Jacques had unloaded the revolver and buried it and six bullets somewhere in the backyard, as if he was burying the terrible past for me. So, despite her demented attempt to murder me, we had pity on her. Our hope was that she would be kept from the world for as long as it took to help her.

I was still stunned, silent, cuddled close to him when we finally relaxed a bit in bed.

"I just pray the so-called press never gets wind of this," I told him. I can see their headlines now: CURRENT DUCHESS OF MARLBOROUGH TRIES TO MURDER PREVIOUS ONE. But she did say something I admired—it is even funny."

"What?" he asked as his warm breath stirred my hair.

"She said she dumped a bucket of water on a reporter once. Not a bad idea."

"I never heard about that one."

"He was probably too embarrassed to report it or file charges. Well, we shall keep them away as best we can when we invite our fellow villagers into the château, especially if I can pull off this annual fete."

"You will, my love. We will together."

"And Mother. She insists on helping, of course, but I am worried about her health again. And you know something else I picked up from Gladys's tirade today? She said the duke is ill, even in pain."

"Can you trust anything she says?"

"Who knows? She hates him, so perhaps she is making it up. I only know you keep me safe, and I love you and . . . ."

I am not certain what else I said, for I was so emotionally spent that I think I fell asleep in that thought and in his arms.

FOR SEVERAL SUMMERS in Saint-Georges-Motel, Jacques, Mother, and I welcomed our neighbors to the château and its spacious grounds. Mother, to the amazement of the local folk, had even widened the river along her property nearby. It might have shocked people, but it hardly surprised me. Even nature couldn't stop Alva Belmont from getting what she wanted!

Besides our many summertime garden parties, our annual September party, which came to be known as "Madame Balsan's fete," was eagerly attended by all. Villagers came in all their costumed finery to mingle with our Parisian and English guests. Each year, we sent out open invitations giving the time—from four to seven in the evening—for the villagers to celebrate with us and were rewarded with a procession to open the festivities.

Promptly at four, up the avenue to our open gate, came a parade of people, many of whom we came to know by name, especially the children. I gave gifts to each one of the young ones, something for school or just for play, a book, crayons, mittens for the coming autumn winds.

We erected a dancing platform on the east lawn next to a pavilion decorated with flags where our staff served many kinds of cakes washed down by choices of champagne or cider. When the children ate ices and tortes at long tables on the lawn, I came to know the ones who were ill or somehow troubled. Katrine, a darling, pretty girl of six, had contracted tuberculosis, but was supposed to be "better." I seated her away from the others and pretended I just wanted to spend time with her myself, which I did.

Later that day I asked her mother, "Are you certain Katrine

is cured?" The woman had three other young children and such a disease could be terribly contagious, though I was not certain that was the child's problem. I hoped it was only chronic bronchitis. I determined to somehow have her diagnosed and treated locally—if I could find a good place in this area.

"We are not certain, but there is no place else for us to go," she told me. "Well . . . clear to Paris, but we cannot afford or do that with us tied here. Cannot keep a sick child in the one local doctor's office, that's for a certain."

Twin boys with the name Marchand also had wracking coughs. All that gave me an idea that I filed away for now as we ourselves were feted and blessed by the children singing "The Star-Spangled Banner" in English for me and in French "La Marseillaise" for Jacques. Since we had donated items to the school, we realized their teacher had planned that in gratitude for us. I was so deeply touched—and damned determined now on what I must do for these dear children and their families.

It WAS AT our home in Paris a few days later that I decided to tell my mother what I planned and how she could help. But she sat just staring at me, not reacting nor speaking. I thought she did not hear me or was thinking my proposal over.

"So, don't you think that our area could use a hospital for children, including a tuberculosis sanatorium attached or even separate but nearby?" I asked her again, still writing a letter to a magistrate about that very subject. "You know, for ill children, even some with communicable diseases. I can fund it, oversee it near the château, but if you want to help, that would be lovely. That region has nothing of the sort, so . . . Mother?"

I turned around to look at her. She just stared past me and began to drool. I jumped up and knelt before her, put my hands on her slumped shoulders, then took her hands. Thank God, she was not dead, but her left side seemed like stone. Her body was so heavy when I tried to sit her up. She must be partly paralyzed.

I lay her back on the couch and rang for my maid. I kneeled beside Mother again and held her hands. When Rosemary came in, I cried, "Ring the doctor at once! I think she's had another stroke!"

Chapter Thirty-One

y brothers came to visit Mother as they had at her previous stroke, but when she neither improved nor faded, of necessity, they went back home to family and duty. I visited her often, usually with Jacques, sometimes alone, as she lay in the bedroom of her Paris home—as ever, not far from us. Did she think that close proximity would patch up our broken past? Over the years, I had grown to admire the woman who became Alva Belmont, but I'd never quite let her be "Mama" in my heart again.

One cold January day in 1933, as I sat alone with her, I realized she could not last much longer. She usually lay silent, so I was surprised when she opened her eyes and began to mutter. I leaned close to see if I could hear what she was saying. She had her earthly goods in order, and I thought she had made her peace with God, but she seemed suddenly so troubled.

"I knew it was wrong," she said, looking straight up at the ceiling.

Oh, I thought. Will this be a deathbed confession that she

should not have forced me to marry the duke? But she went on, disturbed, almost raving.

"My papa said it was not wrong—having slaves. I had my own slave, a little girl, Suley. But I knew it was wrong and I was angry."

I pulled my chair closer to her bed and took her right hand, for her left one was stiff from disuse. I told her, "That was long ago, Mother, before the North-South War. Slavery is long over. You never had any slaves once you grew up."

Even as I said that, I remembered when I was very angry in my youth, too, when she ordered me about like a slave.

"I tried to make up for it," she whispered, sounding so desperate. "Others hated me when I said women's rights were pointless unless Negro rights came, too. It was wrong to have a slave."

"I understand, but you were just a child then. I agree, but—"

"It ruined him. Papa. That terrible system ruined him. Our home gone, the cotton fields. Mama dead. So I had to find a way and then I found William K. Vanderbilt. He married me, saved us, but I was still angry, because it was wrong. Papa!" she cried loudly to the room, certainly not to me, for I do not think she even knew I was there. "It was wrong! I tried to earn money another way! Papa, I married money for you, used it for good, but it was all wrong!"

I felt her relax. She had spent her energy and was surely going back to sleep. She did not quite sigh but exhaled. I waited, but she did not breathe again. Her hand went limp. Her eyes stayed open but looked far beyond me. Far beyond, forever now. Why had she never told me all this before? Perhaps she was pleading her case with God.

I sucked in a sob and bowed my head.

So much—so much!—had been wrong in her life, but she had boldly struggled to make some things right.

ALVA SMITH VANDERBILT Belmont was eighty-three years and nine days old when she died. Jacques and I took her casket to New York on the SS *Berengaria* for a funeral and burial she had already planned. Everything went according to her wishes—except for one thing. She had asked for a female celebrant, but we had to settle for a man because the burial was in the same church where I had married the duke, and they did not permit women to officiate. However, her pallbearers were all women, and what a buzz there was over that.

The date was Sunday, February 12. The congregation numbered at least fifteen hundred, a fitting tribute. The choir sang a hymn she herself had composed. For the other songs, she had allowed traditional hymns.

Forty elderly members of the National Woman's Party, the NWP, wearing their traditional purple and gold, lined the way when the coffin was carried in, and many suffragettes passed in homage. They carried tattered, faded banners from their marches, but I stared at the one that seemed yet brand-spanking new and bold as ever: FAILURE IS IMPOSSIBLE, it read. That one was draped over her casket for the service.

I looked around the crowded church, holding Jacques's hand but remembering how young and frightened and, yes, how angry I was—because to quote my mother's final words, "It was wrong!"—that I was forced to marry here. Marry a man I hardly knew and did not love, but at least my sons and Jacques had made up for that.

The trip from the church to Woodlawn Cemetery was quite a parade: the family motorcars; three motorbuses with delegates from the NWP; policemen on motorized bicycles; and some classic, old-style limousines of her friends. A curious crowd, some with cameras, waiting there made me realize the newspapermen she had once manipulated were present. The family led the way into the tomb she had designed and had built—her last constructed, earthly edifice where her dear second husband, Oliver Hazard Perry Belmont, already lay.

Once again, she had planned a short service here in the French Gothic chapel. It reminded me of the Gothic Room at Marble House, with its collection of crucifixes, where the duke had proposed to me. And again, I decided as I had when Papa was buried in the elaborate Vanderbilt mausoleum that I would never be entombed here. I wanted something simple, something outside, not closed in or grand.

A quartet sang two songs even here, then we heard the bugle call of "Taps" played off in the distance as if Mother were some departed, honored war hero. Finally, we left her casket in the tomb next to her beloved Oliver.

As I exited the chapel holding on to Jacques on one side and my brother Harold, called Mike, on the other, I realized he, too, had a bit of Mother in him, for he could be overbearing and difficult to love even though he had a brilliant mind. Our other brother, named Willie for Papa, was like our father, all easygoing charm.

My having been in Europe these years gave me an objectivity about things in America. So what if manners had changed here at home and men no longer doffed their hats to women? I was blessed with a man who spoiled me and adored me. I got on with both of my very different sons and was thrilled to be a grandmother. And, after everything I had been through, I treasured all that.

AFTER THE FUNERAL, I cherished some time with family and friends, especially the week we spent with my brothers Mike and Willie, even some Vanderbilt relatives Mother had been at war with since her divorce.

We also spent a lovely week with Mike's family at his magnificent new house at Manalapan near Palm Beach, Florida. It was there I heard, quite indirectly, some advice that Mother had shared with a friend but not with me.

"Look here, on this condolence card," Mike told me as I sat with him and his wife under a big umbrella on the beach. "It is from a friend of hers, Elsa Maxwell, see?" he said, thrusting it at Jacques and me and then pulling it back to himself and removing his sunglasses to squint at it. "She says Mother wrote her that her trouble with life was that she was born too late to fit into the old days and too soon for modern times, so that she wanted to change the next generation. If you want to be happy, Mother wrote this woman, live peacefully with your own dear ones in your own era."

Peacefully! I thought. Not Alva V. Belmont. Not if you stood in the way of something she wanted. But perhaps I was more like her than I wanted to admit. Because right now, I wanted to fund and build a children's hospital near Saint-Georges-Motel, and I was going to do it!

ON A HILL just outside the village, I bought property and retained an architect, plumbers, and electricians to build the children's hospital and tuberculosis sanitarium. Jacques supported this project of my heart both morally and financially, and, once finished, it housed eighty youngsters, mostly aged one to five years, although several of the initial patients, like dear Katrine from the village, were older.

They were calling it "state of the art," and it boasted wards, playrooms, and nursing staff facilities. I made certain there was also room for outside activities and play, as the young patients' strength permitted.

I was certain there was nothing more innovative or up-to-date in Paris or London. In the sanitarium—our first patient was young Katrine and one of her brothers from the village—patients lived in separate, glass-walled rooms instead of wards. Each chamber had a built-in bath and each patient had toys galore.

"How is my dear Katrine today?" I asked as I stopped by her bed where she was cuddling a cloth doll. A bedspread of Balsan "blue-horizon" color was draped over her.

"Still coughing, madame. And my Dolly is too, see?" she said, giving the doll a few jerks. "But when I am well, must she still be ill and stay for the next girl in this place?"

"No, for you will get well together!" I promised her and squeezed her toes through the bedcovers. "Of course you will take her home with you to keep an eye on her just the way the nurses do you here."

Her face lit in a smile. "Then I must get well soon, so she will too!"

A nurse bustled in. "Your cousin is here, madame, the one who paints and talks so much," she told me as I scribbled in my ever-present notebook to buy more dolls so that they could go home with girl patients. And something likewise for the boys? I would have to ask around, but you might know Winston was here. Not my cousin exactly, but he always made such a stir.

I blew a kiss to Katrine and went out through my office and the back door, without finding Winston. Shaking my head, I strolled quickly back toward our gate, but saw only Clemmie coming out to meet me. I hugged her, and she told me, "He could not wait to get painting and found out you were what he calls 'nursing' again. He is painting the moat, fashioning it into a pond but is quite distressed there are no waves in it today," she added with a little laugh as the two of us headed toward the château together. "But he has solved that handily and said to tell you that necessity is the mother of invention. He insists that is a Churchill quote not one from old times."

"So what has he done now?" I asked as the moat came in sight. Was he clear around the back of it?

But I spotted him, sitting with his easel at the very bend of it around the side. "Consuelo, my dear," he called out when he saw us coming. "I had to catch the light just right to make waves."

"You are ever making waves!" I teased as we joined him, and then I saw what he meant. He had his valet—who was secretly also his bodyguard—sitting in an old rowboat in the moat, making waves with an oar.

"Cannot hug you right now, or I would smear you up with this off-white color I need for whitecaps," he told me and bent back to his work. "When the time is right, carpe diem."

"My," Clemmie said, "but you are just chock-full of old Latin sayings today."

He ignored that but soon turned toward me with a not only serious, but stern and sad look on his face. "Consuelo, we cannot stay long this time. Sunny's ailing—actually, from cancer."

I gasped. "I heard he was ill, but—neither Bert nor Ivor told me."

"He just told them, as I am telling you—so that you can be of support to the boys, I mean. I asked Clemmie not to tell you so that I could. That is why," he said, looking back at his half-finished painting, "the inland seas are rough today. Hell's gates, if that little hospital of yours was not for children, I would admit myself straightaway. A psychiatric ward for me. I am blue in the face from arguing that Germany is out for blood and land again—France's and ours."

"I am sorry about the duke—Sunny—and the new threat to peaceful times," I told him, putting a hand on his shoulder. Clemmie just shook her head as if she had had enough of all this nonstop German raving.

He put his free hand over mine, though that seemed to have blue paint on it. "I will tell Sunny that you said that and meant it," he said with a sniff as he put his brush down on the easel tray. He shouted, "You may stop making waves now, Thompson! Come get one of these damned cigars as thanks!

"The thing is," he said, turning again to face me, "Sunny still misses you, especially after the debacle with—with his second marriage. Well, all water over the milldam now. Time marches on, and death waits for no man, which is what is scaring me about Hitler and the return of the Huns."

His voice broke, and a tear streaked down his cheek. Clemmie put her arm around his ample waist. Pressing his lips hard together, he nodded at me, then flashed me that *V* sign of his that meant valor or some such. I made the same sign back and hurried inside to find Jacques.

EIGHTEEN MONTHS AFTER my mother died, Bert telephoned me at Saint-Georges-Motel to tell me the duke was dead of cancer at age sixty-two. He raised his voice so I could hear and was almost shouting.

"I know you will not come for the funeral, Mother, but please come soon after—to Blenheim. I need you here, at least for a little while. Of course Jacques is welcome too—always.

Besides, your little namesake needs you to talk her out of fearing the ghost, since we will mostly live here now with the boon and the burden of Blenheim."

"Of course we will come," I promised. Tears stung my eyes. I tried to keep my voice steady. "Blenheim will be different now that you are duke, in good and beautiful ways. After the service, when things calm down a bit, including the newspaper coverage, of course we will come."

"There is one other thing. Needless to say, there were several commemorations in the papers as well as the formal obituary. Lord Castlerosse wrote a memorial in the *Sunday Express*, which was terribly critical and cruel, but that is such a sensational rag. Winston wrote for the *Times* something about your marriage, saying it was unhappy and unsuccessful, but that both Father and 'his first wife, had amazing gifts of charm and kindliness.' I want you to know I love you, and I believe Father, in his own way, did too."

"I will thank Winston later for his kind words and I cherish yours, my dear, so let us just say that. You do not need to mend bridges for your father."

"Righto. Well, of course Ivor misses you, obsessed with his art collecting as he is."

"I am glad you called me with the news, however sad," I told him as tears slipped down my cheeks. "I am proud of the new duke and my firstborn son."

I guess I was crying audibly now, for he said, "I cried too. For all he should have done, could have been. But the water terraces here will be his legacy."

A name and a past writ in water, I thought as I replaced the receiver. One man passed, one era past, and a new one begun.

I started to walk away, but just leaned against the wall. My knees began to shake, all of me. Whatever Marlborough—Sunny—had not been to me, he had been the father of my beloved children. He had given me the opportunity to reach outside myself to his dear people, so that I could be to them their "Angel of Woodstock." Poor man, never truly happy, clinging to a past way of life. A difficult first marriage and pitiful second one: I could almost forgive him now that I had someone to truly love, someone who loved me.

Poor man, going soon to dust among the long line of dukes he so venerated who had once held Blenheim. But I had hopes for our Bert's leadership, hopes for the dear people there whom I would always love and cherish in my memory and heart.

Chapter Thirty-Two

ranny, I am so glad you're here!" my beautiful eighteen-year-old granddaughter greeted me with a kiss and a hug and then hugged Jacques, too. "Everything is so exciting!"

The grand staircase she had hurried down to meet me had never looked so lovely or filled with light. The marble bust of the first duke over the Saloon door might even have been smiling, and I felt a great weight lifted to be happy to be back for this event, though we'd visited Bert's family here before. Yet this day with Sarah seemed special. I doubt that the vast building had changed, but with Bert's family here, returning seemed like a homecoming.

This July 7, 1939, we were at Blenheim for Sarah's debutante ball, which was called by some in society the event of the summer season. It was almost like the old days under King Edward, I thought, as Sarah rattled off the names of guests who would be here. "Oh, and Father is so excited that the Duke of Kent has accepted. Royal family, but then I guess you knew them all!"

"He is one I do not know, so that will be lovely."

As both Bert and Mary greeted us and words flew fast, I was hoping this would all indeed be lovely. Jacques was worried for France, because his countrymen were trying to ignore the German threat, and he had seen that all before. Winston, who would be here soon for this event, was ever dour over Adolf Hitler, who was dictator now, despite the fact that his title Der Fuhrer meant leader or even guide.

We settled in our room, then had iced coffee and cakes with Bert's family on the terrace overlooking the parterres the duke had worked so hard to build. Ivor had joined us now. He was here for the event, too, taking precious time from the art purchasing business he was building. I knew he was still itching for me to fulfill my promise to him, which I had reneged on twice before. He wanted me to visit his father's grave with him. Jacques had said he understood, but I was reluctant.

It was enough to be back in this massive palace with all the memories. At least Bert's family's living here helped to erase the hard times and sad legacy of Gladys, who, we had heard, was still in psychiatric care. We came here several times a year to see the children, and they came to visit us, but each time before this, the huge house itself oppressed me. At least we were outside now, for the views were always grand.

"So, how is the new property you two bought in Florida?" Bert asked. "We shall love to visit you some winter, if we can get away."

Jacques said, "You do know your mother named it Casa Alva, yes? A fitting tribute to someone who was always buying and decorating, part of her mother's heritage, since Consuelo does the same thing."

I reached out to playfully smack his arm. "As if you are an innocent bystander in all of that. Yes, we brought photographs to show you now that Casa Alva is all put to rights. We fell in love with the area—for the winters—when we were visiting my brother. It is a villa fronting the ocean about fifteen miles from Palm Beach with white stucco walls and graceful wrought iron. I must admit I shipped some of my most prized possessions there from Paris and Saint-Georges-Motel in case—well, in case things change," I said with a sideward glance at the younger children who were kicking a football around on the grass while Sarah sat with us adults.

Ivor said, "Wait until Winston gets here tomorrow if you want to hear carping that the British people are not alert to foreign dangers."

"Same with France," Jacques said with a sigh. "Our officials want compromise with Berlin—no more war—but you cannot make friends with the devil. People go about saying '*C'est la vie*' instead of realizing war could come again."

"Let's just talk about tomorrow!" Sarah said, frowning and pouting. "Granny, you should see all the magnums of champagne that are here, the orchestra will be here soon and you simply must see my gown. You had a grand coming out, didn't you? I mean way back when, in America."

"I did," I told her, and described a bit of that day, but my mind skipped to the first time I met and danced with Jacques. And I recalled being here, at Blenheim, when the duke was so thrilled at the Prince of Wales's and Alexandra's first visit. It was hard to believe that my dear friend Alexandra had died fourteen years ago. So many of the important people who had been here then were . . . were simply gone.

I blinked back tears but smiled at Sarah. "It will be a wonderful, memorable event, especially for you, so remember and cherish it always."

Bert beamed proudly, and melancholy Ivor even smiled.

"I promised I would take a walk with Ivor, and so I shall," I told them and stood. "Jacques, would you like to come along?"

"I am dying to tell Bert about the new innovations on the planes," he told me. "The Germans may have their Luftwaffe, but we will not be left behind! So you may leave me behind now, my dear."

Sarah popped up when the motorbus with the orchestra arrived and the others bustled off. It had been a hot summer, so I borrowed a parasol from Mary, took Ivor's arm, and we started out.

"I DIDN'T MEAN to insist," Ivor said as we walked the lane toward Bladon church and its graveyard.

"I know it means a lot to you for me to see his grave."

"Not so much that really, as I just want you to know that I mean to be buried there."

I gasped and turned him to me. "You are not keeping something from me? Your health—"

"As up and down as ever, but no. I did not mean I have an imminent demise on the horizon."

"You would tell me if you did?"

"I swear! Well, you mean that Father kept his cancer a secret."

"I was not part of his life then. He did not have to tell me. Listen, Ivor," I said as we began to walk again toward the gate, "I want you to know that your father loved you very much. I think since you were sickly at first—"

"And now."

"Do not say that. It scared him that he might lose you, so he pulled back a bit, perhaps did not treat you the way he did Bert."

"Bert the bold, Bert the heir—now duke. You know, I have found my own purpose in life, to encourage artists, preserve and even treasure their art, and if I had been the rough-and-tumble sort like Bert, perhaps I would never have seen the beauty in art—in life."

We walked across the road and went into the graveyard through the simple wooden gate that stood ajar. An elderly villager was cutting grass with a scythe around the farthest, oldest tombstones. He almost looked like those drawings of Father Time. Evidently, recognizing us, he snatched off his cap and stopped to stare.

"I vow, 'tis the good duchess, one they used to call the angel," he said.

"It is indeed," Ivor said, "just come to pay respects."

I would have talked to the man and asked his name, but he scurried out. I felt bad about that, but I appreciated his thoughtfulness. How long ago it seemed that I had visited the poor and ill roundabout Blenheim and had spent hours with dear, blind Mrs. Prattley.

The 9th Duke of Marlborough's grave was not grand or great, so I was surprised at that. The stone was fine, though, cleanly incised. Green turf covered it like a blanket. He had been gone six years already, I realized, as I read the dates. Perhaps I should have come sooner.

As if Ivor had read my mind, he said, "If I lie here someday, come and visit. Sit down and stay a while with me."

"Pray God, if you lie here someday, I will be long gone for I wish a full life for you, my dearest. And you must not be so melancholy," I said, squeezing his arm to my rib cage. "You have a long life ahead, and I hope you will find a wife and have a family of your own, for that is something that really matters as well as your pursuit of and love of art. But you know, it is so peaceful and beautiful here . . ."

He bent to kiss my cheek. "Let's go back," he said. "I am grateful, though I do not live at Blenheim, that you are willing to come back. Come on, then, for this is Sarah's special day, and you are special to her—and to me."

We went out the gate to the road. At least a dozen people stood there with more hurrying up. A woman I did not recognize called out, "So glad you come out of the big house to see us like you done years ago. I was Lizzie Millbank then, Your Grace . . ."

Others called out their names or greetings, calling me *duchess* or *Your Grace*. Several said something about my being *the good duchess*. I shook everyone's hands. Of all the accolades and honors I had been given lately, including the Legion of Honour award in Paris for starting my children's hospital and helping with one in Paris, this moved me deeply. So why did I see doom on the horizon and still fear what was coming next?

Despite the warm weather, the high-ceilinged, huge rooms at Blenheim kept us fairly cool, even when dancing. Sarah Consuelo's debutante ball was a smashing success. It was indeed like the old days.

Clemmie, however, was not speaking to Winston because he kept muttering—thank heavens where Sarah could not hear him—things like, "You know Nero fiddled while Rome burned. It is coming, Consuelo, dark days. I have done my last pretty peacetime painting."

Jacques and I relished the music and kept out on the floor, especially for each waltz. I could not believe I was sixty-three and he almost seventy-two, for, I believe, neither of us felt or looked our ages. How long and how far we had come since that first dance we had shared in Paris. As we left the dance floor again, my head was spinning with the "Blue Danube Waltz" and champagne when the Duke of Kent, the king's younger brother, came up to talk more, for we had met him earlier. He and Princess Marina were such a handsome couple, and he greatly resembled his brother, the king.

"You two must come dine with us next time you are in London," he told us. "Consuelo, I have heard you were friends with my grandmother, Queen Alexandra."

"Indeed, for she was very kind to me when I first lived in England and I was a fish out of water. And she tried to help me with my hearing problem."

"Ah, she would. If this were a Catholic country, I would nominate her for saint. Without her love and that of my wonderful nanny, Charlotte Bill at Sandringham—of course my parents too—who knows what sort of layabout or ruffian I would be."

So he had a good sense of humor amid all the war talk. As for considering Alexandra a saint, I wondered if he was referring to King Edward forever "cheating" on her, as they put it now. But it was not long before the duke and Jacques were talking aeroplanes, for the duke said he had long been fascinated by flying.

"I earned my pilot's license in twenty-nine," I heard him tell my husband, "and two years ago I became a Royal Air Force group captain."

And so, they were off to the races—the flying races. After a half hour of such chatter with much gesticulating while I talked to Princess Marina, the duke turned to me again. "I apologize for 'capturing' your husband," he told me. "The next time we are in the same vicinity, as I said, both of you must be our guests. Either I will take your Jacques—and you—up in an RAF plane or he will take me up next time I am in France—

that is decided. God bless you ladies who put up with the avid airmen the likes of us."

He took my hand, then started away. Soon I saw Jacques dancing with Sarah. She looked so young, so happy, and I prayed that is the way she would stay.

OUR LAST NIGHT at Blenheim I felt like a silly schoolgirl sneaking out with Sarah at the top of the stairs, but she was still so excited she knocked on our door because she could not sleep. She and I were in nightgowns and robes, for the halls were cool at night. Because of the rising national tensions I was not sure when I would see her again, so I was happy for more private time with her.

"You have a wonderful, blessed life ahead of you, my dear," I told her. "But do not just be a social butterfly or gadabout. Find some way to help other people, and if—when—you find someone to love and make a home with, make your family your very first priority."

"I will, Granny. But did you miss your family terribly when you wed and even had to leave your home and country?"

"Yes. My father and brothers at least, for I had a difficult mother."

"I remember hearing all that. I think I have rather a good one, because we have girl talks, just like you and I . . ."

Her voice trailed off and she stared down the staircase into the darkness. No, not darkness for someone was coming up toward us, the footsteps clear, the old staircase creaking a bit. But there was no solid form there, only the shape of a woman with one hand on the banister and her head held high. She wore a tiara like the one passed down by Marlborough duchesses and a pale, flowing silk gown.

Sarah gripped my hand so hard I flinched. I shuddered with goose bumps and scooted closer to her, pushing her over as a strange coolness wafted at us and I felt the air move.

"No peace," I thought I heard a female voice say, an angry voice, but then there was nothing.

"It was her!" Sarah said, so quietly I could not really hear her, but I knew what she had said. "I think she said something, didn't she? Well, I guess you couldn't hear her, Granny. I think she was looking for a piece of something."

"Yes, that must be it," I told Sarah. "And we shall tell no one of this, because they will think we are daft. She let us see her, hear her, so that is special that we were together. As I told you years ago, never be afraid of Duchess Sarah."

But I was afraid now. Here I was partially deaf without my hearing aid, and I would have sworn I heard "No peace," a terrible omen from beyond.

IN EARLY SEPTEMBER of that year, I held tight—very tight—to Jacques. We stood on the front lawn of our château while his motorcar loomed nearby. Jacques was in uniform, a colonel in the French Air Force. He had been away on duty but had come home and was leaving me here now. Germany had invaded Poland while France and England were waiting for Herr Hitler's next move in a period the papers had dubbed "The Phony War" because we were not yet under attack. But there was nothing phony about Jacques's departing for duty again. I planned to wait for him here at Saint-Georges-Motel, nearest to his airfield where he oversaw pilots, but I could not bear to let him go.

"Consuelo, my love, I will be late, so I must go," he whispered. But he held hard to me, too. "You . . . you do not have some special premonition, do you?"

"About you? No. I just cannot shake this general feeling of doom. But I will keep busy here with the ill children. In case there is an invasion—"

"More likely as the Huns get closer, it will be refugees streaming through here in the thousands, but I am sure our Maginot Line will hold."

"I could help with refugees, too. I just cannot bear it that the places and life we love, and came to so late, should perish."

He stepped back only to seize both my hands hard in his. "Listen to me, Consuelo. France will fight and I with it. And I fight for you, too, my wife and my life. You must be strong for me, because—"

"Pardon, Monsieur Jacques, but there is a phone call for you," our butler called from the front door of the château. "Important, the man insists, else I would not interrupt you now."

I bit my lower lip. He kept my hand in his, and we went back inside to his study where he took the call. I could hear rapid French, a deep voice, but could not catch the meaning of the words.

My heart thudded. Something wrong at Blenheim, something about Ivor? "Yes, of course, I will tell her," he ended the conversation and put the receiver back in its cradle.

"Tell me what?"

He sat at his desk and pulled me onto his lap. "No one is dead or even hurt," he said, his voice tight, his face so stern. "But the Red Cross has learned there is a hostage list of wealthy people the Germans think they can kidnap to extort much money for their war machine."

"I heard they did that to Baron Louis de Rothschild in Vienna. It took his family millions of dollars to get him returned. And you are on that list? Then you cannot leave for duty, but must stay here since it has been deemed a safe area by the government."

"Shh!" he said and put two fingers on my lips. "Yes, I have been told this rural area is safe for now, and they would, no doubt, like to get their filthy hands on me. But the person who is on that Nazi list, my darling, is you."

Part Five

Refugee, 1939–1940

Fight and Flight

Chapter Thirty-Three

hile Jacques was called away to advise reconnaissance pilots, I worked dawn to dark in the children's hospital. Many of our nurses had been called away in case they were needed as French troops massed near the border, though most believed Hitler was all bluff. Some newspapers had been claiming that the real enemy was the Soviet Union with their dictator Joseph Stalin. However, in England, Winston, in speech after speech, harangued Parliament that another invasion of Europe and war could come.

I had mixed feelings about allowing the now healthy ten-year-old Katrine to be my aide after school, since I was overseeing several village women who were filling in for nurses as well as doing my administrative job. But the adoring and adorable child stuck to me like glue, as did the two elderly male villagers Jacques had hired to protect me. We did not believe I was in imminent danger of being spirited away by the distant Nazis for ransom, but stranger things had happened.

"Madame, must I wear this mask when you do not wear

one?" Katrine asked, fidgeting with the half-face cotton protection I made her wear.

"Since you have had the disease and insist on helping, my girl, yes. Otherwise, I must banish you to using that typewriter in my office."

"Yes, madame. But I am tired of hearing war, war, war."

"I too, but that is the way things are now. So we shall all stick together, like you and I do."

"No matter what," she said and pulled down her mask for a moment so I could see her smile.

She was like a bright and sparkling jewel to me, like another granddaughter, which made me miss Sarah even more. I felt so alone without Jacques, and missed Winston too. I could understand why he was on his own warpath, despite the fact even Clemmie had told him to tone down his inflammatory rhetoric. Hitler had taken Austria last year and was in league somehow with the Italian dictator Mussolini who had annexed Ethiopia, of all places. At least the German border was not near our part of France, for Belgium was closer here. Yet most people, Jacques included, believed that since we lived near Normandy, our little village would be safe.

I put on a good front, yet I was secretly afraid. For France, for Jacques, for all we had built here, and for myself. I had told him if the Huns, mostly called the Nazis now, crossed France's borders, we must move the patients in the children's hospital farther south. But to where?

"When I was ill and then got better," Katrine broke into my agonizing, "I learned you keep your promises." She pointed to a soft cloth doll in the arms of a sleeping young patient named Susanne we were watching through a glass divider. "I still have my doll. It meant so much that she could stay with me, and now I want to stay at your side, to help out."

I set the tray I carried aside on a cart and hugged her with one arm. "Little things like that, daily kindnesses and gifts, are more precious than gold," I told her. "We must remember that with big things swirling around us. Come along now, and we will have a quick lunch at the château before we come back here."

Sometimes on weekends she stayed with me there, but I planned to send her home tonight, because I knew she helped her mother with the younger children. Katrine's father had gone into the army and had trained near Paris. When he came home for a brief leave before being stationed in the east, he had assured us there would be no war, for the Parisians were enjoying life to the full, partying, shopping, dancing. His naïve, happy report made me wonder if I had once been like that. Too many grand parties, too much shopping for luxuries, even properties? But never enough dancing, not with my Jacques.

I TOOK MY daily phone call from Jacques inside the château while Katrine sat out on the terrace. She looked so peaceful there, so young and pretty.

"My darling," came his voice over the receiver, "anything doing there? I miss you terribly, but these are terrible times."

"The usual at the hospital. Very quiet, normal, but for lack of men, including my dear husband. Are you quite all right?"

"Flying, training, advising. Listen, Consuelo, I was thinking perhaps you should go to Blenheim to stay with Bert and Mary. You could see Ivor more. Britain is an island nation and, though Hitler has planes that could fly the Channel to get there—"

"Surely not clear from Germany!"

"If so, they will be met by the Duke of Kent's RAF planes, just as we would resist here, but—"

"Jacques, I am needed here. You are here in France. I am staying, as much as I long to see my sons. We decided I was safe here, at least for now, so have you changed your mind on France's borders holding firm?"

"No, but perhaps I have listened to Winston too long. Darling, if things get worse, do not be afraid if I do not call on time or call at all for a while. But now to my real news. I have been informed there will be a high-ranking official who will be visiting you tomorrow, General Armand Fuisse, to advise about a possible evacuation of your hospital."

"Oh, thank heavens! So you are thinking as I do, that if there are any problems at the border, I must move the children farther south. Perhaps he will know where I can take them."

"I do not know, but he is most insistent, and the hierarchy here know you are on that ransom list. I will be eager to hear what he has advised you. I love you, my dearest, and pray we will soon have our life together back."

"I too. Such treasures now, our memories, but we shall survive this and make more."

"I must go. General Fuisse, tomorrow or the next day. I know you will entertain him and win him over."

His tone had become more agitated, even, for my confident Jacques, a bit shaky. Win him over? So did he not like or trust this General Fuisse? And did he not really trust that I was safe here in our haven far from the German border?

"AH, A LARGE château, some outlying cottages too," General Fuisse said, scribbling notes after he had looked around the estate. He had come in a long, black motorcar with a driver and a guard. "And that hospital you have built—excellent."

I was already beginning to think of him as General "Fussy." He was prissy and fastidious, drinking his coffee with his little finger in the air. His uniform boasted a billboard of medals. He had ordered his men to stay with their vehicle, although I had invited them inside, too. I told him, "I worry that if there would be some sort of . . . of invasion, the children in the hospital—"

"If the Huns try," he interrupted, "we will repulse them. But if there are some casualties, if refugees flee south from Belgium, that could be a problem here with our soldiers needing care."

"From Belgium? You do not think Hitler will be content to have Austria but will want Belgium, too? But that is right on our border. Then you agree with Winston Churchill. He is a relative and friend of mine, you see."

"Ah, I did not know that," he said, putting his coffee cup in its saucer and writing on his notepad again. "Quite the rabble-rouser, is he not?"

"And quite right on Hitler's intentions, I believe, though my husband says we will repulse him."

He appeared to shake that off with a little shrug. He did not seem to take me seriously, which would not please Jacques and did not please me. He had skirted the question each time I mentioned protecting the ill children.

"Madame Balsan, should there be casualties, Mother France will need hospitals and rehabilitation sites in the countryside for our soldiers. As you and Colonel Balsan are surely patriots, we know we can rely on you."

"But in what way? Unless I can be certain the children in our facility are carefully and comfortably moved to another, General, I do not see how this could be accomplished."

"I thought an American would be all full steam ahead on this, take charge," he said, looking up and squinting at me. "We may indeed need not only the facilities of the hospital here for France's soldiers but the château also."

I gasped and sat up even straighter.

"I give you the duty," he went on, "for you are, of course, respected and even honored here—of doing what you can to prepare for the worst."

"General, turning out our children would be the worst. The château and its outlying cottages can be used for the nation, but the sanitarium cannot just be requisitioned like that!"

Frowning, he only scribbled away as if I had not protested. I wanted to throw the coffeepot at him. I wanted to argue more, to absolutely refuse giving up the hospital, but I had to speak again to Jacques first. Had he realized what this man would ask—would demand? That Fuisse could commandeer the buildings of our estate was one thing, but is that why Jacques had sounded so nervous at the end of our last telephone call?

"I understand, Madame Balsan, you are on a German ransom list, as they call it. It would do this estate good to be swarming with French soldiers, for you could surely keep a room for yourself and help with the nursing, too."

I stood as he rose. Thank heavens he was leaving, for I wanted so badly to turn into my mother to tell him off and throw him out.

I HIRED SEVERAL villagers—they refused to take payment at first, until I insisted—to store items and some furniture from the château in our cellars, though I made certain there was space for people lest there was an air attack. I even brought in mattresses and cots when I could find them. I had lain awake at night thinking that—as in London during the Great War—the cellar would have to do for a bomb shelter as would those at the hospital. I gave notice to several artists, who were living gratis in our cottages, that they might have to move if there would be any injured French soldiers arriving. The general had mentioned refugees, too.

After speaking to Jacques, who was furious and said he had been misled, I made several phone calls about facilities farther south to move our sanitarium patients if need be. But I got nowhere. I knew I would have to take a motorcar trip to look for sites myself, but Jacques forbid it until he could get a leave. He said he agreed we would have to help with wounded soldiers if it came to that, but he would try to get a promise the ill children would not be evicted.

Yet again today he argued, "You are safe there, Consuelo, I know where you are and it is not far from me, so do not go south on your own or even with a companion or guard."

"I might as well be on the moon, I feel so far from you. And I feel overwhelmed."

"This is not like you, my love. I know times are frightening, but we must hang on. You are a strong woman—have always been strong."

"I do not mean to complain. I want to support you and I know you are under great strain. But, frankly, I just pray the French generals in command of the borders are not like that beastly General Fuisse! I hope they are more like my Jacques!"

"This is a nightmare, I agree. The threat of war . . . our being apart when we were apart for so long. I swear to you I will see you soon, even if briefly. Just pray that the lines will hold. We lived through separation once and built a life together. If the château goes to the state for now—"

"That is one thing, but again, I say, not the hospital!"

"I know. I will inquire. I will even beard old Fuisse in his den if I must, the old— Well, enough said. Enough said, except for how much I miss you and love you. Darling, as I said, if you ever change your mind and want to go to England or even home to America—"

"You are here and that makes France my home."

"Then, someday, I swear to you, I will make America my home, too—you wait and see."

"That is all I am doing here. I wait to see what will happen to these dear people in my care and I wait to see you."

"I will always—" he said and then we were cut off. The line absolutely went dead. I tried to tell myself that was not an omen.

I SLEPT FITFULLY now, even in my exhaustion. Sometimes I dreamed we were under attack as in London. It was dark in the cellar. Where was Jacques? Was he flying in the night sky without me? Despite my weak hearing, I sometimes was certain I heard guns booming, but it was just the wind rattling a shutter or a spring thunderstorm. I wore myself down, caring for the children, visiting the villagers, tiring myself so that I could manage to get some sleep.

Sometimes I lay awake for hours before dawn. Jacques's telephone calls were scarce now. He said he would be home soon, but when? Perhaps never again if the Germans attacked or broke through the French lines.

Dawn came slowly on a day that should have been so pretty. I tried to reckon the date, it was May 16, 1940, I figured. Yes, that is right, because Winston had been prime minister of England for just six days.

I rolled over and curled into a ball on Jacques's side of the bed. I ached from lifting buckets and patients at the hospital. Winston had said that the French trench warfare would never stop the Germans and their Wehrmacht war machine this time. Now, finally, he had been given the power to try to stop them. Winston, like a third brother to me, one who had been closer than my real ones, had said England must be ready to fight, and I knew so must we all.

I heard the door to my room open. A shaft of light leaped across my face. Half asleep at first, I instantly dreamed Jacques had come home to me. Then I feared the Germans had come for me. I sat bolt upright in bed.

"Madame, news!" my maid's voice cut through my half-waking state. "The German invasion through Belgium is progressing with hardly a shot being fired! It is on the radio, and Katrine has come to tell you so! They will try to cross our French lines soon, madame. Oh, what shall we do? Will soldiers be here soon, wounded ones like you said or the enemy?"

Or refugees as Jacques and the general had said?

"I am getting up to make some telephone calls," I told her, sounding quite in command as I threw off my mussed covers and swung my feet out of bed. I always had my clothes laid out nearby, and I scrambled into them. "Feed Katrine breakfast and send her back home," I ordered. "As soon as I can, I will pack a small suitcase of clothes and shoes in case I have to head south to find a place for the children. You should do the same—we may have to flee."

"Flee, madame? But to where and how?"

Exactly, I thought. Doom and disaster could soon be on our doorstep.

Chapter Thirty-Four

he nightmare worsened. The Nazis' blitzkrieg of planes, tanks, and artillery had been mostly unopposed and they'd quickly taken over Belgium, Luxembourg, and the Netherlands. A flood of refugees from Belgium and the French eastern provinces fled past our gates. First came the motorcars of the wealthy, then the wagons of rural folks, then bicyclists, then those walking. From the moment the farm families, traveling in wagons, began to arrive, and knowing that they'd left their crops and livestock behind, I had canteens set up along the road where people could get fresh water, eat bread with jam, and rest.

"*Merci, madame,*" I heard over and over as I gave orders to my château staff and some villagers who came to help. I knew I was making my two, elderly bodyguards nervous as I moved quickly from person to person, but at least I was not worried for myself now. Seeing the plight of others made me temporarily forget my situation, though my prayers that Jacques would come home soon, at least for a visit, never ceased.

"They are coming, the Huns, madame," one distraught, disheveled woman told me. "They take everything, even kill the animals and burn the crops. Cut down trees in the orchards, too."

I overheard a young man with a very pregnant wife and a young child in arms tell one of my guards, whom he thought was my father, "The Germans, they make everywhere they go a no-man's-land by setting explosive mines. One false step—boom! My brother lost a leg then his life. We had to leave."

A wagon drawn by four beautiful Percherons pulled up with household goods piled high. A bearded man drove with a woman in an old-fashioned bonnet sitting next to him. Perched atop bundles of clothing and what looked to be sacks of flour and grain sat an old woman wearing black, tied in a rocking chair that was secured to the sacks.

No doubt her life as she knew it was over. I thought of Mrs. Prattley and of Jacques's great-aunt who had presided over the Balsans' lovely home the day I first met the family. I had thought I had worries and problems then.

"Madame," a young boy said and tugged at the apron I wore over my dress. "My papa, he is so angry with me for bringing these pets of mine along. He says we cannot eat them so I must let them go. But can they stay here, please? Does your house have a pond? I will come back for them later."

He opened a battered cardboard box and within were four soft, golden ducklings. They made little chirping sounds and looked so frenzied, so trapped. Like all of us now.

"I have fountains and a moat, and I promise you I will put them there," I assured him with a squeeze of his shoulder.

Like so many of the others, tears wet his cheeks. "I hope you do not like duck soup," he said. He gave me a little bow as if I were royalty. He thrust the box into my hands, sniffed hard, then hurried off to climb into a waiting wagon.

At night, on the grass beside the road through the village, we put out lanterns and mattresses we hauled from the château. We had been waiting for wounded French soldiers, who had not yet materialized. We had asked so many of the refugees for news of how our troops were doing, but they did not know. They only knew that there was no French border with Belgium anymore and the Germans were coming.

Before I went back to the château to try to sleep for several hours, I checked again on a young woman who had appeared on the road alone. At first I had thought she was deaf or mute, for she just stared off into space, seeing something—or nothing. But this time, her eyes sought mine, so I sat on the grass next to her narrow mattress and took her hand in the wan lantern light. Her eyes looked hollow—haunted. For the first time I was certain she was neither mute nor retarded, perhaps just shattered by all this.

"You are safe here tonight," I assured her. "Would you like some water or tea? In the morning, you can go on. Do you have family somewhere?"

"Did. Two children."

"And you were separated from them?"

"Yes. Forever."

"Oh, I am so sorry. You lost them before you set out?"

"On the road. The Germans—their planes strafing the road near the tracks, wanting to ruin the railroad line. Both killed, my children. Rosette, she died in my arms and people made me leave them—leave them beside the road because the planes came back again, again . . ."

She gasped and screwed her eyes tight shut as if she were seeing it all again. I thought she would become hysterical. I wanted to. But she seemed beyond that, beyond everything.

"Your husband?" I managed to choke out.

"Gone to a soldier. Lost, do not know, but nothing matters now."

She closed her eyes and cried at last, tears squeezing out and running down into her hairline and her ears. I could not imagine the horror, and yet this was just one person, one horrid incident in this huge tragedy that had barely, I feared, begun.

I sat there, chilled by the night air, holding her hand until I heard one of my guards call out, "Here she is, Colonel! Sitting over here."

I snapped alert. I had dozed off in my exhaustion. Had the Germans found me? No, for then I heard a voice I knew, glimpsed the silhouette of a familiar form.

I lay the poor woman's hand carefully down. She slept heavily at last. I started to stand but was swept off my feet and lifted in strong arms. Jacques! That poor woman had no one, but my Jacques had come home!

"I SHOULD HAVE known you would be in the thick of things, even here," Jacques told me as he bathed in the same tub of water he had insisted I wash in first. I am sure I had resembled a farmwife, someone he had never seen with my loose hair and dirty face.

"At least some of the parents of patients at the children's hospital have been coming to get them," I told him. "That will be fewer we will have to be sure to get safely south. I am so glad you are here to help."

I held up a towel for him as he stepped out of the tub. He looked strong as ever, maybe a bit thinner and more muscular. He dried himself off. He seemed well enough fed and not a scratch or new scar on his lean form.

"How long can you stay?" I asked as he tied the damp towel around his waist, ignoring the pajamas I had laid out on our bed. "Long enough for us to drive south to find a place to evacuate the children, I hope."

"Just long enough to follow the orders of my commander, the Ministre de l'Air. It took me hours to get here, as the traffic was nose to tail, and I kept stopping to pick up those who could not walk, if there was room."

"But we need to go south as far as we can to find a haven for the patients, then return here to pack them up and evacuate them."

"When we go south, you will need to stay south. I have received notice that the German High Command knows where you live, but I am hoping and believing our lines will hold. If not, this trickle of displaced and panicked people will become a deluge, and we cannot buck that, trying to come back up north after we flee south."

"It already is a deluge. I have packed a suitcase for myself, so—"

"Let me see what you have put in it," he interrupted, his voice stern as he followed me over to the settee where my suitcase sat open. "Too big, too much—and a designer case by Vuitton, no!" he said without so much as touching it. "It needs to have plain clothes, work clothes. Does it?" he asked, lifting out some items. "This dress is too formal, too well made. We are not going to some party, but we are joining the refugees, so I will buy some things for us in the village."

"And I thought I was done with people telling me what I must wear!" I exploded before I calmed myself. This was my Jacques, not my mother years ago or the duke. "Sorry," I said, but I could tell he was not angry.

"So," I went on, "you think my luggage will be examined and

searched? I am at least going to take one good black dress. What if I need to talk to some magistrate, to finagle a place for the ill children, to convince them I will pay them as soon as I can get some U.S. funds through our Paris bank? And I am going to telephone my brothers to send some funds, if mine are frozen, and pay them back later."

"My darling wife," he said, pulling out a small, silk sack of jewelry I had included, "haven't you noticed this is not business as usual now?" His voice rose in a scolding, exasperated tone much like mine a moment ago. "And . . . you cannot be caught with this!" he insisted, holding up my French Legion of Honour award by its red velvet neck cord. The gold, white, and blue polished medal glimmered in the light.

"It is precious to me! I had a good mind to pack yours for safekeeping, too!" Why was he ignoring the needs of the ill children? Of course I wanted to be safe, but the Germans were not here, had not even breeched the French lines Jacques so believed would hold—or did he? He was more than brusque, he was harsh, and that was so unlike him.

"You are exhausted," he told me.

I knew that was true. I was almost swaying on my feet. My shrill voice was not my own.

He went on more calmly, "I will bury both of our medals in the backyard in a tin box, and we will come back for them when we can. Your good jewelry, too. We need to set out tomorrow. I have orders from the general to keep you safe."

"If you mean that beastly General Fuisse, he just wants his hands on the hospital, let alone the château. I am telling you again, and you can tell him and your higher command, that I am willing to turn the château over to French soldiers or refugees, but not the hospital—not yet at least. Jacques, you and

I have made decisions together, so you can stop ordering me about like some new recruit. I am afraid your French lines will not hold or your planes stop that horrible Luftwaffe. So I will agree to go sometime soon, but I need to have people ready to evacuate here."

"You can argue and try to defy General Fuisse, of course—even me, but there is someone else who is weighing in. Winston was not sure this telegram would get to you here, so he sent it through the chain of French command, and it came to me."

He went over to his battered valise and took out a much folded, beige telegram. My hands trembled as I opened it and read: COL J. BALSAN. GET CONS OUT OF FRANCE. STOP. SHE IS ON HIGH LEVEL GERMAN CAPTURE RANSOM LIST. STOP. ENGLISH CHANNEL DANGEROUS. STOP. GO SOUTH, THEN TO U.S. STOP. W. CHURCHILL

I stared at the words. My heart thudded. All I could manage was to nod.

"I said we need to set out tomorrow morning," he told me.

"Listen to me as well as to Winston, Colonel Balsan! That young woman you saw me with—the Germans killed her children on the road when they were shooting at people from the air to ruin railroad tracks! I will go, but I need just a little more time here, to prepare at least to save the children, especially if the French lines do not hold!"

He turned and seized me, grabbing my arms, hugging me against his chest. "We have to hold the border! France cannot be crushed again, occupied, used and ruined!"

I wrapped my arms around him. "We must not fight each other. I do not know what to do without you."

"You have done splendidly on your own, and that is so hard—so very hard for me to know, to accept, however much I am proud of you, that you do not need me."

I said, "I do. I do!"

He lifted me and carried me to the bed. He ripped his towel away and pulled back my robe. He was desperate, but I was too. Too strong, too fast, but we crested and clung together afterward, breathing hard.

"I did not mean to hurt you—ever," he said. He pulled me tight against him. "We must start south before all this turns worse. Fuisse says we will have the wounded here soon, and he is sending someone to oversee that."

"Will that make the château or the village a target, even with strafing and bombs from their planes?"

"I pray not. Consuelo, we will try to find a place for the children, perhaps at Pau, far south, almost on the Spanish border. But the mission of my heart is to get you away from the Nazis before they get you or us."

"Yes, you are in danger, too," I said as that reality hit me. "They would love to get their filthy hands on a rich Frenchman to ransom, but especially one who trained pilots to help defeat them in the Great War—and now."

"But even if we find a place for the children, then how to evacuate them from here to there? Because once I get you out of France and to the United States . . ."

"Clear to America?" I cried, turning to face him in our twisted sheets. "I cannot leave you!"

"I am to take you out of the country, get you safe, then return. I made a bargain for that, and we must play by their rules."

"But I want you to stay with me!"

"Then let us work on all that together, yes? But you must do as I say when we set out. We can stay with my brothers as we head south, and then, it depends on where we can go after that, but I swear, I will see you safe in America before I return here. I have contacted your brother Mike to work on getting us a plane to evacuate, but the question is, evacuate from where? So, will you agree to my bargain in all this?"

"To be with you clear to America? Yes, and I will even help you bury our honor medals and my jewelry. But, please, one more day here to do what I must, stage a mock evacuation, arrange all that for later. But we will be conspicuous if we take the big motorcar."

"We will take the old Citroën that sits in the carriage house. I will give you only tomorrow here and then we must go. So we are agreed—a bargain—but my first concern must be you. That has been my own orders to myself for years, only now, the odds are huge."

I QUICKLY ARRANGED and staged, with the help of our staff, who did not know Jacques and I would soon be refugees, too, a rehearsal for the evacuation of the hospital. On that last day, for the first time, I realized we were short of foodstuffs and medicines, which had stopped coming into the village. I had already been paying a pretty penny for black market milk—even canned milk—and medicines. Indeed, I was starting to feel like Mother Hubbard in that old Mother Goose nursery rhyme where she went to the cupboard and it was bare. As I glanced at the refugee boy's ducklings swimming in the moat, I wondered if they would get through the war or end up in some starving soul's stomach.

We could hear the sound of distant guns from the north, like the rumbles of thunder. "Ours, not theirs, I hope," Jacques muttered when he came back from filling the Citroën with petrol. "Winston was right that trench warfare is passé. If we hear planes, it is really time to flee, rehearsal or not."

I had commandeered a few ambulances, two trucks, several cars, and even some wagons for this mock evacuation. We lined them all up and timed—without actually disturbing the children—how long it would take to load them with mattresses, boxes of food, milk, and clothing. I entrusted petrol coupons I had saved to each of the drivers.

Thank heavens the vehicles had pulled away to their various hiding places, because German planes circled the village that day. We watched from under a tree. I had already said a silent farewell to the hospital staff and children—and especially Katrine—because we did not want anyone but the château staff and my two, old faithful guards to know that we were leaving or why.

"You are really scared today," Katrine had observed. "You are even shaking, and it is not cold. Do not worry for the château. I heard the Germans do not bomb nice houses they want to make their hindquarters."

I almost laughed. "You mean headquarters, my dear."

"Yes, that's it. So I will see you tomorrow after school. And that lady you made a bed for in your office, the one who lost her children, is she all right? I heard her screaming when those planes flew over."

I was leaving so much undone behind, especially if I had to flee to America. How long would it be before Jacques and I could dig up the treasure of our Legion of Honour medals? How would the nameless woman whose dead daughter had been named Rosette do without me? Would this sweet child Katrine make it through the war?

"I had best go back to the château now," I told her, giving her one more hard hug and kissing her on both cheeks. "I must see how Monsieur Balsan is doing."

"Oh, he is waiting outside for you. I saw him talking to those two friends of yours who always follow you around. So I will see you tomorrow and help Madame Claire, too."

Claire was the woman I had put in charge here, should I go away for a day. A day? How long would it be? How long the refugee road to the south of France and then how to leave the country for America? But how far, how frightening had been my pathways before, and I had somehow come through. Even without my beloved Jacques, even fighting my mother sometimes, I had come through. But now, Winston was right. Damn the German Huns, the Nazis. I would die before they would get their greedy, brutal hands on me!

Holding hands at dusk, Jacques and I walked the grounds of the château. I even could hear the chatter of the fountains. We threw a coin in our moat for good fortune and by candlelight had wine and vegetable stew, which I prayed would not be our last supper.

Chapter Thirty-Five

e drove out of Saint-Georges-Motel at four o'clock the next morning. I tried not to look back. I had left a note for Rosemary to read to the rest of the staff and to give them a month's wages and one for her to give to Katrine with a pearl necklace. Claire at the hospital had her directions. Strong women all, but we had to be. Yet I realized with some shame that I had not been without a personal maid my entire life.

We got a good start, though at dawn, traffic heading south became heavy again, absolutely clogged at times. We sometimes drove around wagons or walkers on the northern lane, for it was usually quite open—no one was heading toward the German invasion but an occasional French army vehicle. We crossed the Loire on the bridge at Blois, refueling our small Citroën with the petrol coupons Jacques parted with reluctantly. Some petrol stations were already low or out of fuel.

"At least we are going to see some family," I told him, trying to buck us both up, for we were to stay with his brother Étienne the first night in Châteauroux, where the Balsan factories were. When Jacques had gone back into service, Étienne had stepped forward on his own to oversee things there. And finally, farther south we would look up his much younger brother Henri, the black sheep of their family, in the town where we hoped to find a refuge for the children.

"Welcome!" Étienne cried when we pulled in near dark. He hugged and kissed us on both cheeks. "Sad it takes a war for a family reunion. I will pull your motorcar into the carriage house where it cannot be seen. Dinner and a safe bed is waiting. Sad to have to say a 'safe' bed here in central France. Come in!"

I tried to broach that subject indirectly that night at a dinner of beef bourguignon, salad, with a lovely wine and then gateaux. "At least," I said, "this is the heart of France, away from the dangerous borders."

"Have you not heard?" Étienne said, putting his wine goblet down. "Sorry to say, but our city has been strafed and bombed, and we are fearful the planes may be back. They just missed the factory. And have you not heard they have bombed the cities of Lyon and Nancy?"

"Rumors but not that," Jacques said. "I feel guilty having such precious time with you and this lovely meal when so many are suffering. But, *Vive la France!*"

"We must keep our spirits up," Marie, Étienne's wife, said. "And the best way to do that is to be with family, eat a good meal—but then I must go to mass again. You two have a good night's sleep now—if you can."

The look that passed between her and Étienne was full of concern if not fear. I hope they were not just putting on a good front for us. How very brave, even stoic, they had seemed, but I had picked up on the fact that she had been to mass twice today already and she kept fingering her rosary beads in her lap with one hand at dinner. Prayer was one way to stay sane in this madness.

We did sleep well at first, exhausted, but were awakened by a *crump, crump* sound. I saw Jacques was already up. He had opened the curtains and was silhouetted by lightning in the dark sky beyond.

"A storm?" I asked, getting up.

"A German storm of bombs. Falling near our factories. And on the neighborhood a few miles away."

"Should we go to the cellar?"

"I will ask Étienne."

When he went out, I heard their voices in the hall while I watched mesmerized and horrified as the sky was lit by distant explosions.

Jacques came back in. "Étienne says this attack is like the one before, more a threat than a danger. The Germans want France's factories intact when they come here. And he says it was just on the radio that our motherland may make a bargain with Germany rather than be pounded to dust."

"A bargain with them? Such as what?"

"They may call it an armistice, but it stinks of surrender." He closed the curtains and sat on the bed with his head in his hands. I had never seen him cry, but he did so silently, with his shoulders shaking.

I went over and sat beside him. The mattress sagged to bump us together. For once, after all the times he had held me, I tried to comfort him.

AFTER AN EARLY breakfast and good-bye hugs, we set out again the next day. "I am afraid to drive even near the factories," he told me as our headlights sliced through the predawn darkness. "The bastards! We French should have fought despite the cost. I hate giving in to evil!"

I was out of reassuring words. I had comforted so many, but fierce fear did more than nibble at me now. Jacques or not at my side, I fought hard to keep it from devouring me.

When daylight came, we saw where traps for tanks had been dug on some roads and had to go around them. I could feel the Germans at our back with their blitzkrieg, their "lightning war," that moved so fast. "Jacques, I will not be captured."

"That is the point of all this, my love."

"But if there is a checkpoint or something like that, if they take my passport and discover I am on their wanted list, I would rather be shot."

"Do not talk like that! We will get to the border, leave poor, sad France." His voice broke, and we drove on.

FINALLY, AFTER ANOTHER grueling stretch on crowded roads, using our dwindling petrol coupons, we arrived in Périgueux on our way to Pau and the Spanish border. We sought out two friends of Jacques's I had never met. They took us down to a café near their building. It was on a side street and, for once, quiet with no poor refugees. As hungry and grateful as I was for the tea and croissants, it was hard for me to enjoy them because I kept seeing in my mind the parade of people, the faces of the frightened and the lost.

"We must tell you something, but wanted to fortify you first," his friend Pierre said while Estelle just kept frowning and nodding. "On the radio, when they are not playing German music already, that horrible 'Deutschland, Uber Alles,' they announced how far the . . . the occupation . . . has come toward us. I regret to inform you that the Germans are in your village already."

I gasped and clutched my throat with both hands. "Saint-Georges-Motel? Are you sure? We were hoping—praying—it would be too small a place, and they would at least just pass through."

Estelle reached over to touch my shoulder. Jacques sat stunned, silent, but I had never seen him more angry. "And bombs?" he asked.

"Yes, but your brother Étienne phoned your château, then here. Your home was not hit, nor was the hospital, Jacques. Some places in town . . ."

I covered my face with my hands. All those ill, innocent children. Katrine and her family, all the others—as good as prisoners. God forgive me, but I also thought of the June flowers, those innocent little ducklings . . .

"We will go on tomorrow, toward Pau where my youngest brother lives," Jacques spoke at last, his voice deadly calm. "I thank you for being in touch with Étienne as I asked. We still hope to find a safe place for the hospital children to live in case the Germans take over that facility—if they even have any wounded in this lightning war they wage."

I reached across the table to grasp his hand. Mine was trembling but his was, too.

"Come stay with us the night," Pierre said. "You cannot push on in the dark with all the danger on the roads, especially now . . . now that France has declared the armistice with Germany . . . now that France has fallen."

We sat there in tears, silent. Then suddenly from a phonograph, or radio, came the strains of "La Marseillaise." Everyone in the café jumped to their feet, the Germans be damned. People in the street came running and stood at attention, too, some with their hands over their hearts. A woman ran through the tables waving a French tricolor flag that had sharp folds in it, as if it had been hidden in a drawer.

Everyone began to sing, but the words stung my soul: *The day of glory has arrived! Against us tyranny's bloody flag is raised!* I only got that far before I could not go on, so I only mouthed the words. Yet, around me, however ragged and tearful the voices, nothing had ever sounded braver.

THE ROAD TO Pau was through beautiful, peaceful farmland, just waiting to be plundered by the German rapists. The city itself was a crowded mess. Jacques said it was because it was on the route to the Spanish border where many desperate people would try to escape the country—including us.

But here we were blessed to find a big, old house large enough to accommodate the hospital children if they could flee south with the Germans nearby, with their planes in the sky. But how to get them here quickly and safely? For once I cursed the Vanderbilt name and my ties to the fortune I sometimes spent so frivolously, though it had gone for good things, too.

The city of Pau gave me a feeling of increasing claustrophobia and dread. Panicked French officers seemed to be everywhere, looking for German loyalists. Thank God, we had a place to stay amid the seething, homeless crowds, for Jacques's youngest brother Henri happily took us in, though he lived in a small apartment.

"We do not mean to crowd you," Jacques told him when he barely cracked opened the door, then his face lit to see us. "But I did not let my sweetheart talk me into sleeping on the floor of an old house we just rented for our children's hospital patients. And we need your help with that."

"But come in, come in!" he cried, kissing us on both cheeks. "You are both welcome, and I have a bed you can use. And to be of help to my big brother, *sacre bleu*—a joy and an honor."

"Not if it is your only bed, Henri," Jacques insisted, clapping him on the back and then hugging him again.

"I am the host and you and your lovely Consuelo will do as the host says!" he declared and dragged us out of the hall. Though he was in his early fifties, he had never married and was estranged from some of the extended family, for what I knew not, though I knew how that felt. He reminded me of Ivor that way, a bit different, a bit of a loner.

Bread, cheese, and hard cider had never tasted so good. As exhausted as we were, catching up on conversation had never been sweeter. Henri promised to phone Étienne, who would phone the hospital at Saint-Georges-Motel to tell them where to bring the children if they could leave the village before the Germans totally took over.

"But this will give us a reason to work together—for you, my brother, and for my dear sister Consuelo's children!" Henri insisted.

Coffee, which usually kept me awake if I drank it late, had no effect, and I fell asleep against Jacques's shoulder in the very middle of his advising Henri how to patch things up with Étienne.

Like a baby, I guess I was carried to the bed Henri loaned us, for I remember nothing after. It felt but a few hours when Jacques shook me awake. How I wished I would be here when— if—the children came, but we had to press on. Henri seemed proud to be able to help, to be trusted with the task of waiting for the children. I hugged him a special good-bye, because, as with leaving Étienne and Marie, who knew when or if we would see our French family—even our English or American ones—again.

Chapter Thirty-Six

fter our five-hundred-mile flight south, more shock and grief. "Oh, no, monsieur," the petrol station owner told Jacques at the fueling station where we used our next-to-last coupon. "You will not be able to pass through the southern border to Spain or elsewhere."

"But my wife is an American citizen."

"We had all best to learn the new rules, no? You must drive to the American consulate in Bordeaux, and get a visa there. I know these things, monsieur, for my cousin, he works there, yes, right in the consulate, but not as an officer. He is a guard and they are besieged now, as are we all, no? Here, I can draw you directions once you get to Bordeaux. It is such a lovely city, but what will become of it now? Besieged by people and panic."

Besieged and panicked, indeed. I was distraught.

"I do not think we have a choice but to go there," Jacques told me when we were back in the Citroën. "Our petrol coupons are running out, our money . . ."

"Our patience, our courage," I added.

He reached over to squeeze my thigh. "For now this Citroën is our home and best friend. We are off to the lovely city of Bordeaux."

IT WAS A beautiful city, but the excellent directions to the American consulate took us to what looked like a mob scene. Motorcars in long lines, people packed around the building. The only comforting thing was that the American flag hung above the door, and it was so good to see it. My longing to escape, to be home safe, was a physical ache now—or was that my exhaustion and fear gnawing at me again?

We stood for three hours in a queue of panicked people waiting to see one of seven officials. God forgive me for wishing I could pull some strings as Mother had more than once with the Vanderbilt name, but it was not on my French passport.

"Yes?" the mustached, chubby man said in a most harried tone when we were finally at the front of the line. "I must tell you at once, that under these circumstances, we officers are struggling with requests and regulations the U.S. State Department keeps sending out and changing. And the border will close soon, hence all the panic, so I know you will be reasonable."

Not a good beginning, I thought, as I began to explain. We had decided not to try to mention our plight of needing to escape the Nazis. Would he even believe such a story?

"Passports, please," he interrupted my explanation that we wanted to go to our home in Florida. "But you will need a visa, too—a visa," he repeated loudly in the noise of the room. I read his lips for the buzz was bothering my hearing aid.

He skimmed our paperwork. "You do not have a visa?"

"No, but I am an American citizen also and—"

"To issue you a visa—for both of you—I would need your birth certificates and marriage certificate."

"But those are with our lawyer in Paris."

He rolled his eyes. "Paris might as well be the moon, madame, until this hellish, so-called armistice is worked out with the Germans. You must come back in the morning, and I will inquire, but there are many more behind you."

Jacques cut in, "We are not giving up our passports. Is there any other way to obtain visas, then?"

"Well, you could have your passports visa-ed for Spain and Portugal but you would have to go to Bayonne where those countries have consulates. Then you could go to Lisbon in Portugal to get your official entry to the U.S. But that is a gamble, because the frontier will be closing soon, very soon, if it has not already. Yes, that might be your best chance. Please move on, then. Next!"

I could have hit the man and yet he had given us a ray of hope to not have to be separated from our passports and to get out of France. But to drive on with our last petrol coupon to another place and the threat of the way being cut off there, too, was daunting.

We walked several blocks to our motorcar, buying a loaf of bread and soda water on the way. We had no place to sleep but in the car. How far to Bayonne? We looked at each other, weary, frightened but determined. We did not even talk it over, for we had no choice.

"Bayonne, it is," Jacques said and started our faithful, old motorcar.

WE DROVE THROUGH a torrent of rain. It seemed the very heavens were against us. I might not be able to hear the swish-swish of our windscreen wipers, but they mesmerized me as I tried to help Jacques navigate the road to the west. And they said it rained too much in England! Strange, but I thought of beautiful Blenheim in the spring rain. I thought of Winston leading the nation through this dreadful war and yet taking time to be worried about me. I missed my English family and wanted to see them all again, desperately.

"I just thought of something," Jacques said, still squinting at the wet pavement and traffic splashing water at us. "My father was friends with the former Spanish ambassador to France. He lives now at Biarritz."

"But we are almost to Bayonne! We will run out of petrol!"

"But you know how things work. I swear, we will find a mess again at the Spanish consulate. But with a paper to take us to the front of the line . . . Consuelo, you know I am not a betting man, but I think we should try. Coupons or not, we can find someone who wants French francs or that little bit of American cash you have."

"I only brought those bills because my father gave them to me, told me to hold them for him one time, then never—never got them back—before . . ."

"We are both exhausted and on edge."

"And hunted."

"Are you with me?"

"I trust you, my love. Biarritz, it is."

WE HAD TO wait an endless day for the former ambassador, Baron Almeida, to return to his home, but we slept in our car and saved our money. Then, armed with the special letter from him and having turned down a night in a lovely home because we were terrified the border would close, we finally reached Bayonne. And found another mob scene to face.

Our hearts fell when we heard the Spanish consulate insisted on there being a visa with the passports, so we rushed on foot to the nearby Portuguese consulate. After all, we had decided to leave Europe via Lisbon—somehow.

We were greeted by a crowd of people chanting over and over, "We want our passports! We want them now!"

We looked at each other in dismay, but we plunged into the crowd. We slid and squeezed our way slowly ahead. My height helped me to navigate. My panic grew that we would be trapped, found, imprisoned. I saw a slight space in the crowd as people shifted, shouting. With Jacques right behind me, I pushed ahead, up the stairs, which were also packed. Would this wooden staircase even hold?

I heard the man just ahead of us tell his younger male companion, "I know how to empty these stairs." He began to shout, "Look out! These stairs are giving way! Too much weight! They will crash!"

Jacques grabbed my arm and turned to flee. "No," I told him, amazed I had heard the man in this din, a gift from God. "That is a lie this man tells. Up, we go up!"

We made it up right behind the shouting man. The first door in the hallway was closed but there was a bell there, and we rang it while the other two men ran farther down the hall. We waved the ambassador's seal on our letter in the face of the first man at the door. He took us in. When we explained, we had our visas in five minutes. Outside, with the rain still pouring down, I sobbed in relief.

BUT I SHOULD have known we were not home free—and certainly not even home yet. Once in Spain, where foreigners like us were frowned upon, we learned we must take a train to get to Lisbon where we could catch a plane. We realized we had not enough money for either, let alone food and a place to sleep before the train left.

We sold the Citroën that day for a wretchedly low price, but what choice did we have? I hated to see it go, our deliverer this far.

The travel bureau now controlling the train station asked an exorbitant price for our tickets. We could not afford a sleeper car but sat in seats as, thank God, the train finally headed for Lisbon. But we were frightened each time the conductor asked to see our precious papers. Here we were, refugees on a train, and it had been trains that had made my family its fortune. How I missed my father, and, yes, my mother too. She would have settled down those confusing and confused people in the places we had just been.

"Señor, señora, I must have your passports, please. You will receive them back later in Lisbon."

"We do not wish to give them up," Jacques argued. "Can you not examine them?"

"Do not worry. I will give you this official paper, and you will have them returned to you at the Passport Office."

My stomach cramped, and I had to rush to the horrid, swaying toilet on the train while Jacques guarded our meager pieces of paper as our precious passports—our safety and our future— were taken away. The train was hours late and the hotels were occupied, but we finally found a single room with a bed so unkempt that we slept curled up together on the small settee. But we were together. We were out of France. But still far from home, and where was home now?

We stood in a long line, which they even dared to close for an hour for a siesta, but at last—at last!—we had what we needed and a moment of help, too.

"Oh," the officer said. Thankfully, he spoke decent English since Portuguese was something neither of us understood well. That alone and his handing over our passports and visas made him a hero in my eyes already. "Here, it is yes—oh, two documents sent for you here."

He squinted at the envelopes and handed them to me. One was a cable from my brother Mike, telling us he had followed Jacques's request—which I had not realized he had sent from Biarritz—and had booked two spaces for us on a Clipper land-and-sea aeroplane to the United States via Lisbon. Even more amazing, the other missive was an invitation to a formal state dinner as the guest of Prince George, Duke of Kent, at a champagne reception and dinner that night, for he was in Lisbon on a diplomatic mission and had heard we were here to leave the country.

Our nightmare, I prayed, was over. I thrust both letters at Jacques and burst into tears.

IT FELT TO us surreal to be greeted by the duke amid happy chatter and the clink of goblets. Jacques wore his uniform, which he had hidden under the seat of the Citroën and had only remembered to rescue at the last moment when we sold it, but here I was at a formal dinner in a plain black day dress and no jewelry but my wedding ring and the family heirloom pin my husband had given me long ago at dear Crowhurst.

The duke understood when we told him what we had been through, but I was the target of a narrow glance or two from the Portuguese guests. Imagine, I thought. Ordinarily, I would have laughed it off, but I still felt so delicate—nearly traumatized. Here was Consuelo Vanderbilt Balsan, once a duchess, hostess of charities and parties, not dressed for the ball.

"Such an adventure," the duke told me. He had kindly seated me on one side and Jacques on his other. "And I fear our beloved England is about to feel the upheaval, too. But with your cousin Winston at the helm, steady as she goes. A shame his influence does not reach here with the visa and passport people, but I fear not. Still, we are hoping your America will help us out as before."

"I feel so out of touch with . . . with home," I told him. "And I leave my family—on my side, not Jacques's side—in England. I know both my sons, the Duke of Marlborough and Lord Ivor Spencer-Churchill, will serve to help protect their homeland."

"I too, in the skies if the Luftwaffe dares to visit us. Jacques, we could use your skills."

"I would fight them on the ground or in the skies."

"I pulled a few strings to find out about your village," the duke said as he slowly cut into his beef, which Jacques and I had tried not to gobble, for it was the best, heartiest food we had eaten in over a week. Still, I was so upset that nothing tasted quite right. Worry. Guilt over those on the roads, those in endless lines, those in our village. I held my breath as the duke went on.

"Ironically, the German general for the air command has taken over your château, but the hospital, which your butler, Albert, mentioned to my aide just before your house staff fled the village—is currently intact and operating, evidently to be left alone for now."

I breathed out a sigh and clasped my hands to my chest.

"Thank you so much for that kindness," I told him. "And for having us here."

"The least I could do for a French hero and an English—and American—duchess," he said.

I ignored the bejeweled woman across the table who alternately glared at or dramatically feigned looking away from me. Here I was in a plain dress, with hardly any money to my name, no motorcar, no plush hotel room, no maid, and only a settee on which to lay my head this last night before leaving. But I had my dear sons and family, I had my beloved hero Jacques, and I had memories of people and places I had loved. In that moment, if I could take on Hitler himself, I would.

"I HAVE NEVER been on a seaplane before," I told Jacques as we boarded and strapped ourselves into our seats at the wharf along the Tagus River in Lisbon the next morning. And I have never flown the Atlantic in a plane—just give me a ship for that."

"My love, you have not stopped talking. I know you are excited but—"

"Just happy. Relieved. Oh, yes, and in love with a Frenchman."

He smiled and exhaled audibly. "I feel as if I am running, but I will come back—if I can help in any way. Winston said when he phoned to tell us he was P.M. months ago that he could use me."

"He finally told me what this means," I said, flashing him the two-fingered *V* sign. "When we were young—when I first knew him—I always thought of it as meaning vim and vigor, that was Winston."

"Still is. If anyone can best the bastard Fuehrer, it is him. It is for victory, yes? He will use it, he will preach it and speak it."

As the engines started, we held hands. I had made so many journeys, seen so much, met so many. Loved many, too, but the best was here beside me. I closed my eyes as we rocked a bit, moving away from the wharf, then I looked out the window as we picked up speed and lifted from the water into the clear, blue sky. I was heading home. Well, to one of the homes of my heart.

Epilogue

November 1943
Casa Alva, Palm Beach, Florida

I sat alone in the winter sun on the patio, listening to a two-month-old speech on the radio by Winston that had been recorded at the Royal Albert Hall in London. London, Blenheim, dear France—all seemed so far away and yet so near.

I had heard this speech before, practically had it memorized. Although Winston was a great orator, I liked this speech especially since he had given it to a meeting of six thousand British women. Mother would have approved. I wished I had been there, but I had promised Jacques, Bert, Ivor, and Winston that I would remain here until after the war.

Damn the war! Damn Hitler. Just when we were finally safe, Jacques had driven me crazy by insisting on going back, not to France right away, but to England to speak out for the French cause. The man was seventy-five, but then he was a man of honor, and I would have him no other way.

I missed my husband terribly. And I prayed he would never discover what I had done. I had telegraphed Winston to please—somehow—send him home. I had also begged Winston not to tell him I had done so.

I leaned toward the radio in the breeze and turned it up even louder as it came to my favorite part of this speech:

> *I have no fear of the future. Let us go forward into its mysteries, let us tear aside the veils which hide it from our eyes, and let us move onward with confidence and courage.*

Tears blurred my view of the palm trees, the beach, and the blue Atlantic beyond our pool and breakwater. But the future seemed frightening with Ivor and Bert serving with the British forces. Ivor had been ill off and on, and my brother Willie, in New York, had a serious heart condition that concerned me, too.

But, I told myself fiercely, I have a strong heart, for all I have yet to face. I was still working on charities here. I planned to at least visit our Paris home someday and see that it went for a good cause, for we had planned to make America our home base now—even if the war ended well.

But poor France: Jacques had telegraphed that he heard the urban populations were close to starvation as were people in many rural areas. I worried over friends I had left behind, even little Katrine. I, too, longed to go back and fight for my two beloved European nations, so I guess I had better accept that Jacques had been driven to return.

I pulled on a jacket but kicked off my shoes and went to walk the beach. That helped—some sort of action. But I too often gazed out to the endless horizon and wished I were "over there."

I strode faster, kicking at the cool winter waves. Pretty shells speckled the sand, especially the tiny coquina that were washed in but quickly upended themselves and dug in again to safety before the screeching seagulls could snatch them up, or before they were ripped away again by the tide. Yes, I would dig in too, but how I missed my man.

I turned to walk back to the villa I had named for my mother, the bane of my early existence and yet the woman who gave me my backbone. I smiled and shook my head. And Papa, so charming and so dear, had given me the gift of love—and the gift of my Jacques.

The wind stung my eyes, but I imagined my husband, as I did in dreams sometimes. Of course, this time, it was just a man I did not know down the beach in salt spray, built like him, when so much reminded me of my dear love.

But this man was wearing shoes, and striding right through in the lapping waves. He was in a uniform, though so many were these days, but not an American one. But as he strode forward, he waved. It was Jacques!

I ran toward him as if I were sixteen again. He was really, really here!

Arms outstretched, I hit into him and almost took him down, but he lifted me off my feet and spun me. "May I have this dance?" he asked, but his voice broke with emotion. I swear, even with the wind and waves, I heard every word he said, felt we had gone back in time.

We stood in the wash of water on hard-packed sand and held and kissed eternally.

"Why didn't you tell me?" I demanded, out of breath, when we finally leaned back a bit to look at each other.

"I came on a transport at the last minute. I have orders from Winston—you will love this, my darling—to work stateside with children's relief work. And I intend to make a case to Roosevelt's government that they must end their food blockade of France. Things are bad there."

"I will help you, write articles to newspapers. Put you in contact with New York and Washington people who can help."

Despite the tears in his eyes, he broke into a smile as, holding hands, we walked back and turned up the sandy path toward Casa Alva. "I will help with all of that," I promised yet again.

"You can help and always have. The allies must win this war together. And we shall be together in whatever we have to face, and not be afraid."

I thought again of Winston's brave words: *I have no fear of the future.*

With my hand held hard in my beloved husband's, I could finally say that, too.

About the author

About the book

Insights,
Interviews
& More . . .

Meet Karen Harper

About the author

Jeffrey A. Rycus

New York Times and *USA Today* bestselling author Karen Harper is a former Ohio State University instructor and high school English teacher. Published since 1982, she writes contemporary suspense and historical novels about real British women. Two of her recent Tudor-era books were bestsellers in the United Kingdom and in Russia. Harper won the Mary Higgins Clark Award for *Dark Angel*, and her novel *Shattered Secrets* was judged one of the best books of the year by *Suspense Magazine*. ∾

Behind the Book

When I visited Blenheim Palace and Bladon Churchyard over ten years ago, I had no plans to write about Consuelo, the ninth Duchess of Marlborough. I wish I had, because I would have come away with more than a few photos, memories, and a guidebook on the palace. I don't even recall seeing her grave, because my husband is a Winston Churchill buff, and we were focused on his tombstone. By the way, there is a lovely photo of a young Consuelo and Winston chatting at Blenheim that can be seen by Googling *Consuelo and Winston Churchill sitting together at Blenheim Palace*. That mere photo told me they were good friends.

Although Consuelo buried Jacques in 1956, as he wished in the Balsan family tomb in the Cimetière de Montmartre in Paris, before she died in December of 1964, she chose to be buried next to Ivor. She did commission a memorial to Jacques, a French hero, in the park at Chateauroux near his family's estate. Despite the fact that Jacques was the love of her life, she did not want to be buried "indoors," though she had three huge family mausoleums to chose from. Despite her problems with her first husband, she did love the grounds and people of Blenheim. How lovely and plain is her grave under the open sky at St. Martin's Church, Bladon, England. Photos of it are available online. ▶

Behind the Book *(continued)*

Sadly, Ivor died at age fifty-eight just two months after Jacques. Ivor had married in 1954 to Elizabeth Cunningham, and they had a son, Robert, that year, but Ivor had an inoperable brain tumor, discovered just when he had decided to be bold enough to fly to see Consuelo in Florida. Nursing Jacques at that time, she did not see her dear Ivor again, but she fulfilled the request he makes to her in this novel when he says, "If I lie here someday . . . stay a while with me."

I came across Consuelo's fascinating story in research for another of my Victorian/Edwardian novels in the book *To Marry an English Lord* by Gail MacColl and Carol McD. Wallace (Workman, 1989). Consuelo and the ninth duke are on the cover, and much about them is written in this photo-filled book. I then pursued this amazing woman's story by reading her autobiography *The Glitter and the Gold* (St. Martins Press, 1953) though I am aware autobiographies can be slanted and even untruthful. Would you write some of the crazy or bad things you have done in yours?

So to balance that out, I also studied *Consuelo: Portrait of an American Heiress* by James Brough (Coward, McCann & Geoghegan, Inc., 1979) and *Consuelo and Alva Vanderbilt: The Story of a Daughter and Mother in the Gilded Age* by Amanda MacKenzie Stuart (HarperCollins, 2006). Besides these excellent resources, I enjoyed researching a woman who has a great online presence in places like Pinterest and in the fascinating Smithsonian Channel Series *Million Dollar American Princesses*. The segment on Consuelo's *Wedding of the Century* is available for free viewing on the Smithsonian Channel website under *Million Dollar American Princesses*.

Besides visiting Blenheim to get a glimpse of Consuelo's "gilded cage," Marble House in Newport, Rhode Island, is open to the public as are other "cottages" there with Vanderbilt ties.

Scholars have long said that Consuelo is the subject of Edith Wharton's *The Buccaneers*, her last novel.

I also found Gladys Deacon to be a fascinating, if sad, character. She died in 1977 at age ninety-six, having spent a lot of time in a psychiatric geriatric hospital. Even in her youth, she had been in a mental facility in France, and yet managed to become Duchess of Marlborough.

George Curzon, a minor and rather likable character in this novel, also appears extensively in my previous book, *The It Girls*. However, another side of him entirely emerges in that novel. Also, I could not resist having George, Duke of Kent, remark on his beloved nanny, Charlotte Bill, who was the heroine of my novel *The Royal Nanny*. I would have given Charlotte a walk-on part in this book when Consuelo and the duke visit Sandringham, but that visit was the year before she arrived there. I do try to keep straight the dates of what happened when.

Winston Churchill also had a nanny who was truly his emotional mother. And I did not call Consuelo's American governess Miss Harper just to please myself; that was the loyal woman's real name. I rather like that bit of serendipity.

What to say about the formidable and amazing Alva Smith Vanderbilt Belmont? She deserves her own story, but I will leave her here as she is seen through Consuelo's youthful and then mature eyes. How admirable that Consuelo could find it in her heart to forgive, admire, and love the woman who had so abused her in her youth. Despite Alva's give-'em-hell reputation, she did a great deal to fight for the rights of all American women.

Many pictures of the famous Consuelo are available online. To see them, search for images for Consuelo and 9th Duke of Marlborough. A bio and excellent pictures of romantic and swashbuckling Jacques can be found by searching for his name.

I am very grateful for the encouragement and support for this novel from Annelise Robey, my agent, and Lucia Macro, my editor. And, of course, to Don for being my companion to all the places we've been in England and France.

Karen Harper ◡

Reading Group Guide

1. How does Consuelo's American democratic background vs. the duke's aristocratic one merge or clash in the story? Should she have handled things differently? Why did the duke hate America?

2. Consuelo's handling of her mother over the years says a lot about both women. Should Consuelo just have cut her mother off after she was forced to marry the duke? Is Alva strictly a villain? Does she redeem her earlier conduct? Why do you think she acted so dictatorially?

3. Do you believe in love at first sight? We know Jacques claimed to, but does Consuelo show signs of this, too?

4. I could not have possibly made up a character like Gladys Deacon. Is she a sympathetic character or just the opposite? Can you understand her being unbalanced? Also, did you suspect she was after the duke? At what point? Before Consuelo realized it? Why didn't she catch on right away?

5. Is it wrong for parents to favor one child over another, or is it understandable or permissible? Why did Consuelo favor Ivor? Did she try to make up for those feelings by bolstering Bert? Have you seen or experienced parents who do this? Also, in what ways did Winston favor Ivor?

6. What does Mrs. Prattley mean to Consuelo? Something beyond mere charity? Why does Consuelo continue to think of the old lady over the years?

7. How much do early relationships affect us in adulthood? How did her governess, Miss Harper, have an impact on Consuelo? What about the ill child she took presents to in her pony cart at Idle Hour?

8. So many of us tend to see war that is distant from us in time or place in abstract generalities. Modern-day media's close-up-and-personal coverage makes the human impact of war more real. How does Consuelo's contact with refugees make the impact of war hit home for her?

9. I knew quite a lot about Sarah Jennings, the first Duchess of Marlborough, because before I visited Blenheim, I had watched the excellent BBC series "The First Churchills." Sarah had quite a temper, almost as explosive as Alva's. Is her "ghost" hostile or friendly to Consuelo and why? Are you aware of any other cases of historic ghosts tied to their homes or to their great achievements?

10. Jacques Balsan's life greatly paralleled the history of early flight from hot-air balloons to war planes with bombs. Since Americans tend to focus on the Wright brothers, I was not aware that France was also key in the race toward modern flight. Did any other historical details surprise you in this novel? For example, I was amazed how many people of this era were divorced.

11. It seems that both Alva and Consuelo changed houses frequently. In what way were their surroundings an extension of themselves? Do you find this is also true about yourself in your choice of home and décor? ∾